About the Au————

Carol Marinelli recently filled in a form asking for her job title. Thrilled to be able to put down her answer, she put writer. Then it asked what Carol did for relaxation and she put down the truth – writing. The third question asked for her hobbies and, not wanting to look obsessed, she crossed the fingers on her hand and answered swimming. However, given that the chlorine in the pool does terrible things to her highlights, I'm sure you can guess the real answer.

When Canadian **Dani Collins** found romance novels in secondary school, she wondered how one trained for such an awesome job. She wrote for over two decades without publishing but remained inspired by the romance message that if you hang in there, you'll find a happy ending. In May of 2012, Mills & Boon bought her manuscript in a two-book deal. She's since published more than forty books with Mills & Boon and is definitely living happily ever after.

Cathy Williams is a great believer in the power of perseverance as she had never written anything before her writing career. From the starting point of zero, she has now fulfilled her ambition to pursue this most enjoyable of careers. She would encourage any would-be writer to have faith and go for it! She derives inspiration from the tropical island of Trinidad and from the peaceful countryside of middle England. Cathy lives in Warwickshire with her family.

Irresistible Italians

Irresistible Italians:
A Price to Pay

CAROL MARINELLI

DANI COLLINS

CATHY WILLIAMS

MILLS & BOON

First Published in Great Britain 2023
by Mills & Boon, an imprint of HarperCollins*Publishers* Ltd,
1 London Bridge Street, London, SE1 9GF

www.harpercollins.co.uk

HarperCollins*Publishers*
Macken House, 39/40 Mayor Street Upper,
Dublin 1, D01 C9W8, Ireland

Irresistible Italians: A Price to Pay © 2023 Harlequin Enterprises ULC.

Di Sione's Innocent Conquest © 2016 Harlequin Enterprises ULC.
Bought by Her Italian Boss © 2016 Dani Collins
The Truth Behind his Touch © 2012 Cathy Williams

Special thanks and acknowledgement are given to Carol Marinelli for her contribution to *The Billionaire's Legacy* series.

ISBN: 978-0-263-31898-2

MIX
Paper | Supporting
responsible forestry
FSC™ C007454

This book is produced from independently certified FSC™ paper
to ensure responsible forest management.

For more information visit: www.harpercollins.co.uk/green

Printed and Bound in the UK using 100% Renewable Electricity
at CPI Group (UK) Ltd, Croydon, CR0 4YY

DI SIONE'S INNOCENT CONQUEST

CAROL MARINELLI

PROLOGUE

MATTEO DI SIONE knew only too well his shortcomings.

He didn't need to have them pointed out to him.

Again.

Summoned by his grandfather, Giovanni, it was with a sense of dread that Matteo drove towards the Di Sione estate—a magnificent, sprawling residence set in the Gold Coast of Long Island.

On the death of Matteo's parents, Giovanni had taken in the seven orphans that his son, Benito, and wife, Anna, had left behind. For Matteo, then only five years old, this place had become home.

Now he had a penthouse apartment in Manhattan with glittering views of the skyline and the city that never slept at his feet.

This was home though.

For better or worse, this was where his fractured, scattered family met on occasion, or returned to at times.

Now, Matteo assumed that he had been called here to be served a lecture.

Another one.

The previous weekend had been particularly wild, even by Matteo's licentious standards. The press, who were eagerly awaiting his downfall, had been watching. They couldn't wait for a Di Sione to hit skid row and so had taken delight in reporting Matteo's million-dollar loss in Vegas on Saturday night. They had, of course, failed to mention that he had recouped the loss twice over by dawn. What hurt him the most, though, was that a prestigious paper had written a very scathing piece.

Arriving in Manhattan this morning, he had gone from his jet to the waiting car and checked the news— the headline he had seen had been the one he had dreaded the most.

History Repeats!

There was a photo of him coming out of the casino, unshaven, with his hair falling over his eyes. He was clearly a little the worse for wear. On his arm was a blonde.

Beside that image, there was another, taken some thirty years ago, in the very same year that he had been born.

Benito Di Sione coming out of a casino, unshaven with the same straight black hair falling over the same navy eyes and clearly a little the worse for wear. On his arm the beautiful requisite blonde, who was not Matteo's mother.

Matteo doubted his father would have remembered who the woman was, whereas Matteo always remembered his lovers.

On Saturday night her name had been Lacey and she had been gorgeous.

He adored women.

Skinny ones, big ones and anywhere in between.

Matteo had a slight yen for the newly divorced—he had found that they were only too happy to rekindle that long-lost flame of desire.

Matteo always made it perfectly clear that he was here for a good time not a long time and he was never with anyone long enough to cheat.

The article had gone on to list the similarities between father and youngest son—the risk-taking, the decadent, debauched lifestyle—and had warned that Matteo was heading towards the same fate that had befallen his father—dead, his car wrapped around a lamppost and his wife deceased by his side.

No, Matteo was not looking forward to speaking with his grandfather; after all, Giovanni often said the very same thing.

He drove into the huge estate and looked ahead rather than taking in the luxurious surrounds, for they held few happy memories.

Still, it was home and, as he parked his car and walked towards the mansion where the Di Sione children had been raised, he wondered as to his reception. Matteo stopped by fairly regularly and took Giovanni out to his club for lunch whenever he could.

He knocked on the door simply to be polite but, as he did, he let himself in with his own key.

'It's Matteo,' he called out as he opened the door and then smiled when he saw Alma, the housekeeper, up on a stepladder.

'Master Matteo!' Alma mustn't have heard him knock because she jumped a little. She was working on a large flower display in the entrance hall and went to get down from the ladder but he gestured for her to carry on.

'Where is he?' Matteo asked.

'In his study. Do you want me to let Signor Giovanni know that you are here?'

'No, I'll just go straight through.' Matteo rolled his eyes. 'I believe he's expecting me.'

Alma gave him a small smile and Matteo took it to be a sympathetic one. Of course she must have seen the newspaper when she had taken Giovanni his breakfast this morning.

'How is he doing?' Matteo asked as he often did.

'He wants to speak with you himself,' Alma said and Matteo frowned at the vague answer.

He walked down a long hallway and then stood at the heavy mahogany door of his grandfather's study and took a steadying breath, then knocked on the door. When his grandfather's voice called for him to come in, he did so.

'Hey!' Matteo said as he opened the door.

He looked not to his grandfather but to the folded newspaper that lay on Giovanni's desk and, even as he closed the door behind him, Matteo set the tone. 'I've already seen it and I really don't need a lecture.'

'Where does lecturing you get me, Matteo?' Giovanni responded.

Matteo looked up at the sound of his grandfather's tired voice, and what he saw made his heart sink in dread. Giovanni looked not just pale, but so incredibly frail. His hair was as white as snow and his usually bright blue eyes seemed faded, and suddenly Matteo changed his mind—he wanted a lecture now! He wanted his grandfather to have brought him here to haul him over the proverbial coals, to tell Matteo that he must grow up, settle down and cease his hedonistic days.

Anything other than what, Matteo had the terrible feeling, was about to come.

'I've asked you to come here to tell you…' Giovanni started but Matteo did not want to hear it. A master in diversion, he picked up the newspaper from his grandfather's desk and unfolded it.

'For all their comparisons they forget one vital piece of information,' Matteo said. '*He* had responsibilities.'

'I know that he did,' Giovanni said, 'but you have responsibility too. To yourself. Matteo, you are heading for trouble. The company you keep, the risks you take…'

'Are mine to take,' Matteo interrupted. 'My father was married and had seven children when he died.' He jabbed at the photo. 'Well, seven that he had admitted to!'

'Matteo!' Giovanni said. This was not going as he intended. 'Sit down.'

'No!' He argued not with his grandfather but himself. 'For all they compare me to him they deliberately omit to mention that I don't have a wife and children. I'd never put anyone through the hell he made.'

He never would.

It was a decision Matteo had made a long time ago.

He was single and staying that way.

Giovanni looked at his grandson and he worried for him.

Fun-loving and charismatic, Matteo not only acted like his father at times, he looked like him too. They had the same navy eyes, the same straight nose and even their hair fell forwards in the same way.

Giovanni, for his own private reasons, had never

bonded with his son. He had never told anyone why; it was a secret he had intended to take to his grave.

In the aftermath of Benito's and Anna's deaths, five-year-old Matteo, a carbon copy of his father, had been too much of a visual reminder of Benito for Giovanni and, rather than learning from his mistakes, he had repeated them, and Giovanni had kept his distance from his grandson.

Matteo had run wild and that irrepressible personality had gone largely unchecked. When he had dropped out of college after just a year, a terrible row had ensued. Matteo had said that he didn't need to be taught about the business world—playing the stock market was in his DNA and he wanted to set up a hedge fund rather than sit in lectures—and Giovanni had told his grandson that he was just like his father and that he feared he was heading the same way. Accusations that Matteo had not needed to hear and certainly not from his grandfather.

It was too late to tame him. Giovanni had shouted at the young man, and Matteo had fought back.

'You never once tried!' It was the only glimpse Matteo had ever given to another of the pain he carried. 'You never once fought for me,' he had shouted. 'You left me to roam this house and make my own way. Don't act now as if you care.' Yes, harsh words had been said and their relationship still bore the scars to this day.

'Take a seat, Matteo,' Giovanni said.

Matteo didn't do as asked.

Troubled by his grandfather's appearance and unsettled as to what was to come, instead of sitting down, he walked over to the window. He looked out to the vast estate that had once been his playground. Matteo's grandmother had died before he had been born, so his younger sisters had been taken care of by his older sister, Allegra, while his older siblings had all headed off to boarding school.

Matteo had pretty much been left to his own devices.

'Do you remember when you used to visit me as children when your parents were still alive?' Giovanni asked.

'I don't think about that time,' Matteo answered.

He did his best to never look back.

'You were very young, of course. Maybe you can't remember...'

Oh, Matteo did.

He remembered only too well life before the Di Sione children had come to live here. He could still recall, with painful clarity, the fights that could erupt at any given time and just the sheer chaos of their existence. Of course, he hadn't understood then that there were drugs involved. Matteo had just known that his family lived on the edge.

A luxurious knife edge.

'Matteo.' Giovanni broke into his dark thoughts. 'Do you remember when I used to tell you all the story of the Lost Mistresses?'

'No.' Matteo shrugged and dismissed the conversation. As he looked out of the window to the lake, his gaze fell on a tree that was so high his stomach churned as he remembered climbing it and falling. A branch had broken his fall. Had it not, he'd probably have died.

No one had seen and no one had known.

Alma, the housekeeper, had scolded him for the grass stains on his clothes and had asked what had happened.

'I tripped near the lake,' he had said.

His ribs and head had hurt and his heart had still been pounding, not that he would let Alma see that.

Instead it had been easier to lie.

The sensation of falling still woke Matteo to this day but that wasn't all that he recalled as he stood there staring out of the window. There was a darker memory that he had never shared, one that could still bring him out in a cold sweat—pleading with his father to stop, to slow down, to please take him home.

From that day to this, Matteo had never again revealed fear.

It got you nowhere. If anything, it spurred others on.

'You surely remember,' Giovanni insisted. 'The Lost Mistresses...'

'I don't.' He shook his head.

'Then I'll remind you.'

As if I need to hear this again, Matteo thought! He said nothing, though, and let the old man speak.

'Don't ask me how I came by them, for an old man must have his secrets...' Giovanni started. Matteo remained standing, his face impassive, as his grandfather recited the tale. 'But when I came to America, I had in my possession trinkets, my Lost Mistresses. They meant more to me than you can ever know but in order to survive I was forced to sell them. My Lost Mistresses, the love of my life, we owe them everything.' Giovanni stopped speaking for a moment and looked at Matteo's pale features and unshaven jaw, which was now clenched. 'You do remember.'

'No.' Matteo was getting annoyed now. 'I've told you I don't.' He loathed delving into the past and he didn't want a trip down memory lane today. 'Do you want to go out?' he suggested. 'I could take you for a drive. We could go to your club…'

'Matteo.' Giovanni cut him off. He knew that Matteo was trying to change the subject. He loved his grandson very much. Even if they had had their problems, still Matteo came by often and took him out. He just, Giovanni knew, let no one in.

Giovanni had to put things right while he still could. 'I have to tell you something.'

'Come on, we'll go for a drive…' Matteo pushed. He did not want to be here and he did not want to hear what he knew his grandfather was about to tell him.

'I'm dying, Matteo.'

Giovanni watched his grandson for his reaction but Matteo never gave his true feelings away.

'We're all dying,' Matteo responded, trying to make light of the devastating news while his heart pounded in his chest, as still his mind fought to deny the truth.

He did not want to have this conversation.

He could not stand to think of his grandfather gone and his family together at another funeral. Images of his parents' coffins and the children all walking behind them still appeared in magazines at times and were always in his mind.

He did not want his grandfather to die.

'The leukemia is back,' Giovanni said.

'What about that treatment you had?' Matteo asked. Seventeen years ago they had nearly lost Giovanni. A bone marrow donor had been needed and all the grandchildren had been tested but none of them had returned a match. It had been then that the eldest, Alessandro, had confessed that he knew their father had another son. They had tracked Nate down and he had returned a match. 'Couldn't Nate...'

'A transplant is out of the question, and I'm not sure that treatment is the best way forward at this stage,' Giovanni said. 'The doctors say we can hope for remission but, failing that, it is a matter of months. The reality is, I have a year at best.'

'You know how I loathe reality,' Matteo said and the old man smiled.

'I do.'

And Matteo escaped reality often—in casinos, clubs, daredevil escapades, constantly pushing both his body and the hedge fund he had set up to the very brink.

How Giovanni wished he could take back the damaging words he had said and handled this complex man so much better. Yes, while there were many similarities between Matteo and his father, there were other traits too—there was an innate kindness to Matteo that had been absent in Benito, a rare kindness of which Giovanni was immensely proud. And though Matteo was eternally restless, in other ways he was the most patient man Giovanni had ever known. As his health had deteriorated, as his stamina had waned, it was Matteo who would come around and take him out, Matteo who fell easily into a slower step beside him and let Giovanni ramble as he had just done.

'Matteo, I want you to do something for me. I have something that I need for you to do if I am going to go to my grave content.'

Matteo took a breath and braced himself for the inevitable. Here came the lecture! He was quite sure he was about to be told to settle down and tame his ways and so he frowned when the old man voiced his thoughts.

'I want you to bring me one of my Lost Mistresses.'

Matteo turned and looked at his grandfather and wondered if he'd finally lost his mind. 'What on earth are you talking about?'

'My Lost Mistresses!' Giovanni went into one of the drawers in his desk and Matteo saw a flare of excitement in the old man's eyes as he took out a photo. Giovanni's hand was shaking as he handed it to Matteo.

'This necklace is one of my Lost Mistresses.'

Matteo looked at the photo. It was a lavish emerald necklace and it was, quite simply, beautiful. 'White gold?' he checked and Giovanni shook his head.

'Platinum.'

The emeralds were amazing—the size of robins' eggs, they sparkled and beguiled. They were so beautiful that even their image made Matteo reach out to run his finger over the stones. 'We thought it was just a tale that you told, that they were some old coins or something.'

'So you *do* remember!'

Matteo conceded that he did with a half smile. 'Yes, I remember you telling us your tale.' He let out a low whistle as he looked at the necklace again. 'This would be worth...' Usually he could pick this sort of thing but in this instance he really didn't know. 'Millions?' he loosely gauged.

'And some.'

'Who's the designer?' he asked. 'What jewellery house...?'

'Unknown,' Giovanni quickly said and Matteo frowned because surely a piece of jewellery as exquisite as this would have some considerable history attached.

'Is this how you got your start?' he asked. He could

see it a little more clearly. Di Sione had started as a shipping empire but now the name was global. If Giovanni had sold pieces as exquisite as this one, then Matteo could see how it might have transpired. Yet, how could a young man from Sicily come to be in possession of this?

Giovanni was less than forthcoming, though, when Matteo pushed for answers.

'I just want you to find it for me,' Giovanni said. 'I don't know where to start. I sold it to a man named Roche some sixty years ago. Since then it's been sold on.' Matteo could see that his grandfather was getting distressed and knew that this necklace really meant something to him.

'How did you come to own this?' he asked again.

'Don't ask me how I came by them, for an old man must have his secrets...' Giovanni said and Matteo gave another half smile.

Now the tale of old made a bit more sense.

'Matteo, I want that necklace. Whatever it takes. Can you find it and bring it to me?'

He looked over to his grandfather.

How he wished he could open up and tell the old man that he meant something to him, that he understood how hard the years had been on him. But Matteo was incapable of giving anyone more than a loan of that smile or body. His mind was a closed door.

So instead he nodded.

This he could do.

'You know that I shall.'

Giovanni got out of his chair and walked over to Matteo and wrapped his grandson in an embrace, something Giovanni wished he had done more of all those years ago.

Just for a moment, Matteo let himself be held, but then he pulled back.

'Come on, then,' he said, pocketing the picture in his jacket.

'Where?'

'Your club,' Matteo said and rattled his keys but then he changed his mind.

His grandfather was dying.

There was no way that he'd be driving today.

Giovanni called for his driver.

CHAPTER ONE

MATTEO DIDN'T LIKE HIM.

Not that it showed in his expression.

He just sat in Ellison's study and glanced up at the hunting trophies that lined the walls and then back to the man.

'Do I look like I need the money?' Ellison sneered.

Matteo shrugged, refusing to let the other man see that he was surprised by his response to a very generous offer.

He had been unable to find out the designer or jewellery house that the necklace had come from but had found out that Roche had sold it on to Hugo Ellison some twenty or so years ago.

Matteo vaguely knew Ellison from fundraising galas he had attended and he also knew that the man was money and power mad. He had been sure it would only take a generous donation to his political fund to secure the necklace and had set off for the meeting cocksure and confident that he would leave with what he wanted.

Now Matteo wasn't so sure.

'It was a gift to my late wife,' Ellison said.

Matteo knew enough about that marriage to be sure that Ellison wasn't crying himself to sleep at night over her death but he went along with the game. 'I'm sorry,' he said and then stood. 'It was insensitive of me to ask.' He held out his hand. 'Thank you for seeing me though.'

Ellison didn't offer his hand and when he didn't conclude the meeting, Matteo knew, even before Ellison spoke, that he held the ace—it was just a matter of time before the necklace was his.

'Actually,' Ellison said, 'it seems a shame to keep it locked up.' He looked at Matteo. 'Sit down, son.'

He loathed it when people said that.

It was just a power play, a chance to assert a stronger position, but Matteo knew he had the upper hand and so he went along with it and took a seat again.

I really *don't like you*, Matteo thought as Ellison poured them both a drink.

'How come you're interested in the necklace?' Ellison asked.

'I appreciate beauty,' he answered and Ellison gave a smug smile.

'And me.'

Ellison knew who Matteo was, of course. Everyone knew the Di Siones and he knew Matteo's reputation with women.

Yes, Matteo appreciated beauty.

'Didn't you date Princess…?'

'I don't date,' Matteo interrupted and Ellison laughed.

'Good call. So, how far are you prepared to go?'

'How much do you want?' Matteo asked.

'Not how much, how far?' Ellison corrected. 'I believe you like a challenge.'

'I do.'

'And from what I've read about you, impossible odds don't daunt you.'

'They don't.'

They thrilled Matteo, in fact.

'See this.' Ellison beckoned for him to stand and Matteo walked over and they stood staring at a portrait of Ellison and his late wife, Anette, and their two daughters. 'This was taken at our charity gala some twelve years ago.'

'Your wife was a very beautiful woman.' And very rich, Matteo thought. A lot of Ellison's wealth had come from her family and Matteo privately wondered just how far Ellison's political career would have gone without Anette's billions.

'Anette knew how to play the game,' Ellison said. 'We had a terrible fight the day before that photo was taken. She'd found out that I was sleeping with my assistant, but you wouldn't know it from that photo.'

'No.' Matteo looked at Anette's smiling face as she stood by her man. 'You wouldn't.'

Ellison's revelation didn't shock Matteo; instead it wearied him.

He peered at Ellison's daughters. They were both immaculate—one was dressed in oyster grey, the other in beige, and both were wearing the requisite pearls. One had her hair neatly up and the other... A small smile played on Matteo's lips as he examined the younger daughter more closely. Her dark wavy hair, despite a velvet band, was untamed and her eyes were angry. Her smile was forced and it looked as if the hand her father had on her shoulder was not a proud display of affection, more that it was there to hold her down.

'That's Abby.'

Ellison's sigh as he said her name told Matteo that Abby was the bane of his existence.

'Look at this one,' Ellison said and they moved on to the next photo. 'It must have been…' Ellison thought back. 'I think Abby's about five here, so some twenty-two years ago.'

Abby's eyes were red, Matteo noted.

Well, they were actually a vivid green but she'd clearly been crying.

'The only way we could get her to sit in a dress for the photo was to give her a toy car. She was obsessed with cars even then.'

Matteo had no idea where this was leading but he had learned long ago that all knowledge was power and so he let Ellison drone on. He could also see that in the photo Anette was wearing the necklace that Giovanni so badly wanted.

'Abby was upset because we'd just fired the nanny. Both the girls were terribly fond of her,' Ellison said. 'My wife insisted on it though.'

Now they were getting somewhere! Matteo guessed that it wasn't just the daughters who'd been fond of the nanny.

'And this,' Ellison said, moving along, 'is the last photo I have of my daughter in a dress.'

There Abby stood on a red carpet, with a good-looking blond man by her side.

A man Matteo thought that he recognised.

'Hunter Coleman ,' Ellison said and Matteo nodded as he now placed him. Hunter was a top racing driver and had a reputation with women that rivalled even Matteo's. 'Abby dated him for a while,' Ellison explained. 'Anyway, as I said, she always had a thing for cars. If I couldn't find her, then she'd be in the garage, pulling apart a Bentley, or taking the engine out of a Jag. I tried to get her out of it—it's not exactly fitting for a young woman of her standing. She went off to college to study fashion and started dating Hunter and finally I thought that the tomboy in her was gone. The trouble is, unlike her mother, my darling daughter doesn't know how to stand and offer quiet support. No, Abby, being Abby, had to offer a top racing driver advice on his racing technique.'

Matteo laughed but then it trailed off.

Hunter's hand was closed tightly around Abby's, and again, despite the smile, her eyes were…not angry. Matteo looked more closely.

Guarded.

It was the best he could come up with—but no, despite the smile for the camera, that wasn't a happy young woman.

'Anyway, she dumped him!' Ellison sounded shocked. 'God knows how she thought she could do better, and then she switched from studying fashion to automotive engineering. Now she's…'

'The Boucher team!' Matteo could place her as well now. Well, not Abby specifically, but yes, he knew a little about the emerging racing team.

'Boucher was my wife's maiden name.' Ellison sighed. 'It's a very expensive hobby…'

'I can imagine.'

'Oh, believe me, you can't.' Ellison shook his head. 'Especially when the owner of the team refuses to play the corporate game and chat up sponsors. As I said to Abby last week, she's going to have to find the cash. I'm not bailing her out.'

'Has she asked?'

'Not yet!' Ellison's smug smile returned. 'But the rest of her mother's trust fund is tied up till she's thirty or married. There's no chance of *that* girl marrying, which means she's got no income for another three years!'

'Why are you telling me this?' Matteo asked.

'Because, as you must have heard, I'm on the comeback trail. In July I'm going to be holding my first political fundraiser since my wife's death. I've told Abby that if she comes, and looks the part, and by that I mean she loses the jeans and oil rags, then I'll give her a cash injection to tide her over.'

'Has she said that she's coming?'

'Not yet,' Ellison said. 'But I need her to be there. Image is everything in politics and I don't want there to be even a whiff of discord, Annabel, my eldest daughter, will do the right thing but I want Abby to be here too. I want my daughter, at my function, wearing her mother's necklace. I want her looking like a woman for once...'

She looked all woman to Matteo.

'Can you manage that?' Ellison asked.

'Sorry?' Matteo frowned.

'You said that you like a challenge. You like women—see if you can sweet-talk her and get Abby to show up here, looking the part. If she does, at the end of the night, the necklace is yours.'

'How am I supposed to persuade her if you can't...?' Matteo started but then, guessing Ellison's intent, he shook his head. 'No way.'

Ellison just laughed. 'I'm not asking you to seduce her. I don't think you'd get very far. Rumour has it my daughter isn't particularly interested in men.'

No, Matteo really, *really* didn't like this man.

'She hasn't dated anyone since Hunter and it hasn't gone unnoticed,' Ellison said, frowning at the photo. 'I want that rumour quashed. I want Abby here, dressed like a woman and with a handsome chap by her side.' Ellison returned his gaze to Matteo and continued. 'You could be a potential sponsor, considering investing in her team.'

'It's April,' Matteo pointed out. 'Your fundraiser isn't until July. How long am I supposed to be *considering* investing for?'

'I'd be giving you the necklace for nothing, perhaps the money you've earmarked for it could go towards convincing my daughter that you want to sponsor the team.'

'And if she doesn't come to your fundraiser?'

'You don't get your necklace.'

Matteo could cheerfully have knocked Ellison's lights out but instead he watched as Ellison went over to the safe and took out a gleaming polished wooden box and handed it to him.

Oh, my God, Matteo thought as he undid the intricate latch and saw the necklace firsthand.

Not even the photos did it justice.

How the hell had his grandfather come by this? Matteo wondered, and he could see now why he would want it back.

Jewellery had never really impressed Matteo.

This piece couldn't fail to.

'I doubt it's possible to get Abby here,' Ellison said.

Matteo looked over to Ellison and then back to the necklace and he took Ellison's words as a dare—which was something he never said no to.

And his grandfather wanted the necklace so badly.

No, he could never be the man his grandfather wanted him to be but this he could do.

'Can you give me your daughter's contact details?' Matteo asked.

His mind was made up—he would get this Lost Mistress back to where it belonged.

CHAPTER TWO

ELLISON HAD BEEN right about one thing—his daughter Abby really was terrible at the corporate stuff.

It had taken two weeks for her to reply to Matteo's email and at best her response had been lukewarm.

Of course Matteo had looked into the Boucher team more closely by then.

He was a risk-taker by nature, but they were, even by his standards, more of a gamble than one should take.

It was their second year in competition and their best was a fifth place last year. Frequently, they placed last or second last. Now they were competitors in the Henley Cup—a prestigious international event, held over three races.

They weren't considered a mention.

Matteo finally decided to call Abby but *effusive* wasn't a word that had sprung to mind when she told him that no, they couldn't meet, given that she was on her way to Dubai.

'So am I,' he, on impulse, had replied.

'Excuse me?'

'I've got a couple of racehorses that I want to look at and my sister Allegra is holding a charity event in May... Hold on.' Matteo checked his calendar. 'Yes, that's on Saturday the seventh. How about lunch on the Friday?'

'I won't be able to get away for lunch.'

'Dinner, then?' Matteo persisted and she returned his offer with a long stretch of silence. 'Breakfast?'

'Just stop by the track.'

'Sure,' he said. 'I'll look forward…'

She had already rung off.

The heat was fierce in Dubai.

And as for the humidity!

Suffice to say, with the hangover Matteo had, he would far rather be in the airconditioned comfort of his hotel than in the goldfish bowl of a racetrack. The sun seemed to be coming at him from all angles as he made his way to the Boucher sheds.

Matteo had been in Dubai for three days and what an amazing three days they had been. The first had consisted of a wild welcome on board his friend Sheikh Kedah's yacht.

Kedah seemed hell-bent on returning the wild week Matteo had given him on a recent trip to New York City. The second day had been spent galloping at breakneck speed with his friend along a beach. Matteo had taken a tumble and dislocated his shoulder. The sheikh had called for his private physician to put it back. With Matteo's arm strapped and a little out of action they had hit the racetracks and placed a few bets on a camel race. The potential two years' jail time for illegal betting had only served to give Matteo an extra high!

It had been a giddy introduction to Dubai but now he had crashed back to earth—the smell of oil was nauseating and the sound from the track had his molars aching. He'd lost the sling that the physician had provided and so his shoulder was killing him.

And Abby Ellison was nowhere to be seen.

It was after four and he wondered if she might have finished for the day. A group of guys were watching as Pedro, the Boucher driver, put the car through its paces. He knew it was Pedro because Matteo recognised the deep green of the Boucher car.

Matteo had done some further research on the team, of course.

They had entered in the prestigious Henley Cup. A series of three races—Dubai, Milan and Monte Carlo. The final race took place in July a week before Ellison's fundraiser.

As newcomers the Boucher team wasn't being taken seriously, especially because the owner was a woman. Just a little rich girl playing with her daddy's money seemed to be the general consensus.

Pedro Sanchez, their driver, was someone who was being watched seriously though, and there were a couple of other teams who had their eye on him.

The group of men all ignored him and that suited Matteo just fine. He just drank from a large bottle of cola and idly watched.

Or rather, at first, he idly watched.

Matteo had never really been in to cars and not just because his parents had died in a crash. His father had once taken a five-year-old Matteo for a joy-ride.

There was no joy in that memory!

Still, this was different—Pedro was really putting the car through its paces now, hugging the bend, belting it down the straight, and the roar of the motor was, as it flew past him, a bit of a turn-on.

'Whoa!' one of the guys shouted as the car lost traction, but then Pedro skilfully righted it and Matteo watched as the car again sped down the straight and then slowed down as it came towards them.

'Hey...'

Matteo turned as someone greeted him and blinked in vague surprise. 'Pedro...' Matteo shook his hand; he recognised the young man himself from his research. 'Sorry for the double take. I thought that I was watching you out there. I didn't realise there were two drivers.'

'No, no...' Pedro said. 'Soon you'll get to see me drive. That's Abby—she's just checking out some adjustments that she has made.'

Matteo looked back at the car and, sure enough, climbing out from it, dressed in tight leather, was *no* man, and the vague turn-on Matteo had felt before was rather less vague now.

He hadn't known that he was in to leather either!

The racing world was looking up, he decided as she took off her helmet and the fire guard and then shook her long dark hair out.

She was tall enough to wear her curves well, and if she only smiled he would return it with the best of his. And Matteo's smile could melt. But then he remembered he was not here to seduce and so he kept his business expression on.

'So,' Pedro said, 'I hear that you have a meeting with Abby.'

'I do.'

'Good,' Pedro responded and he could hear the slight edge to the man's voice. 'Then I guess it's time for me to show you a little of what I can do.' He looked over to Abby, who had reached them now. 'How is she?'

'Oh, she's running like silk now.'

They spoke as if the car was a person!

'I've warmed her up for you,' Abby said and then, as Pedro headed off towards the car, she finally acknowledged Matteo. 'Di Sione?'

'Yes.' He smiled. 'But you can call me Matteo.'

Abby didn't return the smile.

Instead she blanked him and turned her attention to Pedro, who was climbing into the car.

Was she always this polite with investors? Matteo pondered.

'How long has Pedro been out here?' Matteo enquired, wondering how long he'd had to acclimatise to the hot and humid conditions.

'Long enough,' Abby said and then carried on ignoring him as Pedro started to do some laps.

'Why don't we...?' Matteo started but his voice was drowned out by the sound of the engine and he had to wait till Pedro had passed before continuing. 'Why don't we go somewhere we can talk?'

Still she ignored him and watched the track intently and then, when Pedro had finished a few laps, she turned and finally answered him.

'I don't think so.'

'Sorry?'

'I don't need an investor who wants to pull me away.'

'But Pedro's finished.'

'I'm watching the competition,' she said.

'And you *do* need an investor,' Matteo said.

Not this one, Abby thought.

She knew the Di Sione name, of course she did, and she had looked Matteo up.

Of course she had.

Reckless, wild and debauched, she had read, but looking at the photos of him and finding out a little more about her potential sponsor, it didn't take long for her to work out that he was also as sexy as all hell.

And Abby didn't like sexy.

It terrified her, in fact.

Abby had seen and recognised Matteo the second she had stepped out of the car. He was even better in the flesh and her stomach had curled in a way she would prefer it did not.

She had also seen and felt his eyes roam her body as she had walked towards them and had felt her cheeks turn pink from that fact.

'Can I get earplugs?' Matteo asked. Another team was taking their car out and his hangover was making itself known again. 'I guess we can resort to sign language if we're not allowed to go somewhere decent to talk.'

'Decent?' Abby frowned. What sort of a sponsor was he? Didn't he get that she lived trackside?

She watched Evan put his car through its paces. She had been waiting all day to watch this. Evan Lewis, driver of the Carter team, was one of the Boucher team's toughest opponents. Her friend Bella, who she had studied engineering with, worked for the Carter team and had told Abby that the engine, along with the driver, were poetry in motion. Yes, she had waited all day to see this but as Evan in the aqua-blue car tested the track, she found that she couldn't concentrate.

Matteo stood beside her, swigging from his bottle, which made her thirsty, and as she licked her lips he offered her a drink, as if they had known each other for months.

She gave him a terse shake of her head and he moved forwards and leaned on the rail and bent over a little.

And she noticed.

Oh, she tried to watch Evan but her eyes kept flicking to Matteo's long legs and to a white, slightly crumpled shirt that, despite the heat, wasn't damp. He had a bruise over his left eye and she wanted to know where it had come from. He put down his bottle and in her peripheral vision she saw that he was undoing his shirt.

What the hell?

He turned then and gave her a smile as he popped his hand into the gap he had made in his shirt. 'I've hurt my shoulder,' he briefly explained.

She didn't return his smile, nor did she comment.

Instead she walked off.

Matteo had had enough. He'd just have to work out another way to get his grandfather the necklace because if this was the way Abby dealt with sponsors he could just imagine her reaction to him suggesting what she wear to her father's fundraiser!

'Guess what,' he said as he caught up with her. 'You've just lost possibly the most hands-off sponsor you could have ever hoped find...' He looked into the green eyes that would not meet his. 'I'm going. I've decided that I don't want to do business with you. You're rude,' he said and then saw that, just a little, she smiled. 'You're not very nice.'

'I'm not.'

Now she met his eyes and, with contact made, he changed his mind; maybe they could work together after all.

'That's okay,' Matteo said. 'I'll settle for polite.'

Abby gave him an assessing look. She liked it that he had said he'd be hands off—that had been one of the main issues with their previous sponsor; he had demanded so much of Pedro's time. And she liked, too, that Matteo had addressed up front the issue—she'd been rude.

'I can manage polite,' she said.

'Good.' He drained the last of his cola. 'I do need to get something to eat.'

She said something then but it was drowned out by the roar of a car and he couldn't make out the words.

He just watched her mouth.

'I can't hear you,' Matteo said and she had to watch his mouth now. 'Dinner?' he suggested. Finally there was a lull in the noise and he said it again. 'Dinner?'

'Here?' Abby checked and Matteo looked around. The race wasn't till next week and so the corporate caterers weren't here yet.

'Well, I'd prefer a nice lazy meal back at my eight-star hotel but if you insist on here, then I guess it will have to do. Do they have hot dogs in Dubai?'

Abby nodded to a van. 'Not hot dogs exactly…' She took a breath; they were about to talk big business and a takeaway back in the shed really wouldn't cut it. 'When you say your hotel…' She saw him frown, but no, she would make very sure where they would be eating before she agreed to go back to his hotel. 'You do mean the restaurant?'

'What the hell did you think I meant?' Matteo grinned. 'Of course I meant the restaurant. Don't believe everything you read about me, Abby—I'm fast but not that fast.'

She laughed.

Matteo had no idea what a rare sound that was.

'Do you want to meet there?' he suggested, assuming she had a car.

'Sure,' she agreed, and he told her the name of the hotel he was staying at. 'I'll just get changed,' she said, but aware of all she had in her locker she was factoring in a dash back to her own hotel too.

'Please…' He stopped abruptly. Matteo had been about to say, 'Please don't.' She looked amazing in the Boucher green leather after all, but there was something that stopped him and he quickly changed his plea. 'Go ahead,' he said. 'I'll meet you there on the hour.'

Abby felt her cheeks go a little pink again.

'Is it okay if I have a look around before I head off?' he asked.

'Of course.'

One of the mechanics who was peeling a pear offered Matteo half and, when he took it, offered to show him around. It was actually fascinating. There was a whole wall of tyres that would see them through just one race and the science of it all was something Matteo had never considered.

Abby took her time to get ready. Given Matteo had said that they were meeting on the hour there really was no time to go back to her hotel and change. Also, she was incredibly nervous. Oh, she had sat through her share of dinners and lunches, of course, just not with someone as gorgeous as he, and not with someone who made her smile.

Yes, she knew that she came across as brittle at times, but she had been particularly awful to him.

She forgave herself then.

After all, she knew why.

So, what to wear to dinner at an eight-star hotel with a stunning man when you have neither the time nor inclination for a dress but all you have in your locker is a pair of ill-fitting jeans, a massive black T-shirt and flat sandals?

She suppressed a smile because she had known exactly what Matteo had been about to say regarding her leather suit. That was why her cheeks had gone pink. It had felt a little like flirting and Abby wasn't in the least good at that.

She put on some dark glasses and ran a comb through her hair. As she left the locker room she took out her phone to call for a taxi and then startled when she saw that Matteo was still there.

'Sorry, I thought you'd have your own car. Why didn't you say?' he asked.

'I just…' Abby shrugged.

'Come on,' he said and put on his own dark glasses before heading back out in the sun.

What the hell happened there? he thought as they walked to his car. It was as if Abby had done everything possible to look as unattractive as she could. The jeans were massive and as for the T-shirt!

Maybe hot dogs would be a better idea after all.

He glanced down and he didn't think he'd seen an unpainted female toenail before.

Half an hour spent getting ready, for that!

'Will they mind jeans at the hotel?' Abby checked as he drove them there.

'Not the way you wear them.' Matteo turned and smiled. 'You look great.'

Again, she laughed.

'You are such...' She just laughed again. 'I wasn't expecting to go out for dinner, okay? I do know I'm badly dressed.'

'For who?' Matteo shrugged.

He was relaxing to her.

Oh, she was on edge, Abby knew, yet somehow Matteo was relaxing to her.

'What happened to your eye?' she asked.

'I came off a horse,' he said. 'That's how I dislocated my shoulder. I'm supposed to be wearing a shoulder strap.'

'So, why aren't you?'

'I lost it.'

'Oh.'

He was so incredibly handsome and she felt incredibly drab.

'I could stop by my hotel and get changed,' Abby offered, still a little worried that she was way underdressed.

'No need.'

It was, however, Matteo thought, a seriously nice restaurant they were heading to. Seriously, seriously nice but thankfully he'd been here with the sheikh and had lobbed enough tips these past days that he knew they'd give him a welcome smile as they walked in.

But he didn't want her to be uncomfortable.

'We could go to Majlis Al Bahar...' Matteo glanced over and he saw her nervous swallow. 'I'm not getting romantic,' he reassured, because it was possibly the most romantic restaurant on earth. 'It's just that the dress code is more casual and,' he added, 'I kind of want to try it.'

'No,' Abby said. 'The hotel's fine.

So his hotel it was.

'Table for two,' Matteo told the maître d' and such was his confidence that, of course, no one turned a hair and they were shown to their seats.

Her glasses off, those disgusting jeans tucked away, she really was beautiful, Matteo thought. Her eyes were an intense green and thickly lashed and she was the first woman he had ever sat in a restaurant with who wore not a trace of make-up.

He knew what she'd look like in the morning, Matteo thought. Then he reminded himself that he wasn't here for that and so he looked from Abby and out to the view of the Arabian Gulf. 'I love it here,' he admitted. 'I didn't expect to, then again I had no real idea what to expect.'

'I haven't seen much of it,' Abby said. 'We only got here yesterday...'

Matteo was astute enough to frown. 'So how is Pedro doing with the heat?'

She liked that he understood that it mattered.

'A few days more to acclimatise would have been nice,' Abby admitted.

'Is Pedro as temperamental as the press make out?' Matteo asked.

'More so.' She sighed. 'I can't blame him though. He's an amazing talent.'

'You've given him a very early break,' Matteo said, remembering that Pedro had just turned twenty-one and had been nineteen when Abby had taken him on. 'Shouldn't he still be doing the dinky tracks in a go-kart?'

Abby smiled but it was a guarded one. 'He's going to be amazing—he already is.'

He saw her tight smile and read it.

Someone with a far bigger cash pot would snap him up very soon.

'Treat him like a star, then,' Matteo said. 'Make him never want to leave.' He saw the set of her lips. 'What's his latest gripe?' he asked and her mouth relaxed into a soft laugh at his perception.

'Well, some of the other drivers have suites with their own gym and lap pool.' She looked at Matteo, who said nothing. 'These guys are incredibly fit. You have to be to race at that speed. I know how taxing it is just doing a few gentle laps.'

'It didn't look particularly gentle to me,' Matteo said. 'So, what's it like?' he asked. 'Driving one?'

And she knew the line the guys used but that would really tip her into flirting with him.

'It's amazing,' she said, instead of saying that it was better than sex.

It had to be.

Her one experience had been hell after all.

No, she would not be flirting.

'Pedro doesn't like using the hotel pool and gym,' Abby said. 'And I get that, I do, but...' She loathed talking about money, but that was what they were here to do. 'Our budget's tight.'

'And Pedro doesn't want to hear that?'

'He's been really good,' Abby said. 'They all have been. It's hard watching the others swan off to fancy restaurants when we're heading for the burger bar. We all want better things and know that we have to work for it. It's just hard juggling egos. And also I know that Pedro's right—he'd do better with more resources and

I'd do better if I had more time to focus on the car and the opposition.'

'Instead of playing bookkeeper?' Matteo asked and she gave a low laugh.

'And PA, and travel agent…'

'I get it.'

How could he? 'How come you want to invest?' she asked him.

'Well, I think you're going places,' Matteo said. 'And I want to be securely on board when you do. I have a thing for outside chances.' He looked at the wine menu. 'What are we drinking?' Matteo asked.

'Water for me…'

'You're a cheap date.'

'This isn't a date, Matteo,' she said.

'Actually, no, it isn't.' He put down the menu and was serious. He was interested in sponsoring the team. Seriously so. Matteo was a gambler by nature but this was a huge one. He wasn't thinking about the necklace or her father now. Matteo's head was in the game and if he was going to be a sponsor, then there had to be rules. 'My relationships run into hours rather than days. Believe me, you don't want to know…'

'I already do!' she said.

'Which means, if we want this to work, then it's hands off each other.'

'I'm good with that,' she said.

'Anyway,' Matteo added, 'I don't date.'

'And I don't drink.'

'At all?'

'Nope.' She shook her head.

'Ever?'

'Never.' She smiled at his curiosity. 'Well, I tried it and didn't like it.'

'Okay, water for two it is.'

'You can.'

'I know that I can,' Matteo said, 'but I'm keeping my wits about me with you.'

He looked at the menu and groaned. 'Truffle-crusted scallops—I know what I'm having.'

His groan made her stomach tighten; the low sound of his want caused her breath to hold in her throat, and then he looked up.

His eyes were the darkest navy and when he smiled so, too, did she.

'That's better,' Matteo said.

He was nice, her heart said.

Just that.

The food was amazing and the company too, and he really did take her concerns seriously.

'I had a sponsor last year, not a particularly generous one,' Abby explained. 'He rang all the time, wanted constant progress reports. Race day was hell. He wanted me to join him and his cronies for a champagne brunch and Pedro to be sociable...'

'Look, I get you don't want someone sticking their nose in and I can manage lunch by myself. And, for what it's worth, I won't be putting pressure on you or your team. I wouldn't expect much this year...'

'Oh, no,' Abby interrupted. 'We're winning the Henley Cup this year.'

'I'm just saying that I'm patient.'

'Pedro will be off soon,' Abby said. 'He's a rising star and someone will make an offer that I can't match any day soon.'

'Probably.' Matteo nodded. He'd thought the same but now he could really see the problem. 'Hunter's retiring at the end of this year and I guess the Lachance team...' He paused, remembering that Abby had briefly dated him. 'Hey, didn't you two...?'

'We're winning this year,' Abby said, not answering the question. 'I want the Henley Cup—Dubai first, then Italy, then Monte Carlo.'

'Then you need to keep your driver happy,' Matteo said. 'How tight is it?' he asked.

No one knew just how bad it was and Abby was extremely reluctant to tell him.

Matteo watched as she fiddled with her glass. 'The only thing I want in a relationship is honesty,' he said and then he started to laugh. 'I only get to use that line in business.'

Even Abby laughed.

'So, how about we be honest with each other? Whatever you tell me goes no further than here, whatever we then decide.'

She believed him. And, Abby thought, maybe it would be a relief to tell someone the truth.

No one knew just how bad it was.

Her team all thought she was particularly tense; they didn't know that she was waking up in dread every night. Abby was even considering agreeing to her father's ridiculous bribe to go along to his fundraiser just for the injection of cash he had promised if she did.

The very thought of that made her sick.

She wondered if the photograph of her and Hunter still hung on her father's study wall.

Abby closed her eyes for a second, as panic briefly hit.

No, she would not be going cap in hand to her father.

She opened her eyes to Matteo's waiting ones and decided to tell him the truth.

'I can't get us to Italy.'

Matteo said nothing.

'I've got the car and equipment covered but I can't get the team there.'

'The money's run out?'

Abby nodded.

He didn't get up and walk off and he didn't berate.

He just sat there.

Thinking.

Then he gave in on water and called for a large cognac.

And still he sat there thinking.

Not about the necklace that he was supposed to be here for; instead he was thinking about cars and a team and it gave him a buzz that had been missing at the casino of late. He didn't like motor racing. Fast cars were the only vice he didn't have. There were too many painful memories attached.

Yet, he was starting to come around.

Watching Abby and later Pedro putting the car through its paces, speaking with the mechanics, gauging the opposition...

There was an attraction to the sport that Matteo had never anticipated when he had taken the challenge on.

He asked for figures and she went red in the neck but told him, and she watched as he crunched a few numbers on a calculator.

Not his phone, she noted.

And it wasn't a two-dollar calculator either.

He had beautiful hands, Abby thought, and she liked the way his tongue popped out as he concentrated.

Matteo knew he should conclude this meeting now. The type of money that was required here outweighed the necklace and there was practically a guarantee of zero return.

'Why do you think you're a chance?' he asked.

'I built the car,' Abby said. 'I have the most fearless driver I've ever seen. Pedro's a bit raw but that's good. He's unpredictable. No one except for me—actually, not even me—knows what he's capable of...'

Still Matteo looked.

'But he needs the right tool and my car is that.'

Still he looked. His face gave away nothing, Abby thought, but he had demanded honesty and if that was the case there was something rather large that she was leaving out.

'And I've been waiting nine years for this.'

She didn't tell him why; she just told him that she had.

He saw something then and its name was determination.

No, the numbers might not add up but the feeling in his gut tipped the scale.

'Tell you what,' Matteo finally said and Abby found she was holding her breath. 'If you can come in in the top five here in Dubai, then I'll take care of getting the team to Italy.'

'Will you be staying to watch?'

'God, yes,' Matteo said. 'And sorry if you don't like it but if you do place, then I'll be in Italy too. Don't worry though. I shan't be breathing down your neck.'

And for the first time, possibly ever, Abby imagined

just that—a man breathing down her neck, or even *on* her neck…

Not just any man.

Him.

He expected her to backtrack, to maybe push for a lower place, but instead she looked straight back at him.

'We're going to do better than fifth.'

He really, really hoped so.

And so, too, did she.

'Right,' Matteo said and called for the bill and then he asked for her bank details.

'We haven't placed yet.'

'I'm just making sure that you do.'

He paid and then asked for a driver to take her back to her hotel. 'My sister Allegra has got a big charity event tomorrow. I think we should go.'

'You said…' Abby started but Matteo overrode her.

'Everyone will be there, including the press. It might rattle the opposition if they think you've got a Di Sione on board.' He tapped the side of his head. 'Mind games.'

Oh, it would seriously rattle the opposition and Abby would take any edge that she could get.

She thought of Hunter and that terrible night and she *had* to beat him this year.

It was her only chance for revenge.

'Abby, you need to ooze confidence,' Matteo said. 'Doesn't matter how you feel on the inside.'

'Please.' She rolled her eyes. 'It's easy for you…'

'You don't know me,' Matteo interrupted. 'But believe me when I say, never let them smell fear.'

She nodded.

'So will you come?' he asked.

'Yes.'

'Good,' Matteo said. 'After tomorrow I'll leave you alone to do your thing. If I send a car for you at ten would that be okay?'

'There's no need for that. I'll meet you here.'

'Sure.'

When her car arrived it was Matteo, rather than the driver, who opened the door for her, and they spoke for a moment before she got in.

'I'll see you tomorrow,' he said and she nodded and then he shook her hand. 'And you need to dress up.'

'Excuse me?' she flared.

'I don't care what you wear in your down time,' Matteo said. 'But if you want to wear the Di Sione name on your car and your overalls, then you have to look the part when we're out.'

'And I thought brunch on race day was an imposition...' She was about to tell him to get stuffed but not only couldn't Abby afford to, she didn't want to either. He was right; if her team were going to get anywhere, then maybe it was time to play the corporate game a touch and maybe she could do that with him.

He hadn't turned a hair at her jeans; he had made her feel relaxed and comfortable as she had told him the terrible mess she was in.

'Tomorrow is work,' he said as Abby climbed into the car but then, just before he closed the door, he gave her that smile. 'Not that we can't enjoy ourselves while working.'

The car drove off and Abby found her heart was thumping. They had very carefully laid the ground rules at the table—they were completely hands off, she knew that.

Matteo's inference had been that they would simply enjoy provoking the press and the opposition.

It was her own imagination that was for the first time, if not exactly running wild, then peeking out and blinking at the sun.

A dark sun named Matteo Di Sione.

CHAPTER THREE

ABBY DIDN'T SLEEP WELL.

Yes, their conversation last night about money should have reassured her but Abby knew that she'd lied to Matteo.

They didn't really have a hope of making fifth place.

But they had to though.

Not just for the chance of Matteo investing in them.

Her breakfast was delivered and Abby decided to eat it in bed and, as she did, she took out her laptop and read the news.

The sports news, of course.

The Boucher team barely got a mention.

The Carter team were on form, she read, and the Lachance team got plenty of mentions too.

Or rather Hunter did.

She looked at him, dressed in his familiar yellow leather and wearing that cocky, arrogant smile, and if there was such a thing as pure hate, then Abby felt that now.

She wasn't scared of him any more.

It had been nine years since that terrible night and now, instead of scared, she was angry.

And it was such an undiluted, white-hot anger that ravaged her that it required revenge.

Hunter was thirty-four now and, to date, the Henley cup had been his for nine of the past ten years.

The one year that he had lost it had been the night that Abby had chosen to end their brief relationship.

Foolish timing perhaps but she had arrived in Monte Carlo and had sat in a hotel room, knowing their time together had ended.

They had only been going out for four weeks but Hunter wanted to move things along.

He'd invited her to Monte Carlo.

There would be separate hotel rooms, Hunter had assured her, given he needed his space before a race, but Abby knew very well what was going to come after.

She had gone on the pill but even as she had flown there, Abby had known that the nerves she felt weren't the ones you should be feeling when you were about to lose your virginity.

Hunter made her feel nervous, in a way that she couldn't quite define.

It had been cars that that had drawn them together at first but it hadn't taken long to realise he didn't want a discussion.

Hunter talked and she was supposed to listen.

Everything she had said about cars he had dismissed.

Oh, at eighteen, who wouldn't be flattered to be going out with a star and to be picked up and whisked off to Monte Carlo in his private jet?

Only the gloss had already worn off by then.

Abby hadn't wanted to go but her father had been appalled when she'd suggested cancelling.

Hunter's jet was already on the way!

And so, Abby had gone. She had had a few drinks for courage during the race and then back at the hotel, as Hunter had faced the press after his surprise loss, Abby had had a couple more.

He had phoned and said that he was back at the hotel and Abby had taken the elevator up to Hunter's room to tell him that no, she didn't want to go out tonight and neither did she want to stay in.

In fact, Abby had already booked a ticket and was flying home to New York that night.

As her father had later pointed out—you don't tell a man who has just lost a cup that you're breaking up with him.

So what? Abby had thought at the time.

She hadn't wanted to sleep with him and if she'd stayed, then she knew how the night was expected to end. Abby didn't want her first to be Hunter; it had been as simple as that.

And, her father had also added, Hunter's lawyers would make mincemeat out of her, given that she'd gone to his hotel room after all.

Drunk.

'Not drunk, Dad, I was just...' But then she had stopped trying to describe how she had felt that night as she'd knocked on his hotel door.

Abby couldn't really remember how she had felt before it happened.

She simply couldn't remember who the woman was that had stepped into a man's hotel suite and expected to be able to speak her mind.

Which she had.

They were over, Abby had told him.

'Not quite,' Hunter said.

She hadn't fought enough, according to her father.

There wasn't a scratch on Hunter after all.

Abby had frozen when first he had grabbed her and then she had tried to run but had only made it a few steps across his suite and he had pushed her into the bathroom.

And when *it* was over, when she lay on a cold bathroom floor and thought she could not be more broken both inside or out, Hunter had stood and then urinated over her.

Just to be sure.

Absolutely he had broken her.

Not now.

'I'll take that cup from you,' Abby vowed and spoke to the screen. 'You'll go out the loser you really are.'

Matteo was right: it was all about mind games.

Today Hunter and the other teams would find out that Matteo Di Sione was considering coming on board.

And that would rattle them.

The Di Sione empire was amazing—from shipping, to apps, to computers, they had their hand in everything and had money everywhere.

Matteo was right again: she needed to ooze confidence, not dread.

Maybe now was not the time to be spending money on clothes when she was worried about the hotel bill but there were slim pickings in her wardrobe.

There was a dress that might have been handy for dinner yesterday but wasn't suitable for a gala event.

And then there was the dress that Abby had sworn she would wear if they ever made it to the podium.

It was sexy; it was the colour of tarnished silver with a slight green hue and just way too much for today.

Truth be known, Abby could never see herself having the confidence to wear it—wherever they placed.

She knew that she would have to buy something for today.

Abby signed into her bank account and blinked when she saw the balance.

Oh, my God!

Matteo had meant what he said about ensuring they had every chance of winning.

Nervous, excited and more than a little bit relieved, instead of quickly dressing and hitting the shops Abby dealt with serious business first and rang down to Reception. Having made the necessary arrangements, she called Pedro.

'Hi,' Abby said when he picked up.

'Abby, I don't have time to talk.' Pedro's tone was clipped. 'I am just going down to the pool and then I'm hitting the gym.'

'About that,' Abby said. 'Pedro, I've just spoken with Reception and you're being moved to a suite with its own lap pool and gym.'

'You're serious?'

'I am. Someone's already on their way to move your things.'

'Abby, thanks,' Pedro said. 'This will really help with my training.'

'Good.'

It seemed like an unnecessary luxury, but Abby knew that it wasn't. The facilities in Dubai were stunning and she knew only too well that the other top teams would be utilizing them. Pedro would be out running in the midday heat. He would do everything he could to get his body prepared for the race and so it was very nice to be able to give him this.

Now she could concentrate on getting ready for today.

The shopping in Dubai was supposed to be amazing too but Abby really didn't have the time or the inclination to explore. There were, though, some boutiques on the ground floor of the hotel and one had caught her eye when they checked in.

It wasn't one of the famous international designers; instead it was a niche boutique from a local designer and tentatively Abby stepped inside.

The dresses were exquisite and, when the assistant found out where she was going today, she took Abby under her wing.

Abby had studied fashion for a year; she could mentally dress anyone so long as it wasn't herself. Even though she had been pushed into it by her father, Abby had vaguely enjoyed it and knew what she liked—and understated was it!

'This one,' the assistant said, holding up a dress in pale coral. It was a very sheer fabric with a slip dress beneath and it was very feminine and floaty and really not the sort of thing Abby would choose.

'What about this,' Abby suggested and held up a similar dress in grey, but the assistant shook her head.

'Try the coral one on.'

Oh, Abby hated this.

It felt as if she was dressing up for a family photo, she thought as she stepped into a large changing room. But reminding herself it was business, she put the dress on.

'You look very elegant,' the assistant said after she had asked Abby if she could see it on.

'It's a bit much.' Abby shook her head, thinking of it with high heels, but the assistant was far more used to this type of thing and disappeared.

'Try these,' she said when she returned and handed Abby a pair of flat strappy sandals. They were thin jewelled straps and yet somehow very neutral, and when she tried them on the assistant was right—the dress looked more sophisticated than it would with high heels.

'I like it,' Abby admitted.

'You need to get your hair smoothed out and then tied back,' the assistant said and, remembering Matteo's comments last night, Abby wondered if people in Dubai just spoke their mind.

'I really don't have time to get my hair done,' Abby said, given that it was well after nine.

'I can ring over to the salon,' the assistant pushed, 'if you are pressed for time.'

'Sure.' Abby gave a tight smile as she paid.

She then went into the hairdresser's and had her hair smoothed and there she bought a lipstick that would go better with the dress.

Abby didn't have time to be nervous; she was far too late for Matteo for that. But even so, she managed to be as she stepped into his hotel and saw him waiting in the foyer.

'Wow!' he said. 'You're worth the wait.'

Somehow he both welcomed her and told her off for keeping him waiting.

'We need to get going,' Matteo said.

He really had no idea of the effort she had gone to in order to get her looking like this and Abby kind of liked that about him.

Still, she wasn't so much nervous as they walked to

the car; rather she was incredibly aware, not of her unfamiliar attire, more of the man she was with.

Very, very aware.

That was the best way she could describe it.

She was aware of the dry warmth of his hand on her arm as he led her to the waiting car.

And aware of him as he stretched out beside her and then popped a couple of painkillers and took them without water.

'Do you have a headache?' Abby asked, guessing he must have hit the clubs after he had dropped her off last night.

'My shoulder,' Matteo said.

'You should have worn the sling.'

'I know.' He just shrugged and obviously it hurt to do so because he winced, but then he turned the conversation to work as the car moved through the magnificent streets. 'How's Pedro?'

'He's being moved to a better suite as we speak,' Abby said. 'He's much happier than he was this time yesterday.'

'And if Pedro's happy, we're all happy.'

'Thank you,' Abby said. 'Whether or not it makes a difference…'

'Oh, it will make a difference,' Matteo interrupted but then he saw the anxious dart of her eyes and guessed she was worrying what would happen if they didn't place fifth. 'Just enjoy the buildup to the race,' Matteo said. 'We'll see what happens on race day and then we'll speak after.'

The charity gala that his sister had organised was a huge event and must have taken a lot of work to plan.

There were beautiful people everywhere and no,

Abby didn't feel overdressed now; in fact, she was very relieved that she hadn't gone for grey.

It was just such a beautiful summery day and they headed off to find his sister.

'What's she like?' Abby asked.

'Who, Allegra?' Matteo checked and rolled his eyes. 'She's a goody-two-shoes. Don't mention to her that I've hurt my shoulder.'

'Why not?'

'She'll worry,' Matteo said. 'There she is.'

He called out and waved with his good arm, and an attractive woman came over and they greeted each other with a kiss on the cheek. 'This is Abby,' Matteo said. 'My latest venture.'

'Matteo,' Allegra scolded.

'Business venture.' Matteo grinned. 'How are you?'

'Dusy,' Allegra admitted. 'What have you done to your eye?'

'I just knocked into a door.'

'I don't believe you for a moment,' Allegra said. 'And I can't believe you've been here for more than a week and I haven't seen you.'

'Well, you had this to arrange.'

'It's been crazy…' Allegra admitted but didn't finish her sentence—someone was calling out to her and she gave Matteo and Abby an apologetic smile. 'I really would love to stop and speak but I think it's going to have to be later.'

'Allegra,' Matteo said. 'I need to speak to you about Grandfather.'

'Now?'

He nodded and Abby saw that his expression was completely serious. 'He's not doing too well.'

'I know that,' Allegra said. 'Bianca and I have already spoken to him.'

'I think you need to take some time and go and see him,' Matteo said. Allegra closed her eyes and it was clear that she was upset.

'I know he's not well but...'

'Come on,' Matteo said to his sister and he took her by the elbow. 'I won't be a moment,' he said to Abby as he led Allegra somewhere a little more private. Abby tried not to watch but she glanced over once and saw Allegra put her hand on Matteo's shoulder and give it a squeeze.

His sore shoulder.

Oh, poor Matteo!

He didn't wince; Matteo just took Allegra's hand from his shoulder and gently let it go.

They were far from gushing with each other but Abby could tell, even from this distance, that they cared about what was being discussed.

It was so different from her family.

Annabel and Abby could go months without so much as a brief catch-up, and as for Abby and her father...

Maybe she should make the effort, Abby thought.

Yes, he had hurt her a lot when she had told him about Hunter's attack but, trying to be fair to her father, though he hadn't handled it well, maybe he had been grieving.

Never more than at that time had Abby wanted her mother, but she had been dead for three years by then.

Perhaps it was time to try and be family again?

She jumped a little as Matteo came back to her side.

'Sorry about that,' Matteo said. 'Allegra already

knows that my grandfather is ill but I don't think she knew just how bad things have got.'

'Is he very sick?'

Matteo nodded and for a moment, just a brief moment, he looked at Abby and wondered if he could tell her about the necklace and the real reason that he had made contact.

It almost felt as if he could.

But then he remembered the brittle woman he had met yesterday and decided that no, it was far too risky to chance it.

He was here for the team; he really was. There was no need to confuse things by bringing up the necklace just yet.

All that could wait.

'Come on...' Matteo said.

'Where?'

'To the sky.'

There were helicopter rides and he took her on one, and Abby, who apart from the racetrack had only seen one restaurant and one boutique during her time in Dubai, was treated to a bird's-eye view.

Over the artificial Palm Islands they flew and Abby had never seen anything more stunning. And she also saw where Matteo had suggested they go to dinner. The city seemed to glitter gold and silver and they flew, too, over the racetrack where the first leg of the Henley Cup would be held.

This time next week, she'd be down there, Abby thought with a flurry of both nerves and excitement.

They stepped off the helicopter and Abby took a moment more than Matteo did to find her land legs.

'It makes you dizzy, doesn't it,' Matteo said. 'Let's go and find something to eat.'

They didn't have to look very far; there was plenty to choose from, and though they had lunch it was a quick one because, as Matteo leafed through a glossy program, he decided that he wanted to look at the racehorses that were being paraded.

'Oh, look at that one...' Abby said. It was a stunning, white, purebred Arabian stallion, so highly strung that he looked as if at any moment he might take off.

'Bastard!' Matteo said but didn't get a chance to explain as someone tapped him on his shoulder.

The sore one.

'Kedah!' Matteo grinned as he turned around and saw who it was and he introduced them both. 'Abby, this is Kedah. We studied briefly together in New York.'

'Until you dropped out.'

'I'm still standing,' Matteo said. 'And this is Abby, owner and manager of the Boucher racing team.'

'It is very nice to meet you,' Sheikh Kedah said. He was incredibly handsome, Abby thought. He was beautifully presented, dressed in a robe of pale gold with a *keffiyah* tied and skilfully draped but he had that same wild gleam in his eye as Matteo and they made an extremely good-looking pair. Abby could only imagine the sort of trouble these two got into. 'Your driver did well here last year. Fifth, if I remember rightly?'

Abby nodded, surprised that he knew and pleasantly surprised also that Kedah didn't mention that, after that race, Pedro had gone on to place nowhere.

Kedah turned to Matteo. 'How is the shoulder?'

'Still sore.' Matteo smiled. 'Black and blue...'

'The doctor said you would bruise.' Kedah nodded. 'So do you still want him even after he threw you?'

'Absolutely,' Matteo said and then looked back to the stallion. 'Abby and I were just admiring him.'

At ten minutes to three, two thoughts hit and both unsettled her.

That the horse Matteo had fallen off was a thorough-bred racehorse. What the hell would have possessed him to be riding that?

But she couldn't dwell on it because another thought was invading.

She wanted to see his shoulder.

Abby, who just pushed down all thoughts of sex, who actually felt sick at the thought of intimacy, suddenly wanted to go back to the hotel and peel off his shirt and touch that bruised skin.

With her mouth.

'Are you okay?' Matteo checked, picking up on the sudden tension in her.

'Sorry?'

'Kedah was just saying he'd love to come to the race...'

'Oh!'

'We're not allowed to talk to Abby on race day though,' Matteo warned him.

'I'd love to be there,' Kedah said to Abby and then addressed Matteo. 'If the Boucher team make the po-dium, you get the horse,' the sheikh said and they shook hands.

'Do you bet on everything?' Abby asked when Kedah had gone.

'Not everything,' Matteo said and then he met her eyes and again stopped what he was about to say.

He'd never have put money on enjoying today.

Usually, often, always, he'd be bored by now and would have run out of things to say.

Usually, often, always, he'd be glancing at his phone and wondering if they went back to the hotel now and slept together, then he could drop her back and hit the town with Kedah.

Usually, often, always, he'd have said hi to his sister, stayed for half an hour and then said goodbye.

Instead today felt like the best of days and there was but one reason why.

'What the hell were you doing riding him?' Abby asked, tearing her eyes from his gaze and looking back to the magnificent stallion. 'Do you ride?'

'Not really,' Matteo admitted.

'When you say "not really…"?' Abby checked.

'No.'

'You could have been killed,' Abby said and she was far from joking. This beast would test the limits of the most experienced rider. 'Why would you take such a risk?'

'Do you say the same to Pedro when he stands on the gas?'

'Pedro's skilled and trained,' Abby retorted. 'You're a bit tall to be a jockey.'

Her cheeks were that lovely shade of turned-on pink, Matteo thought, and he was quite sure that it had nothing to do with the sun.

He wanted to turn her around and speak into her ear and put on a high voice, just to make her laugh as he told her what a *fabulous* jockey he was. And then Matteo wanted to be warned that public displays of affection could not happen here.

And then…

'Come on,' Matteo said. 'The fashion show's starting. You used…' He faltered; it had been her father who had told him that she'd once studied fashion.

'Used to what?'

'I thought I read somewhere that you used to study fashion?'

'I did,' Abby said. 'Where did you hear that?'

'I can't remember.' Matteo shrugged. 'I must have come across it when I was researching the team.'

He'd lied.

Matteo sat there beside her and he knew he'd lied, only not in the same way that he had to his sister—that had been about protecting Allegra, this had been about protecting himself.

It didn't matter, Matteo told himself.

He and Abby weren't going anywhere.

Even if they slept together, and from the heat between them that was becoming increasingly likely, he knew that they wouldn't last.

Matteo meant it—he would never get close to another.

Abby didn't notice the silence. It was actually so nice to be away from cars and she had never felt like that. Cars were both her work and her hobby but it was just nice to take a day off, but more than that, she knew it was because of Matteo.

They watched the fashion show and every second model who walked out onto the runway Matteo said, 'You'd look good in that.'

And then out came the underwear and he made no comment.

Not one.

They were both trying so hard to behave and, for Abby, to even have to *try* to behave was a revelation.

Finally, with the fashion show over they decided to call it a day.

'I just want to say goodbye to Allegra...'

'Go,' Abby said.

'Thanks.'

He appreciated it.

She wasn't needy and he liked that.

He liked her.

As they sat in the car on the way back to her hotel, he handed her his phone and Abby looked at a photo of the two of them, both laughing as they sat watching the fashion show.

Neither with a care in the world, it would seem.

Business or Romance? the headline said.

'Oh, no,' Abby wailed. 'Why would they jump to that?'

'Don't worry about it.' Matteo shrugged.

'But we want them to think...'

'Oh, they'll be thinking,' he said.

The car pulled up at her hotel and Abby wondered if he'd suggest dinner and she wondered if she might accept.

But Matteo, being Matteo, skipped entrée, main and dessert and, after such a lovely day, for him the ending was inevitable.

'We could,' Matteo said, 'always go to mine.'

That delicious mouth moved in for the kill and what startled Abby the most was that she wanted to accept, to just close her eyes and give in to the bliss he offered, except she jerked her head back.

'I'm assuming we're not talking about the restaurant at your hotel?'

'We're not.'

For Matteo sex was as straightforward and as simple as that.

'What happened to keeping it strictly business?' Abby asked.

'I can juggle both.'

He looked into green eyes that had been relaxed and smiling all day but now had turned to sleet.

'I'll see you on race day.' Abby's voice was tart—he could feel her anger and indignation emanating—and Matteo, who only ever played with the willing, leant back. 'If you're still interested, that is.' She didn't wait for the driver to open the door for her; instead she got out and slammed the door shut.

You're not here to seduce, Matteo reminded himself as the driver took his rarely rejected passenger back to his hotel.

Matteo never misread signs.

Today the two of them had blasted a heat to rival a Dubai sun.

It was better this way, he conceded as he climbed out of the car and headed to his luxury suite.

If ever he'd been glad that he hadn't told Abby about the origins of them, then it was now, because he was seriously interested in the Boucher team.

And, far more worryingly for Matteo, he was also seriously interested in Abby herself.

Which was, for a die-hard bachelor, very troubling indeed.

He was now terribly glad that Abby had said no.

CHAPTER FOUR

HOW HAD HE ever lived his life without this? Matteo wondered when racing day dawned.

It made the casino look like a playground.

The noise, the crowd, the scent, just the complete buzz was made all the better for having a stake in it, Matteo thought as he made his way to the Boucher shed.

He wondered as to his reception but soon found out he needn't have.

It was quite refreshing to have no one remotely interested in him.

Pedro was playing video games and just blocking out everyone as he did what he had to do to get himself into the zone. Abby, dressed like some man in bottle-green trousers and top, with a baseball cap on, was doing some last-minute checks on the computer. The team were working on the car and Matteo knew when to stay back.

Of course she noticed him.

Abby had been wondering all week if she'd blown her chance with an amazing sponsor. Absolutely she knew she had been giving out mixed signals the entire time they spent together.

Matteo just didn't need to know why.

Yes, it was a relief to see him and an even bigger relief when he left without demanding an update or even a minute of anyone's time.

Matteo and Kedah went for lunch and then placed their bets. Matteo decided to bet on the Boucher team placing. But then, as the cars all took up their positions, and just before betting closed, just for the hell of it, Matteo placed a ridiculous amount on a win.

Dubai had turned it on and as the cars took off, the roar that went up combined with the engines and there was a new love in Matteo's life.

Motor racing.

He looked to Abby; she was lost to him for the next couple of hours, her focus on the race, and Matteo was fine with that.

He'd apologise later, he decided, glad that she had drawn the line.

He could understand now her obsession with the sport. *Neck and neck* took on a whole new meaning when it went for two hours and Abby never broke her focus, not once.

They were going to place, Matteo thought as he glanced at the times and the top four came into the second-last lap.

Better than that, they might hit the podium.

Pedro overtook Evan just as they came into the final lap. The Boucher team was a split second behind Lachance. Pedro was biting at Hunter's heels though, just waiting for that chance to take him.

And then, when Hunter refused to give him that chance, Pedro made his own.

Young, brave and foolish, at the final turn he took Hunter!

The roar from the Boucher team drowned the engines, and even Abby stopped working. There was nothing she could do from here except scream her lungs out.

Pedro gunned it.

He simply took the engine that she had designed, the car that she had built, the driver that she had nurtured and the team that should lose right into the history books, and Abby just stood there screaming as Pedro took her baby home.

They had won!

Not only that, Evan had overtaken Hunter, who had struggled to right his car from Pedro's brave manoeuvre.

The noise was deafening but all Abby could hear was silence.

She was being thumped on the back, lifted up; she was screaming but she could not feel or hear a thing.

And then she saw Matteo, right there in front of her.

For the first time today, she properly saw him. He was wearing black jeans and a black shirt. Dark, dangerous and unshaven, the only safe thing about him was that those full blood-red lips were smiling.

At her.

'You did it,' he said, moving that final step into her space so that his voice was all she could hear.

Matteo didn't even get what she had done—that she had finally beaten Hunter—but right now she didn't even care about that.

'I'm sorry about the other night,' he said, his eyes intent on hers.

'I am too,' Abby admitted, to her own surprise.

Elation enabled honesty and with those words she admitted the truth she dared not, even to herself—she was sorry that she had said no.

And then there was no space between them. They were wrapped in each other's arms and the mouth she had wanted from the night they had met was on hers, crushing hers. Had she imagined a kiss over the years it had always been a gentle one.

This was not that.

It was consuming, blatant and very fierce and, unthinking, her mouth opened in delicious reflex. His tongue was straight in, and yet she, too, sought his, like some exotic sword fight, where both were winners as they partook in the deepest, sexiest kiss.

God, he was shameless, Abby thought. He removed her cap and his hand pressed her head further in so she could feel the skin shredding on her jaw. Then he took the energy of their kiss and didn't just sustain it; Matteo heightened it. He was hard and pressing into her and she could feel every delicious inch. His hands were now travelling down to her bottom and pulling her into him. Yet, rather than pull back, Abby was just as on fire and as sexed up as he.

And then they remembered the rules and pulled their mouths rather than their bodies back.

'When we win…we kiss…' Matteo said.

She could live with that.

They were breathing so hard just staring at each other.

'When we place, we kiss,' he said, kissing her cheek as if it were her mouth and that made her laugh. 'And if we lose,' he continued, making out with her ear, 'then we have to commiserate…'

He was still hard and still there, nudging her stomach, and there was the beautiful absence of fear, even when he pulled back and looked right into her eyes.

'What does it feel like to win?' Matteo asked.

'Better than sex,' Abby said, no longer scared to throw a flirty line.

And she expected him to laugh or to haul her closer in for more of a feel of his erection but instead he looked deeper into her eyes.

'Then someone hasn't been doing you right,' Matteo said.

He intended to remedy that later tonight.

CHAPTER FIVE

HUNTER SAW THEM.

He got out of his car and looked over and saw the woman he had left lying bruised and bleeding on a marble bathroom floor, and then pissed all over, now happy and free.

'Whoa!' The reporters shouted in several languages as Hunter kicked his car and threw his helmet down to the ground and then stormed off.

Abby and Matteo didn't see a thing.

They were too busy laughing as Kedah informed them that Matteo was now the owner of an extremely temperamental horse!

'Her name is Abby,' Matteo said but she deliberately missed the inference.

'I'm not temperamental.'

Or maybe she was, because Abby, who didn't cry, almost did when she watched as Pedro stood in first place on the podium.

'I almost want a glass of champagne,' Abby admitted as Pedro sprayed the crowd with the same.

The Carter team was in second place and Evan grinned and waved and took the dousing.

Hunter attempted to do the same.

It was a good day.

A brilliant day.

And the world was waiting for the press conference.

Oh, they were an arrogant lot, Matteo thought as the drivers came in and took their seats.

Pedro sat there grinning; so, too, did Evan. Even Hunter had recovered from his hissy fit and that assured smile was back on his face.

'I have to congratulate Pedro…' They were the first words out of Hunter's mouth.

He was charming, said a reporter standing to the side of Matteo and Abby.

'Narcissists generally are,' Matteo drawled.

He didn't like him.

'I lost my focus for a second,' Hunter conceded, 'and Pedro took his chance.'

Hunter made it sound like he had lost rather than that they had won and Matteo felt Abby tense beside him.

'Don't worry about him,' Matteo said, without looking over to her. 'You know you won.' He then listened as a reporter asked Hunter a question.

'What about your reaction after the race? You seemed pretty angry.'

'Ha.' Hunter shrugged and then spread his hands, holding his palm to the sky. 'I guess I'm not used to it…' And then he put down his hands and looked straight over to Matteo as he spoke on. 'I tend to get there first.'

Matteo didn't know that he had hackles till then, yet he felt them rise and he watched as Hunter's gaze moved to the woman who stood beside him.

'That was for me…' Abby said and Matteo frowned because her voice was slurred.

His newly discovered hackles were still up and Matteo put an arm around Abby.

'It's okay.' He didn't know what was going on but he could feel Abby's distress and he tried to reassure her.

But all she could hear was *Wah-wah-wah...*

The rest of what Matteo said she lost.

There was a roaring in Abby's ears and her chest felt closed and she could feel that her lips were tingling.

'I can't breathe...' she gasped.

'Abby...' Matteo said, but then she lost track of his deep smoky voice again and she made one last desperate plea.

'Don't let Hunter see me like this.'

Matteo got her out of the press conference and to a horrid plastic seat, where he sat her down and told her to cup her hands over her face. 'You're having a panic attack.'

He was just calm.

On the outside.

Matteo never let anyone glimpse his fear.

He went over to a guy who was walking past and tipped the man's burger into his hand and returned to Abby with the paper bag. 'Breathe into this...' Matteo said and he just kept on talking in his lovely deep voice and telling her she would soon be okay. 'It will pass soon,' he assured. 'My sister Natalia gets them and they pass. I promise.'

He just sat with her the entire way through it. Abby was sweating and white and her eyes were wide open and looking into his as she breathed in and out of the paper bag and then moved it aside.

'He lost,' Abby said and, with a sinking feeling, Matteo knew, he just knew, that they weren't talking about Hunter losing the race today.

Matteo felt sick; he actually did but he just looked back at her.

'He lost a race...' Abby said. She could not do it in full sentences. 'I was ending it. We'd only gone out a few times. We'd never...'

And he didn't know what to say.

'He got so angry.'

Matteo just didn't know what to say.

'I told my father. He said not to report it.' She shook her head. 'You see, I was drunk...'

And now Matteo did know what to say.

It was his first rule.

'Then he should have seen you safely home.'

'I was in his hotel room.'

No, he would not let her go there.

'Then he should have checked into another or put you to bed and slept in the chair,' Matteo said. 'There's no excuse for what he did.'

'It was *so* violent.' Abby relived it just for a second and she watched Matteo blink, not once but three times, and then he responded.

'He should have treated you like glass,' Matteo said.

'It was my first time...'

'Crystal glass, then,' Matteo amended. 'And that was *not* your first time—that's not sex.'

'It's the only sex I know.'

And then her panic came back because they were coming out of the press conference. 'He can't see me like this.'

Yet she couldn't stand.

'What if we look like we were having an intimate

moment—is that okay?' Matteo gently checked and she nodded.

He just wrapped her in his arms and she saw the yellow leather of Hunter walking past and she heard the increasing *thud, thud, thud* of Matteo's heart and his breathing firing into rapid. Abby felt the tension in him and she knew that Matteo wanted to drop her and run and do what her father should have all those years ago.

For her sake he didn't.

But then, at the last moment, when he recalled Hunter's "I tend to get there first" line, Abby felt the rip of tension in him.

'Please don't,' Abby begged when she felt him move to run but then his arms came tighter around her.

'I won't.'

He wanted to though.

Matteo now could barely breathe.

Abby could feel him struggle to contain himself. Matteo even with a hangover in fierce heat did not break a sweat, yet he was swimming in adrenaline and his shirt was drenched and his breathing was coming fast and shallow.

'I might need to borrow that paper bag...' Matteo said.

Still he could make her smile.

And she waited for the questions to start but when her breathing was normal and she peered out from his chest, the only thing Matteo asked was if she wanted some water.

'Please.'

He went off to a vending machine and got her a drink and Abby drank it down thirstily, and Matteo was right; the panic had passed.

'Better?' Matteo asked.

'Much,' Abby said, though she was now incredibly embarrassed at what she had told him.

'So, where do you want to go now?' Matteo asked.

'Go?' It was the last thing she'd expected him to ask her but Matteo squatted down in front of her and looked right at her when, embarrassed by her revelations, she could barely now look at him.

'We're still celebrating your win.' Matteo was insistent. He looked briefly over to the team, who were all on their phones and buoyantly posing for the cameras and Kedah was with them. 'I'm guessing that you don't want to go out with that lot...'

'No.'

'But you won,' Matteo said. 'And you have every day since that bastard did what he did, and do you know what? You deserve to celebrate.'

'I do.'

'So, go and congratulate Pedro. Tell him it's covered tonight, whatever he wants.'

'Er, I don't know if you know what you're agreeing to.'

'You're talking to me.' Matteo smiled. 'I know what a wild night is. Seriously, with the bet I put on I'm even more loaded than usual. I'll get Kedah to go along with them. He runs wild but he's a good sort. He'll keep an eye.'

Matteo didn't, Abby thought, look at her like she had two heads; he just chatted away as if she hadn't just told him her darkest shame. 'You're sure?' she checked.

'Of course,' Matteo said. 'Kedah will cover it and then I'll see him right.'

He went to the vending machine again and bought

a cola for himself and another water for her, and then Abby did what she properly wanted to do but hadn't had a chance to until now!

'Pedro!' She went over and gave him a hug.

'How good was that?' Pedro grinned. 'Hunter's spewing.'

'I know that he is. You were amazing, Pedro. I couldn't believe it when you took him. I still don't know how you did that.'

'I'll tell you in detail over dinner tonight,' Pedro said.

'Actually, I can't make dinner. I'm going to go out and chat up our sponsor,' Abby said. She saw a little flare of relief in her crew that she wasn't coming out with him, though they did their best to hide it.

'Oh, come on, Abby,' Pedro insisted but she shook her head.

Yes, they all got on, but it was a very male world and she saw the tiny smiles as they realised that they wouldn't have to behave as they always did around her.

And that thought brought a lump to her throat.

But these were nice tears that she was holding back.

They all *did* behave around her; she already knew that but she fully realised it then.

Abby's team really were amazing.

'Go and have the best night,' Abby told them. 'It's all covered, whatever you want. Kedah will pick up the tab and Matteo will cover it.'

Pedro frowned. 'Are you sure?'

'Yes! Now go and have a brilliant night!' Abby said. 'God knows you deserve it but,' she warned, 'remember that we've got an official breakfast tomorrow.'

'Tell Matteo,' Pedro said, 'that I'll take him out in the car next time.'

'I shall.' She gave Pedro another hug and then she turned and went back to Matteo.

'Okay, where are we off to?' he asked.

'I don't know.'

'I do.' Matteo had just decided. 'First, though, we'll swing by my hotel and I'll get changed.'

'I need to get changed too.'

He looked down at her oily bottle-green overalls. 'Absolutely, you do!'

'Buy a dress here…' Matteo suggested as they pulled up at his hotel. 'There are plenty of boutiques for you to choose from.'

'No, I bought a dress ages ago and I promised that if we ever got on the podium…' Abby shook her head. 'I just never expected it to be tonight.'

She simply couldn't believe it.

Podium would have been brilliant—it would have shown that they were serious contenders—but to have come first was beyond her wildest dreams!

For others it was a nightmare—the bookies were panicking, the other teams were regrouping. Tonight, only the Boucher team was floating on cloud nine.

As they got out of his car Matteo was about to ask if she wanted to come up and have a drink while he changed but then he decided against it. Now her comment that first day, about their meeting being held in the restaurant rather than his hotel room, made sense.

God, he could kick himself now for the other night but instead he saw her to a seat and gave her a smile.

'I shan't be long.'

Abby sat in the lovely foyer as he went and changed and as she did she saw that she had about fifty missed calls, some from her father, and loads of texts offering congratulations. Where had they all been prior to this victory? Abby thought.

She turned her phone off and then she looked up as a man who had been there for her came out of the elevator. He was wearing black pants and a white shirt and dark tie but he was carrying the jacket to his suit, and he'd shaved.

For her.

And she remembered their kiss and her response and there were just too many feelings for Abby to explore right now, and so she chose to just do her best to enjoy the night.

Matteo had ditched his car and they were driven to her hotel and, instead of sitting in the car while she changed, he came into the foyer.

'My turn to wait,' he said.

Matteo sat down as she headed off to the elevators but he watched as Abby was called back by the concierge and signed for something and then, a few minutes later, she was handed a parcel and took the elevator up.

Abby stepped into her room .

She was dizzy both from elation at winning and her revelations about Hunter but it was the kiss that had taken place between her and Matteo that had her slightly breathless with recall.

Being kissed by Matteo had been amazing, showing her a side to herself she hadn't known existed.

Did it even matter, now that she'd told him the truth? That there had been no one before or after Hunter.

She thought about what he said, how Hunter didn't

count, and she liked that. Even if it made her a twenty-seven-year-old virgin.

She took the dress out of her wardrobe and, given today's events, decided that the dress was too much.

Much too much.

It was seductive, provocative and sexy and it was everything Abby had hoped that she might one day be able to be.

Not yet though.

She was scared of her own sexuality, scared that if she dressed up tonight, then somehow Matteo might think she was leading him on.

To nowhere.

Oh, she was messed up, Abby knew.

She opened the package that she had signed for and her teeth ground together as a formal invitation from her father, inviting her to his fundraiser, fell out. It was written on a thick cream card but there was also attached to it a letter, or rather a note.

Abby.
As discussed.

No signature, no kisses, no *Love from Dad*. Just the reminder that if she wanted money to support her team, then it came with conditions attached.

She didn't need the money so badly now but her decision not to go was starting to waver. Seeing Matteo and Allegra together, trying to do the right thing by their grandfather, had served as a very poignant reminder as to how far Abby's own family had fallen apart, particularly since her mother had died.

Abby peeled back the paper to reveal a walnut box

and she undid the tiny clasp and the lid sprung open. Her legs folded beneath her and she sat on the bed staring at her mum's necklace...

With the silver metal, white diamonds and the green of the emeralds, it was, like her mother had been, beautiful. And, Abby thought, holding it up so it caught the late-afternoon sun, it was possibly the most perfect accessory for her dress.

It was like a sign—not that she should attend her father's function; that decision she would make later—it just felt as if her mother had stopped by to tell her well done.

'Oh, Mum.'

She thought of Anette, her mother, and how her marriage had been such an unhappy one.

Her father was a cruel, egotistical man and her mother, with all her family and support in France, just hadn't found it within herself to leave. Anette had known that Hugo would have made her life hell if she did. So she had settled for a quieter version of hell—a marriage for the sake of the children.

Abby had loved her mother so very much.

She still did.

Had she been alive, Abby knew that what had happened with Hunter would have been handled differently. Oh, Anette had been weak where her father was concerned but not when it came to her girls.

Wear the dress, Abby.

She could almost hear her mother's voice.

Be who you are, not who others dictate that you be.

Abby *could* hear her mother's voice now.

She had been fifteen when her mother had died but

now she remembered a long conversation they had had and her mother's advice.

It hadn't made sense; even in her darkest days, Abby hadn't been able to unravel her mother's words. Abby had tried to be herself and speak her mind and look where that had got her.

At twenty-seven those words made far better sense now.

Abby showered and then pinned up her hair and put on her make-up and with nervous hands pulled on some panties that were a touch too sensible for such an amazing dress but which were all that she had.

And then she slipped on the dress and the feel of cool silk on her skin had her face on fire. It was backless and so there was no bra that would work with it. She could see her nipples.

It wasn't slutty; it really was incredibly beautiful.

She wore the flat jewelled sandals that she had worn to Allegra's gala and they worked better with the dress than heels.

It didn't need heels; what it needed, Abby knew, taking the necklace from the box, was this.

The necklace hung as if it had been designed solely for this night.

It drew the attention from thick nipples and it made her eyes a deeper green. Abby was almost scared of her own reflection because she looked sexy and wanton and she did not want to tease the tiger.

Yet she trusted Matteo not to bite.

It was the most contrary feeling in the world, given all she had been through, and with only instinct to guide her, Abby listened to her own voice now.

Both she and the dress would celebrate tonight.

* * *

Matteo waited.

Oh, he waited for way more than half an hour this time.

He wondered if Abby was having trouble getting into a denim dress and Doc Martens but just as he smiled at that thought the elevators opened and a shining, shy beauty stepped out.

She was in a dress that was a bruised shade of silver, just one polish away from gleaming, and around her throat was the reason Matteo had first made contact.

Not now.

Oh, he watched her walk towards him—too nervous and shy to be sexy. She was utterly gorgeous—and how the hell did he tell her the truth?

Never had he been more grateful for a goldfish attention span when it suited him. Matteo just dismissed the Lost Mistresses from his mind and dealt with now.

'You look…' What? Often Matteo stopped himself from saying what he wanted to with Abby; he didn't tonight. 'You are the most beautiful woman I have ever seen.'

And he felt the most responsible that he ever had towards another.

This was her night.

It wasn't a restaurant like any other that Abby had ever been to.

White, candlelit tables were set on a private beach. It was an outdoor restaurant that combined fine dining with a sunset that fired as pink as her cheeks as they were shown to their seats.

'Champagne?' Matteo asked, and it was as if they were starting again.

Which they were.

He knew the truth now and, more importantly, Abby felt safe to let down her guard with him. She knew, Abby just knew, that she could strip naked and dance like a banshee and still he would see her safely home.

'That would be lovely.'

The champagne was poured and the first thing he did was raise a glass.

'To the Boucher team. Well done, you!'

They ate delectable seafood and their fingers met in the fragrant bowls and they flirted a little but more than that they talked and they celebrated her win.

'Pedro's happy,' Matteo said.

'For now.' Abby nodded. 'I've been watching him for years, since he was about sixteen. I know he's good and that he's thrilled with the win but he's not going to hang around for long and I can't blame him for that.'

'Is *that* why it has to be this year that you win the Henley Cup?'

That being Hunter.

Abby hesitated and then nodded.

'He retires this year. I want my revenge,' she admitted. 'I know it's supposed to be healthier to forgive…'

Matteo snorted, which told her what he thought of that!

'You're going to do it,' he said. 'But if not this year, there's still next. Don't make your life about him.'

'I know.'

'Concentrate on keeping Pedro sweet,' Matteo said. 'Spoil him. You've got winnings now.'

'He placed fifth here last year,' Abby said. 'It was

our first race and he should have been way back but, like today, something happened. He's a genius and now everyone really knows it.' She told Matteo something. 'The next night, after he placed fifth, he took me out for dinner. He was just twenty then and I'm his manager and yet he got the bill and I knew that I was being served notice. He told me that he'd already been approached by the Lachance team. We came to a deal and I asked for this year, for the Henley Cup.'

'Things are different now,' Matteo said. 'He's part of a winning team and it *is* a team—a progressive one. The Lachance mob are sticking to the same old formulas. Remind him of that.'

'I shall,' Abby agreed. 'Pedro wants to take you for a spin when we get to Milan.'

'No, thank you,' Matteo said, and Abby raised her eyes in surprise. She had thought, given his daredevil nature, that he would jump at the chance, but he'd shaken his head at the offer.

'Thanks for today.' Abby addressed what she had to, glad that it was getting darker and so he hopefully couldn't see that her face was on fire.

'For what?'

'I've never had a panic attack before, not a full-blown one. I thought I was going to die.'

'I told you that you wouldn't.'

'You said that your sister got them?'

Matteo nodded but said no more.

'I didn't expect to react like that. I've seen him around before, of course.'

Matteo didn't like that and he frowned.

'We're on tour at the same time,' Abby pointed out. 'I always make sure that we're in separate hotels. I only really see him trackside and usually I'm fine. Well, not fine exactly but I've never had that happen to me.'

'He was angry today,' Matteo said. 'Even if he was trying to hide it.'

'Yes.'

'And I would expect that brought some stuff up for you.'

'I guess,' Abby said. 'I hate how he's messed me up.'

'Messed up?' Matteo checked. 'Hardly! Your team just won—you're coming into your own.'

'You know what I mean.' She had said way more than she had wanted to today but she *had* said it—there had been no one since Hunter.

'It's just a matter of time,' Matteo said.

'It's been nine years!'

He actually grinned. 'How the hell do you sleep?' he asked. 'I need a drink or sex, preferably both.' He thought for a moment. 'You're not frigid. Had there not been one hundred thousand people watching on, I could have had you this afternoon.'

'Exceptional circumstances!' Abby said.

He just spoke about it in such a matter-of-fact way that it made the world a bit nicer but she shook her head at the impossibility. 'He seriously messed with my head.'

'We're all messed up, Abby.'

'You're not.'

'Of course I am. My whole family are.'

'Because your parents died?' Abby asked.

'Because of how they lived.'

It was Abby who didn't know what to say now.

Matteo never opened up to anyone. He could talk for hours and still reveal little about himself but with all she had told him today, well, it seemed wrong to hold back. He looked at her, so stunning on the outside and so churned up within, and it felt unfair to let her think that the polished, carefree man who sat before her didn't have dark memories of his own.

'Do you know why I said no to Pedro taking me for a spin?'

She shook her head.

'Because the thought of having someone drive me around at high speed makes me ill.'

'But riding a thoroughbred racehorse doesn't?' Abby frowned.

'When I was five my father woke me up in the middle of the night. Now, when I look back, he was high on cocaine but I didn't know about drugs then. I just knew there were times we avoided him and that this was one of those times. He'd won a car.' Matteo sat there for a moment and remembered his bewilderment at being woken up. 'We had loads of cars, but no, he had to show me this one. He took me into the garage and I remember that the car was silver. He told me how fast it went and just all this stuff and then he told me to climb in. I did…' He looked at Abby, and Matteo was probably more confused in hindsight than he had been at the time. 'Do you know, he didn't even check if I was belted in? He just revved that engine and took off.'

'To where?' Abby asked.

'Everywhere,' Matteo said. 'It was the longest night of my life, changing lanes, swerving, all the lights blurring. I wet myself,' Matteo admitted. 'He just kept going faster. He was laughing and shouting. I swear I knew we were going to die that night but somehow we made it home. A few weeks later there was a huge fight and my father got loaded. My mother got in the car, apparently to sort things out once and for all. They say the car skidded out of control but I always wonder...'

'If she was as scared as you had been?'

'Yep,' Matteo said. 'She'd got clean by then, well, apart from spending...' He saw her slight frown. 'Believe me, I almost wish she hadn't though. I can't stand the thought that she might have been as sober and as scared as I was that night.'

'What do your brothers and sisters say?'

'There are some things that you just don't discuss. We talk about other things, but the past is there—we all know it. I'm sure they have their own memories and issues. I've never told anyone about that night.' He gave her a wry smile. 'So, no—tell Pedro thanks but no thanks. I shan't be taking him up on his offer.'

He tipped the last of the champagne into her glass.

'Enough of the sad stuff,' he said. 'We're supposed to be celebrating.'

They danced on the beach, a lovely long, slow dance, and Abby was celebrating not just the win, nor that she was out in her sexy silver dress and necklace, drinking champagne and relaxed, but turned on in his arms. But that this emotionally elusive man had told her something about himself.

Something that not even his family knew.

It was, without doubt, for Abby, the perfect end to the perfect day.

Matteo thought it less than perfect. Not the day, nor the night—more what he had found out. What had happened to Abby was criminal, not just the event but the effect that it had had on her.

For the first time that he could remember he wanted

to step up, but that would mean offering more than he had sworn to ever do.

He remembered their kiss and could feel the attraction but the cruellest thing in the world would be to let her think he was capable of even a short-term relationship. And so, when the music ended Matteo did as promised.

He took her safely home.

CHAPTER SIX

ABBY WOKE AND stretched and looked over to her lovely silver dress that was draped over the chair and she was more mixed up than ever.

Matteo confused her almost as much she confused herself.

She wanted him.

Oh, my, she wanted him, and last night had been perfect.

Absolutely perfect except for one thing.

Unlike the sensual kiss they had shared after the win, at the end of last night, when he'd taken her back to the hotel, Matteo had briefly kissed her on the cheek like he was saying goodbye to some elderly moustached aunt.

Maybe all that she'd told him had been a bit too much.

And, Abby conceded, Matteo was way too much to be cutting her teeth on. He didn't do relationships—he had made that blatantly clear—and Abby really was the last person to consider a casual relationship.

Except she was.

She was lying in bed, in pyjamas, and wondering what it would be like to have sex with Matteo.

In fact, since the first night they'd met she'd often found herself lying in bed wondering the very same.

Instead of dwelling on that lovely thought, when there was a knock at the door she pulled back the covers and answered it.

It wasn't breakfast, just the coffee she had ordered, given that they had an official breakfast starting in less than an hour.

She wondered how the team would shape up this morning.

Abby got dressed. There were several issues being a woman in a very male world and the Boucher corporate wear was one of them.

Bottle-green men's trousers.

Yum.

A bottle-green shirt and a black belt and lovely flat black shoes.

She headed down to the restaurant and there, looking very seedy but dressed in bottle-green, were her team.

'How was last night?' Abby asked.

'Kedah's a bad influence,' Pedro said. 'I can see pink elephants.'

'Just keep smiling,' Abby said.

'Kedah wants to sponsor us too!' Pedro told her.

Breakfast was long and there were an awful lot of photos and after that there were even more interviews for poor Pedro.

'How's Pedro doing?' Abby jumped at the sound of Matteo's voice.

'Very well,' she said. 'I wasn't expecting to see you this morning.'

'We'll talk in a moment,' Matteo said. 'I just want to catch up with Pedro.' He went over and whatever he had to say to Pedro took ages and then finally he came over to her.

'Can we go somewhere?' Matteo asked and Abby nodded; he had his business face on and looked tired.

They found a table and she ordered tea and Matteo did the same.

'You don't look like you've slept,' she commented.

'I haven't,' Matteo admitted. 'And neither has my lawyer.'

Abby frowned.

'I'm in,' Matteo said.

'Officially?'

'Yes.' He handed her a very thick contract. 'In a nutshell, I'll be your sponsor for the next eighteen months. You can back out at any time. I can't. Take your time to go through it though.'

She skimmed the first couple of pages and saw the figures he was talking and, no, she couldn't imagine backing out.

'What do you get out of it?' Abby asked.

'The Di Sione name on your car and Pedro, as well as your disgusting shirt...' He looked at her attire. 'Can we add a clause about your clothes? You're wearing the same as the men.'

'We can!' Abby smiled. 'What else?'

'That's pretty much it. Abby, I love the racing world. I can see why you're completely hooked.'

'It's not always this good,' she warned. 'In fact, it's never been this good till now and it might not be again.'

'I get that,' Matteo said. 'I've just spoken to Pedro and when we're both in New York I'm taking him shopping for a car. I'll deal with his ego,' he said and Abby let out a breath of relief. 'You can concentrate on the cars.'

It felt too good to be true and she waited for Matteo to reveal the catch as he carried on speaking. 'Now, go through the contract and flag any concerns that you have but when you read it, know that I'm in, no matter what happens between us.'

Abby looked up from the contract she was reading. It had been business but now he had sideswiped her. 'Us?'

'Do I have to spell it out?'

'I think so.'

'I don't do relationships,' Matteo said. 'I never have and I never will but I think we both know we're heading for bed.'

'I don't know that,' Abby flustered.

'Of course you do.' Matteo stated it as fact. 'And, as I said the day we met, I am very patient. So, don't stress about cup-winning performances on that front either. We'll take it slow, get you enjoying it. Just know that when we're miserable exes, and loathe each other, I'll still be here for the team.'

He meant it.

For the best part of the night and well into the morning he had been speaking with his lawyer and playing email ping-pong with him.

In between all of that though, he had been thinking about Abby.

A future for the two of them was impossible but a future for Abby he could envisage, and he knew that much he could help her with.

'Matteo...'

'I have to go,' he said. 'I'm heading back to New York. I've got a big meeting tomorrow. I know no one thinks I do anything but I do work...'

He'd just offered her millions in sponsorship and a few sex lessons to boot and now he was dashing off.

'Get yourself on the pill,' he said. 'I'll do all the health checks.'

'Health checks?'

'They're not really necessary,' Matteo said. 'I always wear a condom but I shan't with you.' He gave her a smile that had her thighs squeeze together at the top. 'We don't want a break in proceedings,' Matteo said and in the most awkward of subjects still he made her smile. 'No pit stops to change the rubber. We'll just keep the momentum going.'

Pedro came over then. 'Are you okay, Abby?' He checked, no doubt, because her face was on fire.

'I'm fine.'

'Well,' Matteo said in his best business voice. 'I've given you a lot to think about, Abby. I'll see you in Milan.'

It was a month away!

'As I said,' Matteo carried on. 'I shan't be breathing down your neck.'

He shook her hand, shook Pedro's and then he was gone.

'Matteo said I could have his jet at my disposal for a week if I bring in the Henley Cup,' Pedro said. 'He's my man crush.'

Abby shot Pedro a look. 'Hands off,' she said and they both laughed.

It was the first time she'd laughed with a friend about something so basic and nice.

CHAPTER SEVEN

MATTEO DID EXACTLY as he had said he would and was completely hands off.

Abby was the recipient of several emails from some virtual assistant with flight itineraries and suchlike.

The contract was signed and countersigned.

Sheikh Kedah wanted to sponsor them too, but of all the amazing things that were happening, the one that had Abby reeling the most was that she was ankles in stirrups and having a pelvic exam and that she left the clinic with six shiny packets of contraceptive pills.

She still didn't know what would happen between them.

And that wasn't Abby being coy or naive. She was seriously crazy about Matteo but she was also seriously crazy about her work. Yes, the contract might be watertight but sniping at her sponsor she didn't need.

And Abby *would* snipe.

Oh, the giddy high of being with Matteo would be wonderful, Abby knew, but she'd been clearly warned that it would only be temporary.

Abby *was* a sore loser; it was the reason she'd got as far as she had in the racing world.

Losing Matteo, or rather the flirting and friendship

and fun of them…well, it was something she treasured and Abby wasn't completely sure she wanted to mess with what they had.

And he was reckless.

The more she knew him, the more she read about him, the more debauched Matteo's lifestyle appeared.

Still, it was bliss to know that the flights were covered, and with that weight off her mind the race ahead had never had greater attention.

Abby even found the time for coffee with her friend Bella one morning, while Matteo took Pedro out for that shopping spree. Given that Bella was an engineer on the Carter team they had a *very* strict no-inside-info rule, but it was lovely to catch up.

'Are you still walking on air after Dubai?' Bella grinned.

'I think we're all just trying to get our head in the game for Milan, but yes,' Abby admitted. 'It still feels brilliant.'

'And how on earth did you land a Di Sione as a sponsor?' Bella couldn't help but pry. 'I'm not sharing details but you must surely know that everyone is put out? Who wouldn't want a Di Sione sponsor? Even one as wild as Matteo.'

Abby smiled. 'Just luck. I think he likes taking risks and, given our new status, we're the biggest risk of them all.'

'I think he's the risk rather than you,' Bella said and rolled her eyes. 'Front page again.'

Abby frowned and Bella groaned. 'Sorry, I thought you would have already seen the news. It's everywhere,' Bella said and handed Abby her phone.

There was Matteo, staring at the camera, but instead

of his regular suit or slightly bleary-eyed look as he came out of a casino, this image told her that he came in just under the six-foot-three line.

It was a mug shot.

Abby briefly scanned the article and found out that Matteo had been arrested last night after a fight in a very exclusive restaurant broke out and management had had no choice but to call the police.

Patrons were shocked and distressed.

'That's Matteo.' Abby shrugged and handed back the phone, and she managed a wry smile and a roll of her eyes while on the inside her heart sunk.

He was supposed to be picking up Pedro now and her young driver had been looking forward to the day with Matteo so much.

It wasn't just that he had let down Pedro that upset her. Matteo created chaos; a night in wasn't enough for him, nor a nice meal by the looks of things. It had to be drama; it had to end on a dangerous high.

That was the man she was considering sleeping with!

Well, not any more.

Abby truly didn't know what to say. She could hardly tell Bella how crazy she was about him, nor how disappointed she was in him too.

Instead she called Pedro but, unable to get hold of him, she gave up and Abby did her best to forget about Matteo and whatever the latest trouble he found himself in. They chatted about some of the other teams, leaving their own out, and Bella also told her that she was serious about someone.

'In the racing world?' Abby asked.

'Oh, no!' Bella shook her head. 'I had to change

the battery in his car.' She laughed. 'He hasn't a clue and that suits me fine. I'm keeping romance well away from work—I've had my fingers burnt way too many times in the past.'

It would serve her well to remember that, Abby thought as she drove home.

Tomorrow they flew to Milan. Once there, the car, which had been pulled apart and shipped after the Dubai race, would be meticulously put back together again and training would begin in earnest—fine-tuning the car and ensuring it was perfect for the practice race, and then she would make the final modifications for the race itself.

Now though, there was one brief night to relax.

Not that she could.

Damn you, Matteo, Abby thought as she turned on the news and sure enough the first thing she saw was his mug shot.

Abby switched it off and, when the doorbell rang, she hauled herself from the sofa and there at the door stood Pedro.

A very different-looking Pedro.

His hair had been cropped and he was wearing a sharp suit and, judging by the set of keys he was waving, he was the new owner of a car fit for a soon-to-be racing legend.

'Matteo made it to take you out?' Abby put her own anger aside and smiled as she let Pedro in. 'How was it?'

'It was brilliant.'

'I tried to call you,' Abby said.

'I left my phone at Bernadette's. I'm just on my way there now.'

'So what happened with Matteo?' Abby couldn't stop

herself from asking. 'I saw on the news that he'd been arrested…'

'And released without charge.' Pedro shrugged as he walked into her lounge. 'Some guy was arguing with his wife and got heavy. Matteo stepped in and the guy took his mood out on him. Hey, Abby…' Pedro said to his very distracted manager, who was blowing out a guilty breath at her own presumption. 'I wanted to ask you something—can Bernadette come to Milan?'

Abby guessed Matteo had suggested that Pedro ask her.

Pedro had wanted to bring Bernadette last time but things had been so incredibly tight that there had been no room for wives and girlfriends.

Things were different now.

'Sure.' Abby nodded.

She wanted Pedro to linger, to tell her all about his day, or rather anything else Matteo had even loosely mentioned, but he was soon heading off to show Bernadette his new clothes and car and to tell her the news. Abby spent the rest of the night wondering if Matteo would call.

He didn't.

And so, by the time the team were due to fly to Milan, Abby was in a state of high anticipation at seeing him.

She felt a bit like a schoolmistress at an all-male school as they boarded the Di Sione jet. Everyone was in high spirits, everyone except Abby, because there was no sign of Matteo.

Abby sat in a plush leather seat and rolled her eyes as Pedro looked around the jet.

'Who gets the suite?'

'You do!' The attendant smiled.

It was then, Abby knew, Matteo wasn't joining them.

Milan she glimpsed from the inside of a luxurious coach that took them from the airport to the hotel.

Abby knew the hotel the Lachance team stayed at and she had chosen another one, as she always did, which gave her one less thing to worry about.

Everyone was checked in but Abby lingered till they had all headed off to their rooms and then she asked the receptionist if there were any messages for her.

There weren't.

'Is Matteo Di Sione here yet?' Abby made herself ask.

'No.'

'Do you know when he's arriving?'

'We can't give out that sort of information.'

'I'm a colleague,' Abby attempted but she was no match for the tight security around the Di Sione name. 'A close colleague.'

'Then ask him.' The receptionist's smile did not waver. 'Is there anything else that I can help you with?'

It was a busy week with little waking time to dwell on Matteo and when and if he would arrive.

Despite their amazing win, Abby did know it was unlikely to be replicated.

Pedro had raced the Dubai course but never Milan and, though they went over and over it and watched endless recordings of previous races, she could feel Pedro's tension.

'I shouldn't have brought Bernadette,' he admitted to Abby before he put on his helmet for the practice run. 'She's going to see me place last.'

'Don't think about that,' Abby said.

'I just got a text from Matteo, wishing me luck…'

It was more than she'd had.

'I've a feeling I shan't be getting his jet for a week.'

'Listen,' Abby said to Pedro. 'You won last month. Nothing can take that away.'

'Yeah, but I've got a whole lot more to prove now. Hunter reckons it was a fluke—he was talking in Reception loud enough for me to hear.'

Abby took a steadying breath. Apparently there had been a problem with the Lachance team's hotel security and yesterday they had moved to the one Abby's team were staying at.

Still, her own nervousness as to that wasn't the issue now.

'Don't listen to anything Hunter says.' Abby spoke firmly. 'Don't even look at him. Just give him the finger in your head any time you pass him. Maybe not today, but any time in your career that you pass him, then that's what you'll do.'

And so, too, would she.

The practice run didn't go particularly well and Abby spent ages trying to soothe Pedro, who was seriously rattled, but finally at six he headed back to the hotel for an early dinner and then bed. Abby worked till late making modifications to the car.

By the time she got back to the hotel Abby was hungry, tired and certainly not looking the way she would want Matteo to see her, but there he was checking in at Reception.

Abby kept walking.

A month of no contact and she didn't know where

they were at and so she made her way to the elevator and pressed the button and stood.

'Don't you say hello?' Matteo asked and she turned and smiled as he came and stood beside her.

'I didn't know if you'd just wanted to go up to your suite and crash,' Abby admitted.

'I do.' Matteo yawned. It had been a very long day. 'So, how's the race preparation going?' he asked as their elevator arrived and they stepped in.

'It hasn't been the best day.' Abby sighed. 'Pedro's convinced that he's peaked too soon, though he seems a bit calmer now.'

'Yes, I saw the press conference,' Matteo said. 'He looked like he was about to throw up. What have you been doing?'

'I've been working on the car.' The elevator stopped at her floor. 'Do you want to get dinner?' Abby suggested.

'I'm just going to get room service,' Matteo said. 'Do you want to come up…?' He stopped. 'Sorry, that was thoughtless of me.' It had just seemed a natural solution—he was tired and hungry and he guessed, given the late hour, that Abby felt the same. He just didn't want the bother of going down to the restaurant.

He thought she'd be offended but Abby just smiled at his discomfort.

'Matteo, it's fine,' she said. 'Room service sounds great. I'm starving.'

It was actually the nicest thing that he could have said to her, Abby thought—part of the difficulty of re-vealing such sensitive secrets was the aftermath.

She had been worried that he might look at her dif-ferently or think of her in different ways, but clearly it wasn't at the top of his mind and that suited Abby.

They went straight up to his floor and to his suite and everything was better in Matteo's world. Abby had thought she'd ordered the best suite for Pedro but clearly there were others tucked away for the likes of the Di Siones.

It was huge, more like a stately home than a hotel suite. The shutters were open to a stunning view of Milan at night but Matteo went straight over and closed them. 'I'm sick of views,' he said.

Matteo's cases had already been brought up and the butler was putting his stuff away but stopped what he was doing and asked if he could get Matteo a drink.

'Please.' Matteo nodded.

Unlike the bar fridge in Abby's room, here there was a crystal decanter, presumably filled with Matteo's preferred cognac, but Abby shook her head when offered one. 'I'd love a cola.'

'And me,' Matteo said, and before too long they had been served their drinks and were alone, Abby with a lovely iced cola, Matteo with both of his favourite brews. He drained the cola and then took the cognac more slowly as he asked about the practice run.

'I have to say I'm not expecting a repeat of Dubai.'

'Pedro knew that track,' Matteo said and Abby gave a relieved nod, glad that he understood.

'I am worried though. Now that we've had a win there's so much expectation...'

'Not from me,' Matteo said. 'I just called Pedro before and said he's got the jet for a week whatever happens on Sunday. I suggested that he tell Bernadette that *after* the race, wherever he places.'

Matteo took off his jacket and kicked off his shoes.

'You look tired,' Abby commented.

'I am. It's been one hell of a week.' Matteo yawned. 'Family stuff.'

'As well as getting arrested. How was lockup?'

'Same old.' Matteo shrugged.

He didn't want to think about that night. Not the arrest, but the fight that he'd been privy to as he'd gone to the restroom.

Would he have turned away, if Abby hadn't told him what had happened to her?

No.

He might have called management or...

Matteo didn't know. All he did know was that he had seen red and pulled an angry man off his partner and told him to take his temper out on someone who stood a chance.

The bastard had taken him up on the offer.

Still it wasn't just the other night and his family that were on Matteo's mind though—even with an arrest and many nights out it had been a very long month.

A very tame month.

On many occasions he had wanted to pick up the phone and call Abby or step on a plane. He was walking a very fine line because sex was the easy part for Matteo.

Business he had taken care of through his lawyer and the contract was watertight.

It was the feelings he didn't know how to handle. It was Abby he couldn't get off his mind, Abby who he wanted to spend time with. Matteo knew his own reputation though, and he didn't want to give mixed messages—such as how much he'd missed her, how she stayed on his mind.

Instead he stood up and flicked through the restaurant menu but looked up when Abby, who was wandering around the suite, caught sight of her reflection in a mirror and let out a little yelp—her face was streaked in oil.

'I think I should go have a bath and get changed before dinner,' Abby said.

'Have a bath here...' Matteo said and then grimaced. God, every time he said something it came out wrong. 'I meant...'

'I know,' Abby said. 'And I know, given all I've told you, that being in your hotel room should be awkward, but honestly, Matteo—' she gave a tight shrug, unsure just how to voice it '—it isn't.'

She just didn't feel nervous around him. It was during times apart that she did.

'Matteo?' Abby checked because he really was behaving oddly. 'Is everything okay?'

'No,' he admitted and came over to her. 'This is how I wanted to say hello.' He put his arms around her and it was the nicest place to be and he kissed her, a slow gentle kiss, the type that chased the day away. 'I've missed you.'

'You could have called.'

'I thought you said that you wanted a hands-off sponsor.'

He was very hands on now—they were resting on her waist and she could feel the weight of them and the heat of his palms.

'You don't just have to call about the team.'

'I know that,' Matteo said, 'but then I'm not really big on the "how was your day" type of phone call.' He was as honest as he could be about something he didn't really understand, because he'd never really felt the need to be in touch with another, for no reason other than to be in touch. 'And then if I call one week and then don't the next...' He gave a tense shrug. 'I don't do all that.'

And therein was the difference, Abby thought. Matteo was struggling to commit to a call a week! Their heads were in completely different spaces. The way Abby felt, a call an hour would barely do.

'You've got oil on your face now,' Abby said and they peeled apart enough to see the mess she had made of his shirt.

'Have a bath,' he said, because hell, he wasn't letting that bastard change how he spoke to her or the things that he did. 'Either go down and have one, or have one here, but I'm wrecked and I'm having dinner in bed, or rather on top of it, and you're not getting on covered in oil.'

'Didn't you sleep on the plane?'

'No,' Matteo said. 'I had some work to catch up on.'

He let her go and picked up the menu and read through it.

'Sometimes all you need is a good steak,' Matteo said.

'Sounds great,' Abby said. 'I'll have mine well done.'

'Philistine.'

He rang and ordered as Abby headed off to the bathroom and, yes, it was so nice to peel off filthy clothes and step into a deep, fragrant bath and know that dinner was on the way and that Matteo was here.

Abby lay there, eyes closed, just enjoying the sensation of the water and the low sound of Matteo chatting on the phone on the other side of the door.

Then she heard a knock on the door to his suite and from the sound of it dinner had arrived. Abby hauled herself out of the bath.

It had done its magic.

She was clean and scented and all the tension of the day seemed to have gone, Abby thought as she pulled on a robe and opened up one of the hotel combs and ran it through her hair.

She came out of the bathroom and saw that he wasn't in the lounge but it didn't take long to find him. There was Matteo lying on the top of the bed with a large silver trolley by its side and he'd taken his shirt off.

'It had oil on it,' Matteo said as she tried not to look at his naked top half. 'And,' he added, 'I have to sleep in this bed tonight—you don't.'

'I'm very used to the smell of oil,' Abby said and, as he'd more or less told her that it would be closing time in the Di Sione suite soon, she relaxed. Dinner smelled amazing and she handed him his rare steak and she couldn't help but look at his chest. He was slender but muscular and her eyes were drawn to his ribcage and she saw an old yellowing bruise there, she presumed from the fight the other night.

God, that body took a battering.

'How's the shoulder?' Abby asked.

'I have near-full range of movement,' Matteo said.

Even that sounded suggestive as she took her plate to the other side of the bed and climbed on.

'I love having dinner in bed,' Matteo said, showering his steak in pepper.

'I don't think I've ever had it.' Abby thought for a moment. 'Well, unless I've been sick.'

'You know that full feeling when you just want to lie down?' he asked. 'I was going to open a restaurant once, just beds. Dante and Dario talked me out of it.'

'Your brothers?' Abby checked.

'They're far more savvy than me. They started Libertine?'

'The app for the wealthy?' Abby had heard of it. His family really was everywhere!

'Yes, it provides anything for anyone, just so long as you can afford it. Anyway, I accepted their advice that my bedside restaurant chain wasn't the best idea, though I still think it could work.'

'Nobody would ever leave.' Abby smiled.

She didn't want to leave.

'What about…' Matteo had been about to ask about her sister but he kept having to remind himself of what Abby had told him and what her father had. 'What about you?' he asked instead. 'Any brothers or sisters?'

'An older sister,' Abby said. 'Annabel. We've never really got on.'

'Because?'

'Because I make things complicated apparently. She's married to my father.' Abby rolled her eyes. 'Well, not my father exactly but…'

'I get the picture.'

'She's pregnant,' Abby said. 'With her first. At the end of October I'll be an aunt and I haven't seen my sister in years.'

'At all?'

Abby shook her head. 'We talk on the phone at

Christmas and things but I haven't been home for a long time.'

'Years?'

She nodded but didn't elaborate.

Abby didn't want to spoil this night with people who weren't them.

It was just so nice to eat and then to lie there side by side and to talk.

And because it was so nice and they were both so relaxed Matteo tried to tell her some of what was on his mind.

The Origins of Them, as he called it.

'Hey, you know your necklace…'

'It's not actually mine,' Abby said. 'It's my father's.'

'Yes, but…' He hesitated for a beat too long and Abby continued speaking.

'My mother left it to him. He's got a big do in July and has told me that he wants me there, looking presentable and wearing the necklace.'

Matteo swallowed.

'I'm not going to go though.'

He breathed out a sigh of relief. 'How come?'

'We don't really talk. Well, not since…' She didn't want to discuss it again and so she changed the subject a little. 'There's a huge party in LA on the same night. Anyone who placed in the Henley Cup will be there and so now I've got a legitimate reason not to go to my father's function.' She looked at him. 'You should come.'

'Why?'

'You're our sponsor…'

'And?'

The relief that she wasn't going to her father's function, just the little rush of being let off the hook, had Matteo stop worrying about the problems that beset them, and he moved a little closer and started playing with the tie to her robe.

Yes, Matteo decided, he'd tell her about her father and the necklace but at a better time.

After the race, maybe?

'Have you thought about what I said about us two?'

'I have.' Abby answered him as casually as she could—as if she hadn't spent way too many hours poring over his words. Now was the time to say no, that it was perhaps the most stupid of ideas, yet, side-on facing each other, his fingers found the swell of her nipple, even through the thick robe, and he stroked it, just not enough for Abby.

'And?' Matteo asked.

'I don't know,' Abby admitted.

'Better than a no,' Matteo said. 'At least it's something to work on.'

Which he was. She could feel his fingers at the very tip of her breast but as his lips found hers, Matteo's hand flattened and the pressure of his warm palm was divine. It was a different kiss to the one they'd shared earlier; this was a sexy kiss and his naked torso she now explored beneath her hands and he let her. Odd that at twenty-seven it was more than she'd done with a man. His leg came over hers and then Matteo's fingers were at the tie of her robe, but he held back from peeling it open.

Abby wanted him to.

God, she loathed that she tied double knots.

His lips moved from her mouth and to her neck and

Abby's hands drifted down, feeling his toned stomach right to the edge of his belt, and she wanted so much to move her hand farther down but resisted.

Matteo had endless patience but that didn't make him blind to need and if she so much as moved to halt him, then he would, but instead they just carried on kissing as he made light work of her robe.

Now he peeled it open and so their chests were naked and touching, just enough to ensure it was not enough.

'Don't rush me,' Abby said, which was contrary to how she felt.

'I'm kicking you out in five minutes,' Matteo said and then he took her hand and placed it where she wanted it to be. His tongue caressed hers and she explored him through the fabric, hard and straining, and she ached to set him free but opened her eyes and met his gaze.

Oh, she wanted.

But she wanted more too.

More than Matteo would ever give.

'I don't want to lead you on,' Abby said, 'if I don't...'

'You can lead me on any time.'

'I'm going to go down,' Abby said, her hand still on him and his smile made her smile. 'I meant to my room.'

'I know,' Matteo said. 'A guy can dream.'

He made her feel sexy, so much so that she wanted to do just what the suggestive air called.

He could actually feel her reluctance as Abby got off the bed and it felt like a win to Matteo. He'd never really got the saying "it's worth the wait." Matteo waited for no one, impulse never lasted that long and he went with them at whim.

She would be worth the wait though.

As Abby went into the en suite to retrieve her clothes Matteo called her back.

'You can't put those back on.'

'Well, I'm not going down in my robe.'

'Send the butler to get you a change of clothes, then,' Matteo said and went to reach for the phone but Abby halted him.

'No, he'll think...'

'Who *cares* what he thinks?'

'I care.'

'God, you're a prude,' Matteo said but not nastily. 'I'll go and get something for you to wear.' He really was nice like that, Abby thought as he got out of bed and put on a fresh shirt. 'I can have a little rummage through your underwear drawer while I'm there!'

She handed over her room card and Matteo headed out to the elevators.

He wanted her to stay, yet he didn't want to push, Matteo thought as he pressed the button for the tenth floor.

And then, as the elevator stopped at the eighteenth floor and Hunter stepped in, Matteo changed his mind.

He wanted Abby in his room and the thought that she might be here, in this elevator dressed in her robe and alone with Hunter right now, had Matteo holding his breath.

He leaned back on the brass rail of the elevator as Hunter stared ahead and Matteo's eyes never left his face.

Yes, Hunter knew who he was, Matteo knew, because he could see a muscle flickering in his cheek and the tension was near boiling point.

He could take him here now, Matteo thought.

Wipe him out of any chance of racing tomorrow, but Abby would hate that, he knew.

She wanted to beat him herself, in her own way.

The elevator stopped at the tenth floor, only Matteo didn't get out; he didn't want Hunter to even have a hint that this was Abby's floor.

The doors closed again and it was then that Hunter spoke.

'Problem?' Hunter asked because Matteo's stare could blister paint.

'Just the smell,' Matteo answered and then, as the elevator opened, when Matteo knew he should just let Hunter go, instead he offered a very choice word.

Hunter stiffened but he didn't turn around; instead he carried on walking but there was a dangerous, unchecked energy between them and Matteo could feel his heart thumping as he pressed floors five through to twelve and the elevator started moving again.

Matteo got to Abby's room.

The turn-down service had been and there was a chocolate on her pillow and it was all calm but his heart still thumped in his chest and so he poured a glass of water and took a drink.

Abby had told him that they always stayed at different hotels.

He closed his eyes and tried to tell himself to calm down. They were in the same profession, Matteo said to himself. Of course their paths would cross.

The self-talk didn't reassure.

Matteo went to the wardrobe and pulled out a top and a skirt and then he went to her underwear drawer.

Next he went over to the bed and wrote a silly note and left it on her pillow, then back up to his suite he went.

One look at his face and Abby knew something was wrong.

'Here.' He handed her her clothes; he was about to suggest that she get changed and then he would walk her down, or maybe that it wasn't such a good idea for her to be staying at this hotel and that they could switch, but the long sentence sort of shrunk into three words.

'Stay here tonight.'

'Matteo?'

'Hunter's here.'

'There was a problem with security and so they...'

'No, no...' Matteo wasn't buying it for a moment. 'Did you really think he was just going to let you take him down without a fight, Abby? Did you think, when you were hatching your master plan, that Hunter was just going to sit back and let you beat him?'

'It's not going to happen again,' Abby said.

'I'm not saying that it is,' Matteo said. 'But you've stirred up a hornet's nest and he's angry.'

'Did you say anything?' Abby demanded.

'He knows that I know what happened.'

'What did you say to him?' Abby shouted. 'Matteo, you didn't do...'

'I didn't do anything,' he snapped. 'He already thought I knew at the press conference. I just let him know tonight that I did. Abby, that guy swaggers around...I swear that he's going to do whatever it takes to mess with your head.'

'He's already messed with Pedro's,' she admitted.

Matteo was right, Abby realised—it was no accident that Hunter was here.

'Stay,' Matteo said. 'I'm not going to try anything.' And then he shouted, nicely if that was possible, 'I just want you in my bed with me!'

'Matteo, you're not always going to be around,' Abby pointed out.

But he was the master of instant fixes. 'Let's just get through tonight.'

Matteo was shaken, in a way that he never had been about another.

Sex really was the last thing on his mind tonight.

It wasn't anything to do with that.

In fact, for Matteo, it was more concerning than that, because when he stripped off and got into bed, he just needed her skin beside his.

Abby stood there as Matteo stripped off.

Completely.

She guessed it wouldn't enter his head to get into bed any other way.

She could ask for pillows between them, or get into bed, her robe tied and her reluctance evident, only she wasn't reluctant.

It was her feelings for Matteo that scared her.

Not him.

She took off her robe and got in beside him and he switched off the light and just rolled into her.

He kissed her shoulder, the back of her hair and he ran a hand the length of her thigh and to her waist and then the *thump, thump* of his heart slowed and Abby lay there, listening to him sleeping with his hand resting on her stomach.

Abby slowly acclimatised to the feeling of sharing a bed with someone. She kept waiting for his hand to move, or for Matteo to change his mind about not trying anything. But Matteo was sleeping the sleep of the dead and so she found out what it was like to be held naked through the night with no expectation.

It was possibly the nicest gift of all and in that moment her world was the nicest place.

In the dark, next to him.

CHAPTER EIGHT

AT FIRST ABBY thought that she had jolted awake but then realised that the movement had come from Matteo.

He was still asleep but Matteo just had the familiar sensation of falling.

Only it wasn't him falling from a tree this time.

He was standing at the door to an elevator and watching the carriage drop down with Hunter and Abby in it and grabbing out for the cable and missing.

Yes, he jolted but then in that same instant felt her warm next to him and knew it was a dream and straight back into deep sleep he went.

Abby lay there, not thinking of the race ahead today but instead the man next to her now, and she didn't want the alarm to go off.

Of course it did.

Matteo groaned at the intrusion and pulled her closer into him.

Their temperatures matched, their muscles were loose and relaxed and she felt him slowly harden and the nudge of him at the back of her thigh, which seemed to Abby to be at odds with his regular breathing.

Her breathing wasn't in the least regular. She could feel his hand on her stomach and she lay locked in pri-

vate thoughts and aching with want. She lay in a body
that was finally ready to commit, next to a man who
never would.

Abby turned over to face Matteo and his arms, even
in sleep, moved to accept her.

He really was asleep.

All the tension from last night had left and his mouth
was just a little open and she was so close to leaning
over and kissing him awake, just giving in to and exploring the want that hummed through her now.

The snooze alarm went off and she watched his face
screw up and his hand reached for a pillow, pulling it
over his head and, in that moment, Hunter left every
equation.

There were no more thoughts of revenge, no past to
overcome, just the quiet of morning and a feeling of
peace as she lay next to a man who plucked the strings
of her heart.

Just that.

Abby rolled over and turned off the alarm and he
pulled her back to his side. 'Matteo, I've got to go.'

He fought to wake and the events of last night started
to filter in. 'I'll walk you down,' he mumbled and
moved to sit up.

'Stop it,' she said. 'I don't need a bodyguard.'

She just needed *him*; yet Abby knew Matteo had
checked out on love.

'Go back to sleep.'

She went and had a quick shower and dressed in the
clothes that he had fetched for her last night and then
came back into the bedroom, where he lay awake now,
looking at her. He looked sulky and angry and she knew
why—Hunter was around.

'You're going tomorrow, Matteo. I'm here for a few more days, dismantling the car and then straight on to Monte Carlo, so it seems a bit stupid to be walking me to my room today.'

He said nothing.

Matteo didn't know what to say.

Abby was right—tomorrow at six in the morning he'd be gone and, more to the point, he had never been another's shadow.

Silence hung between them.

It wasn't a row; it was Check.

His heart was under threat of capture and Matteo didn't like that feeling in the least.

'Good luck today,' Matteo said but it came out in a rather forced voice.

So, too, was hers. 'Thanks.'

He lay there when she had gone. Yes, tomorrow he would be back in Manhattan and, Matteo decided, he was going to go and get laid.

It had been...

He didn't really want to do the math. Matteo didn't want to admit that since their first dinner in Dubai, he'd lost interest in that half of the world population that had once been his playground.

No, he wouldn't be getting laid any time soon.

Matteo knew he was lying to himself. Instead the next couple of weeks were going to be spent stressing at the thought of her in Monte Carlo with that animal around.

He reached for the hotel phone.

Abby stepped into her hotel room to change into her lovely bottle-green outfit. She opened the chocolate that was on her pillow and as she popped it into her mouth she picked up the note that was beside it.

Dear Abby,
You need new underwear. Shall I take you shop-
ping or can I choose?
Matteo

And then her phone rang.

'Did you get my note?' Matteo asked.

She knew he was ringing to check that she'd got back okay, but it was nice that he didn't have to admit it.

'I did.' Abby smiled. 'You can choose.' And then she was serious. 'Nothing's going to happen today, Matteo. All anyone is thinking about is the race.'

'I know and I meant what I said, even if I didn't say it very well—good luck today.'

'Thanks.'

Matteo had quite a morning in a very lavish boutique.

A few women nudged and laughed but he cared not and amassed quite a collection, which he asked to all be wrapped and then sent up to her room. Then Matteo had lunch and finally he took himself trackside.

The streets were packed and lined with spectators and when he finally made it to the Boucher sheds he, as always, stayed back, though Pedro stopped playing video games and came over and they chatted for a few moments.

Abby saw Pedro was smiling at something Matteo had said, and whatever her personal feelings were towards Matteo, she was very glad to have him as their sponsor. He was very good with Pedro, unlike the sponsor they had had last year who had demanded far too much, especially before a race.

But then, as the race commenced, there were no thoughts of Matteo, nor revenge—all Hunter was, was the car that was ahead of them.

As were eight others.

For the next two hours the team worked intently, working out the best refuel times. Matteo watched Abby relaying instructions and giving Pedro some insights as to the cars ahead of him.

The Italian crowd were even more vocal than in Dubai and it was a loud, exciting couple of hours and by the last three laps Pedro had inched the car into fifth place.

Hunter's experience on the course showed, yet Evan pushed him hard and suddenly a roar went up as Pedro overtook into fourth.

Matteo found that he was chewing his nails.

And then it was into the final lap.

He looked over to Abby, whose face was pale but she was talking very calmly to Pedro through her mouthpiece, even though she must be feeling frantic. Hunter was well ahead of Pedro, Evan was in close second; it was a battle for third and, holy smoke, Matteo thought as Pedro accelerated out of the turn, he was going to get there.

Abby was right; this kid was a genius. The pale, sickly faced twenty-one-year-old that had climbed into the car, sure he would place last, got out a triumphant third, as the Boucher team cheered and embraced.

And no, Matteo wasn't on her mind right now because Abby nearly broke her neck just to get over to a jubilant Pedro.

'What the hell!' she screamed at him, her face split in a shocked smile.

'She flew!' Pedro roared back, simply elated. 'She just took off.'

And they were back to talking about the car as if she were a person. This third was even sweeter than placing first.

The press conference was very different to last time. Abby and Matteo were out and stood hand in hand as Hunter droned on and on about his experience. Evan, a man of few words, just shrugged when asked his predictions for the final race.

They were neck and neck—it could be any one of the three.

Pedro sat with a satisfied grin.

'We'll just have to wait for Monte Carlo,' was not just the gist but practically all Pedro said.

Yes, it was a different type of celebration tonight.

The Boucher team filled a gorgeous restaurant. Abby didn't have time to change but no-one cared. She had the best squid pasta she had ever tasted and Pedro made a speech and said that she, the car, was perfection.

It was wonderful; the party was moving on now to wild and Abby and Matteo decided to head back to the hotel but, before they did, Matteo pulled Pedro aside and had a word.

'Another shopping spree?' Abby checked but Matteo just shrugged.

Oh, he'd been speaking with Pedro but about something rather more serious than shopping, not that he'd tell Abby that.

Yes, things felt different tonight and as Abby and

Matteo got out of the elevator at the tenth floor Matteo reminded her of their deal.

'What happens when we make podium?' Matteo asked and, because there was no one around, he reminded her what happened with his mouth.

Hot and sexy, they were straight back to where they had been in Dubai as he kissed her up against the wall.

Only this time there wasn't the surprise element of his kiss, just hungry need, and she held his cheeks in her hands and kissed him back, her shoulders digging into the wall but her groin pressed hard into his.

It seemed miles to her hotel room and so they continued to kiss while walking—a hungry, laden kiss that had them tripping over a tray the next room had left out until finally they fell into her room.

'Hell,' Matteo said as he backed her to the door, undoing the black belt and buttons on her men's bottle-green trousers, and as he looked down he even laughed. 'This feels wrong...'

It felt pretty right to Abby.

He just kissed her until they stood, breathless and facing the other and both half-dressed.

'I'm not ready.' She was panting, feeling a tease but consumed with want.

'For what?' Matteo checked, slipping his hands into her trousers and feeling her as damp as he knew she would be. He stroked her clitoris through her panties and resumed the kiss, probing her mouth with his tongue for a moment and feeling the tightening of Abby's thighs. He pulled back his mouth but not his hand as she simmered nicely.

Oh, Abby simmered. She wanted to, she wanted,

wanted, wanted, but she was more scared of losing her heart than her control.

'How about a fashion show?' Matteo said and she glanced over his shoulder and saw for the first time all the parcels lying on her bed as his hand remained between her legs, his finger lightly stroking her and teasing her, while teasing himself, but then he removed it.

It was do up her trousers or take them off and Abby chose the latter.

'You're quite neat, aren't you,' Abby commented as he picked up her shoes and trousers and threw them in the wardrobe.

'A bit,' Matteo admitted. 'But I've made a lot of mistakes in my life and I'll scare the hell out of myself if I wake up tomorrow and see them by the bed.'

He made her laugh.

Matteo made her feel fine, just fine, to be wearing nothing except ugly panties and the dark green shirt.

She opened the parcels one by one as he did the same with the buttons to her shirt.

Some of the underwear he had chosen was the colour of summer—gorgeous lemons and pale mint greens—while others were the shades of sin.

'Do you know why I chose those,' he said, having peeled off her shirt so she was down to her bra as Abby held some dark violet panties.

'Because they're crotchless?' Abby laughed when she poked her fingers through the hole.

'Actually, I didn't know they were,' Matteo said. 'I chose them because they're not just velvet on the outside.'

They weren't. The inside was just as soft and hidden-seamed.

'I thought they might feel nice.' Matteo explained his thought process.

Abby swallowed.

'Put them on.'

'I'm not ready to sleep with you, Matteo.'

He just shrugged and removed her bra so that her breasts dropped that aching inch and he toyed with her nipples, stretching them out. 'A lovely come would be nice though.'

He said it as if he were choosing from the restaurant menu, only some things weren't as easy as picking up the phone.

Or were they?

She thought of this morning—how turned on she'd been and how turned on she was now—and Abby handed herself over to him and nodded.

Even a little come would be a miracle!

Slut that Matteo was, the second that Abby nodded her consent he was happily stripping off and turning the heating up to rival Dubai at midday.

And then he told her that was his intention exactly! 'Remember that fashion show we had to sit through?' he reminded. 'I kept picturing you in all the underwear they were parading. Most uncomfortable half hour of my life...' He gave her a smile that had her nearly rock on her heels as she knelt on the bed. 'You were my Dubai fantasy—look how far we've come.'

Clearly they were here for the night.

He was almost clinical about it.

It was a very sexy clinic she was in though, Abby thought as Matteo chose a brandy from her minibar and then lay on the bed, naked, his erection lifting off his thigh, and she took her underwear and headed to the bathroom.

'Take some heels with you,' Matteo called.

Yes, look how far she'd come! Abby stood in the sexiest underwear in the world and added said heels. She even clipped up her hair and put on some lipstick.

It was a game to him and that helped Abby—why, she didn't know, but it just did.

Maybe because it was about fun, rather than Matteo throwing in sentiments that could never be met by the cold light of day.

And so she came out of the bathroom and as she did, Matteo remembered the shy, nervous beauty who had walked out of the elevator in a silver dress.

That woman had gone for good now.

Abby stepped out and briskly walked the length of the room and then turned.

Nervous but not shy.

'They walk more with their hips,' Matteo said and took a sip from his bottle as she crossed the room. 'That's better, but more slowly.'

'Are you going to model for me?' Abby checked, strutting her stuff.

'Any time,' Matteo agreed and she looked at his erection and that he was playing with himself and her lips pressed together, wondering if she could ever lie there and do the same with him.

God, it was hot.

'Take off your bra.'

Even with double velvet her nipples were sticking out, and as she took off her bra he could see the spread of colour on her chest and that her stomach was taut with desire, and he could wait no more.

'Get here.'

She nearly ran.

To him.

Matteo guided her so that she sat on his stomach and he poured the last of the brandy onto his hand and then rubbed it into her breasts.

'The only way to drink brandy.'

She knelt over him as he made sure there was no brandy left on the left. Abby's thighs were shaking, her neck was arched. One hand was on her hip as the other went straight for the kill. His hand slid past her exposed clitoris, leaving his thumb there while his fingers burrowed deep inside.

He changed breast.

She nearly lost her mind.

He just worked her as skilfully as she'd tune an engine. It hurt, the nicest hurt, and then he left her swollen, wet, slightly bruised breasts and his free hand started stroking himself again.

'Matteo…'

'I'm not going to.'

Abby's head lowered, just to watch them. Who was this woman, in obscene panties and loving it?

'Oh…' She just moaned as his fingers and thumb seemed to meet in the middle of a wedge of intimate flesh. He stroked her deep on the inside; he exerted pressure on the outside till her stomach seemed to meet her spine.

And yet, she couldn't—she let out a sob, borne of desire and frustration, and then felt as if she were choking, because everything in her tightened as Matteo started to come.

He had felt her tip—thank God, he thought, because

it was past the point of no return, but he had never enjoyed himself more in the bedroom. Or anywhere else come to that.

Abby closed her eyes, regretting that she had no choice but to, because the feel of him hot and pulsing against her was surely a sight to be seen as everything that had been missing spasmed.

Then she opened her eyes to the lovely sight of him pulling out the last of his come and then stroking it into her and she sank down on him rather than pull back. The intense feelings were better shared and then Abby sat back on her thighs and tried to drag in air.

Half an hour ago, she had glimpsed what it might be like.

Now she knew.

'What does it feel like,' Matteo asked, remembering the power of his own first come.

'Better than sex,' Abby said as he pulled her down, but to the side of him.

He knew how to do her right.

CHAPTER NINE

MATTEO WOKE FIRST.

They hadn't had much sleep.

The fashion show had continued until the early hours and they had pretty much done everything but make love.

Sex.

It felt like more than sex, even if they hadn't.

Whatever they had done, and they had done plenty, it had been amazing for both—oral sex had never tasted so good and Abby had just spent the last half hour before dawn, on her back, with Matteo's fingers over hers and, yes, she would sleep easily at night now.

But Abby wanted more than a part-time lover as her first and he respected that.

Matteo didn't like it but, yes, given that she had waited so long, he understood that she might want a little more than the occasional phone call, or the promise of more when he arrived in Monte Carlo.

The easiest thing now would be to turn off the alarm, cancel the jet, kiss her awake and let her team start to work on dismantling the car, as he set to work on the walls that came between them.

Yet he lay there, staring up at the ceiling and remembering the promise he had made a very long time ago.

Oh, Matteo loved a gamble but as he looked over to where she was waking he knew that the stakes were too high.

He wasn't going to risk hurting an already damaged heart.

'You have to go?' Abby said.

She had woken to the pensive air and guessed he was wondering how to politely kiss and leave.

'I do,' Matteo said. 'And you've got a car to dismantle.'

Abby lay listening to Matteo in the shower and she knew she'd been right to hold back.

She didn't regret what had happened, but it did change things irrevocably.

There was an unfamiliar hollow feeling inside her because what had taken place last night felt very different this morning. There was little closeness now as Matteo came into the bedroom and quickly dressed.

'If you need anything for Monte Carlo...'

'We're pretty much sorted,' she said.

'Good,' he said. 'Well, if Pedro wants...'

'He's going to Rome with Bernadette for a few days,' Abby interrupted. 'The team will all be together again five days before the race.'

'I might not be able to get there until the day or so before.'

'Or an hour or so before,' Abby said.

'I didn't say that.'

'You didn't have to.'

'I'll just see what happens with work.'

It was a horrible end to a blissful night. He went to kiss her but she just turned her face away and, in truth, he was relieved she did.

He simply couldn't go through the motions with Abby, even in that.

Matteo was glad she'd insisted on no sex last night. He'd promised to sleep with her, no strings attached.

For the first time, Matteo wondered if he'd be able to.

It was surely better to stay back.

He didn't call.

Abby knew that he wouldn't. Matteo was a master at setting his boundaries, and that he wouldn't do relationships was his big one.

Somehow she had to accept that fact.

The circus moved on.

Pedro and Bernadette flew to Rome for some romantic downtime while the rest of the team went straight to Monte Carlo. Usually she'd be there, overseeing the car's arrival, but Abby had put it off.

There were a lot of bad memories in Monte Carlo; Matteo knew that and yet, still, he did not call.

He wanted to.

Or rather he wanted a life that had existed before April. One where the Lost Mistresses had been just an old tale that his grandfather had told. He wanted the life he had once led back—fast paced, lots of sex, not getting off to a memory.

Matteo was angry.

Every time he thought of calling Abby he would pull up the image of himself and his father coming out of a casino some thirty years apart and, if that wasn't enough of a reminder, the arrival of an email from Ellison was.

Any progress? Abby has formally declined my invitation.

Good for her, Matteo thought. It was Ellison's do the Friday after the race and he was tempted to reply to the email with two choice words.

Yet, he was as complicit in the attempt to get her to the function, wearing the necklace, as her father was.

Even Giovanni had called wanting an update and Matteo had been unusually terse with the old man.

Matteo knew that he had to speak properly with his grandfather.

Yes, he was angry.

Abby deserved better—someone who would deliver on the relationship front and, according to his lineage, Matteo never could. Even if by some miracle he could negate that fact, he knew that the moment Abby found out about the origins of his supposed interest in her team, it would end them.

Checkmate.

And so the day she got to Monte Carlo he fired one very rapid text.

Hope preparations are going well. I'll try to make it for the practice race.

And then he fired another text to Pedro, reminding him what they had discussed, and the best that Matteo could do was hope Pedro would take his request seriously.

Pedro did.

Abby hated being here.

She woke up and let out a tense breath as she checked her phone and of course Matteo hadn't called.

Only it wasn't just Matteo's imminent arrival that had Abby in knots.

Matteo had been right; Hunter was playing mind games because he'd changed hotels again and two days before the race had checked into the one that the Boucher team were staying at.

Yes, it was a different hotel than the last time she had been here, but just being in a hotel in Monte Carlo already had Abby on edge.

There was a knock at the door and it was the Perpetual Pedro wanting to go down to breakfast.

'I just want to run through a few things,' he said.

'Sure.' Abby nodded. 'I'll meet you down there.'

'I'll wait.'

'How's Bernadette?' Abby asked, because last night when Abby had headed back early from dinner, Bernadette had said that she had a headache and had joined Abby on the walk back to the hotel. Bernadette had even come up to Abby's room for a cup of tea and a chat about the press conference tomorrow and the practice race.

'She's doing great,' Pedro said.

'Good.'

Abby left Pedro in the corridor and grabbed her bag and then they headed down to the restaurant.

'Ready for the press conference?' Abby asked when they had been shown to their seats, and Pedro nodded but then he looked up and smiled, and Abby saw why.

Matteo was here.

'Hey!' Pedro said.

'How are you?' Matteo asked him.

'I'm confident,' Pedro said. 'Actually, I think I might take breakfast upstairs. Is that okay?' he checked with

Abby and, as she nodded, it dawned on her then the reason Pedro or Bernadette had barely left her side.

'Did you tell him to watch out for me?' Abby challenged as Matteo took off his jacket and took a seat.

'Yep.' He met her angry gaze. 'I'm not going to apologise.'

'What on earth did you say to him? You didn't tell Pedro...'

'Of course not,' Matteo said. 'I just told him that I'd had a couple of choice words with Hunter and that I didn't trust his temper. Pedro agreed with me!'

'He did?'

'Yep. He knows what a bastard he is.'

'I've been managing fine for the past eighteen months...'

'You weren't winning then,' Matteo pointed out.

He looked terrible, Abby thought.

There were black smudges under his eyes and she guessed he hadn't shaved for the best part of a week.

'What time's the press conference?' he asked.

'Eleven.'

'I'll stay for that and then I have to head off. I'm catching up with Kedah and we're going out on a friend's yacht. I'll be back tomorrow for the race but then I have to fly out straight after.'

'Matteo.' Abby took a deep breath. They hadn't even slept together and they were sniping and avoiding the other and so she told him what she had been building to since the morning he had left her hotel room.

'Can we just take it back to business?'

He closed his eyes and then nodded.

'You don't have to avoid me,' Abby said. 'Look, as much as you turn me on, I don't want to sleep with you.'

She just said it, not knowing that the waitress was standing beside her waiting to take the breakfast order and
then he laughed and said that he'd like his eggs sunny-
side up please as Abby just about face-planted the table.

And then, just like that, they were friends again, but
even as they smiled, there was, though, for Abby, something more that needed to be said. 'Matteo, thank you
for the other night. I mean that. I have no regrets—it
was amazing but...'

'There's always a but.'

'Not really. I know you don't want to take things any
further and I get that. I respect that...' She gave him a
smile. 'I don't have to like it.'

He liked that she was honest.

'I need more though.' Abby told her truth. 'I've
waited a long time. Or rather I've been so messed up
that I've missed out on an awful lot and I just want,
well, when I do sleep with someone, it has to mean
something.'

'I understand.'

'So thanks for the offer of a sex lesson but I shan't
be taking you up on it.'

Matteo let out a breath of both relief and regret.

Relief that they were finished with.

Regret that they would never be.

'Are we good?' Abby checked and he took her hand
and gave it a squeeze.

'All good.'

And so they stood, side by side, but not holding hands,
as the stars of the show took their places.

It was the deciding race tomorrow and Evan, Hunter
and Pedro were all a chance.

The winner would take all.

But though the desire to win burnt bright, it was no longer driven by revenge. There *was* next year, Abby thought.

It didn't all have to be now.

She wanted next year. More than that, she wanted the team she had built to all be together, but then a journalist asked Pedro the question that was on everyone's lips.

'Are the rumours true about you signing with the Lachance team next year?'

Pedro looked over to Abby and she gave him a smile and a very slight nod, letting Pedro know that he could answer with the truth—they had made a deal after all.

'I've been approached.' Pedro shrugged.

'And?'

'In fact, they asked to speak with me yesterday,' Pedro continued, 'but as I said to them—their cars are as dated as their drivers.'

There was a small stunned silence at the obvious provocation and then the cameras started flashing and Hunter got up and walked out.

'Game on,' Matteo said.

The practice race went well and then Matteo disappeared to get ready for his night on the town. Abby had a lot of work to do on the car and so it was Perpetual Pedro who hung around.

'Go!' she said to Pedro when it was close to seven. 'I don't need a babysitter and you need to sleep.'

'Abby…'

'Pedro,' she warned. 'I have every right not to walk in fear and I'm exercising it. Go.'

Reluctantly, Pedro did and Abby worked till after ten,

fine-tuning the engine till she was as happy as she could be with it and then she took a cab back to the hotel.

She was ready simply to go to bed and to do her best not to think of what Matteo was up to now that she had let him off the hook.

Abby climbed out of the cab, wondering if she could be bothered to get room service. The moment she walked into the foyer though, there was Matteo walking with Kedah, both looking like the two play-boys they intended to be tonight.

Clearly they were just heading out.

Matteo had shaved and was wearing a suit and had that arrogant, rich gleam in his eye and he was, Abby knew, about to exercise *his* right to get royally laid.

'Abby?' He frowned as she passed them and he saw that she was alone. 'Where's Pedro?'

'In bed, where he's supposed to be before a race!' Abby angrily answered. 'Don't ever mess with my team and tell them what to do. You were supposed to be hands off, remember!'

'I was just…'

'Well, don't! It's not your job to look out for me and neither do you have the right to interfere with Pedro's build-up to the race.'

A car was waiting for them in the forecourt and as Kedah climbed in he waved to Matteo to get a move on.

'Your friend's waiting for you,' Abby said. 'Have a *great* night, Matteo.'

She just brushed past him, loathing herself for the anger and jealousy that had shot from her lips. He didn't deserve any of that. They had agreed to no-strings sex and she had been the one that had backed out.

What the hell was he supposed to do? Abby thought as she closed the door to her room and stripped off her greasy overalls.

She ran a bath and, as it filled, sat at her desk, trying to type up the adjustments she had made to the car but the figures all blurred before her eyes. There were emails she had to answer about order of events for after the race but all she could think about was Matteo and where he was right now. Then she suddenly remembered the bath.

Thank God for the overflow, Abby thought, and then she climbed in the overfull bath and cried.

For him.

For them.

And for the wish that she had at least slept with him. Once.

Her first because, if not technically, Matteo would have been her first, and the way she felt about him it felt right that it be him.

It was his lack of feelings for her that hurt.

She lay in the bath and let the hot water relax her and over and over she topped it up and tried not to think about Matteo and Kedah in some sordid hot tub.

Bastard!

Except he wasn't.

He had been completely lovely with her.

She got out of the bath and it was close to one and she knew that she had to be up at five and was just about to take her robe off and climb into bed when there was a knock at the door.

And despite brave words that she was fine without a bodyguard, Abby felt a prickle of fear.

Matteo was out, Pedro would be asleep. She knew

that because he was always in bed by seven the night before a race.

The knock sounded again and she was sweating, Abby realised. Her legs wouldn't move and she just stared at the door, too frozen to go to the peephole and see who it was.

'Abby?'

She just about dropped in relief when she heard Matteo's voice and wrenched open the door.

He saw her terror.

'I thought...'

'Sorry, sorry...' He took her straight in his arms. 'I should have called.'

'I thought you were on the yacht.'

'I couldn't get it up.'

He was so crude and yet he made her laugh.

'I didn't even try,' he admitted and then, because he was holding her, because they had missed each other, for even as his mouth moved to hers Abby was reaching for him and they kissed intensely, hurriedly, before logic moved in, before they thought of the many reasons they should not. His arm curled around her waist as he pulled her in. The fear that had gripped her turned to angry passion and as she kissed him back Abby pushed Matteo's jacket down and it fell to the floor. She didn't care about tomorrow when she could have tonight. 'Abby...' She was opening the buttons to his shirt, her mind made up, yet Matteo refused to give her even a moment to regret and he peeled his mouth away. 'I need to tell you something.'

'You don't.'

They were panting, both breathless, and she didn't

need to hear now that he didn't love her and never would.

'Abby,' Matteo said. 'You do deserve better than this.'

She did, because he was hard and his hands were bunched into the gown so as not to tear it off and they could be over and done with—Abby up against the wall, he could be taking her now—but he would not allow another morning between them like the last one, where the air was awkward and the conversation wooden. He would not do that to her.

'We need to talk.'

'Said the playboy.' And then she saw that he was in as much of a mess as she, Abby realised. 'Matteo, I don't need to hear it. I know we're going nowhere.'

'And I'm trying to tell you why it has to be that way.'

It was possibly the most responsible decision in his life and regrettable at that because there was so much energy and want between them that it felt almost criminal to pull back. His shirt was undone and damp from her wet hair but he took a seat beside the desk as Abby straightened out her robe and then took a seat at the desk in front of her laptop. 'It's like a doctor's visit,' he said and she smiled but they were both hurting so much that their smiles didn't last. 'I know you should be asleep but I needed to say this. I really do have to leave tomorrow straight after the race so if I don't say it now...'

'Are you drunk?'

'A bit.' He nodded. 'Look, you know how everyone says, "It's not you, it's me"?' he said and now Abby really smiled.

'Well, in this case it *is* me,' she said. 'I have more baggage...'

'No,' Matteo interrupted. 'It *really* is me.' He took a breath before continuing. He had never fully had this conversation in his head, let alone with another. 'I made a decision a few years ago...'

'You don't have to do this, Matteo,' Abby said because she could see his discomfort and reluctance to reveal more of himself.

'I want to though,' Matteo admitted. 'I know that you've got baggage and I don't want you thinking that my reluctance to get involved with you had anything to do with what's gone on between us, or that what's happened to you in the past has any bearings on my choice. You're right, you should hold out for someone who can give you all that you deserve and I truly can't. I don't want a relationship.'

'I know,' Abby said, yet there was this tiny part that hoped one day he might change his mind.

He answered it there and then.

'Ever.'

There wasn't even a sound as that little flame died; she just silently acknowledged its passing.

'My father had a lot of affairs,' Matteo said. 'I don't even know if you could call them affairs. Just one-night stands, parties, drugs, alcohol...' He closed his eyes as he had to the drama all those years ago, but then he had been lying in bed listening to the fights; now he was doing his best to block out thoughts of a beautiful future with Abby. 'You never knew what you were going to get,' Matteo explained. 'I never knew who would be there in the morning—Mom, Dad, neither. Sometimes, for days on end it was just the nanny. Really, the older ones looked out for the younger...' He wasn't explaining this very well. 'I always knew that in the morning they might not be there. One morning they weren't but this time it was different. My grandfather was there as well as other relatives and outside there were reporters. But I knew already—I used to sleep with the radio on, I liked the voices and the music—I'd heard it on the news...'

Abby sat there.

She could remember the shock of her mother's death. It had been expected. She had been older but she could still remember the shock and finality of it.

Imagine losing both at five and to hear it read out as a headline on the news?

She tried to but couldn't quite grasp it.

'There was a huge funeral. The press were everywhere and it was on the television constantly, as I expected it to be,' Matteo said. 'It was the biggest news in my life and because I was five I actually thought that it *should* be everywhere...' He gave a wry smile. 'You know how small your world is when you're a child?'

Abby nodded.

'But then we went to live at my grandfather's and life went on but it had changed. The older ones all went off to boarding school and Allegra looked after my little sisters.'

'You?'

'I just did what I wanted and I was always getting into trouble but never really told off. I never got why my grandfather could hardly bear to look at me. No matter what I did, no matter how much trouble I got into, he hardly addressed me.'

'I thought you two were close.'

'We're not close, but we're closer now than we were.' Matteo nodded. 'While I was growing up he just stayed back. I started studying and after a year I realised I already knew how to make money. I had my start-up from my parents' estate, but I didn't need to sit in a lecture and be taught what I already knew and so I dropped out.' He looked up at Abby and he told her about a row that repeated in his head to this very moment. 'For the first time my grandfather got angry with me. We had a huge row. He told me I was wasting my life, I was heading for trouble and that he'd seen the signs, should have stepped in earlier...'

Abby swallowed.

'"But you didn't," I said to him. I told him he had never cared about me so why start to worry now? I told him that I knew he couldn't stand to be near me. I just didn't know why.'

Abby sat quietly, remembering Matteo's patience when she had told him what had happened in her past

'My grandfather said, "Every time I look at you I see Benito."'

'Your father?'

Matteo nodded. 'He told me that I was just like him. A gambler, a liar, a risk-taker. He said that I was on track for disaster and he was tired of sitting back and watching history repeat...'

'Matteo.' Abby wouldn't buy it. 'Just because...'

'Abby,' Matteo interrupted her. 'I am *all* of those things. When my grandfather said what he did, it just confirmed what I already knew. I decided then that I would never let myself be like my father. Yes, I might have his traits but I won't get so involved with another that I'm capable of coming close to the damage that he did.'

'Matteo...' Abby started but then she halted herself. Matteo had let her speak; he had let her work out what she wanted for herself. It wasn't her place to tell him how he felt, even if she thought he was wrong to be so down on himself, but she did say a little. 'Your father had children and a wife—you don't.'

'And I intend to keep it that way,' Matteo said. 'He killed my mother. She had straightened herself out and his depravity and temper took her to an early grave.' And then Matteo did what he never had; he exposed his fear. 'I can't take that risk, Abby...'

'You're the biggest risk-taker I know.'

'Not with love.' Matteo shook his head. 'The stakes are too high. I'm sorry I can't give you what you deserve. I never set out for us to get involved, but then, on sight I did. For the past couple of months, since the day we met...'

She waited.

'It's been you,' Matteo said.

'Just me?'

'Abby, I might not be marriage material but it doesn't mean that I'm not crazy about you. I'm just here to explain why it could never last. I don't want to sleep with you tonight and for you to expect things to have changed tomorrow. They shan't have. I'm flying back and the next time I see you...' He shrugged, but it was a desperate one and Abby looked at a man who dealt in hours rather than days.

'Do you see why I had them pull up such a watertight contract? I'm good for business, not much else...'

'Matteo, I'm not holding out for a ring.' She wasn't sure at first what she was saying, but then Abby looked into the dark eyes of the man who had stayed loyal, who had listened, who had helped her work through dark, dark times to a point where a future seemed possible.

Even if it might not be with him.

And she was sure.

Very.

'I'm going to go,' Matteo said and he stood.

'Please don't.' Abby looked up at him. 'I heard the lecture...' Their eyes met. 'And I get it. I just want it to mean something...for us to mean something...'

'You know that we do.'

'And that's all I need to know.'

It was.

Whatever they had amounted to more than a time-frame, what they felt for the other might not ripen with age but could be celebrated now.

They kissed in a way they had both tried not to, slow, precise and affirming. A kiss that was so tender that the only place it could possibly bruise was your heart. And it punctured his because never, not once, had Matteo allowed himself to even glimpse what another with heart exposed might taste like.

'Sure?' Matteo checked but Abby had already jumped.

The haste in his breathing as her hands stripped him of his shirt had their mouths mesh in hot wet kisses that tasted of no holding back.

Abby's hands roamed his skin and pressed into his chest, feeling his tension and strength as he dealt with the last of his clothes. Haste left then; still kissing he undid her robe and she shrugged it off like a burden and wrapped her arms around his neck so their tongues could caress as their bodies met. His fingers strummed up her ribs and Abby rose to her toes just so that they might repeat that final ascent to the tender top again before he played her breasts.

And when his mouth lowered, when she ached for a bruising kiss, he just caressed one nipple with his tongue, over and over. Abby's knees wanted to give way, but she stayed standing, simply for more, till she bit back the urge to beg. So desperate for more that when his face returned to hers, his kiss drowned her demand and he led her to the bed.

Matteo's hand moved between her thighs and he played her so slowly, stroking her slick warmth, till her knees pulled up. She wanted to scream that she would not break. His skin, his scent, his want, did not match this slow perusal. He came over her and parted her legs wide. Abby met his navy eyes and she looked right at him as he first took her. She watched as he drove in slowly but as he met the depth of her desire, as welcoming muscles gripped, the crystal shattered for them both.

He kissed her eyes and her face; he moved to his side and turned her with him. Matteo stroked her thigh slowly and then down to her calf as he moved within. He positioned her leg higher and brought it onto his hip so he could thrust deeper.

Abby had given in trying to hide her feelings, and anyway there was nowhere to hide. She was moving with him, sharing intimate kisses, glad of his hands that pushed her hair back just so he could better see her come.

It felt like no other time; it *was* like no other time, because the feel of him swell inside her and the sudden haste in him had her sob as she tightened. Her thigh over his cramped but it only heightened the intensity as he parted her wider with deft hips that only angled to get him in deeper as Matteo came hard into her.

It left him dizzy; it made her the same. It was so intense that for a blind moment Matteo believed all things possible. He straightened her cramped limb; he bought her back down with a kiss—each pain he ironed, while still within, except for the big one.

And when he went to fix that, when in the rush of a high, he almost lost his head and told her the one thing she wanted to hear, Abby stopped him with a kiss, a hurried one, a necessary one.

Not for Matteo's sake, but hers.

No lies, no promises.

That it meant something precious was enough.

CHAPTER TEN

'YOU'RE NOT VERY good for my race preparation.' Abby
sighed as she stretched her body and tried not to give
in to temptation and sleep.

They hadn't slept, and if she did now, then she might
just wake up to a call from Pedro to ask where the hell
she was.

'I'm going to ring down for coffee,' she said, deciding caffeine was in order before facing the world. 'Do
you want one?'

'No.' Matteo yawned. 'It will ruin the very long lie-
in that I intend to have.'

'How long?' Abby groaned and pulled a face as,
having briefly opened his eyes, Matteo closed them
again as he spoke.

'Well, it's nearly five now and Kedah doesn't get
here till around midday, so about seven hours…' he
said, rubbing in just how little she had slept.

Yes, it was incredibly hard to peel herself out of
bed but she did so and showered and tried to get her
head into what had once been the most important day
of her life.

It still was, Abby thought as she showered.

Last night made it more so but for different reasons.

By the time she came out, her coffee had arrived. Abby took it out onto the balcony and looked out to the beautiful old buildings and the sparkling Mediterranean and, yes, Monte Carlo truly was beautiful.

It matched her memories of it now.

And whatever happened from here on between herself and Matteo, she'd be okay. The last time they had awoken together it had been awkward and difficult. It wasn't now and Abby was determined to never let it get to that again.

She did not regret last night and surely never would.

It had been a very deliberate choice that she had made.

Abby went back in and Matteo was sleeping and so she dressed in her race-day bottle-green and then headed out to face the most important day of her life.

Her working life, Abby amended.

There was more now.

The build-up to the race passed in a blur.

Pedro was locked into his video games and Bernadette was doing her own thing, catching up with friends on her phone and present but not getting in the way.

She was good to have around, Abby thought.

Matteo and Kedah arrived just after one and there was a sense of calm in the Boucher camp.

Even if they came last they'd already won.

They were more united than they had ever been. Pedro was staying on and they had two amazing races behind them.

As the starting time to the final race of the Henley Cup approached, Pedro came out in his leather and he looked determined rather than tense. Bernadette gave Pedro a kiss for luck and everyone else wished him well but then it was just him and Abby for that last little talk before he took his place.

This time Pedro's teeth weren't chattering with nerves and there was no need to talk him down. Still, Abby carried on with what she had planned to say, that it was the taking part that counted and to remember how far they'd come. The Henley Cup would be the icing on the cake, she told Pedro.

'You always eat the icing first.' Pedro grinned as he put on his helmet.

'Okay, I lied,' Abby admitted and gave up on her losers-are-still-winners approach. 'Bring it home.'

It was a spectacular race. How could it not be? The scenery was straight from a travel brochure, the weather perfect and the car that Abby loved so took off like a bullet from the chamber and left half the field behind.

They were off.

Matteo juggled cola and binoculars as the cars took to the gorgeous hilly streets and then later wished that he hadn't had so much cola because, with only five laps to go, and the top five a close pack at that, he had to excuse himself, leaving Pedro in fourth.

Matteo returned to Kedah's side to be told that Pedro was now third.

The Lachance team and Hunter were first, the Carter team with Evan at the helm in close second.

Matteo glanced over to Abby and saw her concentration as she spoke into her mouthpiece.

Not a stolen glance between them.

And he loved that about her—her drive, her focus—and so he got back to watching the race but, as he did, something happened.

Not on the track.

Well, yes, something happened on the track, because Pedro overtook Evan but, as he did so, hope overtook fear for Matteo.

Just this quiet second in a noisy world where Matteo lost the dread that he never showed, or rather, his fears that he had shown only to one other—Abby.

And if Pedro won, he was going to do it, Matteo told himself.

He was going to somehow put everything right.

'Come on,' Matteo shouted and it felt like Pedro must have heard because, just past the final bend, Pedro not just overtook Hunter, he almost blew him off the track.

'Bring her home!' Matteo shouted and, yes, now even he was talking about the car as if it were a person.

She won!

It was delicious; it was chaos.

As Hunter tried to right the car, Evan screamed past and the Carter team took second place.

There was music and champagne and the cup held high and it was all just a gorgeous blur until it was time for the press conference.

Abby was trying to locate Pedro and found him talking with one of the organisers and so Hunter and Evan had already taken their places as the victor walked in to applause.

Abby stood to the side and Matteo, in the middle of the room, looked at her unreadable expression and wondered what was going on in her mind as the questions commenced.

'Congratulations to Pedro,' Hunter said. 'He's an amazing talent. Without him...'

Hunter looked directly at Abby and tried to tell her she was nothing, that were it not for their driver...

And Matteo watched as…no, she didn't struggle to breathe, and neither did she mouth an obscenity, or do any one of the things that she would be more than entitled to do.

There was more in her armoury than that.

Abby smiled.

For one reason only—she was happy.

And if looks could kill, then a well-timed smile could maim, because after the press conference, to Matteo's relief, Hunter's jet took off a lot faster than the Lachance car and finally there was this little moment when it was just Matteo and her.

'You beat him,' Matteo said.

'No.' Abby shook her head. 'We won.'

She wanted to better explain the change in her, the changes to her heart that he had helped make—to say that, even if there was no future for them, she would treasure the past for ever, but there wasn't time to do that now.

'Hey, Matteo…' Pedro shouted over. 'How about it?'

'How about what?'

'I just got permission, before they take the barriers down. Do you want that ride now?'

'Matteo has to head off,' Abby said, covering for him, as she knew that the very thought of a ride in a racing car made him feel ill, but then, as always, Matteo surprised her.

'I'd love to, Pedro.'

Matteo suited up and the face that disappeared into the helmet was grey but this was something he wanted—no, needed—to do.

Abby watched as he came out of the shed and her

eyes drifted over his leather-clad body just as his had over hers that first day.

'Is it wrong to say just how much I fancy you now?' Abby asked.

'You're not doing it for me, Abby,' Matteo said and blew out a breath.

'You don't have to do this.'

'Oh, but I think that I do.'

He climbed in and took his seat and pulled down the harness and then Pedro did something—he came over and carefully checked Matteo's helmet and harness before getting in himself.

And therein was the difference.

Pedro was nothing like Matteo's father.

Pedro was an expert.

He trained for this, slept for this; every morsel that passed his lips was to better himself for this and Pedro kept to the rules.

And so, too, could Matteo.

Matteo wasn't his father either.

All those thoughts buzzed louder than the engine as Matteo found out firsthand just how fit you had to be to deal with the G-force and heat and demands on the body as the vehicle cornered, as well as that Pedro had to focus.

Yes, it was terrifying but exhilarating and it was one of the best experiences of Matteo's life, and as he climbed out it was to a world that looked different.

'I feel like I've laid a ghost to rest,' he admitted to Abby as he took off his helmet.

Abby nodded.

Last night, so, too, had she.

CHAPTER ELEVEN

As MUCH AS he had wanted to stay and join in with the celebrations, Matteo really did need to leave and head back to New York.

Even more so than before now.

With time differences and flying time, it felt odd that it was still Sunday, albeit late in the evening when he drove towards the Di Sione estate.

Giovanni had appointments all week and, if Matteo wanted to speak with him, then it had to be tonight.

Matteo had told Giovanni that he was coming and he knew that the old man would be hoping it was because Matteo had good news for him.

He wondered how his grandfather would take the news.

Alma let him in and said that Giovanni was in the lounge and Matteo thanked her and walked through.

Giovanni was sitting, staring out to the lake, and Matteo knocked on the open door to alert him that he was here.

'Matteo!' He turned and gave a smile of delight and went to stand but Matteo waved him down and went over and kissed him on the cheeks.

A pang of guilt hit Matteo when he felt the frail

shoulders beneath his hands and saw his grandfather's tired, lined face.

'You've been busy,' Giovanni said.

'Yes, I have to say I like the motor racing world.'

'I see your team won the cup. I got up early and watched the race.' Then Giovanni's face grew serious. 'It's not good news, is it?'

It felt like good news to Matteo.

He was crazy about someone for the first time in his life but, no, there was no need for Giovanni to know all that.

'Not really,' Matteo said and he took a seat. 'I tracked down the necklace. It had been bought by…'

'Ellison!' Giovanni rolled his eyes. 'I guessed that much when I saw you with his daughter. I don't think you've ever been with a woman that long.'

'Her name's Abby,' Matteo said. 'And I've been sponsoring her team. When I first met with Ellison he said that he wanted me to get his daughter to a function that he's holding this Friday. If Abby's wearing the necklace, then it's mine.'

'And?' Giovanni frowned. He didn't see the problem. 'Surely she can wear it for just one night?'

'It's her mother's necklace,' Matteo said. 'Abby wore the necklace the night that her team placed first. I'm sure it must mean a lot to her and I'm not going to take it from her.' He continued. 'I can't.'

'Even though you know it means everything to me.'

'Even knowing that,' Matteo said.

'You're in love?'

'I think so.' Matteo admitted as much as he dared, because love wasn't a place that he knew. 'What I do know for sure, though, is that I care about her and I'm going to do whatever it takes not to cause her pain.'

He was not his father's son, Giovanni realised.

Matteo was very much his own man.

'I hate letting you down.' Matteo continued to speak as Giovanni took the news in. 'I know that I told you I'd bring the necklace to you but, at the end of the day, I can't do that to her.'

Giovanni sat back in the chair and looked out to the lake. He wanted the necklace so badly. A part of him had hoped that finding the Lost Mistresses, and having them together again, might somehow heal his fractured family. And yet, while he ached to have the necklace that meant so very much back in his possession, maybe its magic had already worked. Giovanni had never heard his youngest grandson speak of anyone in this way.

'Could I see it again,' Giovanni asked. 'Do you think, if you explained things to Abby, that maybe she would let me hold it one more time?'

'I think so.' Matteo's response was cautious. 'The thing is...' He blew out a breath. 'It might take a bit of time to get her to agree. I'm going to have to tell Abby that the necklace is the reason I first got in touch. If I know Abby at all, then that isn't going to go down very well.'

'You're going to be in trouble again.' Giovanni smiled.

'For sure,' Matteo agreed. 'Let me work on it.'

And work on it he did.

It was quite a busy few days for Matteo but he did make the time to call Abby and he could hear the surprise in her voice.

'I just wanted to see how everyone pulled up after the celebrations,' Matteo said.

'Well, I don't think anyone has pulled up yet,' Abby admitted. 'I don't think anyone's coming back to earth any time soon. We've got the big presentation and party in LA on Friday. You could come...' She tried to keep her voice light, to not build her hopes up that he had called her.

Actually, Matteo couldn't be there for the presentation in LA, not that he could tell her why.

'I can't make it on Friday. Will Hunter be there?' he checked.

'Nope,' Abby said. 'He's gone to ground.'

'Good. So when will you be back?'

'On Saturday afternoon.'

'Would you like to go out for dinner?' Matteo casually asked, as if he hadn't already booked the restaurant, as if all the plans he had made this week didn't depend on her response.

There was a long stretch of silence before she answered.

Long, because she hadn't expected his call and now an invitation to dinner on the very night she got back was a little more than she dared to glimpse.

He might just want to discuss the team, Abby attempted to warn herself, but her heart refused to be reeled in.

Oh, please don't hurt me, Abby thought.

Please don't get my hopes up high because I accepted a one-night stand when you said it could be no more than that.

'Yes.' Abby cleared her throat and did her best to

sound as if it wasn't such a big deal. 'Dinner sounds great.'

'Saturday, then. Text me your address. I'll be there about eight.'

He didn't await her response; Matteo, too, was having trouble keeping things even.

On Friday he walked into a very exclusive jewellers.

'I've never worked so hard,' the jeweller said and when he showed Matteo the final piece Matteo could see the hours and skill that the jeweller had put into this masterpiece.

Even though the jeweller had only a photo to go on, it could have been made by the same designer!

The emerald sat up high on a platinum setting and it really was a work of art.

No, he hadn't had a replica of the necklace made.

You could never fully replicate the real thing.

And the necklace was the real thing, Matteo was very sure.

And so he'd had made a ring.

'I can't see anything on the photograph of the necklace to indicate origins,' the jeweller admitted.

'It's all a bit of a mystery.' Matteo was also bemused but his grandfather had remained unforthcoming.

'She's a very lucky lady,' the jeweller said as he nestled the ring into a box Matteo had had designed to match the case for the necklace.

'I might have to remind her of that,' Matteo said, imagining Abby's reaction when he told her the truth.

He was nervous to tell her about the necklace—of course he was—but with this ring…

He got back to his apartment and put the photo of the necklace and the ring in his safe and then lay back on the bed and tried to plan his speech for tomorrow. Matteo didn't get very far. He could never quite get past the bit where he told Abby that he'd stood in her father's study and come up with a plan to sponsor her, without imagining his face being slapped.

Deciding that he'd just have to wing it at dinner tomorrow, he dozed off.

Matteo woke to his phone buzzing and the sight of a skyline that was backed by a dusky pink sky.

'Abby?' he said, sitting up. 'What time is it there?'

'Eight,' Abby said and Matteo frowned because it looked as if it was evening and LA was a few hours behind them but then she explained. 'Matteo, I'm already in New York.'

'How come?'

'Hunter arrived this morning and—do you know what?—I just didn't want to be around him. It's Pedro's night and I don't want anything to get in the way of that and so I decided to head for home.'

'Good.'

'I need a favour,' Abby continued. 'Well, I don't need one but it would mean a lot if you could do this for me.'

'Name it.'

'I'm on my way to my father's…' Abby took a breath. 'I know I said that I wasn't going to go but I've changed my mind. It's not such a big deal. I'm just going to put my head in for a couple of hours. It would be great if I could say that you were coming too.'

'Abby.' Matteo was already off the bed. 'I'll come with you. I'll just get changed and then I'll pick you up.'

And 'fess up!

He was already undoing his belt as he spoke but speed wasn't going to save Matteo.

'No, there's no need for that,' Abby said. 'He wants me there by eight and I'm already running late. Look, I get it if you don't want to come but it would help a lot if you could. I'll text you the address...' She looked out of the window of the car and saw that she'd arrived. 'I'm here now. Wish me luck.'

It really had been a last-minute decision.

Abby had arrived home and opened up her case and had seen the gorgeous silver dress that she had worn on the night they had won in Dubai.

Why not? Abby had thought.

She had pinned up her hair to show off the necklace to full effect and had just decided to play the game for one night.

No, she had long ago realised her family would never be close but surely an occasional function or get-to-gether was doable.

Now the car that her father had sent for her pulled up at the house that had never really been a happy home and the door was opened for her.

It had been years since Abby had last been here.

Emails and the occasional phone call had been all she could manage since that terrible time, sitting in her father's study and being told Hunter wouldn't be called to answer for his actions.

She was ready to put it all behind her and, nine years on, Abby felt a lot more together and capable than the last time she had walked up the stairs to the entrance of her family home.

'Abby!' Cries went up from everywhere as she entered.

'Congratulations' were offered from all directions, as well as, 'Wow, look at you!'

'Abby!' Her sister, Annabel, came over and gave Abby a kiss on the cheek but it felt like a sting. 'You changed your mind about coming?'

'I did.'

'The prodigal daughter returns triumphant!'

Abby could have given a bitchy retort. She guessed Annabel thought she was only here to gloat because her team had won but, no, it had nothing to do with that.

'Just try and behave tonight,' Annabel said. 'This is important for Daddy.'

Annabel's husband came over and gave Abby a very guarded smile. 'Abby.'

Aside from that frosty greeting the night went well. Her father was too busy chatting people up to pay Abby much attention, which suited her fine.

Abby's phone buzzed and she saw that it was Matteo texting her.

I'm on my way.

She fired a text back.

No rush.

And then Matteo sent another.

Abby, we need to talk.

Abby frowned at the second text and then wondered if Matteo was doing one of his *I don't do relationships* things, and was maybe annoyed that she'd asked him to come. She decided she would explain when he arrived that this really wasn't a meet-the-father moment.

She was soon distracted when one of her father's friends called her over and asked about the race in Dubai.

'It was amazing,' Abby said for perhaps the fiftieth time that night but she was more than happy to talk about it. Realising that Matteo would be here soon she went upstairs and took a moment to refresh her make-up and check her hair and then stepped back and looked in the full-length mirror.

Yes, the necklace and dress worked but it was the woman wearing them who felt so different tonight.

She remembered coming down in the elevator and the smile on Matteo's face when he saw her and the wonderful times they had shared and she simply couldn't wait to see him again.

Abby went to head back down to the party. Oh, she would never be one who loved these types of events but she was glad that tonight she had made the effort. She felt confident...

Happy.

For the first time she could remember she felt happy, confident and beautiful in her own skin and then she looked over and saw the man who had made all three possible walk into the Ellison home.

He was wearing a smart suit and his black hair flopped forwards and he brushed it back with his hand as he stood for a moment looking around, Abby guessed, for her.

'Matteo!' Her father saw him and Abby frowned at how pleased her father seemed to be that he was here.

Of course they would know each other from similar functions but it was a very friendly handshake that he gave Matteo. Her father even patted him on his shoulder and, as Abby walked down the stairs, she watched as her father and Matteo disappeared into his office.

Matteo had very much been hoping to speak with Abby before her father but, without that chance, he followed Ellison in, determined to have his say.

'Congratulations,' Ellison said.

'It was an amazing win,' Matteo agreed and then he looked to the photos Ellison had walked him through on the day they met and anger grew in his stomach. There was the photo of Hunter with Abby and this bastard knew what he had done to his daughter and yet still had that photo on the wall.

'I'm not talking about the win,' Ellison said. 'I was referring to your achievement in getting Abby here. I have to hand it you—I thought she might come tonight, albeit reluctantly, but she's been the belle of the ball. The necklace is yours… You've certainly earned it.'

Abby stood at the ajar door and somehow stayed standing as the floor seemed to disappear from beneath her.

What achievement?

It didn't make sense.

Yet it was starting to.

Her father had wanted her here tonight wearing the necklace and she knew—oh, yes, she knew—how low he could stoop.

Why had she thought better of Matteo?

Because, despite clear warnings, she'd gone and fallen in love.

She was tempted to turn, to just walk away and pretend she hadn't heard what was said and to simply make it through the night without creating a scene. It had nothing to do with the fact she was on strict instructions to behave tonight; it was more than that—she didn't want the dream to end.

The dream that Matteo had actually cared about her.

She thought of her mother, smiling for the camera, pretending all was well in a messed-up world, and Abby refused to let that legacy live on.

'What did you just say?' Her voice was very clear as she walked into the study. Matteo's back was to her but she saw it stiffen at the sound of her voice.

'Abby...' he started but Ellison spoke over him.

'I was just congratulating your sponsor,' Ellison said, not remotely bothered that they'd been overheard.

But then, Matteo thought, if he was insensitive enough to have Hunter's photo on his wall, what was another layer of hurt to add to the mix.

'What does my wearing my mother's necklace have to with this?' Abby asked. She had walked right over and stood aside the two men and confronted her father first. 'What do you mean when you say that the necklace is Matteo's?'

'Can we talk away from here?' Matteo suggested.

'Why?' Abby checked. 'I think here is the perfect place. Why spread my misery outside the grounds of this home.' She asked the question again, her voice rising. 'Why would you tell Matteo that my necklace is now his?'

'It's actually *my* necklace,' Ellison corrected. 'Your mother left it to me. I knew that you needed money, Matteo wanted the necklace and I said if he could get you here wearing it for the do...' Ellison shrugged. 'It's no big deal.' As Abby's eyes filled with tears Ellison misread them. 'Oh, don't go getting all sentimental, Abby. Your mother loathed that necklace.'

'And I know why she did!' Abby was shouting now. 'Because, yet again, you'd been unfaithful and, yet again, you thought another trinket would put things right.'

'And it did,' Ellison said. 'Your mother knew how to behave, as does Annabel. Whereas you, Abby…'

'Whereas I,' Abby interrupted, 'don't simply turn a blind eye to everything!'

'Abby,' Matteo said. 'I can explain.'

'No,' Abby said. 'I don't want your charming lies. I want to hear—' her voice was rising further '—the truth from my father. At least *he* doesn't sugarcoat things.'

'Abby,' her father warned. 'Keep your voice down.'

'Then give me an answer. Are you telling me that you bribed Matteo?'

'It was a gentleman's agreement,' Ellison said.

'I've got this, thanks,' Matteo said to her father and taking Abby by the arm he tried to steer her away but she shook him off.

'And this gentleman's agreement happened…when?' Abby demanded.

'Matteo came and saw me in April to purchase the necklace…'

Hearing that a meeting had taken place even before she had met Matteo, Abby didn't need further details; she was already walking off. She had nothing, *nothing*, left to say to her father, and she had just one parting line for Matteo as she brushed past him.

'Screw you!' Abby said.

She stepped out of the study and walked briskly towards the entrance and out the front door. Guests were staring and Annabel was throwing fire with her eyes as, yet again, Abby created a scene.

'Will you stop?' Matteo called as he ran down the stairs after her and then overtook. Abby stood on the bottom step as Matteo reached the ground and so he was right in her face but she just stared coolly back, refusing to break down.

'I hate you.'

'No, you don't.' Matteo took her arms and almost shook her to listen to him. 'You hate what I've done, you hate that I set out to deceive you, but I never have.'

'How can you say that when you met him in April? You were never interested in my team.'

It was simple maths to Abby.

From the very start Matteo had never been interested in her.

All the joy, all the memories, dissolved like soap left in the bathtub.

She remembered sitting in jeans in a stunning restaurant and the joy that it hadn't seemed to matter. Oh, there was a reason he hadn't cared what she wore—Matteo had had other things on his mind that night.

Was the necklace the reason he'd been prepared to take things so slowly?

She felt sick with recall as every sweet memory of them soured.

'Abby.' Matteo would not give in. 'My grandfather is sick and more than anything he wanted the necklace. I was going to pose as...'

'Pose,' Abby sneered. 'You started lying even before we met.'

'Yes, but I *stopped* lying an hour after we met,' Matteo said. 'You know that! By the next morning I was already head over heels with your team and by the next week I was struggling because I cared more about you than them...'

'Leave me alone.'

She was humiliated, embarrassed and more hurt than she knew how to be.

'I've been trying to tell you about the necklace...'

'When?' Abby demanded.

Matteo blew out a breath. He knew that he hadn't really tried; he had left it in the too-hard basket, it would seem, for too long.

'Have it...' Abby said, yanking off the necklace, and she tossed it at him but it clattered onto the ground. 'Take it to the old bastard. Tell him he's got his precious necklace now. I hope you're all happy.'

Matteo stood as Abby picked up the hem of her dress and walked briskly off.

He had a ring in his pocket but, no, some trinket wasn't going to fix this and maybe full disclosure might prove too little too late but nonetheless he went after her. 'If you think the past three months have been a sham...' Matteo started but Abby was too angry to let him speak.

'That's exactly what they have been. A sham. And you're the biggest sham artist of the lot.'

'I can't believe you won't even hear me out.'

'I don't *need* to hear you out,' Abby shouted. 'You're all the same!'

Even as she said it, even before Abby saw the expression on Matteo's face as the words hit, she wished she could scramble on the floor, not for the necklace but to retrieve her own words.

'Don't you *dare* compare me to them!'

And when she had every right to be angry—furious,

in fact—she saw his anger. But it didn't scare her—in fact, it shamed her as Matteo continued.

'Don't you ever put me in your father or Hunter's league...' He was sick to death of it. He was sick of being blamed for others' mistakes and tired of being compared to his father. 'I would never knowingly hurt you.'

'You have hurt me though,' Abby said as tears started to fall.

'It's called a row, Abby...'

'And I don't need it!' She walked off to her car and, now furious himself, Matteo stood there and let her leave.

'Problem?' Ellison walked down the steps and retrieved the necklace and held it out to Matteo as he spoke. 'That's Abby—drama as always. Still, you kept to your end of the deal. You've got what you wanted.'

Matteo said nothing as he pocketed the necklace.

It was far safer.

But instead of getting into his car, he took the steps in three strides and, with Ellison following, he walked back into the home and straight into the study from where they had just come.

'What do you think you're doing?' Ellison asked as Matteo ripped the photo of Abby and Hunter from the wall and smashed it over his knee. Not content with that he took out the image and he shredded it over and over and then tossed the pieces at Ellison.

'What you should have done years ago.'

But shredding a photo of Hunter wasn't enough for Matteo.

It was far from enough!

Matteo got in his car and drove, not to Abby's but towards the airport and, as he did, he summoned his jet.

'Now!' Matteo roared and then having ended the call he threw his phone out of the car window.

The bastard was in LA.

Oh, this had nothing to do with making things right.

This was just about catching up on so many unattended wrongs.

CHAPTER TWELVE

ABBY WOKE AFTER MIDDAY.

Like a sad Miss Havisham she was still wearing her silver gown and her face was all swollen from crying till dawn.

Matteo hadn't come dashing to her door to explain, when she had hoped he might, but Abby understood why.

And he hadn't answered his phone when she'd tried several times to ring, and she understood why too.

She had put him in the same league as her father and, worse than that, Hunter, and that was the very last place he deserved to be. To a man like Matteo, who had been put in the same league as his father his entire life, it had been a very low blow she had served.

Abby simply didn't know how to put this right.

Yes, he had lied to her, but now, every time she got cross, every time a rush of anger rose, she remembered his kindness, his sexiness and how he had helped her to find herself.

She had everything she thought she ever wanted.

The Henley Cup.

A winning team.

Revenge.

Her sexuality back.

But not him.

No wonder he didn't want a relationship, Abby thought, only she tried one more time to reach him on his phone.

It was the Monopoly of love because she got sent straight to voicemail.

'Matteo, it's Abby. Last night...' She'd taken the low road. 'Last night,' Abby attempted again, 'I said some things that you didn't deserve to hear. I'm sorry for that and...' What else? Abby thought. The truth. 'I don't know what else to say. You're right, I can't believe that I didn't hear you out. I want to though.'

She rung off and sat there, then pounced on her phone when a text came through but sagged when she saw it was just Bella.

Have you heard the news? :-)

Abby frowned.

What news?

Turn it on.

Abby did and saw the serious face of a news reporter standing outside the venue where she was supposed to have been for the presentation last night. The reporter was talking about the tight-knit world of the racing community and denying that Hunter had been loaded and got behind the wheel.

'The Lachance team manager insists that he fell...'
And then they flashed to an image of Hunter leav-

ing a medical centre and Abby swallowed because if he *fell*, then it must have been from some considerable height and in several directions!

She called Bella.

'What the hell happened?' Abby said. 'Did he take out a car?'

'Oh, this was no car accident,' came the gleeful reply. 'Your lovely sponsor paid him a visit last night.'

'Matteo?'

'Yep.'

'Oh, no…' Abby felt sick. 'Has he been charged?'

'That's just it—Matteo *wants* to be charged!' Bella laughed. 'In fact, when he'd finished with Hunter he took out a business card and dropped it on him and said that he was looking forward to explaining his actions in front of a judge. Oh, Abby, it was one of the best nights of my life. We're all still drinking and cheering.' But then Bella was serious. 'Hunter came on to me once. God, Abby, don't ask but…'

'It's okay,' Abby said. 'I get it.'

They would talk properly some day.

'Where is he?' Abby asked.

'Having his teeth reimplanted, I think.'

'No, I mean, where's Matteo?'

'I don't know,' Bella answered. 'He just left afterwards and no one knows where he is…'

Abby did.

As she rung off she heard the door and then his voice and there, swaying in the doorway, looking rather the worse for wear, was Matteo.

'I know you hate violence…' he started.

Abby did.

'But he had to pay.'

Matteo had a black eye and bruised knuckles and a chipped front tooth. It would have been some fight; Abby knew how hard Hunter worked to stay in shape and she also knew, firsthand, how violent his temper could be.

'Come in,' Abby said and she held the door open but Matteo shook his head.

'Nope, I'm just here to tell you one thing. Two actually.'

'Well, can we at least do that inside?' Abby asked and finally Matteo nodded and in he came. She spoke first. 'I tried to call you.'

'I threw my phone out the car.'

'Why?'

'Because I didn't want you to talk me down,' Matteo said, 'which you would have tried to and then you'd have worried all night.' Then he was more direct. 'And I was cross with you.'

She'd thought that he might be.

'What Hunter did to you was despicable. What he's still doing to you, you shouldn't allow. Stop wasting your life exacting revenge.'

'I know that now.' Abby was trying not to cry. 'Even when we won the cup, I kept wanting to explain that I was happy, just that we'd won, not because of beating him.'

'Good,' Matteo said and then he gave in standing and went and took a seat on a large dark sofa.

He looked around her apartment and, after the night he had had, it was nice and relaxing just to sit in silence. There must be a huge tree outside because the only view he could see as he stared out was green leaves.

'I'll get to the second thing in a moment,' Matteo said and rested his head back for a while.

'Can I get you anything?' Abby offered.

'A drink.'

She guessed he didn't mean coffee.

'I don't think you should be drinking,' Abby said but then went and poured him a very nice cognac.

'I thought you didn't drink,' Matteo said, taking a long, slow sip.

'I run a motor team,' Abby said. 'They get tired of lemonade. Actually, my friend Bella gave it to me when we came fifth last year. I've been hiding it from them since then.'

'Good.'

But the small talk didn't last for very long.

'Second thing,' Matteo said and he watched as her cheeks went pink and her eyes, which were still red from crying all night, blinked a few times. 'Don't ever again compare me to him.'

'I'm really sorry for what I said.'

'And so you should be,' Matteo responded, 'because I would never treat any woman that way.'

'I get that, Matteo. I was cross, I was upset...'

'No excuse!' he said and he pointed his finger at her. 'Because I love a good row but if you ever hurl that at me again I'll be straight out of the door.'

He served her a very serious warning but even as he did there was this little thing called hope flickering in her heart because...did that mean that they might, just might, have a future?

Oh, not a big one, he'd made that very clear, but he'd lived in her heart for three months yet and she didn't want it all to end on a row.

'And you're never to compare me to your father either.'

'I won't,' Abby said.

'He knows what happened?' Matteo checked. He still couldn't believe it but Abby nodded.

'He just carries on as if it didn't. I hate how he has that photo still on his wall.'

'It isn't any more. I smashed it.'

'Thank you.'

'And I tore it up into a million pieces and it still wasn't enough and so I went and found him and I don't regret it.' Matteo stood. 'I'm going to go.'

He wanted a bath and to tidy up; this wasn't how today was supposed to be.

'Don't go yet.'

'I'm a mess, I want to sleep.'

'I'll run you a bath,' Abby said. 'And you can sleep here.'

She just could not stand another twelve or twenty-four hours', or even, knowing Matteo, several weeks' delay in proceedings.

Abby ran him a bath and he stripped off as easily as he always did and got in and then she sat on the edge in her gown.

'Why are you still wearing it?' Matteo asked.

'I fell asleep with it on.'

'That's very un-Abby.'

'Yes, lately I am.'

He had the loveliest body and she got a very nice view of the best of it as he lay back and ducked his head under the water for a moment and then came up again.

'I know you don't want to hear it,' Matteo said, 'but I am going to explain my version of things.'

'I do want to hear it.'

'Then get my jacket.'

She did and he half drenched it as he went through the pockets and took out the necklace and then dropped his jacket back on the floor.

'You know my grandfather brought us up?'

Abby nodded.

'And I told you about the fight. How, since then, we've worked at things. We don't talk about much, but we do talk. I take him out and I care very much for him. In April he asked me to come and see him and told me that he was very ill.'

She knew that much from his conversation with Allegra.

'When we were growing up he used to tell us this tale about the Lost Mistresses. I never really paid much attention. He'd just say it all the time...'

'Tell me.'

'Oh, no...' Matteo rolled his eyes and put on an old man's voice. '"Don't ask me how I came by them...an old man must have his secrets..."'

Abby laughed.

'Well, he started going on about his Lost Mistresses again. He said he wanted me to find one of them for him. At first I thought he was a bit confused. But no, he showed me a photo of the necklace and said he wanted to go to his grave in peace and he begged me to find the necklace. I tracked it down to your father and I made him an offer, which he refused. Your father said that if I wanted the necklace I had to get you to come to his fundraiser, looking like a woman for once and wearing it.' He looked over to Abby. 'I should have said no then. It was wrong of me, I accept that. I told him that

I wasn't going to seduce you or anything. He suggested that I go in as an investor.'

It hurt to hear.

She couldn't polish his words up like a stone.

The very first time they met he had lied to her.

'I thought you were interested in the team,' Abby said...and it sounded so pathetic, but not as pathetic as admitting, she had hoped, almost from the start, that he had wanted her. 'You said...'

'Abby, I hated cars. And you know why.' She nodded. 'But I didn't by the time we went to dinner.'

Still, she recalled him saying how great she looked in those awful jeans and the ease he had put her at.

To know it had all been a lie hurt like hell.

'Abby, I thought you were the rudest woman I'd ever met. I had a hangover, and your attitude made it very easy to walk away. I was going to tell my grandfather there was no chance, or make your father a better offer. But the moment we started talking, I mean, really talking, I was in. I wasn't pretending any more.'

'Yet you still didn't tell me,' Abby said, and she wasn't cross, just confused.

'When?' Matteo demanded. 'When was I supposed to tell you?' And then he told her something about himself. 'I'm a good liar, Abby, and I don't usually have much of a conscience. I say what I have to to get what I want and I'm very good at avoiding things. When my parents would fight I'd just go off into my own world. When my grandfather tells me he's dying, I suggest we go out for a drink. When the woman I'm crazy about tells me all that's happened to her and then comes down, so shy and nervous and wearing that necklace...should

I have told you that night?' he asked. 'Would you have taken it well then?'

'No.'

'On Sunday night, as soon as I landed back in New York, I went and spoke with my grandfather,' Matteo said. 'I told him that he wasn't getting the necklace, that I wouldn't do it to you.' He handed it to her. 'It's yours.'

'Technically it's yours,' she said. 'Gentleman's agreement and that.'

'Your father's no gentleman, so that nulls that. It's yours.'

Abby took it. 'What did your grandfather say when he found out he wasn't getting it back?'

'He was upset, I guess, but he'll live.' Matteo closed his eyes. 'Actually, he won't.' He gave her a half smile. 'He asked if he could see it one more time—is that okay?'

'I think we could manage that.' Abby stood.

'Do you get now why I didn't tell you?'

Abby didn't answer him; instead she stood and walked to the bathroom door.

'You're going?' Matteo said.

'Yep.'

Matteo lay back in the water and closed his eyes again.

Of course she was.

CHAPTER THIRTEEN

ABBY WENT INTO her bedroom and the same tree that filled the view from her lounge was there in her bedroom window.

They could never end on a row.

In a few days the bruises would be gone, that gleaming smile would be back in place and Matteo would be off to pastures new.

Now though, even if he had lied to get past the locked door to her heart, she was very glad that he had.

In the past few weeks she had opened up and become more trusting, less wary. Matteo was right—had he told her then she would have walked away.

She had changed.

Everything had changed.

Right down to the fact that she took off her dress and she put on the necklace and then naked, save for the Lost Mistress, she walked back into the bathroom.

She loved him.

He had stood up for her, fought for her, and completely he accepted her and she accepted him.

Not quite perfect.

She wouldn't have him any other way.

For however long they had.

Abby didn't want to change him, nor for Matteo to change for her. She just hoped that one day he might lose his dark self-image and know the amazing man he was.

He was lying, dozing in the steamy water, but he opened his eyes when she walked in.

Yes, that shy nervous beauty had gone, as had that guarded woman, yet her eyes were a bit wary, no doubt wondering as to her reception as, for the first time, she initiated things.

'Do you be naked, Miss Abby?' Matteo said in a servant's voice and he held out a hand and helped her into the bath.

'Enough of that talk, young Matteo,' Abby said and any trace of awkwardness cvaporatcd like the steam from the water as they made each other laugh. She sat between his big long legs as he eased himself up and she just wished they could stay in the bath for ever and that he would never have to leave.

'Oh, and you be wearing that lovely necklace,' he said. 'Can I feel your jewels?'

'You can.'

His hand slipped under the water.

'That's a fine one there,' Matteo said and he watched her bite on her lip.

God, it felt good, Abby thought as he moved deeper inside and his legs hauled her closer towards him.

'Can I show you something, Miss Abby?' Matteo asked and she could only guess what it was.

She was wrong.

'Lose the voice,' Abby begged. She didn't want to play servants any more and, as she climbed on, Matteo completely forgot he'd been about to produce a ring.

They couldn't kiss, given his swollen mouth, and so she just held on to his shoulders and moved on him at whim and then bent her head and bit him on the shoulder and wished, how she wished, she'd seen it in Dubai.

His fingers now dug into her buttocks and he said words that were going to really hurt her later, because he told her that he loved her.

'And I want to be with you for ever,' Matteo said.

He was a liar, Abby knew. He would say anything to win, and of course he did, as he pulled her down harder and faster. She was coming, and as he came he told her he loved her again.

'You don't play fair,' Abby said, her head on his shoulder, feeling the last flickers of them, and then she pulled back and looked at the most complex man she could meet.

'Can I show you something, Abby?' Matteo said in his lovely, normal voice.

'Yes.'

'You have to get off,' he said and, as she did, he added, 'While you're up...'

He made her, dripping wet, get out of the bath and into his jacket.

'I was going to show you this before you so rudely interrupted me,' Matteo said as she took out a small wooden box that was different, yet somehow the same, as the one she knew.

'What this?' Abby asked, opening the catch, and what she saw had her body tingle with goose bumps.

'What does it look like?'

'My necklace,' Abby said. 'Except it's a ring.'

It was the most beautiful emerald that she had ever

seen, and the setting was the same as the necklace that they had fought over.

The necklace that had brought them together, even if it had torn them apart for a while.

'You had this made for me.'

'No,' Matteo said. 'I was walking past a shop... Yes.' He stopped teasing her. 'I had it made for you when I got back from Monte Carlo. I was going to tell you about the necklace and your father, tonight, in fact, and then I was going to give you this...'

How badly she had judged him.

She went to slip it on to her middle finger but it was too small.

'It's not a dress ring, Abby...' Matteo said and there was no tease in his voice. 'It's an engagement ring.' All joking was aside. He was as nervous as he'd expected to be, not because of what he was asking her—Matteo knew what he wanted. He was nervous that his past, that his father, that the doubts his own grandfather had about him, that he had had about himself, might have crept into her.

'You want to marry me?' She couldn't quite believe what she was hearing.

'More than *want* to marry you,' Matteo said. 'I have to have you in my life. I was going to ask you tonight.'

'I thought it was just dinner.'

'Just dinner?' Matteo checked. 'Or did you want sex too?' he said and Abby smiled as he pulled her back into the bath.

'I wanted sex too,' Abby said.

'And?' Matteo pushed.

'Some more time,' Abby said but then she looked at Matteo and days, weeks or months could never have been enough. 'I hoped for more but I never dreamt of this.'

'Dream bigger, then,' Matteo said. 'And when you can't, then I'll do it for you.'

He always had.

EPILOGUE

'ABBY!' MATTEO WAS very firm. 'You don't have to give the necklace to him. It was your mother's.'

'I want your grandfather to have it though.'

They were in his car, outside the Di Sione mansion, and Abby took the necklace out of its box and held it in her hands. She looked at the stunning emeralds, the colours that she had based her racing team on, only the necklace wasn't her mother. She didn't need jewels to remember Anette.

'I can remember the arguments,' Abby said with a wry smile. 'Not the one where he gave her this, but that was what my father did time and again. As beautiful as this necklace is, there weren't many happy memories attached for my mother. I know she'd be thrilled to make your grandfather happy. Clearly it means an awful lot to him.'

'It does,' Matteo said. 'I don't really know why.'

'Why don't you ask him?'

'One day,' Matteo said.

Except those days were running out, Matteo thought as Abby carefully placed the necklace back into its box.

'Come on,' Abby said.

'You're sure you want to do this?' Matteo asked.

Only he wasn't asking about the necklace this time. 'I'm certain.'

It had been two weeks since that terrible row when they'd both thought they had lost everything.

These were different times now.

Matteo knocked and then he let them into the house he had grown up in and smiled to Alma, who was walking towards them and beaming.

'You look beautiful,' she said to Abby and then she looked at Matteo. 'You've shaved!'

'I have.'

'Signor Giovanni's all ready for you,' Alma said. 'He's in the main lounge. Shall I let him know that you're here?'

'No.' Matteo shook his head. 'We'll go straight through.'

Matteo was nervous, wondering how his grandfather would react, not just to the necklace—Abby was the first woman he had brought to his grandfather's home.

'Matteo...' Giovanni went to stand but Matteo told him to save his energy and went over and kissed him on both cheeks.

'Nonno, this is Abby...'

'Abby Ellison,' Giovanni said. 'Owner of the Henley Cup. Congratulations! That was an amazing win.'

'Thank you.' Abby smiled and decided that she liked him.

When she had heard that Giovanni had compared Matteo to his reckless father and had caused Matteo so much pain and to doubt himself, she had been cross with the old man. Now though, she had come to understand that Giovanni had done his best with all that had been thrust upon him in what should have been his declining years.

Seven children.

Eight, if you included Nate, his son's illegitimate child.

'I've had many visitors this past couple of weeks,' Giovanni said.

'That's good.' Matteo sat down and Abby took a seat to his right and Matteo held her hand.

Matteo really was nervous, Abby realised as he addressed his grandfather. 'We've got some good news for you.'

They didn't drag it out. Abby handed over the magnificent box and Giovanni let out a small cry of recognition.

'This is the box...' Even that thrilled Giovanni.

It was walnut and gleaming and his fingers struggled with the small clasp and Matteo watched as Abby helped him to open it and the necklace was finally revealed to him.

'Oh...'

Had Abby doubted—and she *had* doubted whether or not she should give up her mother's necklace—those last niggles left her then.

Giovanni's blue eyes filled with tears and his old hands took out the necklace and he gazed upon stones that would never diminish with age.

'You cannot know what this means to me to hold it again.'

'We don't need to know,' Abby said. 'An old man must have his secrets after all.'

'Matteo told you the tale?'

'He did.'

'Matteo told me that he couldn't remember.'

'I know I did,' Matteo said. 'Of course I remember.'

Giovanni looked from the necklace to his grandson, who he had struggled so hard to love.

'I was wrong,' Giovanni said. 'To compare you to your father...'

'Can we leave it?' Matteo said, as was his preferred method.

'We've left too many things unsaid,' Giovanni responded and then he looked down to the necklace as if it gave him strength to speak from the heart.

'To see the damage my son did was more than I could take. When I took in his children I wanted to put things right but I was lost in my own regret and grief.'

'I know.'

'You look like him,' Giovanni said. 'You laugh and you act like him and I was scared for you.'

'I know that you were,' Matteo said. 'But you don't need to be now. I've got a new addiction.'

'Motor racing.'

'Two actually,' Matteo said but Giovanni was looking at the necklace and back in his own world again.

'If I could have a day with it,' Giovanni said and he looked to Abby. 'Just some time to remember...'

'It's yours,' Abby interrupted.

'No.' Giovanni shook his head. 'It was your mother's. Matteo told me he would never take it from you, that you had based your racing team around these stones.'

'My mother had green eyes,' Abby said. 'I remember them. I don't need this necklace to do that. It's yours. It's back where it belongs.'

She looked to Matteo because Giovanni was crying and really was distressed and maybe now wasn't the time to tell him the rest of the news that they had to share.

'Abby should have it to give it to her children...' Giovanni insisted.

'Maybe she shall,' Matteo responded. 'Given that it's staying in the family.'

Giovanni frowned.

'We're not just here to give you the necklace,' Matteo said.

'You two...' Giovanni had been accused one too many times of jumping in and he was struggling not to now. 'You are engaged.' His eyes lit up again as Abby held out her hand for Giovanni to admire the ring. 'When did this happen?'

'Two weeks ago,' Matteo said. 'We're getting married in, oh, about ten minutes from now.'

'I don't understand.'

'You don't have to,' Matteo said. 'Alma has everything ready, the celebrant is here...'

'Your brothers and sisters...' Giovanni went to rise, to share the news with family, but Matteo shook his head.

'We want it to be very small,' Matteo explained. 'Abby has been through a lot and we don't want to make a big fuss. The press will no doubt find out but it will be long over and done with by the time that they do. We're marrying now, by the lake with you and Alma as our witnesses...'

The drapes had been drawn and now Matteo pulled them back on a delicious setting sun.

Beneath the tree he had once fallen from was an arch of white roses and soon they would stand there and make their vows.

Alma had already changed and had a suit waiting for Giovanni.

Abby's hair had already been done and she changed into a very simple, coffee-coloured chiffon dress and the same jewelled sandals that had seen her through favourite days.

It was as simple and as beautiful as that.

Abby topped up her lipstick and the least nervous bride walked slowly with Matteo and his grandfather outside and then Giovanni took a seat with Alma.

It was the smallest, most intimate of weddings.

Abby didn't wear the necklace; today it was *their* memories they made. Instead Giovanni held one of his Lost Mistresses in his hands as he sat and watched his wayward grandson stand before the woman he loved and offer his vows.

'I will always take care of you,' Matteo said. 'I know that I shall. You have made love possible for me and I will never forget that. I love you.'

Abby's words were similar. 'I will always be there for you as you are for me. You have made love possible for me and I will never forget that. I love you too.'

She looked into his dark eyes and she had never known such pure happiness, acceptance and absolute trust.

He slipped on a ring—a very simple band was all that was needed to set off such a magnificent engagement ring—and then Abby slipped a somewhat heavier band on his finger.

Matteo examined it.

It was a simple platinum band but there was just the tiniest emerald set into the metal.

'That's a bit blingy.' Matteo smiled, because not only

hadn't he seen it, he'd never, not once, envisaged wearing a ring.

Proceedings paused for a moment but no one seemed to mind.

'Wear the stone facing down, then,' Abby said and Matteo did so.

It was never coming off!

And now, the celebrant told them, they were husband and wife.

'We should call the family…' Giovanni said to Alma as the bride and groom kissed. He wanted dinner, celebrations, but though Matteo loved his grandfather tonight was theirs.

'We're going to go,' Matteo said, holding Abby's hand. 'We just wanted to share the special day with you.'

He gave Alma a kiss and thanked her for helping in the arrangements and then he embraced his frail grandfather.

'What had happened to the other Lost Mistresses?' Abby asked as she said her goodbyes.

'Another time,' Matteo hastily broke in. They'd be here for hours if Giovanni started and Matteo had other plans for tonight! 'We've got our honeymoon to get to.'

They left his grandfather smiling, holding on to the necklace and sitting looking out across the lake and, yes, they had a honeymoon to get to, but Matteo went back for one more goodbye.

'I love you.'

He did.

It didn't roll off his tongue easily as it did when he said it to Abby, but Matteo meant it.

'I love you,' Giovanni said.

That was all.

They had come full circle and there were no more sorrys to be had.

Matteo drove them to the airport and in his complicated, somehow seamless world, there a driver was waiting to return the car to his home.

Their home.

Abby's head was still spinning; she hadn't come back to earth since the day that they had met and she somehow doubted she ever would.

At least not to the same one he had swept her away from.

'Where are we going?' Abby asked as they took their seats and, because it was a private jet, in a matter of moments they were heading off. As they hit cruise level the flight attendants moved into the sleeping area and then the captain's voice came on.

'Congratulations, Mr and Mrs Di Sione, on your marriage. With a tailwind our flight will take approximately seven hours.'

Matteo took her hand and led her to the sleeping area and the crew had done them proud.

There were petals strewn on the bed and there was a feast of champagne and so many delicacies that for a moment she took her eye off the groom.

There were cupcakes that looked like miniature wedding cakes but when Abby bit into one it was filled with a rich chocolate mousse.

'Seven hours' flying time,' Matteo said and he took her in his arms. 'Whatever will we do?'

'Is this a mystery flight?'

'No.' Matteo shook his head. 'We're going to Paris, the city of romance. I think it's time to make up for some lost time—neither of us have ever really dated. I'm going to put that right.'

He put her whole world to rights and Abby did the same for him.

'So no mystery,' Matteo said. 'It's just the start of our adventure.'

* * * * *

BOUGHT BY HER
ITALIAN BOSS

DANI COLLINS

For my editor, Kathryn, because she
'loved, loved, loved' it.

CHAPTER ONE

GWYN ELLIS LOOKED from the screen to Nadine Billaud, the public relations manager for Donatelli International, then back to the screen.

"This is you, *oui*?" Nadine prodded.

Gwyn couldn't speak. Her heart had begun slamming inside her rib cage the moment she had recognized herself. Cold sweat coated her skin. Air wouldn't squeeze past her locked throat, let alone words.

That *was* her. *Naked.* Right there on that computer, the line of her bare bottom clear as the crack of dawn, neatly framed by her hot pink thong. Everyone had a backside that looked more or less like that, but she was extremely selective about showing hers to *anyone*. She certainly didn't email shots like this to men she barely knew. Or post them online.

Her whole body felt like a frozen electrical current was vibrating through her, paralyzing her.

The photo changed and that bare torso with the sheet rumpled across her upper thighs was all her, too. The way her breasts lifted as she arched her back and ran fingers through her hair bordered on deliberately erotic, coupled with that blissful, upturned expression. She looked like she'd been making love all day—as if she even knew what that felt like!

Then the final one came up again. She was adjusting the band of her hot pink undies across her cocked hip, looking like she was teasingly deciding whether to keep them on or remove them, eyes still lazily drooped and soft satisfaction painted across her lips.

The lighting was golden and her skin faintly gleamed—with oil, she realized as her brain began to function past the shock. These had been taken at the spa where she'd had a massage, trying to fix the ache between her shoulder blades that had been torturing her for weeks. She was sitting up and dressing after her appointment, relaxed and comfortable in what she had perceived as complete privacy.

The massage table had been cropped from the images, leaving muted sage-green walls and indistinct, blurred flowers in the background. It could have been a hotel room, a bedroom—whatever the viewer wanted to imagine.

Her stomach roiled. She thought she might be hyperventilating because she could hear a distant hiss. She wanted to throw up, pass out, *die. Please God, take me now.*

"Mademoiselle?" Nadine badgered.

"Yes," she stammered. "It's me." Then, as the sheer mortification of the whole thing struck, she added a strident, *"Can you close that, please?"*

She glanced at Signor Fabrizio, her supervisor. He sat next to her with a supercilious expression on his middle-aged face.

"Why are you showing those like that? With him

in here?" Gwyn asked. "Couldn't we have done this privately?"

"They're available to anyone with an online connection. I've seen them," Fabrizio said pithily. "I brought them to Nadine's attention."

He'd already taken a long look? *Gross.*

Tears hit her eyes like the cut of a hard, biting wind. An equally brutal blow seemed to land in her stomach, pushing nausea higher into the back of her throat.

"Surely you knew this could happen when you took those photos and sent them to Mr. Jensen?" Nadine said.

Nadine had kept her snooty nose high in the air from the moment Gwyn had followed Fabrizio into her office. Fabrizio kept giving her darkly smug looks, like he was staring right through her perfectly respectable blue pencil skirt and matching jacket.

He made her skin crawl.

And worry for her job. Her palms were sweating.

"I didn't take those photos," she said as strongly as her tight throat would allow. "And you think I would send something like that to a client? They're—oh, for the love of God." She heard the door opening behind her and shot to her feet, reaching to push the lid of Nadine's laptop down herself, wishing the images could be quashed that easily.

Deep in the back of her psyche, she knew she was going to cry. Soon. Pressure was building behind her collarbone, compressing her lungs, pushing behind her eyes. But for the moment she was in a type of shock. Like she'd been shot and still had the strength to run before the true depth of her injuries debilitated her.

"Signor Donatelli." Nadine rose. "Thank you for coming."

"You notified him?" Signor Fabrizio jerked to his feet, sounding dismayed.

Whatever remained of Gwyn's composure went into free fall. The *owner* of the bank was here? She tried to gather herself to face yet another denigrating expression.

"It's protocol with something this dangerous to the bank's reputation," Nadine said stiffly, adding to the weight on Gwyn's heart.

"She's being dismissed," Fabrizio hurried to assure Signor Donatelli. "I was about to tell her to collect her things."

Time stopped as Gwyn processed that she was being fired. Stupid her, she had thought she was being called in to talk about a client's possible misappropriation of funds, not to be disgraced in front of the entire world.

Literally the entire world. This was what online bullying felt like. This was persecution. A witch hunt. Stoning. She couldn't take in how monumentally unjust this was.

The only experience she could liken it to was when her mother had been diagnosed. Words were being said, facts stated that couldn't be denied, but she had no real grasp of how the next minute or week or the rest of her life would play out from this moment forward.

She didn't want to face it, but she had no choice.

And the silence around her told her they were all waiting for her to do so.

Very slowly, she turned to the man who'd just entered, but it wasn't Paolo Donatelli, president and head of the family that owned Donatelli International. No, it was far worse.

Vittorio Donatelli. Paolo's cousin, second-in-command as VP of operations. A man of, arguably, even more stunningly good looks, at least in her estimation. His features were as refined and handsome as his Italian heritage demanded. He was clean-shaven, excruciatingly well dressed in a tailored suit and wore an air of arrogance that came as much from his lean height as his aloof expression. His ability to dominate any situation was obvious in the way they all stood in silence, waiting for him to speak.

He didn't know her from Adam, she knew that. She'd smiled brightly at him not long after arriving here in Milan, forgetting that secret crushes didn't know they were the object of such yearnings. He'd looked right through her and it had stung. Quite badly, illogically.

"Nadine. Oscar," Vittorio said with a brief flick of his gaze to the other occupants of the room before coming back to give Gwyn a piercing stare from his bronze eyes.

Her heart gave a skip between pounds, reacting to him even when she was verging on hysteria. Her mouth was so dry she couldn't make it stretch into a smile. She doubted she would ever smile again. The strange buzz inside her intensified.

"Miss Ellis," he said with a hostile nod of acknowledgment.

He knew her name from Nadine's report, she supposed. The furious accusation in his eyes told her he'd seen the photos. Of course he'd seen them. That's why he had stooped from the lofty heights of the top floor to the midlevel of the Donatelli Tower.

Gwyn's shallow breaths halted and her knees quivered. She was weirdly shocked by how defenseless the idea of his seeing her naked made her feel, but the effect this very perfect stranger had had on her from the start was unprecedented. She'd seen him stride through the offices in Charleston once and that simple glimpse of an incredibly handsome and dynamic man had made her view the postings at the head office in Milan that much more favorably than any other branch in the organization. She had wanted to advance, would have taken whatever promotions she could land, but this was her dream location.

Because it gave her the chance to see him.

Be careful what you wish for. She mashed her lips together into a hard, steady line, heart scored, then turned her face away, trying to recover.

He was, quite obviously, nothing like the man she'd constructed in her mind. Italian men were warm and gregarious and adored women, she had thought, expecting he'd flirt with her if they ever actually spoke. She had expected him to give her a chance to intrigue him, despite the fact that she worked for him.

But the man she had been obsessing over had not only glimpsed her naked, he was completely unmoved by what he'd seen. He was repelled. Blamed her. Was privately calling her a whore and worse—

She stopped herself from spiraling. The pieces of her shattered world were being kicked around enough. She had to keep a grip.

But she wasn't used to being rejected out of hand, seeing no interest whatsoever from a man. The reaction was usually the opposite. Her body had always pulled a certain amount of male attention. She didn't encourage it and was pretty boring personality-wise. She worked in *banking*, for heaven's sake. Her hair was the most common brown you could find and she wasn't terribly pretty. Her face was only elevated from plain to pleasant by her mother's exceptionally good skin and a cheery nature that usually kept a smile on her mouth. So she shouldn't be that surprised when a man who could have his pick of women showed no interest in her.

It made her ache all the same.

Think, she ordered herself, but it was hard when she was stuck in this swamp of feeling so thoroughly scorned by a man who enthralled her.

"I want a lawyer," she managed to say.

"Why would you need one?" Vittorio asked with a wrathful lift of his brows, so godlike.

"This is wrongful dismissal. You're treating me like a criminal when those photos are illegal. They were taken at a spa without my knowledge. They're not selfies, so how could I have sent them to Kevin Jensen? Or anyone? His wife is the one who recommended I go there for my shoulder!"

Vito flicked his gaze to the laptop, mentally reviewing images that would have been very titillating if they were a private communication between lovers. For long seconds as he'd reviewed the photos, he'd been captivated against his will, having to force himself to move past his transfixion with her sensual figure to the fact that this was a hydrogen bomb aimed directly at the bank that was his livelihood and the foundation that supported his entire extended family.

But the photos weren't selfies. That was true. He had thought Jensen must have taken them.

Nadine seemed to think his shift of attention was a prompt for her to bring them up for another look. She started to open her laptop.

"Would you stop showing those to people, you freak?" Gwyn cried.

"Let's keep this professional," Nadine snapped.

"How would you react if you were me?" Gwyn shot back.

Gwyn Ellis was not what he had expected. There was an American wholesomeness to her that neutralized some of the femme fatale that had come across on-screen. He had expected, and received, an impact of female sexuality when he had entered the room. He'd felt the same thing the day she'd smiled at him in the lobby.

She'd already been under suspicion, so he'd pretended not to notice her, but nothing could downplay her allure. That body of hers didn't stop, with her firm, well-rounded breasts that sat high beneath her neatly cut jacket and her waistline that begged for a man's hands to clasp before sliding down to the flare of her hips and her gorgeously plump ass that he dreamed of kneading. Knees were not something he'd normally catalogue, but she had cute ones.

An image of cupping them as he held them apart drifted through his brain.

She was a very potent woman. Her shoulders were stiff, her frame tense and defensive, but her slight stature and smooth curves announced to the animal kingdom that she was undeniably a female of the species, of fertile age and irresistibly ripe.

She called to the male in him, quickening the blood of the beast that he suppressed at all costs.

Visceral reactions like lust were something he indulged in very controlled quantities. This was not the time and, judging by his reaction to her, Gwyn was not the woman. High-octane risk-taking was his cousin's bailiwick. Vito controlled his bloodlust ruthlessly—even though there was a part of him that beat with excitement for the challenge of throwing himself into this perfect storm of chemistry to see if he could survive it.

What they could do to one another...

He turned his mind from speculating, hearing Nadine aim a very pointed barb at Gwyn. "I wouldn't sleep with a married man. This wouldn't happen to me."

"Who said I slept with Kevin Jensen?" Gwyn challenged hotly. "*Who?* I want a name."

So indignant. This was not the reaction of a woman who had posed for a lover, running the risk of exposure. She ought to be furious with Jensen or his wife, perhaps tossing her hair in defiance of judgment over her decision to pose naked for her paramour. Instead, she was a woman on the edge of her control, reacting to a catastrophe with barely contained hysteria.

"His wife said you slept with him. Or want to. Obviously," Oscar Fabrizio interjected, "since she posted these filthy photos when she discovered them on his phone. You've been having lunches and dinners with him."

Vito found that attack interesting. He had brought certain suspicions about their nonprofit accounts manager to Paolo's attention a few weeks ago. The assumption had easily been made that the New Girl was in on the arrangement, facilitating.

"Kevin wanted to do things—have our meetings, I mean," Gwyn quickly clarified, "away from the office." She was visibly distraught, looking to Vito in entreaty. "He's a client. I didn't have a choice but to go to him if that's what he requested."

Vito had to accept that. Excellence of customer service was a cornerstone at Donatelli International. If a client of Jensen's caliber wanted a house call, employees were expected to make them.

"You didn't take those photos?" he pressed her.

"No!"

"So they're not on that phone?" He nodded at where she clutched her device in a death grip.

Gwyn had forgotten she was holding it, but she always grabbed it out of habit when she left her desk, and had switched it to silent as she came into this meeting. Now she stared at it, surprised to see it there. At least she could say with confidence, "No. They're not."

"You'll let me confirm that?" He held out his hand.

On the surface it was a very reasonable request, but, oh, dear Lord, *no*. She had something on here that was beyond embarrassing. It would make this situation so much worse... *So much worse.*

She knew her face was falling into lines of panicked guilt, but couldn't help it.

His nostrils flared and his jaw hardened. The death rays coming out of his eyes told her she'd be lucky to merely lose her job.

"This phone is mine," she stammered, trying not to let him intimidate her. If she hadn't already been violated, she might not have been so vehement, but he was going to have to knock her out cold to pry this thing out of her hand if he wanted access. "I get an allowance to offset my using it for company business, but it's mine. You don't have any right to look at it."

"Can it clear you of suspicion or not?" His gaze delved into her culpable one.

She couldn't hide the turmoil and resentment cours-

ing through her at being put on the spot. "My privacy
has been invaded enough."

She was naked. On the internet. She supposed everyone in the building was staring at her image right now.
Men saying filthy, suggestive things. Women judging
whether her stomach was flat enough, saying she had
cellulite, calling her too bony or too tall or too something so they could feel better about their own body
issues.

Gwyn wanted to hang her head and sob.

All she could think was how hard she'd worked not
to be pushed around by life the way her mother had
been. At every stage, she'd tried to be self-reliant, au-
tonomous, control her future.

Breathe, she commanded herself. *Don't think about
it.* She would fall apart. She really would.

"I think we have our answer," Fabrizio said pitilessly.

She was starting to hate that man. Gwyn wasn't the
type to hate. She did her best to get along with everyone. She was a happy person, always believing that life
was too short for drama and conflict. Being the first to
apologize made her the bigger person, she had always
thought, but she doubted she would ever forgive these
people for how they were treating her right now.

A muted buzz sounded and Nadine looked at her
own phone. "The press is gathering. We need to make
a statement."

The press? Gwyn circled around Fabrizio to the window and looked down.

Nadine's office was midway up the tower, but the
crowd at the entrance, and the cameras they held, were
like ants pouring out of a disturbed hill. It was as bad
as a royal birth down there.

She swallowed, stomach turning again.

Kevin Jensen was an icon, a modern day, international superhero who flew into disaster aftermath to offer "feet on the ground" assistance. Anyone with half a brain saw that he exploited heart-wrenching situations on camera to increase donations and boost his own profile, but the bottom line was he showed up to terrible tragedies and brought aid. He did real, necessary work for the devastated.

But lately Gwyn had been questioning how he spent some of those abundant donations.

Had this been his answer? A massive discrediting that would get her fired?

She hugged herself. This sort of thing didn't happen to real people. Did it?

Her gaze searched below for an escape route. She couldn't even leave the building to get to her rented flat here in Milan. How would she get back to America? Even if she got that far, then what? Look to her stepfather to shelter her? Who was going to hire her with this sort of notoriety? Ever?

She'd be exactly what she'd tried so hard to avoid being: a burden. A leach.

Oh, God...oh, God. The walls were beginning to creak and buckle around her composure. The pressure behind her cheekbones built along with weight on her shoulders and upper arms.

Nadine was talking as she typed, "...say that the bank was unaware of this personal relationship and the employee has been terminated—"

"Our client has stated that the photos were *not* invited," Fabrizio interjected.

Gwyn spun around. "And your employee states that

she's been targeted by a peeping tom and an online porn peddler and a vengeful wife."

Nadine paused only long enough to send her a stern look. "I strongly advise you not to speak to the press."

"I strongly advise you that I will be speaking to a lawyer." It was an empty threat. Her savings were very modest. *Very.* Much as she would love to believe her stepbrother would help her, she couldn't count on it. He had his own corporate image to maintain.

The way Vittorio Donatelli continued to emanate hostility made her want to crawl into a hole and die.

"How long have you been with the company?" Nadine asked.

"Two years in Charleston, four months here," Gwyn said, trying to recall how much room her credit card balance had for plane fare and setting up house back in Charleston. Not enough.

"Two years," Nadine snorted, adding an askance. "How did you earn a promotion like this after only that short a time?" Her gaze skimmed down Gwyn's figure, clearly implying that Gwyn had slept her way into the position. Night school and language classes and putting in overtime counted for nothing, apparently.

Fabrizio didn't defend her, despite signing off on her transfer and giving her a glowing review after her first three months.

Vittorio's expression was an inscrutable mask. Was he thinking the same thing?

A disbelieving sob escaped her and she hugged herself, trying to stay this side of manic.

While Vittorio brought his own phone from his pants pocket and with a sweep and tap connected to someone. "Bruno? Vito. I need you in Nadine Billaud's office. Bring some of your men."

"For my walk of shame?" Gwyn presumed. Here came the tears, welling up like a tsunami with a mile of volume behind it. Her voice cracked. "Don't worry. I plan to leave quickly and quietly. I can't *wait* to not work here anymore."

"You'll stay right here until I tell you to leave." His tone was implacable, making her heart sink in her hollow chest while another part of her rose in defiance, wanting to fight and rail and physically tear at him to get out of here. She was the quintessential wounded animal that needed to bolt from danger to its cave.

To Nadine, he added, "Confirm the photos belong to one of our employees. For privacy and legal reasons we have no other comment. Ask the reporters to disperse and enlist the lobby guards to help. Issue a similar statement to all employees. Add a warning that they risk termination if they speak to the press or are observed viewing the photos on corporate equipment or company grounds. Oscar, I need a full report on how these photos came to your attention."

"Signor Jensen contacted me this morning—"

"Not here." Vittorio moved to the door as a knock sounded. "In your office. Wait here," he said over his shoulder to Gwyn, like she was a dog to be left at home while he went to work. He urged the other two from the room and pulled the door closed behind the three of them.

"Yeah, right," Gwyn rasped into the silence of Nadine's empty office, hugging herself so tightly she was suffocating.

A twisting, writhing pain moved in her like a snake,

coiling around her organs to squeeze her heart and lungs, tightening her stomach and closing her throat. She covered her face, trying to hide from the terrible reality that everyone—everyone in the world—was not only staring at her naked body, but believing that she had had sex with a married man.

She could live with people staring at her body. Almost. They did it, anyway. But she was a good person. She didn't lie or steal or come on to men, especially married ones! She was conservative in the way she lived her life, saving her craziest impulses for things like her career where she did wildly ambitious things like sign up for Mastering Spreadsheets tutorials in hopes of moving up the ladder.

The pressure in her cheekbones and nose and under her eyes became unbearable. She tried to press it back with the flats of her hands, but a moan of anguish was building from the middle of her chest. A sob bounced like a hard pinball, bashing against her inner walls, moving up from her breastbone into her throat.

She couldn't break down, she reminded herself. Not here. Not yet. She had to get out of this place and the sooner the better. It was going to be awful. A nightmare, but she would do it, head high and under her own steam.

Gritting her teeth, she reached for the door and started to open it.

A burly man wearing a suit and a short, neat haircut was standing with his back to the door. Guarding her? He grabbed the doorknob, keeping her from pulling it open. His body angled enough she could see he also wore some kind of clear plastic earpiece. His glance at her was both indifferent and implacable.

"Attendere qui, per favore." Wait here, please.

She was so shocked, she let him pull the door from her lax grip and close her into Nadine's office again.

Actually, it slipped freely from her clammy hand. The room began to feel very claustrophobic. She moved to the window again, seeing the crowd of reporters had grown. She couldn't tell if Nadine was addressing them. She could hardly see. Her vision was blurring. She sniffed, feeling the weight of all that had happened so deeply she had to move to the nearest chair and sink into it.

Her breath hitched and no amount of pressure from her hands would push back the burn behind her eyes.

The door opened again, startling her heart into lurching and her head into jerking up.

Hc was back.

CHAPTER TWO

GWYN ELLIS LOOKED like hell had moved in where her soul used to be, eyes pits of despair, mouth soft and bracketed by lines of disillusion. Her brow was a crooked line of suffering, but she immediately sat taller, blinking and visibly fighting back her tears to face him without cowering.

"I want to leave," she asserted.

The rasp in her voice scraped at his nerves while he studied her. Vixens knew how to use their sexuality on a man. If she was a victim, he would expect her to appeal to the protector in him. Either way, he wouldn't expect her to be so confrontational.

Gwyn was a fighter. He didn't want to find that dig-deep-and-stay-strong streak in her admirable. It softened him when he was in crisis control mode, trying to remember that she had, quite possibly, colluded to bilk the bank and a completely legitimate nonprofit organization of millions of euros in donations.

"We have more to talk about," he told her. He had made the executive decision to question her himself, like this, privately. And he wasn't prepared to ask himself why.

"An exit interview? I have two short words," she said tightly.

That open hostility was noteworthy. Oscar Fabrizio had been full of placating statements until Paolo had been patched through on speakerphone. Then Oscar had seemed to realize he was under suspicion. He'd asked for a lawyer. Sweat had broken across his brow and upper lip when Vito had ordered his computer and phone to be analyzed. Both were company issued and it had been obvious Oscar was dying to contact someone—Kevin Jensen perhaps? A plainclothes investigator was on the way. A full criminal inquiry was being launched down the hall.

While here... Vito was sure she was an accomplice, except...

"You say you had no knowledge of those photos," he challenged.

"No. I didn't." Her chin came up and her lashes screened her eyes, but there was no hiding the quiver of her mouth. She was deeply upset about their being made public. That was not up for dispute. "They were taken after a massage. I didn't know there was a camera in the room."

The images were imprinted on his brain. The photos would have made a splash without Jensen's name attached, he thought distantly. She was built like Venus.

But he saw how they could have been taken during a private moment and manipulated to appear like shots between lovers. He had made certain presumptions on sight: that she was not only having an affair with a client, but was engaged in criminal activity with him. If Jensen was prepared to steal from charity donations, would it be such a stretch to photograph a banking underling in an attempt to cover it up?

Powerful men exploited young, vulnerable women. He knew that. It was quite literally in his DNA.

"Are you picturing me naked?" she challenged bitterly, but her chin crinkled and she fought for her composure a moment, then bravely firmed her mouth and controlled her expression, meeting his gaze with loathing shadowing the depths of her brown eyes.

Such a contrary woman with her wounded expression and quiet, forest-creature coloring of dark eyes and hair, then that devastatingly powerful figure of generous curves and lissome limbs.

"Wondering if you are having an affair with Jensen," he replied.

"I'm not!" There was a catch in her voice before her tone strengthened. "And I wasn't trying to start one, either. I barely know him." She crossed her arms. "I actually think he's been skimming funds from his foundation for himself."

"He is." He steadily returned the shocked brown stare she flashed at him. Her irises had a near-black rim around the dark chocolate brown, he noted, liking the directness it added to her subtly tough demeanor.

Her pupils expanded with surprise, further intriguing him.

"You know that for a fact?" Her brows were like distant bird wings against the sky, long and elegant with a perfect little crook above her eyes. She was truly beautiful.

He wanted her. Badly.

He ignored the need pulling at him, stating, "We also know someone in the bank is colluding with him. We've been conducting an extremely delicate investigation that blew up today, thanks to your photos."

Vito was angry with himself. He was a numbers man, calculating all the odds, all the possible moves an opponent might try, but he hadn't seen this one coming.

"I'm not colluding with anyone!" Her expression was earnest and very convincing. But he was a mistrustful man at heart, too aware of the secrets and lies he lived under himself to take for granted that other people weren't self-protecting or withholding certain facts to better their own position.

"And yet you won't let me look at your phone," he said pointedly.

Her jaw set and she turned the device over in her hands. With a shaky little sigh that smacked of defeat, she tapped in her access code, surprising him with her sudden willingness.

"Look at my emails," she urged. "You'll see I was counseling him that certain requests could be interpreted as shady." She offered him the phone.

Gwyn didn't know much about climbing out of a hole, but she knew you had to bounce off rock bottom, so she went there. At least this humiliation was her choice and only between the two of them, now that the room was empty. At least she was getting a chance to speak her side. Maybe he'd see that she didn't have anything to hide except a stupid attraction. Hopefully he'd read between the lines and also see that she wasn't the least bit interested in stupid Kevin Jensen.

Still, it was hard to sit here with the anticipation of further shame washing over her. He would see that her handful of texts and emails with friends back home were innocuous and seldom. She was friendly with many, but actual friends with very few. It was a symptom of moving so much through her childhood, as her mother had tried to find better positions for herself. Gwyn kept in touch with people she liked, mostly through social media, but she didn't bond very often. She had learned early that it hurt too much when she had to move on. The person she was closest to, her stepfather, didn't "do" computers. They talked the old-fashioned way, over the phone or face-to-face.

If Vittorio glanced through her social media accounts, he'd see she followed liberal pundits and quirky celebrities. If he looked at her apps, he'd discover she kept her checking account in the black, played Sudoku when she was bored, read mostly romance and had finished her period three days ago.

And if he looked at her photos, he'd see that she had been taking in the sights of Milan on lunches and weekends. Sights that included his extremely handsome head shot hanging in the main foyer of the Donatelli International building.

Her cheeks stung as she waited out his discovery of the incriminating photo. She'd taken it in a fit of infatuation the other day. After passing the fountain in the lobby a million times since her arrival, she'd noticed someone taking a selfie with the burbling water in the background. It had made her realize she could *pretend* to take a selfie and capture the image of her obsession on the wall.

Why? Why had she followed through on such a silly impulse? It had been as mature as pinning up a poster of a movie star in her bedroom and talking to it.

Especially when he'd been so dismissive the one time she'd smiled at him, like he couldn't imagine why she, a lowly minion, would send such a dazzling welcome his direction. He worked at such a high level in the bank, he barely showed up to the offices at all. He didn't consort with peasants like her.

How many times had she even seen him since arriving here? Four?

She mentally snorted at herself. Like she hadn't counted each glimpse as if they were days until Christmas. She looked for him all the time. It was a bit of a sickness, really. Why? What on earth had convinced her that she had anything in common with a man like him?

Her heightened awareness of him picked up on the subtle stillness that overcame him.

She refused to look at him, certain he was staring at his own image. He must be thinking she was a weird, stalker type now. By any small miracle, was he also noticing that she didn't have those stupid nudes on there?

"Today is full of surprises." Vittorio clicked off her phone and tucked it into his shirt pocket, drawing her startled glance. His hammered-gold eyes held an extra glitter of male speculation, something dark and predatory, like he'd just noticed the plump bird that had landed nearby.

Her stomach swooped.

"Did you read the emails?" she asked shakily.

"I glanced over them."

"And?"

"They appear to support your claim that you weren't involved."

"*Appear* to support," she repeated. "Like I wrote those emails as some kind of premeditated attempt to cover my butt?" Her translucent skin was growing pink with temper. "Look, you have to know it's tricky to tell a client an outright 'no.' I've been trying to do it nicely while Mr. Jensen and Signor Fabrizio—"

Her face blanked. She touched between her furrowed brow.

"They've been setting me up this whole time, haven't they? That's why I got this promotion. They thought I was too inexperienced to see what they were up to. As soon as I proved I wasn't, they turned me into their fall guy. They just pushed me off the roof!"

She was very convincing, right down to the way her trembling hand moved to cover her mouth and her eyes glassed with anxious outrage.

He tried to hang on to his cynicism, but he was entertaining similar thoughts. The very idea ignited a strange fury in him. He knew better than most what happened when a corrupt man took advantage of an ingenuous woman. His father had done it to his mother and she had wound up dead.

His phone vibrated. He glanced at the text from his cousin. Fabrizio claims it was all her. Any progress on your end?

Vito glanced at Gwyn, at the way her shaking fingers smoothed her hair behind her ear while her concubine mouth pouted with very credible fear.

He wasn't without concern himself. Even if Paolo managed to build a case against Fabrizio, Kevin Jensen had positioned himself very well to walk away along the high ground, leaving the bank wearing a cloak of muddied employees. An institution that staked its success on a reputation of trustworthiness would cease to appear so.

Vito refused to let that happen. He protected his family at all costs. They would, and had, done the same for him.

And this *would* cost him. Gwyn was dangerous. The

fact that he was drawn to her, looking to see her as an innocent despite the very real fact she might be involved in crimes against the bank, was unnerving. Being close to her would be a serious test of his mettle.

But his glimpse into her phone had revealed a move to him that even a master chess player like Kevin Jensen wouldn't see coming, even though it was one of the basic rules of the game: if a pawn was pushed far enough into the field of play, she could be promoted to a formidable queen.

CHAPTER THREE

VITTORIO PLUCKED HIS handkerchief from his jacket pocket and moved to dampen it under the tap of the water cooler.

Gwyn watched him, wondering what he was doing, then noticed her purse was over his shoulder, looking incongruous against his tailored charcoal suit.

"Did you get my stuff from my desk?"

Fabrizio seeing her naked was creepy. Vittorio touching her possessions was…*intimate*. Disturbing.

"I did." He came back to tilt up her chin and started to run a blessedly cool, damp, linen-wrapped fingertip beneath her eye.

His touch sent an array of sensation outward through her jawline and down her throat, warm tingles that unnerved her. She tried to jerk away, but he firmed his hold and finished tidying her makeup, telling her, "Hold your head high as we walk to the elevator."

His tone was commanding, his mouth a stern line, while he gave her a circumspect look and tucked a loose strand of her hair behind her ear.

She knocked his hand away, chest tightening again. "I just explained that they're using me. You won't even take a second to consider that might be true? You're just going to fire me and throw me to the wolves?"

"Your termination can't be helped, Gwyn. I have to think about the bank."

His detached tone sent a spike of ice right into her heart. "Thanks a lot."

They wound up in another stare down that pulled her already taut nerves to breaking point. She hated that he was standing while she was still seated. He seemed to have all the power, all the control and advantage.

She hated that, with their gazes locked like this, her mind turned to sexual awareness, refusing to let her stay in a state of fixed hatred. She wondered things like how his lips would feel against hers and grew hot as an allover body flush simmered against the underside of her skin.

She stood abruptly, forcing him to take a step back.

"Good girl," he said, moving to the door.

"I'm not *obeying* you. I—" She cut herself off. She wanted to leave, she did. She wanted to lock herself in her flat where she could lick her wounds and figure out what to do next.

"The reporters won't leave until you do," he said heartlessly. "People will be trying to go for lunch."

Don't inconvenience the staff with your petty disaster of a life, Gwyn. Think of others in the midst of your crisis.

"Everyone's going to stare," she mumbled, trying to find her guts, but her insides were nothing but water.

"They will," he agreed, still completely unmoved. "But it's only two minutes of your life. Look straight ahead. Come. Now."

Her heels wanted to root to the floor in protest. She

wanted to beg him to let her hide here until after closing, but he was right. Better to get it over with.

She knew then what it was like to walk toward execution. While her low heels took her closer to the door, her heart began slamming in panic. Sweat cooled the ardor she'd experienced a moment ago, leaving her in something close to shock.

She sought refuge in her old yoga lessons, concentrating on breathing in through her nose, out through her narrowly parted lips, holding reality at bay, picturing the crown of her head being pulled by an invisible wire toward the ceiling.

"Good," Vittorio said as he opened the door, then settled his arm around her, tucking her shoulder under his armpit as his hand took possession of her waist.

She stiffened in surprise at the contact. A disconcerting rush of heat blanketed her, making her knees weaken.

He supported her, forcing her forward and keeping her on her feet when she would have stumbled. He matched their steps perfectly, as though they had walked as a couple many times before.

Two minutes, she repeated to herself, leaning into him despite how much she resented him. She'd never realized how long a minute was until she had to bear the rustle of heads turning and chairs squeaking, conversation stopping and keyboard tapping halting into a blanket of silence.

Vittorio's aftershave, spicy and beguiling, enveloped her. It was dizzying. An assault to already overloaded senses. Were her legs going to hold her? Amazing how being escorted like this made you feel like a criminal as well as look like one.

Her eyes were seared blind. She couldn't tell who was looking, couldn't really see the rest of the open-plan office because Vittorio kept her on his side closest to the wall and stayed a quarter step ahead of her so his big shoulders blocked her vision of the rest of the floor.

Another man paced on his far side, broad and burly and carrying a file box that held a green travel cup that she thought might be hers. Had they also collected the snapshot of her with her mother and stepfather, she worried?

The elevator was being held open by another hitman type with a buzz cut. He couldn't care less about her silly scandal, his watchful indifference seemed to say. He was here to bust heads if anyone stepped out of line.

The elevator closed and she let out her breath, but rather than dropping as she expected, the elevator climbed, making her stagger and clutch instinctively at Vittorio's smooth jacket.

He cradled her closer, steadying her, fingers moving soothingly at her waist. Disturbing her with the intimacy of his touch.

"Why aren't we going down?" she asked shakily.

"The helicopter will avoid the scrum."

"Helicopter?" she choked out, mind scattering as she tried to make sense of this turn of events.

"Thirty seconds," he warned, tone gruff, and nudged her a step forward as the elevator leveled out with a *ding*.

His arm remained firm across her back, urging her through the opening doors.

She trembled, trying not to fold into him, but he was the only solid thing in her world right now. She had to remember that despite his seeming solicitude, he wasn't on her side. This was damage control. Nothing more.

The refinement at this height in the building was practically polished into the stillness of the air. Nevertheless, humans were humans. Heads came up. Eyes followed.

Vittorio addressed no one, only steered her down a hall in confident, unhurried steps, past a boardroom of men in suits and women with perfectly coiffed hair, past a lounge where a handful of people stood drinking coffee and into a glass receiving area beyond which a helicopter stood, rotors beginning to turn.

The security guard took her box of possessions ahead of them and tucked it into a bulkhead, then moved into the cockpit.

Wow. This wasn't a helicopter like she'd seen on television, where people were crammed into three seats across the back wall, shoulder to shoulder, and had to put on headphones and shout to be heard.

This was an executive lounge that belonged on a yacht. She didn't have to duck as she moved into it. The white leather seats were ten times plusher than the very expensive recliner she'd purchased for her stepfather two Christmases ago. The seats rotated, she realized, as Vittorio pointed her to one, then turned another so they would sit facing each other.

There was a door to the pilot's cockpit, like on an airplane. An air hostess smiled a greeting and nodded at Vittorio, taking a silent order from him that he gave with the simple raising of two fingers. She arrived seconds later with two drinks that looked suspiciously like scotch, neat.

Vittorio lowered a small table between them with indents to hold their glasses.

Gwyn took a deep drink of her scotch, shivering as the burn chased down her throat, then replaced her glass into its holder with a dull thud. "Where are you taking me?"

"This isn't a kidnapping," he said dryly. "We're going to Paolo's home on Lake Como. It's in his wife's name and not on the paparazzi's radar."

"What? No," she insisted, reaching to open her seatbelt. "My passport is in my apartment. I need it to get home."

"To America? The press there is more relentless than ours. Even if you managed to drop out of sight, I would still have an ugly smudge on the bank's reputation to erase."

"I care as much about the bank as it does about me," she informed him coldly.

"Please stay seated, Gwyn. We're lifting off." He pointed to where the horizon lowered beneath them. "Let's talk about your photo of *me*."

A fresh blush rose hotly from the middle of her chest into her neck. "Let's not," she said, squishing herself into her seat and fixing her gaze out the window.

"You're attracted to me, *sì*?"

She sealed her lips, silently letting him know he couldn't make her talk.

Nevertheless, he had her trapped and demonstrated his patience with an unhurried sip of his own drink and a brief glance at the face of his phone.

"You smiled at me one day," he said absently. "The way a woman does when she is inviting a man to speak to her."

And he hadn't bothered to.

"I play a game with a friend back home," she muttered. "It's silly. Man Wars. We send each other photos of attractive men. That's all it was," she lied. "If it makes you feel objectified, well, you have a glimpse into how I feel right now."

Her insides were churning like a cement mixer.

"You're embarrassed by how strong the attraction is," he deduced after watching her a moment. He sounded amused.

Her stomach cramped with self-consciousness. Could her face get any hotter?

"This releasing of compromising photos is very shrewd," he said in an abrupt shift. His tone suggested it was an item in political news, not a gross defilement of her personal self. His finger rested across his lips in contemplation.

"Jensen has very cleverly made himself appear a victim," he said. "The moment we accuse him of wrongdoing, he'll claim he only took advice from you and Fabrizio. Fabrizio may eventually implicate him, trying to save his own skin, but Jensen has this excellent diversion. He can say you came on to him, maybe that you were working with Fabrizio, that you sent those photos to ruin his marriage. Perhaps they were cooked up by the two of you to blackmail him into skimming funds. Whatever story he comes up with, it will point all the scandal back to you and Fabrizio and the bank."

"I'm aware that my life is over, thanks," she bit out.

"Nothing is over," he said with a cold-blooded smile. "Jensen landed a punch, but I will hit back. Hard. If he and Fabrizio were in fact using you, you must also want to set things straight? You'll help me make it clear you had zero romantic interest in Jensen."

"How?" she choked out, wondering what was in his drink that he thought he could accomplish that.

"By going public with our own affair."

Gwyn pinched her wrist.

Vittorio noted the movement and his mouth twitched.

She shook her head, instinctively refusing his suggestion while searching for a fresh flash of anger. Outrage was giving her the strength to keep from crying, but his proposition came across as so offhanded and hurtful, so cavalier when she couldn't deny she was weirdly infatuated with him, it smashed through her defenses and smacked down her confidence.

"I don't *have* affairs," she insisted. She looked out the window at the rust-red rooftops below. The houses below were short, the high-rises in the center of the city gone, green spaces more abundant. They were over outlying areas, well out of Milan. *Damn it.*

She wanted to magically transport back to Charleston and the room where she had stayed during her mother's short marriage to Henry. She wanted to go back in time to when her mother was still alive.

"It's such a pathetically male and sexist response to say that sleeping together would solve anything. To suggest I do it to save my job—no, *your* job—" She was barely able to speak, stunned, ears ringing. Her eyes and throat burned. "It's so insulting I don't have words," she managed, voice thinning as the worst day of her life grew even uglier.

"Did I say we'd sleep together? You're projecting. No, I'm saying we must appear to."

Oh, wonderful. He *wasn't* coming on to her. Why did she care either way?

"It would still make it look like I'm sleeping my way to the top," she muttered, flashing him a glance, but quickly jerking her attention back to the window, not wanting him to see how deeply this jabbed at her deepest insecurities.

From the moment she'd developed earlier than her friends, she'd been struggling to be seen as brains, not breasts. A lot of her adolescent friends had been fair weather, pulling Gwyn into their social circles because she brought boys with her, but eventually becoming annoyed that she got all the male attention and cutting her loose. The workplace had been another trial, learning to cope with sexual harassment and jealousy from her female coworkers, realizing this was one reason why her mother had changed jobs so often.

Her mom had been a runner. Gwyn tried to stay and fight. It was the reason she had stuck it out in school despite the cost. Training for a real profession had seemed the best way to be taken seriously. Yet here she was, being pinned up as a sex object in the locker room of the internet, set up by men who believed she lacked the brains to see when people were committing crimes under her nose.

And the solution to this predicament was to sleep with her boss? Or appear to? What kind of world was this?

She looked around, but there was nowhere to go. She might as well have been trapped in a prison cell with Vittorio.

He swore under his breath and withdrew her phone from his shirt pocket, scowling at it. "This thing is exploding." His frown deepened as he looked at whatever notification was showing up against her Lock screen. "Who is Travis?"

His tone chilled to below freezing and his handsome features twisted with harsh judgment. She could practically see the derisive label in a bubble over his head.

"My stepbrother," she said haughtily, holding out her hand, not nearly as undaunted as she tried to appear. Her intestines knotted further as she saw that she'd missed four calls and several texts from Travis, along with some from old schoolmates and several from former coworkers in Charleston.

All the texts were along the lines of, *Is it really you? Call me. I just saw the news. They're saying...*

Nausea roiled in her. She clicked to darken the screen.

Travis had been vaguely amused with her concern over not having every skill listed in this job posting for Milan. *Do you know why men get promoted over women? Because they don't worry about meeting all the criteria. Fake it 'til you make it,* had been his advice.

Really great advice, considering what such a bold move had got her into, she thought dourly.

But his laconic opinion had been the most personable he'd ever been around her. He was never rude, just distant. He never reached out to her, only responded if she texted him first. He didn't know that she'd overheard him shortly before her mother's wedding to his father, when he'd cautioned Henry against tying himself to a woman without any assets. *There are social climbers and there are predators.*

Henry had defended them and Gwyn had walked away hating Travis, but not really blaming him. Had their situations been reversed, she would have cautioned her mother herself. It had still fueled her need to be self-reliant in every way.

She had been so proud to tell Travis she'd landed this job, believing she'd been recognized for her education, qualifications and grit. *Ha.*

"I guess we can assume the photos have crossed the Atlantic," she muttered, cringing anew.

It was afternoon here. Travis would be starting his day in Charleston, and the fact that he'd learned so quickly of the photos told her exactly how broadly these things were being distributed. Maybe reporters had tracked down the family connection and were harassing him and Henry?

Damn that Kevin Jensen. His headline name was turning her into a punch line.

She set her phone on the table, unable to think of anything to say except *I'm sorry*, and that was far too inadequate.

She swallowed back hopelessness, realizing a door had just closed on her. She could go back to America, but she couldn't take this mess to Henry's doorstep. He'd been too good to her to repay him like that. Travis might make her cut off ties for good.

"You're not going to call him?" Vittorio asked.

"I don't know what to say," she admitted.

"Tell him you're safe at least."

"Am I?" she scoffed, meeting his gaze long enough for his own to slice through her like a blade, as if he could see all the way inside her to where she squirmed.

And where she held a hot ember of yearning for his good opinion.

"He's not worried," she dismissed, feeling hollow as

she said it. "We're not close like that. He just wants to know what's going on." So he could perform damage control on his side.

She had worked so hard to keep Travis from seeing her as a hanger-on, so he wouldn't think she was only spending time with his elderly father in hopes of getting money out of him and possibly cut her off. She was vigilant about paying her own way, refusing to take money unless it was a little birthday cash which she invariably spent on groceries, cooking a big enough dinner to fill her stepfather's freezer with single-serve leftovers. She always invited Travis to join them if she was planning to see Henry, never wanting him to think she was going behind his back.

Now whatever progress she'd made in earning Travis's respect would be up in smoke. But what did that matter when apparently no one else would have any for her after this?

"Do you have other family you should contact?" Vittorio asked.

"No," she murmured. Her mother, a woman without any formal training of any kind, had married an American and wound up losing her husband two years into her emigration to his country. He'd been in the service, an only child with elderly parents already living in a retirement home. They had died before Gwyn had been old enough to ask about them.

With no home or family to go back to in Wales, her mother, Winnifred, had struggled along as a single mom, often working in retail or housekeeping at hotels, occasionally serving for catering companies. She'd taken anything to make ends meet, never deliberately making Gwyn feel like an encumbrance, but Gwyn was smart enough to know that she had been.

That's why Gwyn was so determined to prove to Travis her attachment to Henry was purely emotional. It was deeply emotional. Henry was the only family she had.

"You do make an easy target, don't you? A single woman of no resources or support," Vittorio commented. Perhaps even desperate, she could hear him speculating.

"You must think so, offering an affair when I'm at my lowest," she said. "You might as well hang around bus stations looking for teenaged runaways."

Something flashed in his gaze, ugly and hard and dangerous, but he leaned forward onto the table between them and smiled without humor.

"It's not an offer. Until I say otherwise, you're my lover. I'm a very powerful man, Gwyn. One who is livid on your behalf and willing to go on the offensive to reinstate your honor."

His words, the intense way he looked at her, snagged inside her heart and pulled, yanking her toward a desire to believe what he was saying.

"You mean the bank's behalf. To reinstate the bank's honor," she said, as much to remind herself as to mock him. Her prison-cell analogy had been wrong. This was the lion's cage she was trapped in with the king of beasts flicking his tail as he watched her.

"You understand me," he said with a nod of approval. "We've been very discreet about our relationship, given that you work for us," he continued in a casual tone, sitting back and taking his ease. "But I assure you, I'm intensely possessive. And very influential. This crime against you—" the *bank* "—won't go unpunished."

He was talking like it was real. Like they were actually going forward with this pretense. Like they were really having an affair.

She choked on a disbelieving laugh, pointing out, "That just switches out one scandal for another. It doesn't change anything. I still look like a slut."

She might have thought he didn't care, he remained so unmoving. But sparks flew in the hammered bronze of his irises, as if he waged a knife fight on the inside.

He still sounded infinitely patronizing when he spoke.

"Sex scandals have a very short lifespan in this country. A little one like a boss-employee thing, between two single adults?" He made a noise and dismissed it with a flick of his fingers. "Old news in a matter of days. I would rather weather that than have the bank suspected of corruption. The impact of something like that goes on indefinitely."

"Do you even care if I'm innocent? All you really want is to protect the bank, isn't it?" She looked at where she'd unconsciously torn off the whites of two fingernails, picking with agitation at them.

"Of course the bank is my priority. It's a *bank*. One that not only employs thousands, but influences the world economy. Our foundation is trust or we have nothing. So yes, I intend to protect it. The benefit to you could be exoneration—which I would think you would pursue whether you're guilty or not. We'll imply that Paolo knew of our affair and that's how he and I were made aware of Jensen's activities. We kept you in place to build the case."

"Will I keep my job?" she asked, as if she was bargaining when they both knew her position was so weak she was lucky she wasn't being questioned by the police right now. Or being hurled from this stupid helicopter.

"No," he said flatly. "Even if you prove to be innocent, putting you back on our payroll would muddy the waters."

"Let's pretend for a minute that I'm as innocent as I say I am," she said with deep sarcasm. "All I get out of this, out of being targeted by *your* client with naked photos that will exist in the public eye for the rest of my life, is a clean police record. I still lose my job and any chance of a career in the field I've been aiming at for years. *Thanks.*"

He didn't own the patent on derision. She found enough scorn to coat the walls of this floating lounge, then turned her dry, stinging eyes to the window.

After a long moment, he said, "If you are innocent, you won't be left with nothing. Let me put it another way. Cooperate with me and I'll personally ensure you're compensated as befits the end result."

"You're going to pay me to lie?" she challenged, her tone edging toward wild. "And what happens when that comes out? I still look like an opportunist."

He didn't flinch, only curled his lip as he asked, "Which lie is closer to the truth, Gwyn? That you want to sleep with Kevin Jensen? Or that you've been sleeping with me?"

Could he see inside her thoughts? Did he know what she fantasized about as she drifted into slumber every night? She sincerely hoped not. Talk about dirty images!

Blushing hotly all over, she crushed the fingers of one hand in the grip of the other, trying to keep herself from ruining any more of her manicure. Having him aware of her attraction made this worse, just as she had suspected. It was mortifying to be this transparent around him.

All she had to do was picture Nadine's disapproving face to know how far protesting with the truth would get her, though. If she had more time, she might have come up with a better solution, but the helicopter was much lower now, seeming to aim for a stretch of green lawn next to a lakeside villa.

On the table before her, her phone vibrated with yet another message.

It didn't matter who it was from. Everyone she knew was being told she had sent naked photos of herself to a married man. The existence of the photos was bad enough, but she was prepared to do just about anything, as the people in Nadine's line of work would say, to change the narrative. Vittorio said this would cut the scandal down to a few short days and she had to agree that it was a more palatable lie than the one Kevin Jensen had put forth.

"Fine," she muttered, swallowing misgivings. "I'll pretend we were having an affair. Pretend," she repeated. "I'm not sleeping with you."

He smiled like he knew better.

CHAPTER FOUR

HE LET HER into the house, then watched her wander it as he made a call, allowing her to listen as he greeted someone with a warm, *"Cara. Come stai?"*

Gwyn took it like a punch in the stomach, wondering how crazy she was to agree that he could call *her* his lover if he already had one.

The restored mansion was unbelievable, she noted as she clung to her own elbows and stared at the view of Lake Como that started just below the windows off the breakfast nook. The rest of the interior was warmly welcoming, with a spacious kitchen and May sunshine that poured through the tall windows and glanced off the gleaming floors with golden promise. Family snapshots of children and gray-haired relatives and the handsome owner and his wife adorned the walls, making this a very personal sanctuary.

This felt like a place where nothing bad ever happened. That's what home was supposed to be, wasn't it? A refuge?

Would she ever build such a thing for herself, she wondered?

Gwyn moved into the lounge and lowered into a wingback chair, listening to the richness of Vittorio's voice, but not bothering to translate his Italian, aching to let waves of self-pity erode her composure. She felt more abandoned today than even the day her mother had died. At least then she'd had Henry. And a life to carry on with. A career. Something to keep her moving forward. Now...

She stared at her empty hands. Vittorio had even stolen her phone again, scowling at its constant buzz before powering it down and pocketing it.

She hadn't argued, still in a kind of denial, but she was facing facts now. She had no one. Nothing.

In the other room, Vittorio concluded with, *"Ciao, bella,"* and his footsteps approached.

He checked briefly when he saw her, then came forward to offer the square of white linen that was still faintly damp and stained with her mascara.

So gallant. While she felt like some kind of sullied lowlife.

She rejected it and him by looking away.

"No tears? That doesn't speak of innocence, *mia bella*," he jeered softly.

She never cried in front of people. Even at the funeral, she'd been the stalwart organizer, waiting for privacy before allowing grief to overwhelm her.

"Is that all it would take to convince you?" she said with an equal mixture of gentle mockery. "Would you hold me if I did?" She lifted her chin to let him see her disdain.

"Of course," he said, making her heart leap in a mixture of alarm and yearning. "No man who calls himself a man allows a woman to cry alone."

"Some of us prefer it," she choked out, even though there was a huge, weak part of her that wanted to wallow in whatever consolation he might offer. She'd had boyfriends. She knew that a man's embrace could create a sense of harbor.

But it was temporary. And Vittorio was not extending real sanctuary. They were allied enemies at best.

He wasn't even attracted to her. He thought she was a criminal and a slut.

"Just show me where I can sleep." She was overdue for hugging a pillow and bellyaching into it.

His silence made her look up.

"Paolo is still tied up questioning Fabrizio. His wife has very kindly offered her wardrobe." He waved toward the stairs. "She has excellent taste. Let's find something appropriate."

"For?" She glanced down at her business suit, which was a bit creased, but in surprisingly good shape despite her colossal besmirching.

"Our first public appearance," he replied in an overly patient tone, like he was explaining things to a child.

"You said we just had to wait out the scandal for a few days." A strange new panic began creeping into her, coming from a source she couldn't identify.

"Oh, no, *cara*," he said with a patronizing shake of his head. "I said that the worst of the scandal should pass in a few days. We are locked into our lie for a few weeks at least. You don't get seasick, do you? The wind might come up this evening and the dinner cruise could get rocky."

Vito wondered sometimes, when his dispassionate, ruthless streak arose this strongly, whether his father's genes were poking through the Donatelli discipline he had so carefully nurtured to contain it.

The mafiosi were known for their loyalty to family, he reasoned. The ferocity of his allegiance to Paolo and the bank had its seeds in his DNA. Of course he would do everything and anything to protect both. Of course he would do whatever was necessary to neutralize the threat Jensen posed.

Vito was aware of something deeper going on inside him, though. A pitiless determination to *crush* Jensen. It was positively primeval and he wasn't comfortable with it.

He glanced across at the fuel for his suppressed rage and was impacted by intense carnal desire.

Why?

Oh, Gwyn was beautiful. He couldn't deny it, even though she was pale beneath a light layer of makeup. It had been expertly applied by Lauren's very trustworthy stylist from Como. Like anyone who worked for society's high-level players, the stylist knew any sort of indiscretion meant a loss of more than just one lucrative client. Lauren had sent the woman "to help a friend." The stylist kept her finger on the pulse of celebrity gossip. She had recognized Gwyn with a very subtle start, then grinned and put her at ease so Gwyn had been smiling as she emerged as a butterfly from the chrysalis of a guest bedroom an hour later.

Her smile had faded when she had found Vito waiting for her. That had bothered him, making him feel a small kick of guilt, like he was responsible for her unhappiness.

...targeted by your *client with naked photos that will exist in the public eye for the rest of my life...*

He had asked her for the name of the spa and had ordered a team to look into it, wondering if a connection to Jensen might turn up beyond his wife recommending Gwyn visit it for physiotherapy.

Gwyn could have used something to relax her in that moment, as she'd stood so stiffly, projecting hostility as she seemed to wait out his judgment on her appearance.

He could hardly breathe looking at her. She was a vision in a long, sparkling blue skirt with a high slit and a black, equally glittering halter top that clung lovingly to the swells of her ample breasts. Her midriff was bare and her hair loose so her face was squarely framed by the blunt cut across her brow and the straight fall of rich, mahogany brown. She wore silver hoop earrings and a dozen thin bangles supplied by the stylist. Lauren's shoes were a half size too big, but Gwyn's toes were freshly painted a passionate red.

"You're stunning," he had told her sincerely.

Her hands had grown white where she clutched a small black pocketbook. Averting her face, she'd said, "Not sure why I bothered when people are going to look through what I'm wearing."

"Do you need me to tell you you're beautiful either way?"

She flinched. "Took a long look, did you?"

So much resentment. It annoyed him to be lumped in with all the other voyeurs. He had spent the past hour taking stock of how thoroughly Jensen was arrowing those images back at the bank, how the world media was exploiting Gwyn's naked body for ratings. He had looked at everything *but* her photographs, deliberately sparing her one more pair of male eyes and himself the disturbing dual reaction of arousal and fury.

The thought that men around the world were licking

their lips in lascivious heat over her figure was making him grow murderously affronted.

So he didn't appreciate her goading him.

"They're imprinted on my mind," he said without apology, watching something tense and disturbed flash across her expression before she quelled it. "You have nothing to be ashamed of. I don't mean that from a physical standpoint, but that's true, as well."

She reacted with a startled stare of confused vulnerability.

"That sounds almost kind. Are you practicing? Because there's no one here to overhear you being nice to me." Her mouth pouted in consternation, lips possibly trembling a moment before she firmed them.

It struck him that she didn't know he was attracted to her.

He would have laughed if he hadn't been so stunned. Admiration of her figure was a given. Why did she think she'd been chosen for this particular form of exploitation?

But there was more. Tendrils of possessiveness had rooted in him during those first seconds of viewing her pale nudity. A prowling hunger was growing, urging him to make her aware that he ached to touch her. He wanted to see the knowledge, the catch of excitement in her gaze. The exponential increase of passion as it reflected back and forth between them like parallel mirrors.

He didn't know how he knew it would be like that, he just did.

"You'll have to get used to looking insipidly pleased by my compliments," he said to disguise his growing need, grasping at her remark about practicing. "And welcome my touch," he added, giving in to temptation and letting the backs of his fingers graze the softness of her bare arm.

Goose bumps immediately rose on her skin and her nipples tightened.

It was such a visceral reaction he experienced an answering pull in his groin, one that very nearly had him throwing in the towel on his precious discipline. He had wanted to scoop her up and head straight to the nearest bedroom. Hell, the floor.

She blushed. Hard. Hurt flashed across her expression. "I'm already a powerless game piece. Don't make it worse by taunting me with my own stupid reaction to you." Shame darkened her eyes, but she dared to threaten him. "Or we will have a very ugly public breakup."

"And a very hot and public reunion," he responded fiercely, catching at the taut tendons in her wrists where she clenched her hands into fists. Tucking them behind her back, he pulled her in close and slid his lips along her perfumed neck, eyes almost rolling back into his skull as male hunger slammed through him. He *wanted* her. "Because your reaction to me is exactly what will sell this story of ours. So get used to revealing it."

Then, because she strained her face away from him, he sucked a tiny love bite onto her neck where it met her shoulder. Her whole body shuddered and a sensual moan escaped her. Her hips bucked to press her mons against his straining erection and lingered to rock with muted need, teasing both of them.

In that second, they could have both lost it, but he had forced himself to release her, his grip on his control far too tenuous for his liking.

He was unsurprised by the hatred she flashed at him as she took a staggering step away from him. She looked stricken. Shocked by her own reaction. He was unnerved himself. They would tear the skin from each other's bones if they gave in to this thing between them.

That hatred was good, though. It armed him against making love to her. He was driven, not despicable.

She hadn't spoken to him again, moving to the car like an airman with jump orders, sitting stiffly, keeping her stoic expression averted.

Everything in him itched to knock through that wall of hostility with another sample of their amazing chemistry, but he needed time to get hold of himself first.

The driver slowed to a crawl behind the line releasing rock stars, socialites, minor royalty and major league players onto the red carpet.

Vito wasn't on the list, but he knew the American actor hosting the cruise, so he had seized the opportunity to "come out" with Gwyn here. It was a precursor to an international film festival. The guest list was not only small and exclusive, but worldly enough that leaked sex tapes and mug shots were dismissed as "publicity." Nude photos were barely worth mentioning, as common to a portfolio as head shots.

He heard Gwyn's breath switch to measured hisses as she tried to control an attack of nerves. As the car stopped, he took her limp, clammy hand in his—and experienced a thrill of excitement from the contact despite the terror in the gaze she flashed at him.

"Chin up," he reminded her with a patronizing smile, sensing that kindness in this moment would be her downfall. She seemed to find her strength in anger, so he provoked it.

She said something under her breath that wasn't very ladylike, making him want to smile, but that wouldn't do for their purposes.

"Let them know how much you hate them," he said as the door beside him opened. He stood, bringing Gwyn with him, not giving her a chance to chicken out. Then he paused, giving the paparazzi the moment they needed to realize who they had.

The girl from the photos.

With Vittorio Donatelli.

His hand possessively slid so he had his arm around her and drew her closer, dipping his chin to look into her withdrawn expression with just the right level of concern before he lifted a hostile, contemptuous glare to the wall of cameras, silently messaging Kevin Jensen that he had messed with the wrong man's woman.

A buzz of gasps went through the crowd and the bursts of light intensified into a wall of exploding lights. The shouts became a rabid din.

Gwyn swallowed and revealed the barest moment of anguish before she leveled her shoulders and sent a haughty, dismissive glance toward the cameras that was gloriously effective in its disparagement. Her upward glance at Vito was not only a cold, silent demand that he remove her from this place, but a wonderful expression of trust that he would and could save her from it. He doubted she realized how revealing it was, but he saw it, knew the cameras caught it and was deeply satisfied.

She kept her spine iron straight beneath his hand as he steered her through the blinding lights to where the purser stood at the top of the steps to the gated marina.

"I'm not on the list," Vittorio told the uniformed young man. "But I'm on the list."

The purser didn't even relay his name, only glanced at the wild reaction they'd provoked and recognized the value they added to the event. "Thank you, sir. Enjoy your evening."

Vittorio started toward the steps, then turned back. "If Kevin Jensen is on the list, he's not on the list. Understand?"

"Absolutely." The purser nodded and flipped a page, striking through a name.

This morning, life had been normal.

Somehow, in roughly twelve hours, Gwyn had gone from mousy banking representative to notorious internet sensation. Thanks to Vittorio secluding her today, the full reality of her situation hadn't hit her until that moment outside the limo. Then strangers had called her name, clamoring for her to turn, shouting disgustingly invasive questions in a dozen languages.

When did you pose for those nude photos?

How did Mrs. Jensen find out about your affair?

Is Vittorio Donatelli your lover?

She stepped onto the yacht and a murmur rippled through the crowd. Heads tipped together and a few people pointed.

She instinctively edged closer to her date and his fingertips dug into her hip, oddly reassuring.

The last thing she ought to count on Vittorio for was protection. He'd behaved like a bastard earlier, using her own reaction against her like that. She was sick with herself for rubbing into his groin like she ached for his penetration—which she did. She was even sicker that finding him hard had excited her to the point she would have let him have her right there at the top of the stairs if he'd wanted.

Men were simple creatures, she reminded herself. Comedians were always complaining about erections popping up like dandelions at inconvenient times. As much as it would soothe her ego to believe Vittorio was attracted to her, she knew he couldn't possibly feel the same lust that had cut into her like a knife. His reaction had been about as personal as shivering from the cold.

They were united in one thing: pretending they were in a sexual relationship to defuse Jensen's allegations.

So she slithered closer to him, ignoring the fact that she drew genuine comfort from his strength. If he stiffened in a kind of surprise before tightening his arm around her, well, she wasn't a masochist who wanted another mean-spirited lesson in how incapable she was of resisting him. She stood close; she didn't soften and invite.

"Vito!" A gorgeous blonde approached them, tugging a legendary, award-winning, big-screen star in her wake. They turned out to be the host and hostess.

Gwyn silently laughed at herself. If the crowd was goggling at her, she goggled right back. The yacht was full to the gunwales of faces she'd seen in movies and on TV. Hugely famous people. It added a fresh layer of surreal to her already bizarro day.

"Thank you for coming," the tall, stunning supermodel said in a New York accent, kissing Vittorio on the mouth. "We'll have so much more exposure for the premiere now. I didn't see the photos," she said to Gwyn with an offhand shrug. "But my agent represents five of the top underwear models in the world. Judging from your figure, he would love to be your first call if you want to make lemonade out of this. Don't put it off. Attention like this doesn't last. Vito has my number."

"Vito," Gwyn repeated a moment later, when they were alone.

"My friends and family call me that. You should, too."

"Should I call her agent, is the real question," Gwyn said, taking a deeper drink of her champagne than was probably wise, but the impulse to get legless drunk was very strong.

"I would prefer you didn't," he said in a tone that was oddly lethal.

"Call her agent? Why? What other kind of work can I get? Even Nadine thought I wasn't good enough at my job to earn *this* promotion without falling onto my back. Maybe it's time I gave in to what the world has told me all my life and allow myself to be objectified. Make money on God's gift." She waved down her front.

An arc of dangerous fire flashed in his gaze again. "Have you come up against a lot of sexism in your life?"

"Is there an amount that's reasonable and acceptable?"

They were approached by someone else, stealing her moment of possibly taking him aback. They spent the next hour mingling. It wasn't awful, but she was tongue-tied and Vito kept stealing her champagne, setting the flutes out of her reach and giving her sparkling water or fruit juice in exchange.

"If you don't let me drink," she said at one point, fake smile pinned to her face, "people are going to think I'm pregnant. Surely I've hit the redline on scandal for one day?"

"I'm letting you drink. I'm just not letting you get drunk. You'll thank me tomorrow."

"I highly doubt you'll ever hear those words out of these lips," she assured him.

"We'll see," he said, catching at the hand she reached to the passing tray and tugging her in the opposite direction. "Come."

"Where?"

He only drew her from the main deck where glass panels provided a windbreak, keeping the laughing, dancing crowd contained in a pool of colorful light off a rotating mirror ball. A musician who had risen to fame three decades ago was going strong, shredding the piano, playing with a band of indie rockers on guitars and drums.

Vito tugged her down a narrow flight of stairs to where a cool gust raced along the lower deck, making her cross her arms as the chill hit her in the face.

"It did get windy," she said, hanging back in the alcove at the bottom of the stairs.

He removed his taupe linen jacket and draped it over her shoulders, enveloping her in a scent that was both his and something else. His cousin's aftershave, maybe, because he'd also raided the closets in the master bedroom. "We have work to do, now that you've relaxed."

"What kind?"

He drew her toward the stern where foam kicked up in a widening trail behind the yacht. The rush of wind and churning water filled the air. Pinprick lights from distant houses danced against the black silhouettes of the mountain-backed shoreline.

And a handful of smaller boats paced this big one, bouncing on its wake, buzzing like mosquitos. Something flashed. A camera.

"Oh."

"Sì," he confirmed. "We are stealing a kiss, *mia bella."*

"You can try," she said stiffly, turning her head to glare at him with antagonism, hands on the rail. "I've about had it with being robbed of things I'm not willing to give up. This cruise could get very rough indeed."

He leaned his back into the rail and set his feet wide, then indicated she should come into the space. "I'm offering a kiss," he cajoled, surprising her with his tender tone. "Would it be such a chore for you to accept it?"

A spasm of pain went through her, increasing when she saw another flash and suspected her moment of torment had just been caught and would be fed to the online trolls.

She found herself ducking her head, letting him draw her into his chest in an embrace that she knew he staged to look tender, but it *felt* tender. Like a place of shelter. She was on her very last nerve and desperately wanted to believe she was safe with him, but she couldn't. Not by a long shot.

"I don't kiss strangers," she muttered into his chest.

He smoothed her hair behind her ear and his breath warmed her cheek as he spoke. "We're lovers, *mia bella."*

In her periphery, more flashes were sparking, but maybe that was the electric reaction he provoked in her.

"You don't even find me attractive. Can you imagine how it feels to kiss someone you know feels nothing for you? Actually it's worse than that. You feel contempt. This is not a nice place to be. I can't pretend to be okay with it."

His hands stilled on her. "Have you had many lovers, Gwyn? You keep surprising me with what sounds like naivety."

"How is it naive to know that all these seduction moves of yours are motivated by a desire to protect the bank, that you're actually overcoming disgust to touch me?" She lifted her face to glare at him, unable to read his face in the dark. "Are you going to tell me next that I'm being too cynical?" She nearly choked on her own words. She was growing weak just standing against his body heat, reacting to him even though she knew he felt nothing toward her. This was so unequal.

"You're a very beautiful woman. You must know that." He rested the heel of his hand on her shoulder, fingertips toying at her nape beneath the fall of her hair.

The caress was so beguiling, the words so throaty, her whole body responded. Her knees weakened, her skin tightened and her nipples prickled. Deep between her thighs, damp heat gathered. Her breath hitched.

At the same time she heard the levelness in his tone and understood that his body might be growing hard, but his mind was still not affected.

"I suppose this *is* an affair then," she said, feeling him give a small start of surprise.

"What do you mean?"

"Well, it's not a relationship with a future. It's going to serve a purpose then end with neither of us calling or texting. You're right. I haven't had a lot of lovers and they've mostly been hit and runs. That's why I don't date much. I hate the part when I'm left feeling used. That's why I don't want to kiss you right now. I'll just feel dirty after."

"Ah, *cara*, you are very naive," he said with a gentle

laugh. "You're in a position to use *me*. Stop being so nice and do it. You'll feel terrific."

She gave him her profile, staring into the dark, angry that he made being nice sound like a character flaw. Angry that her life had been destroyed. Angry that there was no substance to what was going on between them. She was an object. Nothing real or important. This was how her mother had felt all the time.

A self-destructive impulse rose and she tossed her hair as she looked up at him.

"Fine. We'll kiss."

It was too dark to tell whether his brief hesitation was surprise or something else, but his hand moved to cup her cheek and he bent, capturing her mouth in a firm, hungry possession without a lead-up. No delay.

Because they were lovers, she reminded herself as excitement tore through her veins. According to the illusion they were projecting, they were familiar enough with each other to throw themselves into a passionate kiss without preamble.

Heart pounding, she returned his kiss with all the emotions roiling in her. Fury, mostly. She let her hand go to the short hairs at the back of his neck and increased the pressure, drawing him down to her, hurting herself with the way she mashed her mouth against his, liable to leave both of them bruised as she scraped her teeth against his lips in punishment for all that he'd done to her. For all that the world was doing to her.

He grunted and his hand went low on her back, pressing into her bottom to pull her tighter into him, fingertips flagrantly tracing the line between her cheeks.

She didn't protest. She shuffled closer, shoving herself aggressively into his frame, like they were combatants. She moved her hand to take a fistful of his hair, hoping his scalp stung while she moved her lips under his, mouth burning with avid, angry friction.

With another gruff noise, he lifted his head, let her catch one breath, then closed his arms more tightly around her, swooping into a deep, dominant kiss, tongue spearing boldly into her mouth.

Her reaction might have been frightening to her if she wasn't so close to exploding. She needed this outlet, this contained space of banded arms keeping her from flying apart. She fought letting him take over as long as she could, flicking at his tongue with hers, trying to make him break, but he was too strong willed. Way stronger than her.

With a little sob, she finally capitulated, softening and letting him take control.

Her reward was a wash of delirious pleasure. Suddenly she felt what this kiss was doing to her. Her blood was hot, her erogenous zones sensitized and singing. His body seemed to envelop hers in sexual need. She was so steeped in desire, her knees folded.

She would have gone anywhere with him in that moment. Would have let him do anything. She wanted him to cover her and push inside her and take her to a place where nothing could touch her.

His assertiveness eased. His hand moved soothingly over her back. His damp lips tenderly caressed hers until they broke apart to gasp for air. He tucked her head under his jaw and held her ear against his pounding heart.

She rested there, trying to catch her breath, listening to his heart slam, feeling like she'd been running and now the ache of exertion was catching up to her.

He was hard, she realized, and she panged again with longing for this to be real, for them to make love so she could lose herself in mindless pleasure. She ought to find his desire threatening, she thought. Or offensive maybe. She didn't move away from pressing against him, though, liking that evidence of his reaction even if it was strictly physiological. She stayed in that little cave of safety his arms provided, face pressed to his shirt, body sheltered from the wind by his broader one.

And she started to cry.

There was no stopping it this time. It wasn't a grand storm, just a slow leak of tears that grew into a steady, unstoppable flow. Her control surrendered to exhaustion, like a drowning victim letting go and sinking beneath the surface. She clung with limp arms and leaned her weight into him as pulsing waves of suffering rocked her.

He didn't tell her to *shush*. He held her, rubbed her back and didn't say a word.

CHAPTER FIVE

VITO SAT IN the armchair of the hotel room, feet on the ottoman, wearing only his pants. He was pretending to read emails, but sat angled so he could watch Gwyn sleep.

A full-out rainstorm had manifested while she'd been fixing her face in the head, after their kiss. The yacht had raced to moor at the nearest marina and, while most of the guests scrambled through sheets of rain for taxis to take them to their hotels, he had walked into the yacht club and paid a fortune for a top-floor room. He hadn't been interested in leading the paparazzi back to the mansion and Gwyn had been at the end of her rope.

He could have taken a suite, he supposed, but he didn't want anyone counting how many beds had been slept in. He had shared this one with her—until he'd given up trying to sleep. She'd been emotionally drained and slightly drunk, looking disturbingly vulnerable and wary after she'd washed her face and put on his shirt to sleep in it. She had threaded her bare legs under the covers and kept firmly to her side of the bed.

He'd kept his pants on, since he never wore shorts, and tried not to touch her once he had put out the lights and crawled in beside her. At least until he'd realized she was curled into a ball, shivering from the chill of getting soaked by the rain. He could have risen to turn off the air-conditioning, but he'd spooned her instead.

When she had stiffened, he'd said, "Go to sleep," in the same quietly firm tone he would use on any of his abundant underage cousins, nieces and nephews who might creep down the stairs when they ought to be in bed. Molding Gwyn to him, he'd gone quietly out of his mind while she had relaxed into the hot curve of his chest and thighs.

She had dropped into a deep sleep, leaving him nursing an aching erection, blood burning like acid in his arteries. Every time he dozed, his mind took him back to kissing her on the deck, when she'd aggressively tested his control.

He didn't know how he'd kept from lifting her skirt. Possessiveness, perhaps, because in that moment he hadn't cared if anyone saw his naked ass, but the idea of the paparazzi catching another glimpse of her unclothed had been intolerable.

He'd tried to slow things down while he calculated whether to steal into a stateroom or ask for one to be assigned, so they wouldn't risk interruption.

She had started to cry.

This woman. He was trying very hard to vilify her, to help maintain some distance, but there was no question in him any longer as to whether she had posed for those photos. She was too devastated to be anything less than violated.

Which did things to him. Provoked something that could turn into a blind savagery if he dwelt too much on the injustice.

He sipped the coffee he'd made in the small pot, studying her timeless features, so well suited to her surroundings.

The building was classic Renaissance, imposing and symmetrical. The interior was equally ornate and gracefully proportioned, enriched with dark wood grains and gold accents upon fervent reds and royal blues. The setting made a beautiful foil for her pale skin, pink lips and long dark lashes.

He'd neglected to close the heavy curtains so sunlight poured across her cleanly-washed face. The collar of his white shirt was turned up against her cheek, the unbuttoned sleeve pushed far up her bare arm.

His Lover At Rest, he thought with a sardonic smile, toying with the idea of snapping her photo. His conscience stopped him. *If it makes you feel objectified, well, you have a glimpse into how I feel right now.*

He wasn't bothered by her taking a photo of his photo. He knew he was good-looking. Female attention had always been abundant in his life in the very best way. He wasn't surprised that she found him attractive and certainly wasn't offended by it. He liked it. Too much.

She wasn't as comfortable with their chemistry. She was feeling used and he was being a bastard, not letting her see that he was equally ensnared by lust, but wanting her was weakness enough. Letting her see it would be akin to handing over a weapon, something he was too innately self-protective to ever do.

His phone vibrated in his hand and he dragged his attention off her peaceful expression to see that his cousin was forwarding something.

Can you deal with this? Will talk more when I get there. Leaving in a few hours.

Vito understood by Paolo's desire for a face-to-face that he was being abundantly cautious with traceable, hackable things like texts and emails, but it surprised him that Paolo was coming to Como. He had been working from home, refusing to leave his wife's side as she approached the end of her third pregnancy.

But his cousin was smart enough to see the implication behind Vito's appearance with Gwyn last night. He would want more details, to be sure they had their story straight, especially before he made further statements to the press.

The multitude of demands for more information from all corners was threatening to break Vito's phone, coming from every direction from family to news contacts to the bank's core investors. The story across the sea of media had shifted from lurid curiosity about the woman in the photos to deeper speculation as to who she was and how she had ensnared not just one, but two powerful men into a nude photo scandal. Was she sleeping with both of them?

He stroked his thumb along the edge of his screen, deciding it was time to feed another tidbit to the press, leading them away from Jensen's version of events toward his own.

Yesterday, he had ordered a team to look for a connection between the spa owner and Jensen, suspecting it could be a laundry for some of the funds Jensen had funneled. Even if the spa's only crime was the breach of Gwyn's privacy, he didn't see any reason they should remain open and making money while Gwyn suffered.

With enormous satisfaction, he touched the query from one of his former paramours who worked as an anchor for an Italian morning talk show. Quote me as stating that the photos were taken without her consent at a local spa, he messaged to her.

As the *whoosh* sounded to tell him the text was sent, he could practically hear her spiked heels racing down to her producer's office, intent on identifying said spa and surprising the owner with an early-morning interview. She would seize world coverage with her exclusive by noon.

With a smirk at how easily the press was played, he turned his attention to the email Paolo had forwarded.

It was from Travis Sanders, director of an architectural firm Vito had never heard of. A quick swipe to his browser revealed it was a growing global corporation based in Charleston. Henry Sanders had started in real estate and morphed into renovation and restoration. His son, Travis, had earned his degree then took over his father's firm, expanding into design and engineering. All of their projects were prestigious; the most current one was a cathedral in Brazil.

Vito read Travis's email to Paolo:

I haven't heard from my sister since the tenth of last month. If you're screening her calls, stop screening me. I want to hear from her.

Short and decidedly acrid.

Gwyn shifted on the bed, rolling onto her back and opening her eyes. Confusion quickly fell into a wince of memory. She glanced at the empty spot beside her, sat up, saw him and brought the edge of the sheet up to the buttons closed across her chest.

"I thought you said he was your stepbrother?" Vito said.

"Who? Travis?" She frowned in sleepy confusion. "He is. Why?"

"He wants to hear from you. He thinks we're preventing you from calling."

She sighed and looked at the landline beside the bed like it was a snake he'd asked her to pick up.

Since she'd left her own mobile back at the house, he rose and took his across to her. "Would you rather text?"

Her gaze flickered across his bare chest and wariness trembled in her eyelashes while sexual awareness brought a light pink glow to her skin. He would have smiled with satisfaction if his entire body hadn't tightened in response. Her scent was coming off those rumpled sheets in a way that tugged at his vitals.

She expertly sent off a quick message and handed back the phone, not looking at him.

Despite it being very early in Charleston, the phone vibrated immediately with a response.

Vito glanced at it and couldn't help a dry smirk. "He wants to know his father's birthday. To confirm that was actually you who just texted, I imagine."

"Seriously?" She took back the phone, tapped out a lengthy message and slapped it back into Vito's hand.

He glanced at the exchange, reading that she'd told her stepbrother she was fine, not being held hostage, didn't know what to say and hoped the press wasn't bothering Henry. She wanted Travis to apologize to him for her.

Vito frowned at her expression of misery, started to tell her what was in store for the spa, but another message came through.

"'This isn't like you,'" Vito read.

"How the hell does he know what I'm like?" she muttered, sliding her feet out the side of the bed. "He barely talks to me."

"You're to call him when you can talk freely," he read aloud as she headed toward the bathroom.

She made a noise and said, "I'm going to see if it's possible to drown in a shower."

"Don't take too long. I'm hungry and plan to order breakfast now that you're up."

Funny how something as simple as a shower became a saving grace in a time of crisis. Washing her hair, smoothing a soapy facecloth over her body... It was comfortingly normal. Routine. She took her time, thinking of nothing as water rained down upon her.

Until her mind drifted to hearing the shower in the night.

Why had Vito risen to shower at 2:00 a.m.? He'd been hard against her butt. She remembered that. If she hadn't been so drained, she might have turned and let him do something she would be regretting right now.

Had he touched himself in here? Pleasured himself? When he could have had her out there?

The thought struck like a blow, tightening her midsection, making her miserable all over again. She had to stop thinking there was any sort of potential between them. Maybe sex was an option. He'd told her to go ahead and use him, after all. But that's all it would be: empty sex. There was no room for romance. They weren't lovers. Despite appearances, they weren't dating. They weren't even friends.

This was all fake.

And her life was a complete disaster, she confronted anew as she stepped from the shower and faced a choice between last night's sparkling evening wear and his rumpled white shirt. She was not in a fit mental state to start any kind of relationship.

She pulled on the robe from the back of the door. It had an embroidered sailboat on the left lapel and was made of thick, comforting chenille. She knotted the belt and emerged to scents of ham and eggs, coffee and sweet pastries. Her stomach contracted. When had she last eaten, she wondered? Vito had forced a few morsels on her last night from the extravagant buffet, but she hadn't been interested.

He was closing the door behind someone as she came out and waved at a stack of clothing that had been delivered. "See if that fits."

She didn't know what to say and found herself fingering through the clothes. There was a clean shirt for him, a short-sleeved, collared one in cobalt blue along with clean socks.

For her, he'd ordered clean underpants, a camisole with a shelf bra in butter yellow, palazzo pants with a subtle floral print and a sheer top that picked up the colors in the pants with splashes of emerald and streaks of pink.

"We're going shopping so you won't have to wear it long if you don't like it," he said, making her realize she was frowning.

"No, it's fine. I thought I'd be wearing the robe back

to the house." She looked for price tags, didn't find any and started to worry. How would she pay for this?

"Let's eat," he said, indicating the set table before the now open window.

Their view looked onto the red umbrella tables six stories below, the marina of bobbing, million-dollar boats and the deceptively placid lake glinting in the cradle of mountain peaks.

"Is the shopping really necessary?" she asked, breaking the yoke of her poached egg with the tine of her fork.

He shrugged. "It's a parade for the cameras and you need clothes for all the circulating we'll be doing over the next few weeks, so, yes. I would say it is."

She watched her fork tremble as a fresh wave of helpless anger swamped her.

"I would like to remind you that I don't have a job. How am I supposed to pay for a new wardrobe?"

"You are so cute, Gwyn," he said, *so* patronizing. "I am indulging my *innamorata*. It's what besotted men do."

Her appetite died. She put down her fork, vainly wishing she wasn't sitting here naked under a robe he had funded. She wished she had a better choice than walking out of here in clothes that were borrowed or an outfit chosen and paid for by him. She wasn't used to being this powerless. Even when Travis had been unknowingly annihilating her sense of self-worth, she'd had a job and enough savings to get herself and her mother started over in a cheap room if Henry had called off the wedding.

"Women love shopping, Gwyn. Why are you so upset by the prospect?" Vito asked, tucking into his breakfast with gusto.

"Because this isn't like me," she said, tartly quoting her stepbrother. "My mother didn't have much. She made ends meet, but we lived very simply and I still do."

She typically ate scrambled eggs she cooked for herself, not delicately poached orbs on toasted ciabatta with garlic and a pesto hollandaise, garnished with shallots and plum tomatoes. She drank orange juice she mixed from concentrate, or instant coffee, not mimosas and rich, dark espresso that made her want to moan in ecstasy with the first taste.

She swallowed her tentative sip of the hot, bitter brew and set down her tiny cup, noting that Vito was watching her, like he was deciding whether to believe her. She hesitated to open up, but figured it was better to be honest about her background than to hide it.

"Mom met my stepfather while working as a janitor in his office. Travis was *not* impressed by his father's choice in second wives. He was at university and I moved into his old room for my last year of high school. I guess it was weird for him to suddenly have this geeky girl underfoot whenever he visited his dad. Strangers living in his house."

She had taken refuge in homework when Travis was around, only emerging to eat dinner where Henry had put her at ease and made her laugh.

"My mother genuinely loved his father," she said, silently willing Vito to believe her. "She never would have brought me into any man's home for any reason except to give me a father. I think of Henry that way." She had to drop her gaze as she admitted, "But the day before their wedding, I overheard Travis warning Henry that we might be gold diggers. I thought his mind would change over time, as he saw that we were just trying to be a family, but a year into their marriage my mother was diagnosed with cancer. I was supposed to move out, go to college, but instead I stayed to help Henry nurse her. I took some online courses, but Mom felt like such a burden on us. Travis didn't come around much. I know how it looked to him, like Henry was stuck with a pile of medical bills for someone he shouldn't have to support."

She stared into the harsh glare of sunlight on the water to sear back the tears gathering in her eyes.

"It was such a raw deal that she finally found a man who loved her, who wanted to take care of her, and she died before she could make a proper life with him. Make him happy."

"I'm sorry to hear that," Vito said, sounding sincere, covering her hand.

She removed her hand, forcing herself to shrug off the bleak sadness.

"I'm very conscious of the fact that Travis thinks I'm only maintaining a relationship with Henry because he has money and I don't. I never take any when he offers, so letting you swan me in and out of Italian boutiques is not exactly the picture I want to paint so my stepbrother will let me continue visiting the only father I've ever had."

She looked at him, blinking several times to bring her vision back from a wall of white to see his toughened yet brutally handsome expression.

"But I'm hardly in a position to demand the luxury of pride, am I?" she added caustically.

He was watching her with a gravity that made her feel naked all over again. "Would he really stop you from seeing him?" he asked.

She shrugged. "I don't know," she muttered. "He

loves his father as much as I do and wants to protect him. He wasn't trying to be cruel. I mean, you'd probably say the same thing to your own father in that situation, wouldn't you?"

Vito's stare was inscrutable. He held her gaze for a long time, like he had a million responses and was sifting for the best one. He settled on saying, "Eat," and lowered his attention to his plate.

Well, that settled that, didn't it, she thought facetiously, and forced herself to take a bite.

No matter how sincere Gwyn seemed, Vito couldn't afford to let himself be swayed emotionally. While she finished getting ready, he reviewed her background more thoroughly.

She interrupted, emerging from the bathroom with a more natural look that was infinitely more beautiful than last night's smoky eyes and sharp cheekbones and red, glossy lips painted by the stylist. Gwyn had frowned when he'd handed her the pots of color and paint, grumbling about not wanting to look like a ghost if she was going to be photographed. If not for that, she implied, she wouldn't have accepted the makeup at all.

"What do we do with last night's clothes?" She looked for them.

"I've made arrangements."

She stared at him.

He lifted his brow in inquiry.

"I borrowed something. I want to be sure it's returned in good condition," she said.

"It will be." He frowned, annoyed by what sounded like a lack of faith, but also seeing yet more evidence of the do-it-myself streak of independence she seemed to have. "I reviewed your file and some other details," he told her as they left the room.

She looked over her shoulder at him, dismayed, but not fearful. "Like?"

Her financial situation. Her debt level was low, but she had a little, and hadn't made any significant payments or purchases recently. There had been nothing to red flag her as possessing or spending a sum that might have been embezzled. Instead, he'd found more evidence that she was exactly as she portrayed herself.

"You've worked hard for the education and position you've attained," he acknowledged once they were in the privacy of the elevator. "But Fabrizio signed off on your transfer despite there being two candidates with more experience. It supports what you said yesterday, that you might have been recruited because you were green and possibly more likely to let things slide out of ignorance."

"So you're willing to believe it based on your own assessment of hard evidence, but nothing I say has any bearing. My word means nothing to you. Isn't that the story of every woman's life." She shrugged on the cloak of righteous anger she'd been wearing since he met her, but he could sense the hurt beneath.

He wasn't sure what kind of reaction he expected, but he hadn't expected that. His belief in her *meant* something to her. It made him realize exactly how much power he had over her and he wasn't sure he was comfortable with it.

Since when did he not embrace power? He loved it!

But he was suddenly confronted with how vulnerable she was. To all the men in her life, but especially to him, right now. It slapped at his conscience, made him think again about her saying he would protect his father. The joke was on her. His real mother had been light-years ahead of his father in social status, belonging to the Donatelli banking clan. His father had been on the bottom of society's spectrum. A criminal of the vilest order.

He had cold-bloodedly seduced her with an eye to his own gain.

What are you *doing, Vito?* he chided himself.

He was protecting the bank, he reminded himself. And his blood was decidedly hot when Gwyn's hand was in his own.

He strolled her through the late morning sun, ignoring the cameras, entering every boutique on the promenade and refusing to leave without making a purchase.

But for a woman who only needed to act enamored to get herself out of trouble, she did a lousy job of it. She wasn't outright defiant. No, her resistance was subtle enough to give credence to what she had said earlier about not wanting to look like a gold digger. She needed cajoling to enter a change room, pulled a face at the prices and frowned at the growing number of bags he was having sent back to the yacht club.

It was beyond his experience. Every woman he knew enjoyed being spoiled this way, whether sisters, mother or lovers. He had been raised to be chivalrous, and not only owned a sizable number of shares in the bank, but investing was his living. He made more money in a day than he could spend in a week. This was pocket change.

He began taking special care, looking for items that were particularly flattering to her, complimenting her, trying to soften that spine and coax a smile of pleasure out of her. Why couldn't she relax and see the fun in this?

A motorcycle jacket with a faux fur collar and narrow sleeves that capped the tops of her hands to her knuckles looked genuinely delightful on her. He stood behind her as she eyed it in the mirror.

"It suits you. Makes you look as tough as you are," he said.

She met his gaze in the mirror. "You do this a lot, don't you? I honestly didn't see you as the kind of guy who had to buy his women."

She might as well have butted that hard head of hers back into his lip and nose. He tightened his hands on her shoulders to freeze her in place.

Her gaze met his again and she saw the danger there, stilling, hand on the zipper of the jacket.

"Be very careful what you say to me, *cara*."

"You want those vultures out there to believe this," she said with a small toss of her head to the front of the store, where music was blaring so loudly they could barely hear each other even back here. "I don't have to. Or does your ego demand that I fall for you for real?"

Once again she had him thinking about a powerful man exploiting a vulnerable young woman.

That wasn't what this was.

She moved the zipper an inch then shrugged his hands off her shoulders. "Buy it if you think I should have it. I don't care."

The hell of it was, he believed her.

Gwyn watched cute sundresses and silk scarves, two hats and a designer bag that cost the earth all go into colorful boutique bags. Vito told her they'd buy evening gowns in Milan—for what?—but insisted she get trendy jeans, cocktail skirts and flirty tops, lingerie that she flatly refused to let him watch her try on and shoes. Dear Lord, the shoes.

Deep in her most covetous, most materialistic heart, she adored Italian-made shoes. She'd been saving up for a pair, browsing regularly as she debated whether to be practical and buy something she might wear often or ridiculously capricious and own something that would sit in a box in her closet, to be worn on only a few special occasions.

Vito bought her six pairs of very chic, very expensive day shoes and completely dismissed them as, "They'll do for now." More, he assured her, would be purchased with the gowns in the city.

She might have protested, but he was already angry with her. That moment at the mirror had made her tremble inside, he'd looked so lethal. At the same time, she knew he wouldn't hurt her physically. It was her heart, her own ego and self-confidence that were in peril.

Especially because, despite her nastiness, he didn't let up on his solicitude. They walked from store to store and paparazzi swarmed around them, clicking and flashing and capturing every murmur and expression. One called something particularly disgusting and she flinched.

"Ignore them," Vito growled, drawing her closer to the shelter of his big body, brushing his lips against the tip of her ear as he spoke, then smoothed his fingers through the tails of her loose hair, caressing her waist, so attentive to her needs.

She imagined she looked deeply smitten every time he touched her like this. That's why she'd had to insult him and drive a wedge between them. Her response to his pretend seduction was dangerously real. Her nipples tightened when all he did was touch the small of her back. She flushed with desire when she inhaled the scent of his neck.

How was she so comfortable under his touch? That's what she wanted to know. Normally she was quite standoffish with men. If they so much as took her elbow while they walked her down the street, she found the presumptiveness of it annoying.

Not Vito. Her skin called out for each light graze of contact. She was in a perpetual state of readiness, skin sensitized and aching with anticipation, eager for his merest caress. She wanted him to smother her with his big body. Absorb her.

In some ways it was exhausting. She was incredibly relieved when he pointed to a car with a chauffeur in sunglasses leaning against it, reading his phone. "We'll take a drive to some viewpoints, see if we can lose these cameras before we head back to the house."

Their last two boutique bags went into the trunk where the myriad of other purchases were now arranged along with dry cleaner bags holding the clothing they'd worn last night. The man really was a demigod, taking care of the dreary details of life with what seemed like a magical snap of his finger and thumb. Forget the other conquests who fell for this routine. She was becoming one of them. How could any woman *not* find this level of provision seductive?

She settled with a sigh on the leather seat in the back, pretending she wasn't aware of the scooters that kept buzzing up beside them for the next ten minutes as they drove into the hills. The windows were blacked out, however, so the followers soon fell away, accepting that their opportunity was over and they might as well go file the photos they had and collect their payments.

The car climbed high above the lake, the twists in the road taking them into stretches of quiet thoroughfare, where she finally let out her breath in a sigh.

Vito leaned forward to close the privacy window and poured both of them a water from the bottle in the door.

"Was it so bad?" he asked. "Spending my money?"

"No," she said, adding a sarcastic, "How was it for you?"

She heard how suggestive that sounded and made a noise into her glass.

"Why does everything I say come out sounding dirty around you?" she muttered.

"Freudian slip?" he suggested.

She slid her thumb along the rim of her glass, blushing and saying nothing.

"Your silence speaks volumes," he taunted.

"Am I the first woman to find you attractive? I doubt it," she said caustically.

"You're the first to be so annoyed by it," he said with a hint of laughter in his voice. "Why? Because you're so tempted?"

"I've never been a drug user and that's what it would be," she muttered. "You're sitting there like a giant pain-killer promising to keep me from feeling the bus that's crushing me. So, yes, I'm tempted." She couldn't believe how honest she was being. It wasn't like her to be this blunt, but what shred of dignity was left to lose? "But I've never gone to bed with a man purely for physical release. It makes me feel cheap to consider it."

"You're incredibly insulting when you want to be,

aren't you? The problem, I think, is that you don't know how powerful this particular painkiller will be." He leaned across and set her glass in her door. His was gone and his hands went to her waist. "Come here."

"What—?"

He dragged her to straddle his thighs, making her stiffen in surprise at the sudden intimacy of having her legs open across him, her inner thighs lightly stretched by the press of his thick, hard ones.

She kept her arms stiff, holding herself off him, but she was intrigued despite her wariness. "There's no one to see this performance," she reminded tautly.

"Yes, I know," he said smokily, and stroked his hands up and down her thighs, massaging in a way that sent ripples of anticipation into her pelvis. With a little shift, he slouched and they were sex to sex, her tingling loins firmly seated against the very hard ridge of his erection.

"If only I still worked for you and could charge you with sexual harassment," she said, but her voice had thinned and her twitching thighs wouldn't cooperate enough to lift her away.

"I don't have to buy women, *cara*. They come to me for this." His hips came up just enough to press where too many nerve endings were centered. She bucked in an allover response, gasping.

"You're so full of yourself," she told him, shivering, not fighting the hands that pressed her hips so she felt that delicious grind again.

The corners of his mouth deepened in satisfied amusement. "Let's see which one of us wants to be full of me, hmm?" His hand slid up her side, across her shoulder to cup the side of her neck.

A trail of tingles followed his caress, sensitizing her,

making her go still when self-preservation instincts told her to get the hell off his lap.

As he exerted a tiny pressure, urging her forward, asking for her mouth against his, she gave in.

It's only a kiss. They'd done it before.

But this wasn't a kiss. It was a match to a flame.

As her mouth reached his, he captured her in a hungry kiss, like last night, only hotter. With a confident hand on her butt, he rocked her against his erection, making her shudder and take over the move herself, seeking the rhythm that would build the desire in the heated, dampening flesh between her legs.

Distantly she told herself to be cautious, remember this was about the bank. He was only doing this to prove a point, but her arms went around his neck in a kind of instinctive twine. She pressed to crush her breasts against his chest. Their tongues tangled and they both opened their mouths to deepen the kiss into something flagrant and wildly passionate.

Maybe there was something else she ought to have been thinking about, fretting over, but few thoughts of any clarity stuck after that. She became a being of pure sensation. All her awareness centered on the points where they touched, how he stroked her back and hips, how her body prickled and responded like firecrackers were exploding at different points.

His hand slid to cup her breast, weighing and gently massaging. She rubbed her nipple into his palm, never so free when it came to sex. Maybe if he'd seemed surprised by her lack of inhibition, she would have pulled back, but he groaned with appreciation, encouraging her, giving her all the pressure she needed as he shaped and squeezed her breast. She loved the way the light fabric of her top and silky cami made it easy for him to find and tantalize her nipple, pinching the peak and causing a stab of arousal straight between her legs.

She gasped and moaned approval. More heat rushed to pool in her loins, making her ache there and seek that hard ridge. She rubbed, trying to soothe the needy throb between her legs, unable to remember the last time she'd had any sex, let alone thrown herself into it like this. No man had ever aroused her this quickly and thoroughly with little more than a kiss and a few brazen caresses.

She arched as his other hand found its way beneath her top and pulled her cami askew, so he could pull back and look at her through the translucent film of her overtop. They both watched his thumb circle her nipple, flicking back and forth, stimulating the tight bead so she shuddered and panted, scalp tight, excited beyond what she could imagine could happen from such a simple bit of teasing.

"Come here," he said, urging her to lift on her knees and push her nipple toward his mouth.

She did, bracing her hands on his shoulders, vaguely aware they were in a moving car. Maybe the blur around them was empty of humans, but the darkened glass at her back wasn't. She ought to be showing more decorum, but his tongue moved the silk of her top against her nipple in delicate friction. The dampness of his mouth enclosed her in heat, sucking and inciting. She was lost, groaning with delight as he tortured her, licking and moving that damp fabric, squeezing the swell of her breast just enough to push more blood into the tip.

She was going to climax from this alone, she thought, working her nails with agitation against his shirt, thinking she should stop this, but she was compelled to keep going because it felt so damned good.

Her waistband released and his other hand slid in, confident and possessive, cupping soaked lace, saying something in Italian she didn't have the wherewithal to interpret, but he sounded pleased. Like he was complimenting her. She absolutely flowered when he sounded so appreciative and admiring.

He held his palm steady for her to grind herself into the heel of his hand. She moaned with pleasure as her arousal became acute. She tore at his collar and tried to stroke his skin, wanted to bend and kiss him, but as she pulled back, he stared at her chest.

"Give me the other one," he growled, eyeing her left breast, still tucked away.

With trembling hands, she lifted her top out of the way, pushed the cami down so her breasts were thrusting out the top of it, brazen in the extreme—

He opened his mouth wide on her bare nipple and she nearly screamed at the sensation of his teeth closing softly, dragging all the way to the tip before he sucked her into the deep, wet cavern of heat that was his greedy mouth.

A rush of need flooded into her sex. Into his palm.

He made an animalistic noise and his fingers pushed past silk, fingertips seeking, two penetrating, burying deep, thumb tracing and finding. Circling.

"Yes," she gasped, giving herself up to the stunning height of pleasure, welcoming the thrust of his fingers, clasping him hard to her breast as he nipped in a way that was just short of pain. The sensations he was offering were so sharp and intense it was almost too much to bear. She clenched, trying to hold back, realizing how close she was to losing it. This wasn't what she'd meant to happen.

His arm clamped around her waist and he kept lashing her with those twin sensations until she couldn't hold back. Orgasm crashed over her. Her body nearly buckled under the power of it. Her cries of abandon filled the backseat and she pressed her hands to the ceiling, all of herself offered to him as he pleasured her, nearly bursting into jagged tears at the intensity of her release. Dying. She was dying and would never breathe again.

The paroxysm held her for a long time, until she slowly became aware that his caress had become soothing.

His damp hand moved, sliding onto her hip then cupping her backside, urging her to nestle her tender, throbbing flesh against the aggressive ridge of his erection straining the front of his pants. He lifted his head and licked at her panting mouth, teasing her into kissing him back.

She was still shaking with reaction and kept her eyes closed as she kissed him with swollen, trembling lips, aware of his hardness everywhere: shoulders, arms, thighs. Even his lips were firm where hers were soft with spent pleasure. His heart was pounding while she was still trying to catch her breath, both of them damp with perspiration.

Finally she dragged her eyes open to see he had a very smug, satisfied light in his half-closed eyes. That arrogance was unnerving, making her realize he had completely taken her apart while losing none of his own control. Only his collar was slightly askew, his hair barely out of place.

He told her in a low growl what he wanted to do to her.

What was wrong with her that she responded with an internal clench of anticipation to his dirty talk?

She pushed off his lap and shakily tidied her clothes, avoiding his gaze, trying not to think of where his hand had been. How she'd sounded as she called out with release. Had the driver heard her? How did things just keep getting more mortifying?

She managed to rally, responding to what he'd said with a scathing, "The way you're looking so self-satisfied, I'd think we already did that."

He angled to look at her, reaching to smooth a wisp of her hair from its tangle on her eyelashes. Her pulse leaped with excitement, but his finger didn't even brush her skin.

"It was bothering me that other men had seen you naked. But no man has ever seen you like that, have they? I'm very satisfied."

What an egotistical—

"You're a jerk," she told him, thinking there were saltier words and she was tempted to find them.

"Are you losing the feel-good already? Because I'm right here, ready and willing to take you to your happy place all over again."

"Oh, shut up," she snapped, turning her face to the window. Pride. Who knew it was such an unaffordable luxury?

CHAPTER SIX

GWYN DIDN'T KNOW how close she'd just come to being taken in the backseat under the straying eye of his driver. Oh, Carlo would have known they were petting, would have turned up the music so he wouldn't hear anything indelicate, but neither he nor Gwyn knew that Vito had nearly lost control, so caught up in Gwyn's pleasure he'd almost found his own, fully clothed and completely at her service. He'd barely stopped himself from rolling her beneath him on the seat, stripping them bare and quite possibly planting a baby in her without a single thought for the consequences.

The thought disturbed him. Was that how he'd been conceived? In a fit of blind passion that completely disregarded the impact to the woman in question?

By the few accounts Vito had from his adoptive parents, his mother had been deeply infatuated, if far too young and naive for a thirtysomething gangster with a pitiless determination to get whatever he wanted. He had wanted Antoinietta Donatelli. He had seduced her. His family had always sworn up, down and sideways that Vito wasn't a product of rape. No, he was the product of a man taking advantage of a woman who didn't have nearly the worldliness needed to resist him.

Not unlike Gwyn, who didn't take lovers strictly for the pleasure of physical release.

Because, he suspected, no man had given her a release like that. He probably shouldn't have, but her animosity had been eating at him. That remark about buying women and her resistance toward him on every level had been grinding away at his control. When she had called herself "cheap" for wanting to sleep with him, something feral in him had snapped, demanding that he *show* her how good they would be together.

Cheap? It was unique and precious, beyond even what he had imagined it could be. Disconcertingly powerful.

And honest.

Her reaction now, so taken aback by her own abandonment, told him how thoroughly he had owned her in those moments. He thrilled to it, but it caused a shift inside him. Something he wasn't fully prepared to examine, fearing he was making a rationalization to justify getting what he wanted: her.

But the way she'd ignited in his arms made thinking of anything except possessing her impossible.

They seemed to have left the paparazzi far behind and circled back toward the house. As soon as they were inside, Gwyn went straight through to the small patio outside the back door, where the cool afternoon breeze off the water gave her the first proper breath she'd taken since coming apart at Vito's touch.

She went down the steps to the pool deck where she stared out over the lake, blood cooling, hands curled around the rail to ground her back into harsh reality. Why had she let that happen? And what did it mean for the rest of this pantomime they were acting? Would they become lovers in every way, not just a one-sided grope that only proved his superiority over her?

That was the part that devastated her. She could give herself orgasms if she wanted them. But despite all the ways he'd turned out to be different from the urbane Italian gentleman she'd fantasized about, she was even more in thrall than ever. Would she become his lover?

She couldn't imagine finding the will to say, *No.*

Vito came outside with two wineglasses and a corked bottle. He wordlessly poured and offered her one, not speaking until she took hers.

"Salute," he said, gaze trying to catch hers.

She couldn't do it, too aware of how intimate things had been between them. Too vulnerable to him.

"I keep making you angry because it seems the only way to keep you from falling into despair," he said, as though explaining the answer to a riddle.

"Something else for my own good?" She snapped her gaze up to his.

He smiled faintly. "Whatever works."

She released a shaken sigh, finding his statement not exactly comforting, but oddly bolstering. He wasn't toying with her for fun, but trying to help her in his backhanded way.

She couldn't deny that his lovemaking had, for a few minutes, completely wiped away her anxiety over her nightmare of a life. Now everything was flooding back and she would be very thankful if he did something annoying. Despair hovered like a rain cloud looking to move in and burst over her.

He set his glass on a table and shrugged out of his new jacket, a vintage cut in light wool with leather patches at the shoulders. It was gorgeous on him, very debonair, but the dove-colored shirt beneath was equally smart, clinging to his muscled shoulders, buttons open in a V that showed his throat and collarbone and a few dark chest hairs.

He slung the jacket negligently over the back of the nearest chair, attention shifting to his phone. With a flick of his thumb across the screen, he paraphrased from something he was reading. "The spa is claiming they had no knowledge of the photos, but the press has found the same connection my team discovered this morning. Your masseuse is related to one of Jensen's employees. I'll take you to lodge a formal complaint with the police when we return to Milan so they can look at pressing charges for invasion of privacy."

"Charging the masseuse doesn't put the blame on Kevin, though, does it?"

"He has worked very hard to keep his hands clean, but we'll get there. It's early days yet." He picked up his glass and sipped, continuing to read his emails.

Days. It hadn't even been two full ones, but she'd already gone further with him than most of the men she'd dated for months. She was in so much trouble if that was a precursor of what was to come.

Pensively sipping the pale gold of the wine, she wound up exclaiming a very sincere, "Oh, that's very good!"

Not that she was any sort of connoisseur, but Travis always brought wine when she cooked and he didn't punish anyone with cheap stuff. She'd been enjoying trying bottles here in Italy and hadn't found a bad one, but this surpassed anything in her price range.

Vito glanced up, offering what looked like a very

genuine smile for a change. "It's the private reserve from my great-grandparents' vineyard. One of my cousins runs it and doles the bottles out to family every year. We could make a fortune, but it's too good to sell."

"Do you—" Gwyn forgot what she was going to ask as a flash of movement caught her eye.

Was that a little boy? He touched his lips to signal her to keep quiet as he climbed the rail that bordered the pool terrace then darted behind an oversize terracotta planter.

Vito followed her gaze and glanced backward at the empty landscape, then brought his alert frown back to her. "What's wrong?"

She started to say, "I saw a little boy—"

Before she could get the words out, the boy was barreling straight for Vito's legs.

In the same moment, Vito's expression hardened. He plunked his glass down and spun in a fluid motion, like he knew exactly what was coming. He crouched, grabbed, then threw the boy high into the air as he straightened, then caught him firmly and held him nose to nose.

"You little gremlin. I ought to throw *you* into the pool."

"Do it!" The boy's laughing eyes brightened with excitement. He splayed out his arms and legs, ready to fly through the air into the still, blue water despite being fully dressed.

"I won't," Vito told him, hitching the boy's wiry figure onto his arm so they were eye to eye. "That's your punishment for trying to push me in. No swimming at all. Say hello to Miss Ellis," he said, indicating her with a nod. "This is Roberto. He has all of his mother's sass and twice his father's disregard for danger."

"I was going to come in with you," the boy excused, curling his arm around Vito's neck and pressing his cheek to Vito's with open trust and affection. He was speaking perfect English but could have been Vito's son, his looks were so patently Italian. He turned his attention to Gwyn and pronounced what sounded like a coached speech. "It's nice to meet you. Welcome to our home." He offered his small hand for a shake, making it a firm one.

"It's a beautiful home," Gwyn said, ridiculously charmed, even though he couldn't have been more than five. "I'm very pleased to meet you, too."

Roberto gave her a stare reminiscent of Vito's most delving look.

"Are you American? Mama is Canadian and sometimes people think she's American, but your accent is different. You sound like our housekeeper in Charleston."

"Good ear," Gwyn said with a bemused smile. Honestly, he had more sophistication than some thirty-year-old executives she had met.

"Did you drive here yourself? Where is your father?" Vito asked, giving the boy a little bounce.

"He won't let me drive," Roberto said with a disgruntled scowl, then pointed to the top floor. "He's putting Bianca in her bed. She fell asleep in the car. She has a cold."

"He brought both of you? How is your mother?"

"So pregnant," a woman said, coming out the back door of the house.

Lauren Donatelli was very pregnant, but carried it

beautifully on her tall frame, glowing and graceful as she came down the short flight of steps onto the pool terrace, nary a waddle in her step.

Gwyn recognized her from photos she'd seen in the Charleston news several years ago, along with the odd image published in the company newsletter where Lauren invariably stood next to Paolo looking warm and approachable despite how aloof and distant her husband always seemed.

"Hi, I'm Lauren," she said, offering her hand.

"Gwyn," she murmured, and tried to thank her for the loan of clothes, but was waved off.

"Anything for Vito. Hello, *caro*," she said to him. He stooped a little so she could kiss both his cheeks.

"Should you be anywhere but a maternity ward?" he asked her.

"I offered to check myself into a clinic, but the doctor said there was no point since it will be at least two weeks. Paolo wouldn't let me stay in the city without him, of course. His mother is at the house, but you know what he's like. Won't let me out of his sight." She shook her head in exasperation.

"Roberto was born inside their front door. Bianca delivered in a car," Vito informed Gwyn.

"It was easier to lose the paparazzi waiting at the gate if we made it look like we were going for a simple family outing," Paolo said, arriving with a baby monitor that he set on the table next to Vito's wineglass. "Miss Ellis," he greeted with a cool nod.

"Signor Donatelli," she murmured, intimidated to the soles of her feet.

Thankfully his son pleaded, "May I swim, Papa. *Per favore?*"

"Vito and I must talk about work, but if you put on your trunks you can come to the shore with us and wade."

"Yes!" Roberto dropped out of Vito's arms and started to run toward the house.

"Quietly," Lauren warned, slowing his step. "Don't wake your sister. I'll start dinner," Lauren said with a well-practiced hostess smile.

"You will not," Paolo told her. "I'll cook when I come in. Stay off your feet."

A man willing to cook. Gwyn was so astonished it took her a moment to blurt out the sensible solution that broke the challenging stare between the married couple.

"I can make dinner."

Everyone looked at her. These two men really were too much masculinity in one impactful wall for any woman to handle.

"Unless you need me to be there while you talk?" She had no doubt she would be the topic of their discussion. Frankly, she was hoping to avoid listening to her humiliation being kicked over like something a dog owner had failed to dispose of properly.

"I would appreciate your cooking, if it's something you don't mind doing," Paolo said, then turned to his wife. "You may sit and chop tomatoes if you promise not to put your weight behind it."

She made a face at him.

"If our daughter wakes, would you call me?" he added to Gwyn. "She's under the weather and will want to be held, but Lauren needs to take it easy. At this stage the hiccups will start her labor. I have my hands full enough without catching a baby today."

"It's twenty minutes out of your life," Lauren murmured, looking at her fingernails. "I don't know what you're complaining about."

He caught her hand and brought her curled knuckles to his lips. "I can barely think of anything else as it is. You know that. Try to buy us a few more days while we settle this work crisis? Please?"

The looks they were giving each other were such a mix of open emotion, tender and teasing and loving, Gwyn knew she ought to look away. It was a private couple's moment, but it was so beautiful, she was transfixed. She wanted that. The cajole and silent communication and connection that bound in a thousand ways. The secretive smile. The way they looked like they wanted to kiss, but were in no hurry because Paolo was stroking her bent knuckle against his upper lip and they had an abundance of time and opportunities for loving affection.

"Maybe this one will have my patience instead of your lack of impulse control," Lauren teased. "We could get lucky."

"Do not blame me!" Paolo scoffed. "They wind up with your sense of humor and think it's funny—stop laughing. I'm serious. No laughing. You'll put yourself into labor."

Lauren disobeyed, releasing a hearty chuckle that made Gwyn smile along with her.

Their son came outside in his trunks and Gwyn turned her expression of amusement into a greeting for the boy, giving the couple their privacy to exchange a kiss.

When she glanced at Vito, she saw he was watching her, his expression unreadable.

* * *

A few minutes later, Gwyn was moving around Lauren's kitchen, chatting with her with surprising ease. Perhaps Lauren wasn't resting with her feet up as her husband had demanded, but since she wasn't holding anything heavier than a paring knife, Gwyn didn't say anything. Besides, every birth story she'd ever heard was a lengthy process, happening in the midnight hours. Lauren wasn't complaining of a backache or any of those other things women talked about as precursors to labor. She was relaxed and pleasant and ever so nice!

Feeling as vilified as she did, Gwyn was deeply relieved to be treated like a normal person.

"Did you get that top at the boutique on the far end of the lake?" Lauren asked. "I bought the red-and-gold one two months ago. They have amazing stuff, don't they?"

Gwyn agreed, then, as she set a pot of water to boil and the conversation lulled, she screwed up her courage and said, "I, um, lived in Charleston before I came here. I'm not trying to pry," she hurried to add. "I just thought I should tell you that I couldn't help but be aware of all the coverage about your husband. Um, first husband, I mean."

Lauren's expression smoothed to something very grave, gaze sliding away to hide her thoughts. "It was a heartbreaking time."

"I'm very sorry for your loss," Gwyn said quickly, feeling it was the decent thing to say to the widow of a war hero, but it wasn't why she'd brought it up. She wasn't asking the big question that had been on everyone else's mind at the time: had Lauren slept with her husband's best friend the night she had learned her husband was dead? The answer to that was outside throwing rocks into the lake, as far as Gwyn could tell.

"I wouldn't have mentioned it except... Is it bad taste to ask how you handled all the attention?" Gwyn asked.

Lauren smiled with empathy. "It's exhausting, isn't it? People so love to judge." She opened a cupboard and drew out a box of linguine noodles. "I guess you make peace with whatever you've done to get yourself into that situation and accept that you can't control what others think or say. It's what you think of yourself that matters."

"I'm obsessed with what other people think," Gwyn admitted glumly. She had a childhood full of starting new schools, being teased for being first to wear a bra, then constantly being underestimated because she was smarter than anyone expected from a girl with good looks.

Her mother had nursed the same sort of angst, having quite an inferiority complex due to an orphan's upbringing. Sometimes Gwyn wondered if that had been her mother's reason for moving so often—part habit, but also a continuous attempt to reinvent herself in hopes of ever-elusive acceptance.

For Gwyn, landing this job in Milan had been her first step in believing she really was good enough and smart enough to earn respect on her own merit, but she was seriously struggling to believe in herself now.

And while she could dismiss the dim views of strangers and comfort herself with the knowledge she hadn't done anything to deserve the humiliation she was suffering, she was acutely sensitive to what Vito might be thinking of her.

Why? Why couldn't she shrug off his judgment of her?

Because he affected her on every level, she acknowledged. Because he had literally controlled how she felt in the car today, working ecstasy through her. If he had the power to make her feel good, he also had the power to devastate her.

She started to blush, feeling the heat rise from deep spaces to become a hot glow on her cheeks. *Such* power. She wished she could get him out from under her skin!

"My turn to pry," Lauren said, handing Gwyn a bag of mushrooms, scanning Gwyn's guilty pink cheeks with interest. "This thing with you and Vito. Have you really been seeing him? Or is it just for show?"

"What?" Gwyn said dumbly, nerveless fingers nearly losing the featherweight of the bag.

"You don't have to tell me," Lauren said with a teasing twinkle in her eye. "I'm being nosy because he's one of my favorite people, but I realize there are things at the bank that can't be discussed. Believe me, I know." She made a face of long suffering. "But…" She sent Gwyn a cagey look as she moved to the sink. "I have a feeling that if he'd been seeing you before this story broke, I would have known."

"What do you mean?" Gwyn asked, knocked off balance by something she couldn't identify. Was she suggesting Vito acted differently around her? Lauren had only seen them together for a minute and a half before they'd come inside and the men had gone to the beach.

"I don't know. There's something in the way he looked at you—" Lauren shrugged, starting to wash her hands, then cut herself off as she gave the soap dispenser next to the sink a shake. "I think there's a new one in the upstairs bathroom," she said, turning off the tap.

"I'll get it," Gwyn said, setting down the mushroom she was stemming.

"I'll peek in on Bianca while I'm up there," Lauren said with a wave.

Seconds later, Lauren's voice was considerably less relaxed as she swore loud enough for Gwyn to hear her all the way down in the kitchen.

"Are you all right?" Gwyn called, making a panicked start up the stairs.

Lauren came to the open door of the main bathroom, bracing herself against it with a white-knuckled grip, expression somewhere between exasperated and remorseful.

"He's going to kill me. Tell Paolo my water just broke."

Vito was not a romantic, but he had seen the longing in Gwyn's expression and felt a kick of commiseration. Paolo and Lauren made anyone covetous of their happiness. He envied his cousin himself, not just for finding his soul mate, but for his freedom to pursue a life with her. Even if Vito did find the right woman...

He was adept at not letting himself dwell on such things and cut off the thoughts as he and Paolo took Roberto down to the water and exchanged reports.

Paolo expanded on what he'd already messaged, saying Fabrizio was a tough nut, but cracks were showing in his story. The board of Jensen's foundation was not yet moved to worry about any of this, let alone meeting to discuss Jensen's possible removal. Jensen himself was leaving the country for a minor quake that was more photo op than actual disaster relief, but would bolster his image.

"You haven't frozen the foundation's assets?" Vito asked.

"I don't have grounds. I'll be pushing for a forensic audit once Fabrizio breaks or we're able to prove Jensen was behind the instructions to move funds, but he is definitely playing a rough PR game right now. This—" He chucked his chin back toward the house and Gwyn. "I see where you're going and it would work if it was true, but I can't go on record saying that you've been having an affair with her all along. We all may have to testify at some point."

"Sì," Vito agreed. "But you can state that unnamed sources—me—" he shrugged "—made you aware some time ago that there were worrisome transactions within the account. We put it on a watch list and saw no reason to remove Miss Ellis because she was not only conducting herself with sound ethics, but has since proven to be an excellent source of knowledge with regards to the foundation's legitimate activities."

"You're convinced she has been conducting herself ethically?"

It was the judgment Vito had been avoiding making, aware that Gwyn was already a weakness to him. He wanted her and therefore he wanted to believe her, because how could he have an affair with a woman who was committing crimes against the bank? He couldn't gamble his family's future on his own selfish desires.

But at every stage, if she was the type to manipulate a man like Jensen, her actions would have been different, right up to this afternoon in the car. *He* would have been the one losing control to her hand or mouth, he was sure, if she was the type to lie and steal and wish him to believe otherwise.

At no time since he'd met her had Gwyn acted dishonorably, though. In fact, she was trying to protect the little family she had from the fallout of dishonor that, if she was innocent, wasn't hers to bear.

The problem was, if she *was* blameless, he was going to have to kill the man who had done this to her.

"I believe she is Jensen's victim, yes," Vito said, and heard the cruel edge on his tone. "They gambled on her lack of experience and when she showed her intelligence, they threw her to the wolves."

He understood the expression *bloodthirsty* as he said it. His tongue tingled and his throat tried a dry swallow, but he didn't long for water. He craved the tang of suffering for Jensen and Fabrizio and whoever had helped them by taking those photos.

He felt the quick slash of Paolo's glance before he returned his watchful gaze to his son, but his cousin obviously read his mood.

"So we imply you two have been having an affair all along and she's been feeding us information. What happens when I'm asked point-blank if I condone my VP of operations sleeping with a customer service rep?" Paolo folded his arms, eyes on his son, but his tone added, *Because I don't.*

"You never comment on the private lives of your family or your employees," Vito said, which was true. "But as a rule, you expect to be notified of such relationships in a timely manner and you have no quarrel with when and how your VP of operations has advised you of this connection."

Paolo shook his head, mouth pulled into a half smirk.

"People call me competitive, but strategy plays are your drug of choice, aren't they?"

"Live the lie and it becomes the truth," he said blithely.

Paolo sobered. "The photos certainly look convincing," he said with another pointed look, before returning his alert attention to his son in the water.

Vito had seen the photos online from today's shopping trip with Gwyn and last night's kiss. The passionate embrace on the stern of the yacht still made his pulse pound just thinking of it. His mind went to the car, the wet heat clenching his fingers as she shuddered and cried out with fulfillment.

There were a million reasons why he should merely *act* like they were an item, rather than make the affair real, but they would make it real. He knew it in the same way that adversaries knew a physical confrontation was coming. They could put it off, because they both knew in their gut that neither of them would come away unscathed, but their making love was inevitable.

"No comment?" Paolo prodded. "Because if she's a victim, don't make her more of one."

That stung. Vito hid it, countering lightly, "What do you want me to say? I like women. I can't help that they like me back."

It was the laissez-faire attitude he always affected when discussing paramours. Paolo was the head of the family. He couldn't escape marriage and the duty of producing progeny. Vito didn't have the same pressure to procreate. He was at liberty to play the field the rest of his life if he wanted to.

Paolo sent him a dour look, the one that told him Vito could show the rest of the world, pretend his entire life was one long, lighthearted affair, but he knew better.

Paolo knew him better than anyone. They had been adversaries themselves in childhood, scrapping constantly. Two strong-willed, alpha-natured boys of similar ages would. It had culminated in a fistfight of epic proportions when they were twelve, not far from here, on the property Vito's family still owned, high in the hills overlooking the lake. They had been beating each other with serious intent, their superficial argument transitioning into a far more serious drive for dominance over the other. Neither was the type to give up. Ever.

Paolo's father had stopped them. He'd been a man of strength and drive and purpose, the conservative head of the bank that had been the family's livelihood for generations. He was a loving man, a devoted uncle, a pillar of strength for all of them.

And he'd nearly cried when he'd pulled the boys apart.

You can't do this, his uncle had said. *No more. You're family.*

Vito didn't like upsetting his favorite uncle, but he had had nameless frustrations swirling inside him. He was claimed to be part of their clan, but he wasn't. Something was off and he knew it. He loved his parents. His mother doted on him. His father showed great pride in every one of Vito's accomplishments, but he didn't feel close to them. He was different. Not quite like them, not the same in temperament or looks as his sisters. He felt more kinship toward Paolo's father than his own. When they all came together for these sorts of big, family occasions, he caught watchful looks from some of the older aunts and uncles. It made him tense. Meanwhile, Paolo was so very confident in his own position, Vito was compelled to knock his cousin out of it.

So the angry accusation had come out. *Am I? Family?*

The way Paolo had looked to his father for that same answer, as if he too suspected Vito was not quite one of them, had been the most devastating blow of all.

Paolo's father had stood there with his hand on his hair, like he'd come across a bomb blast and was suffering a kind of shell shock himself, unable to make sense of the broken landscape.

Then, very decisively, he had nodded. *Fine. I'll tell you. Both of you.*

Vito had never questioned such huge news coming from his uncle, rather than his father. It was a Donatelli matter, after all. *He* was a Donatelli. Legally he was a Donatelli-Gallo. Women kept their maiden name when they married in Italy. He and his sisters used a hyphenated version of their parents' names, but he had always felt more drawn to the Donatelli side of his family and used that name to this day.

Because he had no Gallo in him, he had learned, sitting on a retaining wall overlooking the lake, hearing his uncle explain to him that his mother, his *real* mother, was the youngest Donatelli sibling, Zia Antoinietta. The aunt who had died and was rarely mentioned because her loss made everyone so sad. Vito would later look at her photographs and see more of himself in her than in her older sister, the woman who had called herself his mother all his life.

Your father was a dangerous man, Vito. Danger-

ous to us as a family, to the bank and very dangerous to your mother. I pulled her away from him so many times, but she kept going back. She was pregnant. She thought she loved him. I'll never forgive myself for not finding a way... She finally realized what was in store for both of you when he knocked her around and put her into labor. She called me to come to her where she was hiding from him. She died having you. I held her, waiting for the damned ambulance, and she begged me to keep you away from him, to keep you from turning into a mafioso like him. He wanted an heir to his empire, but it's a kingdom built on blood and suffering. We would have called you Paolo's brother, but well, you know the story we tell instead.

Vito did. His adoptive mother, the middle sister, often told the story of how she had thought she had miscarried, but Vito had miraculously survived. In reality, she and her husband had spirited her sister's newborn to the family home at the lake and waited out a suitable time before presenting Vito as their son. His birthday was off by four months.

I paid a fortune to the doctors to write out a certificate that you had died with her. And threatened your father with murder charges if the affair ever came out. I'm certain he would come for you if he knew you survived, Paolo's father had warned.

Vito could only imagine the fortune Paolo's father had paid to keep the liaison from becoming public knowledge and destroying the bank as it was. If online scandal rags had existed then, the affair wouldn't have suppressed as easily, he was sure.

Your mother was too precious to me, you are too

precious to me, for me to watch you two beating each other senseless. Turning to Paolo, he had lifted his shirt, showing a long scar that had always been blamed on surgery, but not today. *Did I take this knife trying to bring home my sister so my own son could kill hers? Save your strength for the fights that matter, then fight them together. Understand?*

He hadn't had to warn them to keep the secret. That was a given. He had risen and urged Paolo to come with him, to give Vito time alone.

No, Paolo had said. *I'll stay.*

They had sat in silence a long time, the space Paolo's father had taken up a wide gap between them. Finally Paolo had said, *Do you want to punch me?*

Yes, Vito had seethed. But he hadn't. They'd never fought again. They rarely mentioned it. Eventually Vito had learned the name of his biological father and the man's predilection for violence had sickened him. Then there was the second son's equally conscienceless disposition.

Vito wanted to believe he was different, but how could he claim to be a better man than what he'd come from when just the thought of those men and their actions put him into a state of mind willing to crush and kill? Vigilante justice was still brute force and only proved he was more like his biological father than he wanted to admit.

So he couldn't in good conscience make children with a woman without telling her what kind of blood he carried and he couldn't reveal the truth without endangering his family and the bank.

Therefore, he was a confirmed bachelor, destined to have affairs with women who didn't expect a future and to commiserate with the struggles of child-rearing from the sidelines.

"Your lips are blue. Come out," Paolo ordered his son.

"Three more," Roberto said, holding up three quivering fingers, teeth chattering, narrow shoulders shaking as he prepared to dive for yet another colored rock.

"One," Paolo said firmly.

"Two," Roberto responded.

"Everything is a negotiation," Paolo muttered, making Vito set his teeth because Paolo was complaining about a privilege not every man had. "Two. Then—"

"Paolo!" Gwyn came to the rail above them, at the edge of the pool deck. Her eyes were wide, her face pale. "Lauren says her water broke!"

Paolo went white and grim, swearing tightly. "Out, Roberto. Now. Stay with Vito," he ordered his son, locking gazes with Vito long enough to cement the command that Vito keep his son from drowning, but also sharing a moment of genuine fear.

It struck Vito that Paolo had never told Lauren why he didn't find these home births of hers as much of a joke as she did. He knew women could die.

It also told him how volatile his secret still was, if Paolo hadn't shared it with the woman who was his other half.

"I'll call the ambulance," he said to Paolo's back, pulling out his phone as his cousin took the stone stairs in great leaps, already pushing back his sleeves.

CHAPTER SEVEN

"THAT WAS THE most remarkable experience of my life," Gwyn said forty minutes later, as the ambulance carried off a grumbling Lauren and an infant boy who had squawked once, latched perfectly, then fallen asleep snuggled against her.

"They're just going to tell me that everything is fine and I can go home if I want to. I wish you hadn't called them," Lauren scolded Vito on her way out the door.

"Humor us, *mia bella*," Paolo said with equanimity, buttoning his clean shirt with hands that might have tremored a little, but he'd barely broken a sweat while carrying his wife to their bed and catching their son minutes later.

He'd been very coolheaded, calling Gwyn to bring him the bag he'd prepared with clean towels and receiving blankets, speaking to his wife in a calm, tender tone, using sterilized clips and scissors from the bag to cut the cord himself, as if he'd been a midwife all his life.

Their daughter slept through most of it, waking in time to glimpse her new brother, but quite content to cuddle with Vito amidst all the activity. Roberto called the little girl Bambi, which was adorable, and both children stayed with Gwyn and Vito while Paolo went in the ambulance with his wife. A car pulled out from the house across the street where the drivers and other ancillary staff were staying, following to bring them back once Lauren and the baby had been examined.

Vito didn't say anything as he closed the door. In fact, his color was down and he took a measured breath as if he'd just dodged a train.

"You're green around the gills, Vittorio," Gwyn chided, amused. "Were you worried?" She hadn't had time to panic and was riding a high of amazement.

"Lauren makes it look easy," he said in a tone that suggested he was well aware labor and delivery didn't always go so smoothly.

"I'll say," Gwyn responded. "I didn't even get the water boiled!" She moved into the kitchen where she had managed to snap off the gas on her way to fetch Paolo. "Shall I finish making dinner?"

"We'll help," Vito said, sliding Bianca onto a stool while Roberto climbed into the one his mother had been using. Vito was very good with the children and they openly adored him, grinning at his teasing, behaving angelically as he gently kept them on task.

Vito exchanged several texts with Paolo, who mentioned that everything was fine but there was a small delay in seeing the doctor.

"Paolo will be taking some family time now that the baby is here," Vito said to Gwyn. "We had planned for this, but we'll have a proper meeting when he gets back to review a few things before I assume his duties. You and I will spend the night here and head back to the city in the morning."

Gwyn nodded absently, too caught up in watching him cut up a little girl's food, steady Roberto's hand as he shook out red pepper flakes then smoothly reached to top up Gwyn's wineglass with a practiced flair. Throw in his ability give a woman orgasms and get the laundry done and he was the perfect man in every way.

He met her gaze.

Her thoughts must have reflected in her it. Building a career had been a dominating goal in her life, partly because she'd seen how hard her mother had struggled to support herself without a proper profession. Gwyn had focused on her degree and finding the right job and chasing opportunities for advancement. It had meant relegating a husband and children to a dreamy "some-day" that she hoped would find her when the time was right.

But she longed for a place to settle and call home. She wanted a family within it that wasn't a tenuous late-in-life connection, but a network of blood ties like this family had, where a woman could be nosy about a man simply because she cared about him. She could leave her children with him in utter confidence that he would keep them safe and give them the affectionate security that fed their souls.

"Be careful, Gwyn," Vittorio said with gentle gravity, holding her gaze.

She scanned for hazards the children might tip before meeting his gaze again, confused.

He wore the tough, circumspect look of the man who'd first stared her down in Nadine Billaud's office.

"This is not our life," he said in the same temperate tone. "Not yours. Not mine. So stop thinking it will happen."

She was far too transparent around him. It was achingly painful to be this obvious, especially when he had touched her so intimately they were practically lovers, then shot down her dreams so dispassionately, leaving her nursing a giant ache that hollowed out her chest.

"Not with you, perhaps," she said, lifting her glass and her chin, holding his gaze even though the locked stare made her stomach cramp. "But there's no reason I can't have something like this, someday. Is there?" she challenged.

He might have flinched, but she wasn't sure.

And the silence went on long enough for her to remember her own notoriety. Would anyone want her after this? Ever?

A noise at the door told them the new parents had returned.

Gwyn rose to set two more places, grateful for a reason to turn away and hide that her eyes were welling up.

"Do you need the address for my flat?" Gwyn asked the driver as they slid into the car the next morning.

"I have it, thank you," the driver assured her as he closed her door for her.

The air was fresh, the sun shining and the children had both hugged her at the door. Nevertheless, Gwyn's good mood took a dip when Vittorio made no protest against her going home.

She wasn't about to ask him what *he* had planned for her, though. She had lain awake a long time last night considering her options. Her life wasn't over, she had concluded. It just needed to be re-envisioned.

As Vito flicked through messages on his tablet, she took a firm grip on the future she had outlined for herself. She opened her social media accounts and started removing objectionable posts. Dear Lord there were some nasty people out there. Some thought she was a harlot, others offered to do lewd things to her...

She didn't realize she was making noises like she was being roundly beaten in a boxing ring until Vito asked sharply, "What are you reading?"

"I want to connect with a headhunter to start searching out a position for when this is over." She winced as an invitation to hook up flashed into her eyes with a photo that couldn't be deleted fast enough. "I have to clean up my news feeds first, before potential employers look them over. It's a minefield."

"*You* don't," he growled, reaching across to click off her phone. "Plumbers exist to clean up sewage. I've already assigned you a PR assistant. She'll meet with you this afternoon and scrub all of this."

The last thing she wanted was to accept more generosity from him, but she was too grateful to refuse.

"And I'll see that you have a suitable position when the time comes so don't put out feelers for a job yet. It sends the wrong message."

"What does 'suitable' mean?"

"Something equivalent or better to the position you had, so you're not set back in your career. I've discussed it with Paolo and you'll receive a glowing recommendation, a severance package and a settlement for the damage caused by our leaving you in the position of working with Jensen despite having him under investigation. We've agreed that if we had removed you when we became suspicious, the photos wouldn't have happened, so we'll be accepting responsibility for that. We'll work out the exact details once we have Jensen on the ropes."

She blinked, stunned. Inside her chest, her heart rose like the sun from behind dark mountains, beaming light through her whole being. Lightness. The weight of being mistrusted lifted and something like hope dawned in her for the first time since she'd walked into Nadine's office and seen those photos.

"You believe me?" The words were very tentative. She could barely take it in.

"I do." His expression was grave, but there was a hard light in his eyes, not hostile, but daunting. It leaned even more impact to his words as he said, "These actions against you will not go unpunished."

She didn't fear him in that moment, but she recognized that he was a man to be feared.

And she was so relieved to have him on her side, so touched that he believed her, she grew teary and had to look away, unable to even voice a heartfelt, *Thank you*.

"But for now your occupation is 'mistress.'"

She flung her head around to confront him. "Did you say that to make me angry?"

He didn't glance up from flicking the screen on his tablet. "I said it because it's true."

"Oh, well, pray tell, what are the duties of that position? Does it come with benefits?" *Shut up, Gwyn*.

He took his time letting her regret that impulsive outburst, slowly lifting his attention to scan her expression while a faint smile played around his lips.

"Amusing me is your primary function," he said, adding a sardonic, "Check."

Then he had the audacity to let his gaze take a leisurely tour down her new top. It was a simple low-necked, peach-colored silk with a pleat at her cleavage. Not particularly sexy, but he seemed to look right through it, making her breasts feel heavy and her nipples tight. She found herself pressing her jeans-clad thighs together as a throb hit where he'd caressed her in this very backseat yesterday.

"We've covered the benefits," he added. "And that you may take advantage of them as often as you see fit."

"And this is supposed to fill up my nine-to-five?" she shot back, trying to cover her pulsing response, flicking her glance at the closed privacy screen while she willed her fierce blush to recede.

"I can't make love to you *all* day, *cara*. I have responsibilities."

She tried to send him a disgusted glare, but anticipation curled through her despite herself, melting her insides and turning her on. Yes, his low voice and sexy promise made her hot, curse him.

"Did you relive it last night?" he asked in a low tone of lusty pleasure. "I did. I wanted you to come to me, so I could feel you fall apart like that again. Under me this time."

Her stomach swooped and she turned her face to the window, trying to hide that she had toyed with the idea of going to him. She had ached with desire and had had to fight against the urge.

"I need to find healthier ways to deal with my situation than cheap sexual gratification," she said.

"Stop calling it cheap." His voice lashed with quick anger, making all the hairs rise on her body.

Now who was angry and who was laughing? She looked back at him and let him see her smug delight in getting a rise out of him.

"I'm sorry," she said with mock regret. "This is becoming quite expensive for you, isn't it? Because if you won't let me get a real job, you'll have to cover the lease on my flat." It was a childish jab and promptly fell flat.

"That's already in the works."

Her smarmy grin fell away.

He smiled at having drawn the wind from her sails. "I've had mistresses before," he added calmly, sobering a few degrees as he added, "Never one who has moved in with me, but we have a message to broadcast. I've assigned you an assistant. She'll send you our calendar shortly."

Moved in? *Our* calendar?

"I thought I was going back to my flat." She glanced toward the driver who had said he had her address.

"To get your passport and any other personal items you don't want to leave for the movers. Am I speaking English? Why are you staring at me like that?"

"When did I agree to move in with you? Do I get my own room?"

"Do you want one?" he asked, sounding oh-so-reasonable against her high pitch of disbelief, but the knowing slant to his half-closed lids made the question not just annoying, but far too rhetorical.

She didn't know how to be sophisticated and blasé about agreeing to be his lover. She was still fighting the longing to. Deep down, however, she knew she wanted to go to bed with him, and very likely would, which was the most aggravating part of it all.

Thankfully her phone buzzed. She glanced to see her new assistant was loading her calendar.

Gwyn scanned through, seeing that she had legal meetings, appointments with her PR assistant, stylists, boutiques—

"A *spa*?" she said sharply to Vito.

"All the women in my family frequent it. Don't worry. It's secure."

Luncheons, dinners—

"Berlin?"

"I have meetings." He shrugged.

London, Paris, back to Milan then three stops in Asia.

"What am I doing while you're working in all these places?" she asked, mind whirling.

"You'll have a security detail. Do whatever you want. Shop, visit the museums. You won't have as much time as you think. I'll need you at my side quite often."

She spent the rest of the drive answering questions for her assistant: Did she have any special dietary requirements or allergies? Any requests for products to have on hand at Vito's apartment or while she traveled? Was she due for any dental or medical appointments that should be scheduled? What about prescription refills?

More birth control pills? Was that what she was asking, Gwyn wondered with mild hysteria?

When they arrived in the city, they went straight to her building where a handful of photographers quickly snapped to attention from slouching on scooters and hovering on stoops. Vito's security guards kept them at a respectful distance and movers arrived shortly after Gwyn entered her flat.

The place was untouched, her plate with toast crumbs from a few days ago still sitting by the sink, but everything had changed. Not just her life, but there was something in *her* that was changing. She was a self-sufficient person, didn't want to look to Vito to rescue her like some kind of damsel needing a white knight, but as he gave instructions and spoke to her landlord to assure him the crowds at the entrance to the building would cease now that she was leaving, she felt grateful to have him on her side.

She hated feeling weak and managed and power-less, but if someone else was stealing control of her life, she was glad the rudder had wound up in his un-erring hands.

She trusted him, she realized. It was a weird sort of trust. He could and probably would hurt her, but he wasn't making any false promises not to. He wouldn't lie to her, even if the truth was harsh and unpalatable.

His governance over her world proved very advanta-geous when she made her statement to the police, too. Had she been merely a midlevel bank employee with no connections or legal team behind her, her complaint probably wouldn't have been such a priority, but she was assured charges against her masseuse would be forthcoming.

The rest of the day passed in a blur. There was a very short press conference announcing the birth of Paolo's son, Vito's assumption of his cousin's position for the next few weeks and he confirmed rumors that a formal internal investigation had been launched against an un-named, but high profile account.

"For privacy and legal reasons, we can't expound on that," Vito said.

Then he sent a look to Gwyn that said everything his mouth did not. His expression spoke of regret and guardianship and the suppressed anger of a warrior who must wait for the war. Which might have been a bit of overacting for the cameras, but she thought it had its seeds in what he had said earlier about Jensen not going unpunished.

And she was touched all over again.

The press conference had been held at a hotel where Vito was due to meet with various heads of the bank's branches before attending a mixer with those same people, their spouses and an exclusive list of their top-tier investors.

"It was scheduled a year ago, long before any of this hit the fan," he said, sending her to a penthouse suite with an entourage who coached her on everything from staying on message—*The investigation is ongoing. I can't comment.*—to how to lengthen her lashes most effectively.

She was mentally and emotionally exhausted when they all finally left her alone, seriously wishing she could go to bed instead of having to go out.

Then Vito materialized from the second bedroom like a freshly groomed panther, his black tuxedo a second skin, the white of his pleated shirt and bow tie a blaze that set off his swarthy skin tone, hollow cheeks and straight black brows. His hair, just a shade too long to be a conservative business cut, gave him the perfect balance between decadent playboy and powerful executive.

His silk pocket square exactly matched the reflective, lake blue of her gown.

She'd never worn anything so elegant or daring, with its strapless bodice and low back. The sweep of the skirt was gathered in loose edges, forming a slit over her left leg, and was ruched together with a sparkling broach on her hip, making her feel graceful and sexy at once.

She felt sensual. Beautiful. And, as she stood looking at the beautiful man before her, she felt for the first time like she was his match.

Vito was trying to make it to the end of a trying day. He understood the concerns of those around him, the questioning of his choice in female companionship, but he couldn't understand why he was so angered by all of it. He kept telling himself it was the bank he wanted to defend. To protect.

But it was Gwyn. He wanted to sweep a sword through the air to cut down all this resistance against his being with her.

And this was why.

She stood before him like a water deity, wearing that swirl of river blue and sapphires that gleamed like bubbles against her neck and ears. Her hair was caught in a low knot against the back of her neck, wisps framing her introspective expression, mysterious and enthralling.

She was a prize, a weapon, an illicit substance. She was something he wanted. Badly.

His libido was becoming a monster, first hooked by spending nearly every moment with her for the past forty-eight hours, then feeling her absence as he'd pushed her to the sidelines to weather attacks from close quarters.

It had left him keyed up, mood balanced on a knife's edge, the outlaw in him looking to ignore any sort of rules or propriety and simply take her, make her his. This wasn't the first time he'd chafed against the constraints he placed upon himself, but he always maintained this veneer of civility painted onto him by the family who had kept him alive, safe and living within the law.

She didn't want cheap gratification, he reminded himself, and heard Paolo again. *If she's a victim, don't make her more of one.* He kept remembering that look in her eye as they'd played house for an hour with Paolo's children. If only the world understood how laughable it was to think *she* was inferior to *him*.

"You look nice," he said gruffly, trying not to let the vision she made break the shackles controlling him. He moved to hold the door. "Let's get this over with."

She made a noise that might have been one of injury and muttered, "That's what she said," as she passed him into the hall.

"*What* did you just say?" he asked tightly.

Gwyn grappled her feelings back into their box, telling herself to quit taking his lack of real interest in her as a slight.

"It's just something people say. One of those online memes," she said, striding purposefully beside him toward the elevator. "Why are you so grouchy?"

The hotel was pure opulence, the carpets cushioning each step, the rail dripping leafy plants in terraced layers down to the lobby forty stories below.

He pressed the call button for the elevator and said, "I'm not."

She glanced around, saw they were alone and said, "You know, we may not have much, but I thought we had honesty. If you don't want to tell me, say it's none of my business. But don't lie."

His gaze widened at her audacity, making her swallow. But honestly. She was doing everything she was told, letting him treat her like a puppet after she'd already been misused. What else did he want from her?

The elevator arrived and an older couple stepped off, leaving them to enter the empty car alone, replacing what might have been an air of relaxed camaraderie with a charged energy that bounced off the refined walls.

At least it wasn't one of those glass boxes that made you feel airsick as you descended. It was red velvet and had mirrored panels split by a flat rectangle of gold for a handrail. A chipper, understated soft shoe drifted from the speakers, sounding incongruous.

"If you must have the truth, *cara*, I've been warned several times today that our relationship is ill-advised," he said, stabbing at a floor number, then thumbing hard into the door close button. "I know they're right, but I don't care. I want you, anyway. If we'd stayed in the room, I would have kept you there."

"Really?" she derided. "I thought I just asked you not to lie to me? Because you've never once acted like you wanted anything to do with me."

"Ha!" He punched the side of his fist into the red emergency button, stalling the elevator with a jar and a short buzz, making her stagger and reach for the rail. "The very fact that you can't read the signs tells me how ill-suited you are for an affair. But, just so we're crystal clear, *cara*, I don't care about that, either. *I want you.*"

She couldn't look away from him, fascinated by the way his gold-brown eyes shot glittering shards of bronze.

He stepped closer, setting one hand then the other on the wall next to her head, leaning in. "I wanted you when you smiled across the lobby and you were already under suspicion, so I couldn't do a damn thing about it. I wanted you when I looked at this..." His boiling metal gaze slid down her front, scalding her. "And I knew every other man in the world was looking at you, too." His gaze flashed up, bright and piercing. "I want to kill each and every one of them," he added tightly. "Especially Jensen."

Her knuckle bumped his side and she realized her hand had lifted of its own volition, moving to press against her chest and keep her heart inside its cage. It slammed hard and fast.

He looked at her splayed fingers. "Scared?"

"I honestly didn't think you..." Her voice trailed off as his expression hardened with accusation.

"How could you not know? You look at me constantly. I *feel* it. How could you not be aware that I'm watching you, too?" He picked up her hand and pressed it to his own chest, where his heart punched against her palm. "You felt this in the car, when just my touch made you scream with pleasure. How could you not know it's the same for me?"

Emotion pressed at the backs of her eyes and thickened her throat.

He watched her struggle to swallow and cupped his hand under her jaw, palm against her throbbing artery, thumb caressing the hollow below her ear.

"The only thing holding me back, *mia bella*, is your indecision. Have you made up your mind yet? Do you want cheap, physical gratification?" The bitterness in his tone scraped at something in her, making her squirm in a kind of guilt.

She had hurt him with that? She searched his eyes, the windows into his soul. "What else would it be?" she asked in a near whisper.

His lips hardened and his brow lowered in consternation. "I don't know. But it would be a hell of a lot more than that."

She lifted her hand to the side of his face, drew him in and pressed a kiss of apology onto his mouth. It was perfect and sweet and healing.

And a mistake.

With a moan from her and a tortured groan from him, they laced themselves together, mouths opening with instant passion, dragged together like magnets meeting its attractor. His fingers dug into her back, her bottom, crushing her close. She arched into his steely body, loving his strength and the smell of him and that firm evidence of arousal that was not purely incidental, but his reaction to *her*.

He pressed her into the wall with his body, stilling the rock of her hips with a hard pin of his own. "You want me," he said against her lips. It was a demand for confirmation.

"I do," she admitted with an ache of helpless need.

"Now?"

"Wh-what?" She opened her eyes to see a fiery passion in him that was barely controlled. This man who seemed to have command of the entire world was so affected by her, he was looking at her with a kind of desperation. She thought she could feel each pulse pound in him, rocking his entire being.

"Here?" she asked. She was achy and heavy and ready. The thought of waiting until they were upstairs— it was too far.

This was insanity. Complete insanity.

"No?" He shuffled closer, feet between hers, one hand going to the slit in her skirt, finding her bare thigh and stroking across her skin like magic. "If not here, say so now."

She might have hung on to a shred of decorum if

he hadn't found the front of her lace undies and traced lightly while his mouth found the side of her neck at the same time. Need flooded through her at that light caress. She gasped with longing, clinging to his shoulders, trying to keep her knees locked so she wouldn't wilt right to the floor.

"Open my pants," he said, breath hot on her skin while the nibble of his lips made her shiver with pleasure and that exploring touch worked past the edge of lace into wetness and need. She made a guttural sound of pure excitement as he circled and pressed the swollen bud he found. His other hand was gathering her skirt out of the way, lifting her bare thigh to his hip, opening her to his flagrant touch.

"We can't," she gasped, but her hands worked the button on his pants, the fly. She had never tunneled her hand into the heated front of a man's trousers, but there was his shape filling her palm, naked and hot and silky. He was commando, shockingly bare to her touch, smooth with a graze of rough hair at the base, so steely and thickly aroused she gasped and clenched in anticipation.

He bent his knees, urging her to line him up as he shifted her underwear to the side. He traced his thick tip along her seam, parted, sliding easily against her then probing. "Do I need a condom?"

Late for that, wasn't it? She was dying! Panting with excitement.

"I'm on the pill," she managed to say, moving in invitation. She wanted him so badly. *Now.*

Their breaths mingled. His nostrils flared as he found her opening and pressed with more purpose. Nerves made her stiffen slightly, but she was eager, anxious as she looked into his eyes, wanting him to like it, wanting this to be good.

"Oh," she whispered as he pushed the tip in, stretching her. Her gaze clouded and her breaths grew uneven. When she clenched on him, little shock waves of pleasure jolted through her. Her eyelids grew heavy and wanted to close.

He pressed farther in, his weight driving her against something that dug into her back. She wriggled, making a noise of discomfort. "The rail—"

He smoothly lifted her, one hand going under her bottom where he balanced her above that infernal rail and then he was firmly seated all the way in, eye to eye with her. It was incredibly intimate. Man and woman. Steel and silk. Their panting breaths humid against each other's lips.

"Hold on to me," he rasped.

She closed her legs around his waist, twined her arms over his shoulders.

He moved, watching her expression as he withdrew and returned, driving in deep, holding there a moment, then dragging out slow, tantalizing her to new heights, arousing her with each thrust. Then he built the tempo to swift thrusts that were exciting and delicious and sent her racing up the slopes of need.

She clung to him with every part of her. He was hard everywhere, tense and determined. Her lips ached to be kissed, but she needed air. She couldn't look away from his gaze, watchful, waiting, demanding. It was too wild, too erotic, too scorchingly fast. She was there, right there, shuddering and flying apart. Finally closing her eyes as the pleasure detonated into something otherworldly.

A deeply animalistic noise left him as he arched deep and pulsed inside her, holding her in that state of ecstasy.

She gloried in the moment, body electrified as they completely possessed each other, united in this moment of culmination.

CHAPTER EIGHT

GWYN COULDN'T BELIEVE she had let him do that to her. Her legs were still trembling as she joined him inside the ballroom, having slipped into the ladies' room the minute they left the elevator to recover herself.

"*Cara*, please meet some friends of mine," he said, settling his arm around her as he introduced her.

It was different. She was different and they were different. Her world had been upended all over again. The sexual awareness was still there, but instead of being a sharp, unmet need, it was a deep, perilous knowledge. She knew what her body was capable of. He did. They both knew what he could do to her, how he could strip her of willpower and blind her with desire. She wondered if she had really done the same to him because he didn't seem as affected.

His arm sat heavier on her, more possessive, but when his glance came into her eyes, his held the light of memory and male satisfaction, but none of her wariness.

She was suffering all the same crush and attraction and fascination, but it was even more painful now. Before, she had yearned for him to match this feeling. Now she knew it didn't matter if he did. She was lost regardless.

It made the stares and the curled lips and the dismissive way people treated her as he introduced her all the harder to bear.

She said nothing, still wondering how on earth she would survive Vito let alone the rest of all that had happened. It made her desperate for reassurance, but he was no help, standing here looking indifferent, letting one of his executives from New York talk his ear off about some policy Vito had assigned him to write.

To her, it sounded a lot like a guy trying to impress the boss by telling him how hard he was working, rather than actually doing the work.

Meanwhile, Gwyn realized she knew the woman from the Charleston branch who had just caught her eye. Here would come a gauntlet of questions. This was going to be the worst night of her life.

The moment she tried to excuse herself, however, Vito's arm hardened on her.

"I should say hello to Ms. Tamsin," Gwyn said, caught between homesickness and dread. She would love to hear the news on her former colleagues, but really didn't want to talk about herself.

"I'll come with you." Vito nodded at the man who'd been pontificating.

"But I want your advice!" the executive blurted.

Gwyn was so far into her own head, she completely misplaced where she was and who they were talking to. In that moment, a coworker was asking for guidance so she offered it. "Why don't you use the UK model as a template? Tailor it to US regulations and plug in that bit about interstate transfers. The section on overseas rates should work almost word for word."

The surprised pause and dumbfounded stares from

both men were almost laughable, except Gwyn realized how badly she'd overstepped and instantly wanted to die of embarrassment. She never would have spoken to Oscar Fabrizio or any other higher-up that way. No, she would have done that work for him, she thought privately, and let him take the credit. Such was the life of lower-level administrators.

The executive was taken aback and glanced between her and Vito, as if to say, *Are you going to let your porn star girlfriend talk to me like that?*

"Excellent suggestion," Vito said. "Why reinvent the wheel? I'll expect to see the draft tomorrow," he told his executive and walked her away.

"I'm sorry," she mumbled.

"For what?"

"Interjecting like that."

"Why? You were right. I would have thought of it myself eventually, but I wasn't really listening. Too busy thinking of something else," he said with a pointed look that shot sexual heat from her heart to her loins. "I've never gone without a condom before. That was exciting. *Grazie, mia bella.*"

Her hand tightened on his sleeve as her knees wobbled, making him smile like a shark.

The rest of the evening was a trial, but she got through it. And when they were leaving, he surprised her by taking her downstairs to a waiting car instead of back up to the penthouse he'd already paid for.

"What about the early morning meetings you have here tomorrow?" She tilted her head at the hotel. "I thought that's why we were staying here."

"I want you in my bed."

Her skin tightened in reaction. "Okay."

* * *

Vittorio was not a weak or needy man. He loved his family and would certainly be a lesser man without them, but he considered himself a supporter of *them*, not the other way around. He wasn't a dependent personality, either. He drank a glass of wine most days because it was a cultural habit, not because he was addicted.

Gwyn was another story.

As he tied his tie, he glanced at her sleeping form reflected beyond his shoulder, brunette hair spilled across his pillow where she'd rolled to hug it when he'd risen, murmuring a sleepy and satisfied, "Thank you," before falling back asleep.

Words she had promised him he would never hear, he thought edgily, still high on the powerful orgasm they'd shared from a very lazy missionary lock in the predawn hour, the paroxysm holding them gasping for long, exquisite moments.

It had been two weeks and, if anything, the chemistry between them was stronger. If he was in her presence, he wanted to touch her. If he touched her, he wanted to have sex with her.

His desire was becoming the sort of all-consuming hunger that he arranged the rest of his life around. If he had other thoughts, they tended to be of the reckoning kind: dark acts of retaliation against Jensen and his cohorts. He wanted justice for Gwyn, but not necessarily the legal kind that would put an end to their reason for being together.

"I'm jealous," Gwyn said in a soft morning voice that lifted the hairs all over his body.

"Of whom?" he asked, reaching for his suit jacket, shrugging it on like armor.

He'd had these sorts of conversations before, but he had to admit to shock that Gwyn would have any reason to feel possessive. Had he even looked at another woman since meeting her? If he had, it was a comparison that Gwyn always won. Not just in looks, either. If he heard a woman laugh, he thought the sound too sharp or coarse, not the perfect joyful huskiness of Gwyn's. None seemed to have her same intuitive ability with conversation either, steering seamlessly from business to small talk to current events. His lack of interest in other women might have worried him if his libido hadn't been showing such vigor and health in bed with this one.

"You," she answered ruefully, rolling onto her back and throwing her arm over her head. "Going to work." She touched the headboard, looking up to the pattern her finger found and traced.

Her remark didn't entirely surprise him. He might have had innumerable mistresses who expected to be supported, but his sisters and the bank's abundance of female employees told him that many women enjoyed their careers as much as men did. Gwyn was bright and confident and had had clear goals before Jensen had derailed her. A life of leisure was not something she had aspired to—which was yet another side of her character that set her apart and shone a favorable light upon her in his eyes.

It was also why he enjoyed supporting her. She didn't expect to be spoiled so her reaction was priceless when he collared her with precious stones and shackled her with gold bracelets. Her protests against his generosity were refreshing, her newness to belonging to a man endearing.

He moved to the bed and lowered to hitch his hip beside hers, splaying his hand over the rumpled sheet that covered her belly. "I thought you enjoyed the art exhibit yesterday?" He had liked watching her face light with enthusiasm as she had told him about it last night.

"I did. I'm not sure your bodyguards did, though." She covered his hand, traced her light touch over the backs of his fingers, sending a ripple of pleasure down his back, as if he was a wolf being petted by a maiden.

"Well-secured places like art galleries make their job easy. They're happy to follow you around one." That wasn't the real issue, he could tell, but he didn't know what else she needed to hear. Perhaps, "Rather than go back to Milan when I finish here, why don't we take a few days on the water?" he suggested. "I'll hire a yacht."

Her gaze met his. "I feel like I'm back in my childhood, moving around before I can establish myself, not even trying to make friends because there's no point."

He frowned, having supposed that she connected with her friends online when he wasn't around, but she never mentioned any conversations or told anecdotes, he realized. She'd already told him that the family she did have was a very loose tie. She was still too embarrassed to speak directly to her stepfather and was keeping to short texts with her stepbrother.

He couldn't imagine living in that sort of social desert. He had curtailed a lot of his nonbusiness dinners because of work pressures and was sidestepping family occasions to avoid awkward questions about his relationship with Gwyn, but he was Italian. An active social life was in his biological makeup.

"Why did you move so often?" he asked her.

She shrugged. "Every reason. Lost job, better job, good luck, bad luck, harassment, location…I think the biggest reason was that Mom had itchy feet. That's why she married my dad, to move to America. She and Henry were going to travel once I finished school." Her fingertips smoothed under his cuff, tracing the band of his watch. "I wanted to see the world, too, but by moving to a new city and settling in, so I could absorb the culture and become part of the community."

Whatever friendships she'd made in Milan had been blown apart by the photos and her termination. He hadn't forbidden her from contacting any of her co-workers or neighbors, but she had isolated herself and he'd been pleased to keep things simple. He wondered now if he should make more of an effort to draw her into his own circles, but to what end? This was a temporary affair, not a relationship.

And knowing their time together was finite, he found himself very unwilling to share her.

"No news from Paolo about how much longer the investigation will take?" she asked.

"No," he said so abruptly her eyes widened and a shadow of injury crept across the back of her gaze. He mentally kicked himself for revealing the brute that he was, but her question almost sounded as though she was anxious to end things and he wasn't ready.

"Living in limbo is hard," she said in stiff explanation, trying to sit up.

He gathered her tense form into his lap, looking at the pugnacious glare she tilted up at him. He pressed a kiss against her firmly closed mouth.

"I'm hearing you," he told her, thinking about those times when he caught a faraway, melancholy expression on her face. He had put those moments down to her distress over the photos, but there was more to it, he realized now. She was a woman longing to put down roots. "I'm not dismissing you. But there's nothing I can do right now."

"And nothing I can do either, apparently."

"Fold my socks?" he suggested, since she often nagged him to pick his up.

She snapped her teeth at him in playful retaliation.

He kissed her again and this time she softened and kissed him back.

But he was still thinking about her discontent when he broke from his meeting with the Hong Kong consortium and picked up a message from Paolo: *Fabrizio is asking for leniency in exchange for full disclosure. We could see charges against Jensen early next week.*

The tide was turning.

The need for their affair was almost over.

Gwyn was in a type of shock as they returned to Vito's penthouse less than a week later, mind still caught up in all that had just been said at the press conference and after it. *Be careful what you wish for,* she thought bleakly. She had been anxious to embark on her future and here it was.

"I wish to say a special thank-you to Miss Ellis for her patience and unwavering integrity during this entire process," Paolo had said. "Due to the sensitive nature of the investigation, we asked her not to make any public comments during a time that has obviously been very distressing for her."

The cameras' lenses had shifted to where she had stood next to Vito, trying to capture her reaction, which she had fought to keep noncommittal. Inside, she'd been screaming in agony and still was. This was it. *The End.*

Paolo's private words to her afterward were what had really done her in. Handlers had moved them into an anteroom and scattered. Vito had stepped away to call his assistant with some instructions.

"Grazie," Paolo had said to Gwyn, not showing any reaction when he shook her hand and found it clammy. "We will pursue defamation charges on your behalf and that could result in prison time for Jensen, but I realize that does nothing to compensate you for all you've lost. Vito promised you a settlement, *si*? Hire a good lawyer and begin those negotiations immediately. I want a number so I can add it to our list of damages when Jensen is tried."

"Of course," Gwyn had murmured, as if she had the first idea how to hire any kind of lawyer, let alone a "good" one. Her mind had started buzzing the minute Vito had called her to say he was sending a car and was bursting with a bigger swarm of bees over how abruptly this press conference ended the need for their affair.

She was devastated. Her very nascent and juvenile crush had become something real and deep and heart-wrenching.

She had started to think of his beautiful apartment as her home.

Vittorio had modern tastes and liked space around him. The penthouse had high white ceilings and three bedrooms, one that he used as an office, off a tiled upper hallway that he called a loft. It was nothing so modest as that. It was a second story. The main bathroom had His and Hers powder rooms on opposite ends of a tub that they easily, and frequently, shared. This flat was wall-to-wall understated luxury, from the designer furniture to the kitchen that sparkled with stainless steel functionality, positioned to allow the cook to visit with guests while stirring and chopping.

High-end art, lush plants and family photos rounded off the space into a haven of warmth and welcome. Her snapshot of her almost family, her own image with her arms around Henry and her mother, sat on the night table next to her side of the bed.

Gwyn swallowed, trying to hide her devastation at leaving all of this, along with the man who lived here, by kicking off her heels beside the front closet, then realized she would have to pack them. She couldn't wrap her brain around what that would entail so she moved to where she'd left her tablet on the sectional before the big screen TV, pretending she was checking email.

"Are you hungry?" Vito asked behind her, shrugging out of his suit jacket and tossing it across the back of the sofa. "I'm going to make coffee."

She wasn't, but she loved cooking with him, enjoying the foreplay of brushing bodies, senses stimulated by the aroma of fresh ingredients, the sizzle of a pan and the rich textures and flavors they seemed to create together.

The full scope of all that she was losing gripped her and she lifted her head to stare blindly through the bright windows.

"Cara?" He was right behind her, making her start. "What's wrong?"

"Nothing." *Everything.*

His gaze dropped to her tablet. "Something has upset you? Do not tell me you're reading reactions to today's press conference. Stop polluting your head that way."

"No, um—" She glanced at the tablet, saw Travis's latest message, started to gloss past it, then decided to confront it. Just pull the bandage off in one ruthless yank. She showed him what Travis had written.

I saw the press conference. Does this mean you're coming home?

Vito's gaze came up and slammed into hers. He was so handsome. Brutally, impossibly handsome with his white shirt and striped tie and tailored pants with their knifelike creases, then black leather shoes glossed to a mirror finish. She didn't know any other man who could wear a vest with the buttons offset at an angle like that, the edge piped in silver, and look so suave.

She longed to trace that piping, touch those buttons. She very much needed the connection that seemed to have been building between them with each physical encounter, but what did they really have? Sex. That was all.

"We haven't really talked about the next steps. I imagine I will be leaving?" she said, insides hollow. "Now that we don't have to pretend anymore?"

They weren't pretending. That's what his cocked brow said.

She licked her lips. "Because it would make it pretty obvious we got together just for show if I left right away, wouldn't it?" Tossing the tablet onto the sofa, she jerked a shoulder. "I could say I'm going to see family and we could let it die off from there."

"We could," he said carefully, so emotionless a scalding pain rose behind her breastbone.

For a moment she couldn't even breathe, let alone speak or move. Then she found a smile of false bravado and brought her hands to the sides of his head.

His hot palms settled on her hips, holding her off as he gave her a questioning look.

She didn't have a very strong grip on her emotions, and keeping anything from him these days was pretty much impossible, but she tried to affect nonchalance.

"Don't worry. I'm not staking a claim. I'll figure it out in a little while. But I'd like to leave you with something to remember."

Then, because she had spent a great deal of time devoting herself to learning what turned him on, she did everything she could to arouse him. She rarely instigated lovemaking unless they were in bed. It was shyness and lack of confidence, but today she left inhibition at the door and pressed herself against him suggestively.

She ran her hands over him with the proprietary touch she usually suppressed. His shoulders were a landscape of masculinity, appealing to the primal woman in her that sought protection and provision. His buttons opened to, first, the warm silk of his shirt, then the satin of his skin, with the fine hairs on his breastbone and a dark arrow to his navel that teased her lips as she kissed what she exposed. His nipples were sharp against her tongue and her teasing made him suck in a quick breath.

She kissed him, not just letting him know she was receptive, but taking the initiative, not hinting that she wanted to make love, but demanding it. It was exhilarating to be this assertive.

He let her bare his chest and open his pants, swiveling so he leaned his hips against the back of the sofa and stepped his feet apart, drawing her into the space. Then he cupped her face so he could kiss her, not taking control, but not passive. Never passive.

Her own clothes loosened, suit jacket falling away, bow at her neck tugging then falling into ribbons of blue polka dots on white. Vito drew back long enough to pull the sheer confection over her head then brought her against him again, skin to skin, both of them murmuring approving noises.

Vito had experienced the advances of women in the past. Often it was a power play or a quid pro quo of some kind. Sometimes he relaxed and enjoyed it, other times he set the pace that suited him.

Gwyn, guileless, sensual Gwyn, undid him. She was so very entrancing in her conservative exterior and her abandonment to lovemaking, especially today as she licked into his mouth, rubbing against him in a way that was not so much practiced as pure. She was trying to turn him on, but the way she grew bright-eyed and flushed with hectic color was even more arousing.

When she released his belt and opened his pants, he let her drag them down his thighs, watching her drop to her knees and loving the sight of her taking him in hand. The sensations of her wet worship, the encompassing heat and delicate suction, had him tempted to let her take him all the way. This *was* something he would remember for the rest of his life. He would never forget her. He had known that before she'd begun anointing him this way.

But if they were saying goodbye, he wanted to do the same to her. To make this last. To create the sort of memory that would sustain them both for the rest of their lives.

That knowledge was a sharp twist in his gut that allowed him to pull her to her feet, turning her so she faced the back of the sofa.

"Wait. I want—"

"Are you not doing what I want, *mia bella*?" He paused in bringing her skirt up, waiting. "Giving me something to remember you by?"

Her knuckles were white where she gripped the leather. "Yes," she whispered. "But I want to see you. Kiss you."

"You will," he promised her, kissing her bare shoulder, then drawing back to memorize the sight of plum wool bunched on the small of her back as he pressed her to bend forward. He stroked his hand over pale white cheeks wearing a line of amethyst lace. Those he dispatched to around her ankles in a moment, caressing her where she was plump and wet, hearing her whimper under his touch, back arching, shoulders shuddering with pleasure.

"We will always have this," he vowed, pressing into her. "Now come for me." He shifted his hand so he was giving her all the pleasure she could bear. "Surrender to me. It's what I love the most," he told her, opening his mouth on her nape, losing himself to the delight of thrusting into her, barely holding on as she suddenly gasped and clenched in strong pulses around him. Her gorgeous cries of fulfillment went through him like church bells.

He petted her as he carefully withdrew and kicked out of his pants. Then he scooped up her still-quivering body and carried her toward the stairs.

"You didn't—"

"I know exactly what I have and haven't done, *mia bella*." His ears were ringing with the pulse hammering upward from the damp, urgent flesh between his thighs. "If you think I'm going to let our last time be a one-sided dalliance in the front room, you haven't learned one damned thing about me or what I expect from my mistress."

It wasn't unusual for them to make love two or three times in a day. Sometimes it was a rush of passion, sometimes a slow, sultry buildup.

It had never been quite such a complete immersion. They ignored the phone when it rang, ignored the growl of their stomachs, barely even spoke except to encourage or compliment or groan incomprehensibly.

Finally, when it was well and truly dark beyond the windows, they landed weak and sated and aching with sensual exhaustion, limbs tangled, quiet and still at last.

The sense of closeness between them was so acute that Gwyn could barely comprehend that it was over, but it was. Those panting moments when their hearts had beat in unison had merely been physical compatibility. Nothing more.

Shifting her arm off her stinging eyes, she decided a trip to the ladies room might be in order to keep herself from revealing how hard this was for her.

"Stay," he said as she began to rise.

A helpless noise escaped her. "Honestly, Vito, I don't think I can. That was…a lot." Her loins were stinging and tender, her muscles quivering with overuse.

A gruff noise escaped him, part humor, part apology. He came up on an elbow and scooped her beneath him, heavy on her as he pinned her to the mattress. "That's quite a compliment if you think I have anything left in me," he growled, nose going into her neck and inhaling. "I mean stay in Milan. This doesn't have to end here and now."

She stilled. "You're asking me to stay as your mistress?"

"*Sì.*"

The room was dark shadows and rumpled blankets; her world narrowed to the warmth of his lips against her collarbone. He didn't see her wince of agony at the term. He might sometimes refer to her as his lover, but that was a euphemism for what she really was. She knew that and she had justified what she was letting herself become as necessary for their ruse.

But that was no longer necessary.

"Because it would look better for the press?" she asked.

"Because we're good together."

That surprised her, making her heart leap as though he'd admitted to deep, abiding affection even though she knew he only meant they knocked each other off the bed with the intensity of physical pleasure they gave each other.

If she stayed with him, wouldn't that allow time for him to develop deeper feelings toward her, though? It was the kind of treacherous, self-delusion all women were capable of, when they were half in love with a man who didn't love them back. She knew it, but she was still tempted to let him talk her into staying. To see.

She traced the line of his spine and lightly searched for proof that he might already be harboring feelings toward her.

"What if I don't want to?" she asked.

His turn to go completely still. He lifted his head and in the muted light she saw his hard mouth twist. "I'm not a man who begs, *cara*. Be careful about bluffing. I'll call you on it."

She ought to be happy he'd gone so far as to tell her he wanted her to stay, she supposed. It *was* quite an admission from such a self-sufficient man. One who could have his choice among women.

"It's not an ultimatum," she said, trying to hide her hurt behind a neutral tone. "I told you when we first met that I don't have affairs. Relying on you goes against everything I've tried to become. I ought to start salvaging my life, not leave it on hold."

His tense hand on her waist grew heavy. "I respect your independence. I do," he assured her. "But your life is already on hold, I carry some of the fault for that and I have the means to support you while you give real thought to your next steps. Let me do this for you, *cara*."

I respect you. Such a small phrase and it moved her so very deeply to hear it. How could she not stay and try to nurture that into something even more meaningful?

"I don't want to lose that respect," she said, hearing his breath catch and taking heart from it. It almost sounded like he was bracing himself. "But I do enjoy the sex."

If the noise he made sounded to her like relief, she knew that was wishful thinking. He was amused, which had been her goal. Keep it light. Don't let him know how emotionally dependent she really was.

"And I'm going to have to insist on more frequent feedings," she added, trying to rise. "I suppose I have to cook again?"

"Two words, *cara*," he growled, flattening her on her back and setting his teeth against her shoulder. "Bite me."

CHAPTER NINE

"GOOD JOB ON the lawyer," Paolo said dryly as he opened the door to his home to them a few nights later.

Gwyn was a bundle of nerves, not quite believing this was a mere social dinner, but Vito assured her it was. All she had done was ask casually how Lauren and the baby were getting on. Vito had called to ask and it had turned into a dinner invitation. Now, here they were.

"She's really nice, isn't she?" she said to Paolo, barely tracking the conversation as the old-world beauty of the house dazzled her. Vito had told her as they drove in that the house had been in the family for generations. It was set on a property that had to be worth millions of euros given its size and location. What charmed her more was the way the high ceilings and Renaissance architecture and formal furniture was peppered with colorful children's toys, a baby swing and the sleek lines of a laptop on an antique escritoire.

"Nice," Paolo repeated under his breath, saying to Vito, "Did you have anything to do with her choice?"

"I've stayed out of it. Why? Are we likely to lose these?" Vito plucked at his shirt.

"My stepbrother found her for me," Gwyn hurried

to say. "I didn't know who else to ask. Why? Is she awful?"

"Depends which side of the table you're on," Paolo said smoothly. "You're on the side where she is very nice. But she's already setting a high bar for our own legal team. It will be a good exercise for them in staying sharp."

Lauren came down the stairs at that point, newborn in her arm.

After a greeting of kisses all around, she brought them through the house to the back to greet the children who were playing outside under the eye of the nanny.

"Ignore the boxes," Lauren said as they came back in, waving at the dozens piled near the back stairs. "One of the aunts has embarked on a family history book. Paolo and I have been digging relics out of attics and pantries that haven't been opened in years. It's fascinating! So many old photos and diaries. *Love* letters."

Gwyn had just taken the baby from Lauren, gathering his warm body close and glancing at Vito like she was the first person to ever cuddle a baby. It was a vulnerable moment of wanting to share her excitement and joy, maybe see what he thought of the sight of her with an infant against her heart, but he wasn't looking at her.

He and Paolo had a lightning exchange that consisted of one look of inquiry and another of an infinitesimal shake of Paolo's head replying, *No.*

If Vito realized she had seen what had just transpired, he betrayed nothing. In fact, his direct gaze, so forceful as he met hers, was a silent declaration that he had nothing to hide.

But she'd seen something. She knew it.

"That's what brought me to Italy, you know," Lauren said, moving through to the lounge where she gathered toys. "Looking up family. My grandmother had a *scandalous* affair with a married man and went home pregnant."

"Here I thought you came to Italy for me," Paolo said, holding up a red plastic bin so Lauren could drop her collection of stuffed toys and books into it.

"You're why I stayed, *mio bello*," she said, offering her lips for a kiss.

The rest of the evening passed in entertaining conversation, excellent food and an invitation from the children to read bedtime stories. It was sweet, yet poignant, making Gwyn recall the way Vito had told her this would never be her life.

Later, as they were readying for bed, she asked him, "Did you ever live in that house?" She was still thinking about that odd moment when Lauren had mentioned love letters. Had he left some evidence of a lost crush?

"I stayed with Paolo's family at different times as a child, wherever they happened to be living. Both of our families traveled a lot, but my sisters and I were well matched in ages to Paolo and his sisters. We often had summer vacations together, that kind of thing. They were our favorite cousins and my uncle…" Vito shrugged. "I looked to him as much of a father figure as my own," he said with a hint of private irony.

"That must have been so idyllic," she said wistfully. "Did you and Paolo play with the girls? Or were you horrible sexists?"

"A little of both," he said dryly, unbuttoning his shirt. "We were never going to play with dolls without lighting their hair on fire, but if the girls wanted to play tag or hide-and-seek, we were up for it."

"And once you discovered real girls, the ones you weren't related to, I'm guessing you were never seen again?"

He didn't say anything, only left his shirt on a chair and bent to peel off his socks, leaving them on the floor. Where did he think those went? She always wound up putting them in the hamper because the housekeeper only came in every other day.

"You're not going to admit to having girlfriends back then?" she asked, brushing out her hair.

"I'm wondering why you need confirmation."

"Okay, I'll just admit that I saw you and Paolo have a silent conversation when Lauren mentioned finding letters. I wondered if you had some kind of scandalous affair in *your* past."

"I've always left it to Paolo to create the publicity stirs, keeping my own behavior to run-of-the-mill, pedestrian affairs that aren't very interesting." He held her gaze as he pulled his belt loose. "Current one being the exception."

She set her jaw, arms crossing. "Am I being too nosy? You're starting to sound hostile."

"Just bored, *cara*."

She set down her brush and worked her silver bangles over her hand, trying to hide how deeply his comment stung.

"Well, it's interesting to me," she said stiffly. "I can't imagine what a project that book will be for your aunt, having so much family history to sift through, so many people of note. I'm envious, if you want the truth. My tree is two people and I could write a single paragraph about each of them. Excuse me for being curious about yours when it has such depth."

She turned to set the bangles on the night stand and pulled off her earrings.

"A clean slate can be a good thing, *cara*. There are some family secrets better left out of the history books."

She shot him a look over her shoulder. "If that's supposed to make me less curious, you're going in the wrong direction."

"You told me you didn't want me to lie to you. Do you remember that?" He came up behind her and found the zip at the back of her cocktail dress. "It was the day we became lovers, in the elevator."

Her dress loosened and all of her tingled with memory and fresh anticipation. How did he do that? Steal the air from her body without really touching her, just opening her dress?

"I remember," she told him, standing very still, closing her eyes because he aroused her just by standing near enough to feel his own arousal emanating off his big body.

"You said if I didn't want to talk about something I should simply say so. I don't want to talk about this, *cara*."

"Okay," she whispered, transfixed by the way her bra tightened, then loosened as he released the clasp.

"I want to suck your nipples, then I want your heels in my back as I lick my way down and make you scream my name."

She swallowed. "Okay."

Vito watched Gwyn charm the head of their legal department. She was praising the man's country after their recent visit to Zurich, where Vito had stolen a day with her for scenic driving, a hike and a picnic, opera in the evening and a late-night dinner of fondue.

It had been a day like, well, he should just admit it—it had been like a honeymoon. She had basked under his attention and he had exalted in hers. He'd never had a woman in his life who was so compatible to him, not just in bed, but out of it. Laughing or silent, naked or clothed, he always felt comfortable around her. He was always proud to have her at his side, loved showing her off.

And was half jealous of that heavyset, middle-aged counselor now, as she poured all her charm and attention in that direction, her flushed pleasure utterly captivating.

At least he could take credit for that allure of hers. Not because he'd paid for the classic suit that was tailored to make the most of her million-dollar figure, or because the smooth chignon and subdued lip color and artistic platinum pendant and earrings were also billed to him. No, he liked to think he was responsible for giving her a place where she could blossom, not just privately in his bed, where she was developing an erotic command with regard to telling him what she liked and wanted, but in public arenas.

Gwyn wasn't a bold person by nature and her photo exposé had left her self-confidence seriously dented. Vito had reminded her again and again that she had no reason to feel shame or think she owed anyone explanations. Under his tutelage, she'd regained her confidence and an attitude of self-possession that was even more hypnotic than her exquisite outer shell. He adored seeing her personality shine through like this.

"She's staying after this?" Paolo asked in an undertone, tucking away his phone.

"You disapprove?" Vito challenged lightly, but with very little actual lightness.

"I don't pass judgments on the private lives of family. You know that," Paolo said with a sardonic twist of his mouth. "If I saw impact to the bank I would comment, but I wouldn't have to, would I?"

No, he wouldn't, but Vito still wound up feeling defensive. He wasn't sure it would matter to him if this affair impacted the bank. He suspected he would carry on with Gwyn regardless.

He had intended to end things after the announcement of charges against Jensen. It would have been a tidy break without loose ends or deeply hurt feelings. Gwyn had been as prepared for it as he had. Even as she had suggested pretending a visit home to see family, he'd been thinking along the same lines.

Then she had touched him, kissed him, somehow stepped inside the shields he wore so easily against the rest of the world and imprinted herself on his very psyche. He had sought satiation that afternoon, certain that when his libido was exhausted, he'd be ready to release her.

But she'd only had to shift away from him in the bed and his entire being had been racked with agony. The single command for her to stay had slipped past his renowned self-discipline, left his lips and landed on her naked skin.

And he didn't regret it. Even though he knew she was falling in love with him. All the signs were there. She wanted to know about his childhood, wanted him to *share*. Aside from dining with Paolo and Lauren, he'd drawn a fine line between her and his personal life, but her yearning to feel connected to the broader landscape of his world, to make her place within it, was obvious.

He couldn't offer her the life she dreamed of when she held his cousin's son and scrambled his eggs in the morning and met him at the door with a kiss when he came home, though.

And cheating her of those things made him reprehensible. If Paolo didn't quite approve of the relationship, that was why. His cousin was an honorable man and knew that Vito was not behaving with complete honor. *If she's a victim, don't make her more of one.*

Vito was implying certain promises that he wouldn't keep, buying time with a woman who could be spending her affection more wisely elsewhere.

But Vito wanted her. His possessive desire was a kind of ferocious pulse beat inside him, territorial and unwavering. He was glad to get this settlement out of the way, glad to put another stage of the scandal behind them. Along with whatever arrangements he made for her when they eventually parted, she would have this very generous cushion for her future, but this was no more an end point to their liaison than the press conference had been.

She was his. He was keeping her. No one would stop him. If Paolo had tried, Vito might very well have shed his cousin's blood for the first time in twenty-odd years.

Gwyn only ever saw her stepbrother in casual clothes, usually wearing stubble and jeans. That's why it took her a full three pulse beats to realize the man who came in behind her lawyer, the man who was clean-shaven, wore a tailored suit as razor sharp as the Donatelli men's and said a grim, "About time," in a voice she knew was Travis.

"Oh, my God! What are you doing here?" She was taken aback, surprised by a light rush of excitement at seeing a familiar face. She almost stepped forward to hug him, but embarrassed realization hit at the same moment, along with the only reason she could imagine he would turn up so unexpectedly. "Is Henry okay?"

"He's fine. Worried sick about you," he said, sending a hostile glance around the conference room. "Why haven't you called him?"

"I…didn't know what to say. You told him I was okay, didn't you?"

"Are you? What is this?" He waved at the conference table where red folders had been set in front of a handful of chairs. "I told you not to sign anything without talking to me first."

"I texted you," she said.

"When I say talk, I mean talk, Gwyn."

Out of the corner of her eye, she saw Vito start forward with purpose, as if he took exception to Travis's patronizing attitude. Paolo stopped him with a hand on his chest and came forward with his own extended.

"Paolo Donatelli. And you are?"

"Travis Sanders. Gwyn's brother." He bit the words off.

Step, she almost clarified, but Travis was still talking.

"I'd like a word with her if you'll excuse us?" So dismissive to the men who owned the skyscraper.

Vito didn't move a muscle, stating implacably, "I'll stay."

Travis tried to stare Vito down. All the hairs on

Gwyn's body stood up, electrified by the open animosity pinging back and forth between the men.

"Look, um—" She glanced to Paolo for help.

"Take as much time as you need," he said, flashing a look at his cousin, but only waving the lawyers from the room and pulling the door closed behind them.

Gwyn looked to Vito, but saw immediately there was no point in asking him to leave. The hostility radiating off him was palpable.

Licking her lips, she turned back to Travis. "I'm *sorry*," she said with deep sincerity. "It's true, I was avoiding you and Henry. This whole thing has been very humiliating. I feel horrible for what Henry and you must be going through."

Vito made a noise that she knew was an admonishment against apologizing for something that wasn't her fault.

"Is that why you haven't come home? Because you were embarrassed?"

She shrugged, as disconcerted by his forcefulness as by the implication that what she considered "home" was her home in his eyes, too.

"Is it?" Vito demanded from his position on the far end of the table. His hot glare was equally unnerving because he looked so stunned.

Hurt, even?

He must know she'd stayed for him. She swallowed, sending him a reassuring look before she turned back to her stepbrother.

"I stayed here for a lot of reasons, but I knew you must be furious—" she began.

"I'm furious because I'm worried, Gwyn!" he cut in. His dark face reddened with deep emotion and his hand waved in the air. "None of this is like you except the part where you refused to pick up the phone and ask me for help! Instead, you're relying on…"

His gaze tracked Vito as he came down the side of the table to where Gwyn stood, closing in behind her in a silent message that might have been a warning to Travis to mind his tone. There was such an air of menace as he looked at the man.

"What the hell is going on here?" Travis asked, shifting his disbelieving gaze to hers. "I mean, I know what it was supposed to look like. Anyone with half a brain can see you were backing Jensen into an admission that he set up the photos, but why are you still here now that that's accepted fact? Why didn't you come home after he was charged?"

"I—" She didn't know what to say. Somehow she was in Vito's grasp, her back against his front, one of his heavy hands on her hip, the other curled around her upper arm.

"Why do you care?" Vito remarked in a dangerous tone.

Travis lifted his gaze to a point past her shoulder, his eyes so cold and deadly, Gwyn tensed and held her breath.

"We're family," Travis said through lips that barely moved. "Maybe we're not related by blood, but we're family. Do you get me? She's not without connections. So whatever the hell you think you're doing with my sister, it ends now."

Family?

Gwyn was dumbfounded by Travis's reaction.

The whole moment was so supercharged with emotion, she almost couldn't speak, thoughts scattered. But these two pitbulls were about to take each other apart, so she covered Vito's hand on her arm and tried to ground out his aggression.

"It's okay," she told him, then turned to Travis. "Your worrying about me is really nice, but it's not necessary. I've been in good hands this whole time."

In her head that had seemed like a sensible thing to say, but the hands upon her tightened and Travis choked out, taking on a thunderstruck expression.

"Have you? Have you really?"

"Yes," she insisted, shifting enough so she could see Vito's stony expression over her shoulder. She wasn't sure what she had expected to see there, but not that cast of iron. For some reason it undermined her confidence in what she was saying. "Paolo and Vito have had my back this whole time."

"That's odd," Travis said, tone dripping sarcasm. "Because what it looks like to me is that a man in a position of power took advantage of a woman who was already in trouble, used her to keep his bank from taking a kick to its reputation, hung on to her to influence the settlement that was being negotiated—" he nodded at the folders on the table "—and *if* he keeps you here, will be using you for reasons that have become far more basic."

"Travis," she gasped, stabbed by his cruel assessment.

"I'm sorry, did I miss a wedding announcement?" Travis asked, flicking his gaze to Vito's. "Are your intentions honorable?"

Vito's hands fell away from her body and stripped her of her skin at the same time. *No.* She wouldn't let Travis ruin this. Why wasn't Vito explaining this wasn't cheap, physical gratification but something so much more?

Public humiliation was a cakewalk compared to losing the regard of people you cared about, she realized, as one man looked at her with pity and the other didn't meet her gaze at all.

"You've always thought I was a gold digger, Travis. Why are you upset to find me exactly where you expected me to be?" she threw out.

"Gwyn," Vito growled in protest while Travis's head snapped back.

"When did I ever call you that?"

"The wedding day. You said Mom and I—"

"I barely knew you!" No apology or denial, she noted. He just railed on. "Now I do and you're as green and idealistic as they come. He's taking advantage of you, Gwyn." And he looked genuinely outraged by it. If she wasn't so furious with him for ruining a good thing, she'd be touched.

"I'm an adult," she asserted. "Perfectly capable of deciding when and with whom I want a relationship."

"Oh, tell yourself that, but this isn't a 'relationship.' It's an arrangement. The most rudimentary kind. He's miles ahead of you and it's all calculated for his best interests, not yours. You will come away with some very pretty material items that I know will mean nothing to you because you are a woman looking for love, not lucre. You're better than this, Gwyn. Don't let him turn you into something you're not."

"You don't know anything about what we have," she said hotly, half turning to snag Vito with her glance, urging him—*insisting*—he defend himself. *Them.*

His jaw pulsed and he stared at Travis, not with heat, not with guilt. Blank.

It hurt. His silence gutted her and his refusal to appear insulted and furious shook her to the core.

"If you have any decency at all, you'll send her home with me," Travis said flatly. "She's better than this."

No, I'm not, Gwyn wanted to say. Maybe she even said it aloud. She knew she argued, "That's a stupid ultimatum. He doesn't have to prove anything to you. *I* decide whether I stay with him or not," she declared.

"Sign the papers when you're satisfied, not before," Vito said, more to Travis than to her, reaching to square one of the folders against the edge of the table, then sending a second look, this one blistering, back to Travis again. "You're wrong about my interfering in this. It's all been negotiated at arm's length, but I'll leave so I'm not a distraction while you finalize it."

"Vito!" Panic edged into her voice as she watched him circle toward the interior door. This wasn't really happening was it? "You're— This isn't—" *Over.* Was it? She couldn't finish the question, afraid she already knew the answer.

He paused, but he didn't turn around. "This was always going to happen, *cara*," he said gently. "You knew that."

She thought of the day when she'd been prepared to leave and had likened it to tearing off a bandage. But genuinely facing The End was a kind of pain she couldn't describe, like her soul was wrenched from her body. Her heart beat outside her chest.

She did the only thing she could. She turned on Travis, the man who had marched in here talking like he cared about her and was destroying her life.

"Why would you do this to me? Do you resent me so much for taking some of your father's precious attention—"

"Gwyn," Vito said sharply, hand gripping the edge of the table with white knuckles, face grim. *This was always going to happen.* Go home with your brother. Let him take care of you. I want to know you're safe there, not being harassed by the press or anyone else."

"Oh, do you?" she jeered. "What am I now? Not just a pawn, but a marble that gets picked up and taken home? *I* decide what happens to me!"

"Do whatever you want," he commanded. "But you're not coming home with me."

He might as well be throwing rocks at the dog that threatened to follow him. His words landed like sharp stones in her throat and her eyes and her glass heart, chipping and cracking it, leaving it in jagged broken pieces as he disappeared through the door and closed it with finality against her.

"Gwyn, I'm sorry," Travis said, touching her elbow.

She shook him off, distantly supposing she looked like someone had died in front of her because that's how she felt.

She had been miserable, absolutely devastated, when her nude photos had appeared. Vito had questioned her like a criminal and she had thought her life couldn't get any worse. Then he'd made everything better. He'd charmed and soothed and ignited her. He had made her fall in love with him. She had trusted him in ways she'd never let herself trust anyone, especially a man. She had offered her heart on a platter, let herself believe he cared for her at least a little...

But she meant nothing to him.

She hated him with everything in her. He was a bastard and she *hated* him.

At least, that's what she told herself.

The door he'd used to exit the conference room led into Paolo's office. His cousin stood up from his desk. "They're ready for us?"

"All I could see was your father," Vito told him numbly, trying to laugh it off, but ghosts were skimming across his skin, leaving it covered in gooseflesh. His chuckle came off his heart like a dry leaf. A kind of pain, the kind he would never let anyone, for any reason, inflict upon him, coursed like poison through his veins. "I can't be like mine, stealing something I'll end up destroying."

Incomprehension crystalized into understanding in Paolo's expression, maybe even something that might have been a protest, but Vito was already on the move again. If he didn't get out of here, he wouldn't be able to leave her.

"Finish without me. Give her whatever she wants."

CHAPTER TEN

NOT LONG AFTER her mother had married Henry, he had said to Gwyn, "Travis can teach you to drive."

Already far behind her age group in getting her license, Gwyn had declined, not wanting to look stupid in front of him, choosing instead to spend her hard-earned tip money on a couple of private lessons. She couldn't count the number of times Travis had offered to buy dinner over the years, but she'd always insisted on cooking. When she tried, she could think of four distinct times when he had asked whether she was looking for work because he'd heard about a particular position and was willing to recommend her. She'd always taken it as a criticism of the work she was doing or a favor that would make her indebted to him.

Not once had it ever occurred to her that he might give one solid damn about her.

He did. He might have blown up her relationship— *arrangement*—with Vito, but he was sorry. He was treating her like she was made of butterfly wings and soap bubbles, barely touching her, moving her with the gentle cadence of his voice. He told her that he shouldn't have waited for her to ask for help, but that he knew how important her independence was to her. He had wanted to respect her choices, but he couldn't watch her get hurt. He told her she could do better.

"I thought he cared about me," she finally broke her silence to say, as they flew first class back to Charleston.

"I know," he said after a surprised pause. She hadn't spoken since Vito had left the conference room, afraid her voice would crack and the rest of her control would follow. "And there are times when an affair like that is harmless. But you weren't coming into it as his equal. By that I mean the position you were in at the time, life experience, money, influence," he said with a glance from the corner of his eye. "You're a helluva better person."

"You don't know him," she mumbled into the drink he'd ordered her.

"I know him," Travis snorted. "It's like looking in a mirror."

For some reason that made her laugh, jaggedly and with fraught emotion, but as powerful and intimidating as she'd always found Travis, Vito was so much more. Everything she felt about him was massive and angsty and not the least bit brotherly.

Travis twisted his mouth and said, "Why is that funny? Shut up."

Which made her laugh more. Because the alternative was to cry and she'd wait to do that when she was alone.

He took her to Henry's and she really only meant to stay a week or so while she sorted out her life and got a job, but Henry practically begged her to stay. Then Travis walked her into an office a few blocks away and told her she was the comptroller for his friend's chain of high-end restaurants.

"Nepotism?" Her ego really needed to earn something on her own merit.

"Don't be like that. You're *over*qualified. But it's close, the money is good and no one will bother you. It's an excellent stepping stone," Travis urged. "It reestablishes you in the field which is something you need. He really needs someone who can upgrade his system and train the team to use it. You'll be doing him a favor."

"Right," she mumbled, but took the job.

It was awkward at first. Not so much at work. Everyone there was quite nice to her, but as she began moving around in public some people had the audacity to stare. Sometimes they asked outright if she was *that* woman. Usually if she replied, "Yes. Why?" it shut the interest down to a startled, "Just wondering."

Then there was the one day when she was feeling really thin-skinned and went off with the kind of fury that Vito had always warned her against.

It happened to be her mother's birthday. Her period had arrived that morning, severing any crazy illusions she had been nursing that she'd have a lifelong tie with Vito. Then a knock at the door had announced her things from Italy. Not just the boxes from her flat that had gone into storage. *All* her things. Gowns that had hung next to Vito's suits. Scarves and scent and sandals.

Her gaze had scanned the entire inventory list, from eyebrow tweezers to toe rings, seeing novels and anklets and flower vases, but no mention of "Vito's heart."

She had asked the men to stack the boxes in the den, closed the door on them, made a huge breakfast for Henry, ate none of it herself and had cried in the shower before forcing herself to leave for work, already thirty minutes late.

So when she parked her car outside her new job and saw the cameras running at her like laser-shooting weapons in a sci-fi movie, she was already on her last nerve. A million babbled questions washed over her, all of them prompted by some shred of news in the Jensen case that she no longer cared anything about. But when one of the voices said, "We deserve to know everything that happened between you and Vittorio Donatelli," she lost it.

"You *deserve* to know? I'm supposed to betray his confidence and my own right to privacy and tell strangers about our personal relationship? What is wrong with you people? Do you understand what a relationship is? You rely on the other person *not* to talk about you. That's why humans make connections, so we have a safe place to be ourselves. Vito Donatelli gave me that. That's what happened between us, okay? *Trust.* What a kinky, filthy concept, right? I'm sure it is to you!"

She used her elbows to get through the crowd, rather pleased when she heard grunts of startled pain and anxiety for their precious equipment.

"You don't deserve one damned thing."

Vito started to replay the moment where Gwyn gave the paparazzi a piece of her mind, but heard a squawk through the closed doors to Paolo's office.

He rose, not getting any work done anyway, and went through to find Lauren pacing in a light, bouncing step, patting the back of her fussing son.

"Hi," she said with a warm smile, coming across to kiss his cheeks. "Paolo's meeting me here with the other two, but I'm early. Sorry if we disturbed you. This one's fighting sleep even though he's overtired and grumpy."

She wrinkled her nose at her son, then kissed his crinkled little chin.

Vito took him and settled him into what he privately labeled The Sleeper Hold. He'd learned it from watching his many relatives comfort his many infant relations. If a baby didn't take to the shoulder or a cradle hold in the arm, they wanted to lie on their stomach across a forearm, head pillowed in the crook of his elbow, limbs dangling.

Arturo made a stalwart effort to keep up his complaints, but settled in short order with one discontented kick of his leg and a weary sigh. Vito kept rubbing his back, pacing laconically to the window and back. Moments later, he held a warm, limp, sleeping baby.

"You're such a natural," Lauren said, stroking her son's hair, stopping short of the words he'd heard from countless women in his family. *Don't you want children of your own?*

"Paolo was visiting the old bank today," Vito said. "He took Roberto and Bianca?"

Lauren nodded. "Your aunt was meeting them there with a photographer."

Erecting this modern building and moving the Donatelli fortune into it had been a massive decision into which the entire family had weighed. While no one could dispute the practicality of bigger rooms and proper air-conditioning, or the SMART Boards and Wi-Fi and improved security, there was something to be said of the old financial district. The community was a tight one there. It had relied for centuries on old-fashioned networking in the narrow, cobbled streets of the city center.

It was how a young, beautiful daughter of an Italian

banker had wound up catching the notice of a mafioso's son looking to launder his own father's ill-gotten gains.

"I've read there are hidden passageways under those old banks where secret deals were arranged back in the day. Paolo won't tell me if it's true."

"If he did, we would have to kill you," Vito said casually. It was a myth that all of Milan enjoyed perpetuating.

"You bankers," she said, with a teasing grin. "You pretend to be so boring, but you're walking secrets, aren't you?"

Vito glanced down at the sleeping baby to disguise his reaction. "Hardly. What you see is what you get, *cara*."

"So you won't tell me yours," Lauren said after a brief, decidedly significant pause.

"Secrets? I have none to tell," he said, lifting his head and looking her in the eye as he spoke his bold-faced lie.

She tilted her head, but her gaze was soft with affection. "I've always imagined you fell in love with someone you couldn't have. That's why you won't marry and have children when you would make such a wonderful husband and father—"

"Lauren," he said gently. "I adore you. Let's keep it that way. Stop now."

"But then I saw you with Gwyn." Here was the woman who was strong enough to be Paolo's match. She rarely had to show this sort of steel because her sweet nature inevitably paved smooth streets wherever she went. But Paolo was not as domesticated as he appeared. A weak woman would not have fared well as his wife.

"Take him," he said, rolling Arturo into her arms.

"We're not having this conversation." He started back to his office.

"I spent five years married to a man who didn't love me because I was afraid of what I felt for Paolo. Five years sleeping with the wrong man," she said to his back. "She'll find someone else you know."

He was at the door, feeling the latch like a knife hilt against this palm. A pain in his chest was the blade. He twisted it himself.

"She'll try to make babies with him," her voice continued in brutal purity behind him. "I did. Because she'll think that any man's baby is better than no baby at all…"

He almost had the door shut on her. Rude, but necessary.

Her voice elevated. "If you won't tell me, at least tell *her* why you're breaking her heart."

He pulled the door closed and turned the lock for good measure. Then he leaned his forehead upon it, blood moving like powdered glass in his arteries, the baby's body heat still imprinted on his aching arm.

CHAPTER ELEVEN

GWYN THOUGHT SHE was doing pretty well. It had been two months and most of the paparazzi vultures had learned that she lived a very boring life, going from Henry's to work to the grocery store to the dentist to the quickie oil change place. Even she was bored with her life.

Which is why she went on a date with a friend of her brother's. She told herself it was any number of things: getting back on the horse, research about a possible move to New York, interest in a career change to landscape architecture—hilarious. As if she had any interest in watching grass grow. But it was also an opportunity to eat in a restaurant where she didn't work, to see a jazz trio and wear one of the dresses she couldn't bring herself to discard.

She also told herself it was a test, to see if she could let any man other than Vito kiss her.

She was honest with him, told him up front that it was her first date since "it" had happened. He was good-natured, kept things casual and friendly, was a gentleman and a pleasant companion, making her laugh. He made her forget for moments at a time that she was pining and lost without the man she really loved.

But at the end of the night, when he moved to kiss her, she balked. It was instinctive. He wasn't Vito. It felt wrong.

He drew back, solemn and knowing, ruefully disappointed. "Not ready, huh?"

"I'm sorry."

"Don't be." He picked up her hand and kissed her bent knuckles. "I'll be back at the end of the year. We can go out again then. See if you feel differently."

"Thank you," she said, privately sighing. *But I won't.*

Then Henry turned on the porch light and they both chuckled.

Travis was at the breakfast table when she walked into the kitchen the next morning.

"Do not look at *anything*," he warned.

She knew the paparazzi had gone crazy. Cameras had been flashing around them all evening.

"He said we could go out again the next time he's in town." She poured a cup from the coffee he'd made. "But he doesn't realize how notorious I really am, does he?"

Travis said it wouldn't matter to his friend and as Gwyn went about her week, she wondered if anything mattered. It certainly hadn't mattered to Vito that she was dating other men.

Because deep in a sick corner of her soul, that was the real reason she had done it. She had hoped he would see one of those images that had been taken of her dining and dancing. She had hoped it would make him react.

Nothing.

Crickets.

Which was as painful and disheartening as the fact

that she'd felt nothing for a perfectly nice man when he'd acted like he liked her, not just her face or body or the bare skin he'd seen online, but her.

With a shaky sigh, she looked down at the payments she was approving and wondered how many times she'd written her initials without taking in what she was actually signing. She started again.

When she walked outside, summer was announcing its intentions with a heat just this side of uncomfortable and a memo that humidity intended to climb to unbearable.

She dug her keys from her purse, ignoring the sound of a car door opening because it was likely yet another paparazzo—

"Cara."

Cupid's arrow, right through the heart. Sweetly painful, painfully sweet.

She turned to regard him and wished she'd taken a moment to find a bored expression. Instead, she was sure he read all the mixed feelings of welcome and yearning and hurt and betrayal. Why would he show up now, as she was finding ways to live without him?

Why like that? So iconic in one of his banker suits, cut to precision on his leanly sculpted form. He wore a hint of late-day stubble on his cheeks and his eyes were the color of morning light on mountain glaciers.

He stepped to the side and indicated the interior of his limo.

She sputtered, arms folding, aware of footsteps running toward them as some lurking paparazzo realized who she was talking to.

"Have dinner with me," Vito said, paying no attention to the click and whiz of the camera.

"It's four-thirty. I have my own car." She showed him her keys.

He turned and leaned down to speak to his driver, then slammed the door, walking toward her to hold out his palm.

"Really," she said, letting the full scope of her disbelief infuse the word. "Just take up where we left off? No."

"I want to talk to you."

"Does it occur to you that I might not want to talk to you?"

"That is a bluff." He met her gaze and there was a myriad of emotions behind that brutally beautiful face and somber expression. Knowledge shone in his eyes, knowledge of her and what he did to her, his patented arrogance, a kind of desolation that stopped her heart. Heat that made it jump and race again.

He took her keys from her limp fingers.

"I said I wanted to talk. You only need to listen." He touched her elbow, turning her toward the parked cars. At the same time, he clicked the button so the lights on her hatchback flashed. Then he held the passenger door for her.

She hadn't sat on this side of her new car, which wasn't bottom of the line, but wasn't the kind of luxury Vito was used to. While he drove, she took out her phone long enough to punch in Henry's number, leaving a message that she wouldn't be home right away because she was going to dinner with Vittorio.

He glanced across as she dropped her phone into her purse.

"Things are well with your family? You're living with your stepfather. Is that because of the attention?"

He knew she hadn't moved into her own place? She hardly stalked him at all.

She shrugged. "He wants me there. I guess if there's a silver lining to the photos it's learning that I really do have a family. I know now exactly what other women mean when they say that older brothers are annoying. Your sisters must say that a lot."

His brow cocked at her cheeky remark, but he only said, "His protectiveness surprised me after the way you sounded so dismissive of him."

"Join the club," she snorted under her breath.

"He knows you went out with a man the other night?"

"I assume the whole world knows it, if you've heard about it." She reminded herself that it didn't matter that he was bringing it up—even if his voice had lowered to a tone that pretended to be casual, but was actually quite lethal. "He's a friend of Trav's so yes, he knows. He set it up." *Chew on that.*

"You had a nice time?" Again with the light tone, but his knuckles were white on the steering wheel.

"I don't talk about the men I date," she said flatly.

Silence for a full minute, until he stopped behind a line of traffic waiting for a light.

"No. You don't. I appreciate that, *cara*," he said softly, and this time his voice was filled with gravity and sincerity. "I know you've had offers for tell-alls. They must have been generous. You wouldn't have to work again, I'm sure."

She only turned her face to her side window. If he thought she was the least bit tempted in profiting from what they had shared, he really didn't know her at all.

"How do you like your job?" he asked.

"It's a job, Vito. It's no pin-up gig as Kevin Jensen's

piece on the side. It's no mistress to a playboy banker. But it pays the bills."

"You're angry that I sent you away."

"I'm angry that you're here," she said, swinging her head around to glare at him. "My life was starting to look normal. Why stir it up again?"

Why? It was a fair question. One Vito couldn't answer. At least, not without admitting to himself that he was a very weak man.

"I want to explain why I sent you away," he said. Even though he had walked out on Lauren that day, telling himself she was wrong. Better to break ties cleanly, to let Gwyn move on with her life without knowing what kind of a near miss she'd had.

Why had he decided, after seeing her with another man, that he should let her know why she couldn't be with him? It was flawed logic.

He had wanted to see her again was the real answer. He could say that he wanted to talk and her to listen, but that was a lie. He wanted her to talk. He wanted her to relay every detail of the minutes she'd been away from him, the way she might have given him the highlights of her day visiting a museum, or conveyed a funny conversation she'd overheard on the street or simply traded views with him that might be more liberal than his own, but were always well thought out and left him with a broader view of the other side.

"I thought we were going to dinner," she said as he turned into the underground parking lot of the Donatelli International building.

"You said it was too early," he reminded, pulling into the spot reserved with his name, right next to the elevator. She scowled so mistrustfully at him, he had to chuckle. "I'm not going to kill you and eat you, *cara*."

No promises against licking and nibbling, of course.

It was all he could do not to pounce on her after he punched in the override code to get him to the floor he wanted. She had come out of her workplace with her jacket slung over her arm. Her black skirt was of a modest length, but narrow and stretchy, clinging to her hips and thighs. She wore a light green top that was so plain it was unremarkable, but the narrow belt at her waist gave it some traction across her bustline, emphasizing her hourglass figure. And those shoes with straps as narrow as her belt were positively erotic.

He hoped like hell he had paid for them, unsure why it mattered, just wanting to know she was still allowing him some place in her life.

She flicked her hair behind her shoulder, affecting cool composure, but her mouth was pulling at the corners as she said, "I know why you sent me away. It was an affair, nothing more. Like you said, it was always going to happen."

"*Sì,*" he agreed, and the word moved up from his chest like gravel. "But for different reasons than you think."

The elevator opened into the private residential floor, where he and Paolo had suites and guest accommodations were made available to other family members. There was a private gym and indoor pool here, a dining lounge with views to the ocean that was closed because he was the only one here. Paolo's suite, where he had taken Lauren the night he'd told her that her husband was dead, was on the far side of the oversize foyer. Vito's was here, to his left, but before opening his door, he paused in the foyer and indicated the portrait on the wall.

It was a print of the original that had first hung in the old bank in Milan and now occupied the main lobby of the new tower.

"My great-grandfather," he said, looking at the man who'd been painted in his middle-aged prime wearing a brown plaid suit and a bowler hat.

He felt Gwyn's gaze touch him, questioning why this might be important, but she gave the portrait a proper study.

"He had two sons and five daughters, but only his sons inherited." He nodded at the two brothers who had cemented the foundation for what Banco Donatelli would become. "This one is my grandfather. His brother only had daughters. We've become more progressive and all share in the dividends now, but my uncle, Paolo's father, was recognized as his successor."

He moved to the photo of his grandfather with his wife and five children. It was a formal color photograph with the family posed for posterity, the fashions laughably dated. His grandfather had long sideburns and his pointed collar jutted out like wings against his tan suit and gold tie. His grandmother wore a floral print dress and Paolo's father, nearing twenty, was dressed like a newsboy. The four teenage girls wore identical dresses in a truly horrid purple.

"You Donatelli men get stamped out with the same mold generation after generation, don't you?" She glanced from his great-grandfather, to his grandfather, then to his uncle and then to him. "The girls take after your grandmother. Except this one." She pointed at Antoinietta, barely twelve.

"Sì," he agreed, giving himself one last moment for reservations, but he had none. "That's why I look so much like a Donatelli. She is my actual mother."

Gwyn didn't know what to say, and Vito's profile gave nothing away as he moved to unlock a door and hold it for her.

She entered a private suite that was much smaller than his penthouse in Milan, but had such a similar decor, was stamped so indelibly as *his*, she felt as though she had come home.

"I don't understand," she told him, and the phrase covered many topics. Why had he told her that; why did it matter?

He moved to a photo on the wall in his lounge. The midnineties fashions weren't quite as painful as the seventies had been. A stout man wore a dark suit with a narrow tie that made his barrel chest seem more pronounced. His wife wore a black dress with a scoop neck. Young Vito actually pulled off the red suspenders over his white shirt, but his sisters' hairstyles, all wisped to look like a sitcom star's, were priceless.

She studied his image, realizing he looked...unlike the others.

Maybe she wouldn't have noticed it if he hadn't told her this was not his biological family, but he was taller, leaner, more intense as he gazed into the camera while the rest of them beamed warmly. They seemed relaxed the way a family should when they were together, but he had that smoldering personality that never stopped emanating danger.

"*Mia famiglia.* I love them. My parents taught me generosity and acceptance. They love me every bit as much as they love their daughters. I would die for any of them. But my sisters have never been told," he said, making her swing her attention to him in surprise. "Paolo knows, but he's likely the only one in our generation or lower who does. He hasn't even told Lauren. I know some of my great-aunts and uncles have suspicions, but none has ever breathed a word..." He shook his head and shrugged. "This is something that was put in the vault and meant to be left there."

"Because your mother was young? Unmarried?" she guessed. His grandfather might have progressed to including his daughters in his will, but illegitimate babies had still been a scandal for a man in such a lofty position. It wasn't a big deal *now*, though. Was it? Why continue to hide it?

"My mother was eighteen. I'm a bastard, yes. And I won't tell you the name of my father, but that's for your own protection as much as mine. He was mafioso, *cara*. A truly dangerous and reprehensible man."

She blinked, shocked, and moved blindly to sit on the edge of the sofa. "How—?"

"—does the daughter of a banker get mixed up with a thug? He singled her out. I'm sure he had his moments of charm. I've seen photos and I imagine any woman would call him attractive. According to my uncle, my mother might as well have been the youngest daughter of a church minister, rebelling at her father's attempts to keep her cloistered. My grandfather was ready to disown her, but my uncle kept fighting to bring her home. I mean that literally. He had scars. She went back, regardless. Again and again."

"Got pregnant."

"Indeed." He pushed his hands into his pockets,

rocked on his heels, scowl remote and dark. "Even though she came away bruised at different times. I will never understand—"

His profile was hard and sharp.

"She was late into her pregnancy when he bashed her around and she left for the last time. She called my uncle to come take her to the hospital, but she was far into labor when he got there. He caught me and held her as she died. She begged him to keep me from my father. If you could have seen his face when he told me these things..."

"Oh, Vito," she breathed, rising to go to him, hand reaching for his arm, but he was a statue, unmoved by her touch, barely seeming to breathe, face still and harsh as though carved into marble.

"This is what I am, *cara*. A mixture of impetuous Donatelli rebellion—have you met Paolo? I have that same cursed need to dominate and it is a monumental task to hold all of that back. Then I have this streak of brutality on top of it. My father killed people. And the dead ones are the victims who got off easy. His other son turned out as conscienceless, trafficking in women and drugs, winding up dead in the gutter outside his own home, like a rat. I even have a nephew. He's already been arrested for assault. There but for the grace of the Donatelli family go I."

"Vito," she chided. He didn't really think he would have turned out like that, did he? She frowned, hurting for him, feeling how tortured his soul was by a bloodline he didn't want and couldn't escape.

He ran his hand down his face. "I cannot perpetuate that sickness into another generation, not into the very family that took me in, kept me this side of the law and out of the hands of a man who would have turned me into himself. I *won't* risk it. Do you understand? Do you see now why I can't marry you and give you that dream I see in your eyes every time you rock a baby or hold a child's hand?"

She lowered her eyes, aching inside. He saw through her every single time.

"When your brother came to Milan that day," he said heavily, "all I could think was that it was better to let our separation happen then, before you were pregnant with an abomination—"

"Don't say that!"

He held up a hand. "But it tortures me, *cara*, that he made it sound like you were only a convenience to me. Our affair served many purposes, not all of them romantic, *sì*. That's true. But to let you think that was all it was is a lie. We are honest with one another if nothing else, are we not?"

"Are we?" she asked, mind reeling from all he'd told her, which made certain suspicions rise that were so sweet and fragile she barely let herself touch them. But why would he tell her all this, with that tortured look on his face, if he didn't care for her, trust her, not just a little, but a lot.

"Does some part of this sound made-up to you?" he asked, voice chilling and shoulders going back.

She made a noise. "Well, it is quite a story. But I do believe you. No, I'm questioning why you've told me."

She thought back to that day in the elevator when he'd been so angry at what she hadn't been able to see in him. All this time he'd presented her with the thick wall of the vault that fronted the man inside. Of course she'd had trouble seeing his true thoughts and feelings.

But now, now she thought she saw very clearly. It wasn't just wishful thinking, was it?

"I just explained," he said testily. "I didn't want you hurting unnecessarily."

"So I'm supposed to not hurt when you leave again? Secure in the knowledge that your rejection is for my own good? You know I love you, don't you?" There. She flung her own vault wide open, crashing it into the wall.

He flinched, dragging in air like he'd taken a knife to the lung. "I hoped that you didn't," he said through his teeth.

"Oh! Another lie!" she charged, stabbing a finger at his chest, hard enough to hurt her fingernail.

He grabbed her hand and glared, dark brows a fierce line. "I'm not lying!"

"You knew I was in love with you and you sent me away to get over it, but the minute you thought I might, you came back to see exactly how deep my feelings went. This—" she pulled free of his grip and pointed wildly to encompass all the photos he'd shown her "—is a test."

"Untrue. I'm explaining to you why I can't marry you and give you the family you've always wanted."

"Fine. I accept," she said, crossing her arms.

He grew cautious. "Accept what?"

"That we'll never marry and have children. Maybe we can talk about adopting someday, but that's not a condition. I'll accept simply living together without all those picket-fence trappings I always wanted."

"No!" he growled. "That's not what I'm saying. You deserve those things, Gwyn. Your brother is right. That's why—" He cut himself off with an impatient noise, palm scraping up his cheek, creating a raspy sound.

"So I should go marry another man and have his babies?" she confirmed.

"No! Damn you, no. I hated seeing you with that man. It made me sick. No. And damn you for forcing me to admit that." He stalked away a few steps, hand raking into his hair. "I'm trying to think of you, Gwyn, but I keep acting for myself. That is who I am. Greedy. Selfish." He pivoted. "Don't you see that's what I'm trying to protect you from? I want that deal you're offering. I want to take you into my home as my lover and shortchange you on all the things you have a right to. What does that make me? How could you love someone like that?"

"What kind of man are you really?" she cried. "One who blames himself for his mother's death?"

He jerked a little in surprise, said, "No," but without conviction. Then hitched a shoulder. "Perhaps. A little. Everyone, the aunts and uncles who knew, always looked at me as if... I used to fight with Paolo. A lot. But then my uncle told me about this and I knew I had to contain this part of myself. Stamp it out as much as possible."

"And you have," she told him. "Are you likely to hit me, Vito?"

"No," he said, his contempt for men who would do such a thing thick in the word.

"What if I provoke you? What if I push you?" she asked, coming across to give him a light shove in the middle of his chest.

He caught her hands and easily twisted her arms behind her back, hauling her close in such a swift move they both released a little, "Ha," as their bodies lightly slammed together.

She tested his hold. "Now what are you going to do to me?" she said, but softly. Knowingly. She was never frightened here, only eager with anticipation.

"Kiss you," he answered. "Make love to you."

"Love me?" she suggested. Begged.

He lowered his head with a groan, capturing her mouth in a way that instantly owned, but gave at the same time. Anointed. Worshipped. His kiss was almost chaste in its sweetness, but so carnal they couldn't help running their tongues together and opening to deepen the kiss until they were both breathless.

Then he released her arms and tucked her head against his chest where his heart slammed, his strong arms enfolding her to him.

She stroked his sides, soothing the beast.

"I could never hurt you, Gwyn. I wanted to carve out my own heart when I saw the way you looked at me that day you left Milan. The thought that I'd left you feeling anything but confident in how very lovable you are was intolerable. I do love you." He touched his lips to her ear. "I love you in ways I didn't know it was possible to love, with my body, with my breath. I ache with love for you every night and every day."

She closed her eyes, savoring the sting of joyous tears. Threading her arms around him, she held on to him and the moment. The strength that had sustained her and protected her and would be hers. Because she would fight for this.

Him.

"Vito, how did the Donatellis keep you this side of the law?"

"I don't know," he muttered, digging his fingers into her hair, petting her like he was comforting himself. "A million ways, I suppose. Redirection, distraction, love."

"I love you," she drew back to say.

His hold on her flexed and he swallowed. "She loved him. He didn't change."

"Look what she was starting with," she said wryly. "What makes you think a child of yours couldn't be molded the way you were? Especially if he or she started out loved, the way you did?"

"Cara—" It was both protest and longing.

"It's not a deal breaker, I swear. I'm just saying you shouldn't write off your genes as all bad. Either way, I'm yours. You're stuck with me, understand?"

"Your brother is never going to— Screw it," he muttered, ducking abruptly to scoop her legs out from under her and give her a toss, catching her in the cradle of his arms, high against his chest. "We're getting married. Maybe we will adopt, but I'm not having you walk around without my ring. No one will call you anything but my wife."

"Was that a proposal? Because I missed the part where I was asked," she said, but it was hard to sound tart when she was grinning and his neck smelled good and she wanted to crawl inside his clothes. Under his skin. "I missed you," she said against his Adam's apple, voice thready with need.

"I'm half a man without you," he said as he strode into the bedroom and placed her on his bed. "I'm only the worst parts of myself. Angry, jealous, miserable." He yanked his shirt open as he pulled it from his pants. "You understand what kind of possessive bastard you're consigning yourself to, don't you?"

"I'd like to say it's my choice, but I don't think I've ever had one." She lifted her hips to reach her zipper, then working her skirt down, enjoying the way his chest swelled at the sight of her bared legs. He hurried to finish undressing. "It has to be you or no one," she told him.

"Are you still on the pill?" he asked.

She nodded while she released the belt that she'd worn over her shirt, but she caught the little something that passed over his expression. It was a brief hesitation, words that rose but were second-guessed. One day, she knew from that tiny moment of betrayed thought, one day he would be ready to think about children. It was okay that today wasn't that day. She wanted him to herself for a little while, anyway.

He skimmed her undies away and settled his hot body over her, his hips between her legs. One arm reached to help her finish pushing off her top. "This is pretty," he said of her bra, tracing the edge of the blue-green lace. "It can stay for now."

He leaned to kiss her, but she drew back, needing to know.

"Does it bother you that so many men have seen me naked?"

"That will always bother me, *cara*. Not just because I am a jealous Neanderthal of a man, but because it hurt you so very badly. I would do *anything* to make that go away for you."

She traced her fingertips along his temple, down the side of his face, then cupped the side of his neck. "But we might not have found each other if that hadn't happened. And you wouldn't be here at all if your mother and father hadn't happened. Life is never going to be perfect and tidy, you know. Bad things can happen. We can only do our best with what we're given."

"Are you giving yourself to me?"

"I am," she said solemnly.

Excitement lit his eyes, but his kiss was tender. "Then I will do my best with you. That is a promise, *mia bella*." He settled his hips low and his hard, glorious length slid into her, slid home, making her groan in welcome. This was where they both belonged.

"Ti amo tanto," he groaned. *I love you so much.*

And later, when they were debating whether to rise and go out to eat, both completely lacking the will to move any more than a hand to caress a collarbone or turn their lips into each other's skin, her ringtone sounded from the other room.

Leaning off the bed for his pants, Vito pulled out his own phone and dialed, saying a moment later, "She's not coming home tonight. We'll come by your father's in the morning on the way to the jewelry store. I'll ask for her hand like a proper suitor. Good enough?"

It must have been because he hung up after one grumbled word from a voice she recognized as Trav's.

"I told you he's annoying," she said.

Vito set aside his phone and gathered her beneath him, bracing himself on his elbow above her, just looking at her in the half light of dusk coming through the uncovered windows.

"I like it, *tesoro*. I'm a competitive man. I will enjoy treating you so well he is forced to eat his words again and again."

She burst out laughing, not asking where his edges and superiority complex came from. At least he was using his naturally dominant nature for good instead of evil.

"I do love you, you know," she told him, gazing into his eyes. "I love you because you told me. You trust me. That means so much."

"I never imagined telling anyone." He frowned across the room, into the middle distance. "It's not about protecting me anymore, but protecting the bank. This could be a very big problem for the family."

"I'll never tell a soul, I promise."

"I know." His brows gave a little pull, like she was stating the obvious. "I knew when I came here that even if you were repelled, the secret would always be safe with you."

She petted his cheek, smoothing his rough stubble, chiding, "But I will take every opportunity to point out things like the fact that you have a crazy fierce capacity for loyalty. If your son or daughter had the same, we'd have nothing to worry about."

His beautiful mouth pursed. "One of the first things I admired about you was that fighting spirit of yours."

"Really?" She tussled with him and he let her win, so she had him on his back and she sat straddled over his thighs. But rather than crow with triumph as she pinned his big hands to the mattress, she leaned down to say against his lazy, satisfied grin, "You changed my world and I'm going to change yours."

"Vows to live by, *mia bella*. I do."

EPILOGUE

"DON'T YOU DARE, you little streaker!" Gwyn said, but her daughter had figured out that her mother was handicapped by a belly the size of Nebraska. She slithered away and left Gwyn on her knees holding a towel and a clean diaper.

"Vito!" Gwyn cried, and awkwardly clambered to her feet, waddling after her just-turned-two-year-old into the hall.

Antoinietta made her way down the stairs with determined little feet, hands gripping each of the uprights in turn, always tenacious about getting what she wanted, but willing to play by the rules once they were given to her.

Vito made no effort to come up to the girl, just stood at the bottom with his hands on his hips. "You really take after your mother, don't you?"

"Oh, you're funny," Gwyn told him, narrowing her eyes in a promise of retribution. "I told her who was coming for dinner. It was supposed to be an inducement to get her into her clothes, but…" She waved to indicate how well that had worked.

"Bea!" Toni called, trying to dodge her father as he made a grab for her at the bottom of the stairs. Then she said a very stern, "No, Papa," when he caught her and carried her up the stairs. The higher he went, the more she struggled and the louder she said, *"Down."*

"Yeah, that's all me," Gwyn said as he took the diaper from her. Their daughter was making a very serious effort to get out of his hold, squirming so hard her face was red, pudgy fists white and tiny brows screwed up with stubborn resolve.

"She's *two*," Vito said.

"She's *yours*," Gwyn said, chuckling when that actually made him close his arms even more tenderly around his adamant little girl.

"She is," he said proudly, and proceeded to speak in a calm voice, explaining that her cousins would be here soon, but she had to dress first.

He wrangled her into her clothes amid a great deal of negotiating and, *"Me do!"*

The bell rang as Vito carried her down the stairs a few minutes later and Toni's excitement soared as Bianca and the boys entered. She spared a moment to hug and kiss the adults, but her adulation was reserved for her true hero, Roberto, her partner in mischief, Arturo, and her dearest and most beloved Bianca.

"Bea." She hugged the girl who knelt to hug her back with every warm and sweet bone in her body.

Gwyn was almost as excited as her daughter when family came over. Henry now saw the advantage of a tablet and connected with them online when he wasn't actually staying at the apartment he'd bought nearby, so he could visit in person and watch his granddaughter grow up. He was flying in next week, anticipating the new baby would be with them. Even Travis had made a point of coming with his father for Christmas this year, since Gwyn had been too far along to travel.

Tonight it was Vito's turn for having family over. All of Vito's relations had made her feel welcome, Vito's parents especially, but Lauren was like a sister to Gwyn. Now that they were both pregnant, they were even closer than ever.

As for the man who was her boss again, after contracting her for a special project he'd offered to her a year ago? She didn't find him nearly as formidable.

"You're as much of a comedian as your cousin, aren't you?" she said to Paolo as he set a bag she recognized inside the door. It was the birthing kit he'd prepared when they had come to the house on Lake Como and Lauren had delivered Arturo. "I'm warning you right now, if your wife has her baby in my home, when I am already eleven months pregnant—" It was an exaggeration, but that was how she felt.

Paolo cut her off by kissing her cheek. "I brought it for Vito."

"Ha!"

"Bite your tongue," Vito muttered.

"The doctor said I'm at least two weeks away," Lauren assured them and they all groaned and rolled their eyes. "But honestly, Gwyn. The second one comes faster."

"So I can count on thirty-six hours reducing to thirty?" Gwyn joked.

"Cara," Vito protested. He had been appalled, genuinely upset that all the pleasure they gave each other had resulted in so much pain for her, but Toni was such a gift Gwyn was more than willing to go through it again to meet the next addition to their family. In fact,

she had a feeling it would be sooner than later. One of the reasons she had invited them for dinner was because she had that low, dull ache in her pelvis that had sat with her for two days before her labor had started for real with Toni.

Soon, she knew, she'd be tied up with a newborn and not entertaining for a while, so she wanted a proper visit with this family she enjoyed so much while she had the time.

Sure enough, a few hours later, as she and Lauren were drying dishes, the first pain hit, a nice strong one that took her breath.

"Vito," Lauren called as she took the plate from Gwyn's hand. "We're going to take Toni home with us. You and your wife have a date with a midwife."

They made that date, with no time to spare. Second babies did come faster and Vito almost had to eat his smug words to Paolo as they'd left, about how some men got their wives to the hospital before their children delivered. His son arrived as Gwyn was being admitted, caught by a startled ER nurse who barely had time to pull the curtain.

"Do you mind?" Gwyn asked Vito when she was settled in the maternity ward, pronounced healthy along with their son, but staying for overnight observation. "That he's a boy, I mean?"

"Why would I mind?" he asked, lifting a sharp gaze from studying the boy.

"You wanted a girl with Toni. I thought…" She had taken it to mean he believed girls were less likely to develop undesirable behaviors.

"Because I wanted to name her Antoinietta. I knew

my mother would be touched to have her sister remembered and she is."

"You're not worried your son will be like—"

"Me?" he cut in, mouth twisting into a wry smirk. "I'm counting on it."

She had to chuckle at that, and leaned forward to kiss him. "Me, too."

* * * * *

THE TRUTH BEHIND HIS TOUCH

CATHY WILLIAMS

case which behaved like a recalcitrant child, stopping and swerving and doing its best to misbehave.

Anyone with a less cheerful and equable temperament might have been tempted to curse the elderly employer who had sent them on this impossible mission, which was frankly way beyond the scope of their duties. But Caroline, tired, hot and hungry as she was, was optimistic that she could do what was expected of her. She had enormous faith in human nature. Alberto, on the other hand, was the world's most confirmed pessimist.

She very nearly missed the building. Not knowing what exactly to expect, she had imagined something along the lines of an office in London. Bland, uninspiring, with perhaps too much glass and too little imagination.

Retracing her steps, she looked down at the address which she had carefully printed on an index card, and then up at the ancient exterior of stone and soft, aged pinks, no more than three storeys tall, adorned with exquisite carvings and fronted by two stone columns.

How difficult could Giancarlo be if he worked in this wonderful place? Caroline mused, heart lightening.

'I cannot tell you anything of Giancarlo,' Alberto had said mournfully when she had tried to press him for details of what she would be letting herself in for. 'It is many, many years since I have seen him. I could show you some pictures, but they are so out of date. He would have changed in all these years... If I had a computer... But an old man like me... How could I ever learn now to work one of those things?'

'I could go and get my laptop from upstairs,' she had offered instantly, but he had waved her down.

'No, no. I don't care for those gadgets. Televisions and telephones are as far as I am prepared to go when it comes to technology.'

Privately, Caroline agreed with him. She used her computer to email but that was all, and it was nigh on impossible trying to access the Internet in the house anyway.

So she had few details on which to go. She suspected, however, that Giancarlo was rich, because Alberto had told her in passing that he had 'made something of himself'. Her suspicion crystallised when she stepped into the cool, uber-modern, marbled portico of Giancarlo's offices. If the façade of the building looked as though it had stepped out of an architectural guide to mediaeval buildings, inside the twenty-first century had made its mark.

Only the cool, pale marble underfoot and the scattering of old masterpieces on the walls hinted at the age of the building.

Of course, she wasn't expected. Surprise, apparently, was of the utmost importance, 'or else he will just refuse to see you, I am convinced of it!'.

It took her over thirty-five minutes to try to persuade the elegant receptionist positioned like a guard dog behind her wood-and-marble counter, who spoke far too quickly for Caroline to follow, that she shouldn't be chucked out.

'What is your business here?'

'Ah...'

'Are you expected?'

'Not *exactly*...'

'Are you aware that Signore de Vito is an extremely important man?'

'Er...' Then she had practised her haltering Italian and explained the connection to Giancarlo, produced several documents which had been pored over in silence and the wheels of machinery had finally begun to move.

But still she would have to wait.

Three floors up, Giancarlo, in the middle of a meeting with three corporate financiers, was interrupted by his secretary, who whispered something in his ear that made him still and brought the shutters down on his dark, cold eyes.

'Are you sure?' he asked in a clipped voice. Elena Carli seldom made mistakes; it was why she had worked for him so successfully for the past five-and-a-half years. She did her job with breathtaking efficiency, obeyed orders without question and *seldom* made mistakes. When she nodded firmly, he immediately got to his feet, made his excuses—though not profusely, because these financiers needed him far more than he needed them—and then, meeting dismissed, he walked across to the window to stare down at the paved, private courtyard onto which his offices backed.

So the past he thought to have left behind was returning. Good sense counselled him to turn his back on this unexpected intrusion in his life, but he was curious and what harm would there be in indulging his curiosity? In his life of unimaginable wealth and vast power, curiosity was a rare visitor, after all.

Giancarlo de Vito had been ferociously single-minded and ruthlessly ambitious to get where he was now. He had had no choice. His mother had needed to be kept and after a series of unfortunate lovers the only person left to keep her had been him. He had finished his university career with a first and had launched himself into the world of high finance with such dazzling expertise that it hadn't been long before doors began to open. Within three years of finishing university, he'd been able to pick and choose his employer. Within five years, he'd no longer needed an employer because he had become the powerhouse who did the employing. Now, at just over thirty, he had become a billionaire, diversifying with gratifying success, branching out and stealing the march on competitors with every successive merger and acquisition and in the process building himself a reputation that rendered him virtually untouchable.

His mother had seen only the tip of his enormous success, as she had died six years previously—perhaps, fittingly, in the passenger seat of her young lover's fast car—a victim, as he had seen it, of a life gone wrong. As her only offspring, Giancarlo knew he should have been more heartbroken than he actually was, but his mother had been a temperamental and difficult woman, fond of spending money and easily dissatisfied. He had found her flitting from lover to lover rather distasteful, but never had he once criticized her. At the end of the day, hadn't she been through enough?

Unaccustomed to taking these trips down memory lane, Giancarlo shook himself out of his introspection with a certain amount of impatience. Presumably the woman who had come to see him and who was currently sitting in the grand marble foyer was to blame for his lapse in self-control. With his thoughts back in order and back where they belonged, he buzzed her up.

'You may go up now.' The receptionist beckoned to Caroline, who could have stayed sitting in the air-conditioned foyer quite happily for another few hours. Her feet were killing her and she had finally begun cooling down after the hours spent in the suffocating heat. 'Signora Carli will meet you up at the top of the elevator and show you to Signore De Vito's office. If you like, you may leave your…case here.'

Caroline thought that the last thing the receptionist seemed to want was her battered pull-along being left anywhere in the foyer. At any rate, she needed it with her.

And, now that she was finally here, she felt a little twist of nervousness at the prospect of what lay ahead. She wouldn't want to return to the lake house empty-handed. Alberto had suffered a heart attack several weeks previously. His health was not good and, his doctor had confided in her, the less stress the better.

With a determined lift of her head, Caroline followed the
personal assistant in silence, passing offices which seemed
abnormally silent, staffed with lots of hard-working executives who barely looked up as they walked past.

Everyone seemed very well-groomed. The women were
all thin, good-looking and severe, with their hair scraped
back and their suits shrieking of money well spent.

In comparison, Caroline felt overweight, short and di-
shevelled. She had never been skinny, even as a child. When
she sucked her breath in and looked at herself sideways
through narrowed eyes, she could almost convince herself
that she was curvy and voluptuous, but the illusion was
always destroyed the second she took a harder look at her
reflection. Nor was her hair of the manageable variety. It
rarely did as it was told; it flowed in wild abandon down
her back and was only ever remotely obedient when it was
wet. Right now the heat had added more curl than normal
and she knew that tendrils were flying wildly out of their
impromptu braid. She had to keep blowing them off her
face.

After trailing along behind Elena—who had introduced
herself briefly and then seen fit to say absolutely nothing
else on the way up—a door was opened into an office so
exquisite that for a few seconds Caroline wasn't even aware
that she had been deposited like an unwanted parcel, nor did
she notice the man by the window turning slowly around
to look at her.

All she could see was the expanse of splendid, antique
Persian rug on the marble floor; the soft, silk wallpaper
on the walls; the smooth, dark patina of a bookshelf that
half-filled an entire wall; the warm, old paintings on the
walls—not paintings of silly lines and shapes that no one
could ever decipher, but paintings of beautiful landscapes,
heavy with trees and rivers.

'Wow,' she breathed, deeply impressed as she continued to look around her with shameless awe.

At long last her eyes rested on the man staring at her and she was overcome with a suffocating, giddy sensation as she absorbed the wild, impossible beauty of his face. Black hair, combed back and ever so slightly too long, framed a face of stunning perfection. His features were classically perfect and invested with a raw sensuality that brought a heated flush to her cheeks. His eyes were dark and unreadable. Expensive, lovingly hand-tailored charcoal-grey trousers sheathed long legs and the crisp white shirt rolled to the elbows revealed strong, bronzed forearms with a sprinkling of dark hair. In the space of a few seconds, Caroline realised that she was staring at the most spectacular-looking man she had ever clapped eyes on in her life. She also belatedly realised that she was gaping, mouth inelegantly open, and she cleared her throat in an attempt to get a hold of herself.

The silence stretched to breaking point and then at last the man spoke and introduced himself, inviting her to take a seat, which she was only too happy to do because her legs felt like jelly. His voice matched his appearance. It was deep, dark, smooth and velvety. It was also icy cold, and a trickle of doubt began creeping in, because this was not a man who looked as though he could be persuaded into doing anything he didn't want to do.

'So…' Giancarlo sat down, pushing himself away from his desk so that he could cross his long legs, and stared at her. 'What makes you think that you can just barge into my offices, Miss…?'

'Rossi. Caroline.'

'I was in the middle of a meeting.'

'I'm so sorry.' She stumbled over the apology. 'I didn't mean to interrupt anything. I would have been happy to wait until you were finished…' Her naturally sunny personality rose to the surface and she offered him a small smile. 'In fact, it was so wonderfully cool in your foyer and I was just so grateful to rest my legs. I've been on the go for absolutely ages and it's as hot as a furnace out there...' In receipt of his continuing and unwelcoming silence, her voice faded away and she licked her lips nervously.

Giancarlo was quite happy to let her stew in her own discomfiture.

'This is a fantastic building, by the way.'

'Let's do away with the pleasantries, Miss Rossi. What are you doing here?'

'Your father sent me.'

'So I gather. Which is why you're sitting in my office. My question is *why*? I haven't had any contact with my father in over fifteen years, so I'm curious as to why he should suddenly decide to send a henchman to get in touch with me.'

Caroline felt an uncustomary warming anger flood through her as she tried to marry up this cold, dark stranger with the old man of whom she was so deeply fond, but getting angry wasn't going to get her anywhere.

'And who *are* you anyway? My father is hardly a spring chicken. Don't tell me that he's managed to find himself a young wife to nurse him faithfully through his old age?' He leaned back in his chair and steepled his fingers together. 'Nothing too beautiful, of course,' he murmured, casting insolent, assessing eyes over her. 'Devotion in the form of a young, beautiful, nubile wife is never a good idea for an old man, even a rich old man...'

'How dare you?'

Giancarlo laughed coldly. 'You show up here, unannounced, with a message from a father who was written out of my life a long time ago... Frankly, I have every right to dare.'

'I am *not* married to your father!'

'Well, now the alternative is even more distasteful, not to mention downright stupid. Why involve yourself with someone three times your age unless you're in it for the financial gain? Don't tell me the sex is breathtaking?'

'I can't believe you're saying these things!' She wondered how she could have been so bowled over by the way he looked when he was obviously a loathsome individual, just the sort of cold, unfeeling, sneering sort she hated. 'I'm not involved with your father in any way other than professionally, *signore*!'

'No? Then what is a young girl like you doing in a rambling old house by a lake with only an old man for company?'

Caroline glared at him. She was still smarting at the way his eyes had roamed over her and dismissed her as 'nothing too beautiful'. She knew she wasn't beautiful but to hear it casually emerge from the mouth of someone she didn't know was beyond rude. Especially from the mouth of someone as physically compelling as the man sitting in front of her. Why hadn't she done what most other people would have in similar circumstances and found herself an Internet café so that she could do some background research on the man she had been told to ferret out? At least then she might have been prepared!

She had to grit her teeth together and fight the irresistible urge to grab her suitcase and jump ship.

'Well? I'm all ears.'

'There's no need to be horrible to me, *signore*. I'm sorry if I've ruined your meeting, or…or whatever you were doing, but I didn't *volunteer* to come here.'

Giancarlo almost didn't believe his ears. People never accused him of being *horrible*. Granted, they might sometimes think that, but it was vaguely shocking to actually *hear* someone come right out and say it. Especially a woman. He was accustomed to women doing everything within their power to please him. He looked narrowly at his uninvited visitor. She was certainly not the sort of rake-thin beauty eulogised in the pages of magazines. She was trying hard to conceal her expression but it was transparently clear that the last place she wanted to be was in his office, being interrogated.

Too bad.

'I take it my father manipulated you into doing what he wanted. Are you his housekeeper? Why would he employ an English housekeeper?'

'I'm his personal assistant,' Caroline admitted reluctantly. 'He used to know my father once upon a time. Your father had a one-year posting in England lecturing at a university and my father was one of his students. He was my father's mentor and they kept in touch after your father returned to Italy. My father is Italian. I think he enjoyed having someone he could speak to in Italian.

'Anyway, I didn't go to university, but my parents thought it would be nice for me to learn Italian, seeing that it's my father's native tongue, and he asked Alberto if he could help me find a posting over here for a few months. So I'm helping your father with his memoirs and also pretty much taking care of all the admin—stuff like that. Don't you want to know…um…how he is? You haven't seen him in such a long time.'

'If I had wanted to see my father, don't you think I would have contacted him before now?'

'Yes, well, pride can sometimes get in the way of us doing what we want to do.'

'If your aim is to play amateur psychologist, then the door is right behind you. Avail yourself of it.'

'I'm not playing amateur psychologist,' Caroline per-

sisted stubbornly. 'I just think, well, I know that it probably wasn't ideal when your parents got divorced. Alberto
doesn't talk much about it, but I know that when your
mother walked out and took you with her you were only
twelve...'

'I don't believe I'm hearing this!' Intensely private,
Giancarlo could scarcely credit that he was listening to
someone drag his past out of the closet in which it had been
very firmly shut.

'How else am I supposed to deal with this situation?'
Caroline asked, bewildered and dismayed.

'I am not in the habit of discussing my past!'

'Yes, well, that's not *my* fault.' She felt herself soften.
'Don't you think that it's a good thing to talk about the
things that bother us? Don't you *ever* think about your dad?'

His internal line buzzed and he spoke in rapid Italian,
telling his secretary to hold all further calls until he advised her otherwise. Suddenly, filled with a restless energy
he couldn't seem to contain, he pushed himself away from
the desk and moved across to the window to look briefly
outside before turning around and staring at the girl on the
chair who had swivelled to face him.

She looked as though butter wouldn't melt in her
mouth—very young, very innocent and with a face as transparent as a pane of glass. Right now, he seemed to be an
object of pity, and he tightened his mouth with a sense of
furious outrage.

'He's had a heart attack,' Caroline told him abruptly, her
eyes beginning to well up because she was so very fond
of him. Having him rushed into hospital, dealing with the
horror of it all on her own had been almost more than she
could take. 'A very serious one. In fact, for a while it was
touch and go.' She opened her satchel, rummaged around

for a tissue and found a pristine white handkerchief pressed into her hand.

'Sorry,' she whispered shakily. 'But I don't know how you can just stand there like a statue and not feel a thing.'

Big brown eyes looked accusingly at him and Giancarlo flushed, annoyed with himself because there was no reason why he should feel guilty on that score. He had no relationship with his father. Indeed, his memories of life in the big house by the lake were a nightmare of parental warfare. Alberto had married his very young and very pretty blonde wife when he had been in his late forties, nearly twenty-five years older than Adriana, and was already a cantankerous and confirmed bachelor.

It had been a marriage that had struggled on against all odds and had been, to all accounts, hellishly difficult for his demanding young wife.

His mother had not held back from telling him everything that had been so horrifically wrong with the relationship, as soon as he had been old enough to appreciate the gory detail. Alberto had been selfish, cold, mean, dismissive, contemptuous and probably, his mother had maintained viciously, would have had other women had he not lacked even basic social skills when it came to the opposite sex. He had, Adriana had wept on more than one occasion, thrown them out without a penny—so was it any wonder that she sometimes needed a little alcohol and a few substances to help her get by?

So many things for which Giancarlo had never forgiven his father...

He had stood on the sidelines and watched his delicate, spoilt mother—without any qualifications to speak of, always reliant on her beauty—demean herself by taking lover after lover, searching for the one who might want her enough to stick around. By the time she had died she had been a pathetic shadow of her former self.

'You have no idea of what my life was like, or what my mother's life was like,' Giancarlo framed icily. 'Perhaps my father has mellowed. Ill health has a habit of making servants of us all. However, I'm not interested in building bridges. Is that why he sent you here—because he's now an old man and he wants my forgiveness before he shuffles off this mortal coil?' He gave a bark of cynical, contemptuous laughter. 'I don't think so.'

She had continued playing with the handkerchief, twisting it between her fingers. Giancarlo thought that when it came to messengers, his father could not have been more calculating in his choice. The woman was a picture of teary-eyed incomprehension. Anyone would be forgiven for thinking that she worked for a saint, instead of for the man who had made his mother's life a living hell.

His sharp eyes narrowed and focused, taking in the details of her appearance. Her clothes were a fashion disaster—trousers and a blouse in a strange, sickly shade of yellow, both of which would have been better suited to someone twice her age. Her hair seemed to be escaping from a sort of makeshift braid, and it was long—really long. Not at all like the snappy bobs he was accustomed to seeing on women. And it was curly. She was free of makeup and he was suddenly conscious of the fact that her skin was very smooth, satin smooth, and she had an amazing mouth—full, well-defined lips, slightly parted now to reveal pearly-white teeth as she continued to stare at him with disappointment and incredulity.

'I'm sorry you're still so bitter about the past,' she murmured quietly. 'But he would really like to see you. Why is it too late to mend bridges? It would mean the world to him.'

'So have you managed to see anything of our beautiful city?'

'What? No. No, I've come directly here. Look, is there anything I can do or say to convince you to...to come back with me?'

'You have got to be kidding, haven't you? I mean, even if I were suddenly infused with a burning desire to become a prodigal son, do you really imagine that I would be able to drop everything, pack a bag and hop on the nearest train for Lake Como? Surprise, surprise—I have an empire to run.'

'Yes, but...'

'I'm a very busy man, Miss Rossi, and I have already allotted you a great deal of my very valuable time. Now, you could keep trying to convince me that I'm being a monster in not clapping my hands for joy that my father has suddenly decided to get in touch with me thanks to a bout of ill health...'

'You make it sound as though he's had a mild attack of flu! He's suffered a very serious *heart attack*.'

'For which I am truly sorry.' Giancarlo extended his arms wide in a gesture of such phoney sympathy that Caroline had to clench her fists to stop herself from smacking him. 'As I would be on learning of any stranger's brush with death. But, alas, you're going to have to go back empty-handed.'

Defeated, Caroline stood up and reached down for her suitcase.

'Where are you staying?' Giancarlo asked with scrupulous politeness as he watched the slump of her shoulders. God, had the old man really thought that there would be no consequences to pay for the destructive way he had treated his wife? He was as rich as they came and yet, according to Adriana, he had employed the best lawyers in the land to ensure that she received the barest of settlements, accessed through a trustee who had made sure the basics, the *absolute* basics, were paid for, and a meagre allowance handed over to her, like a child being given pocket money, scarcely enough to provide any standard of living. He had often wondered, over the years, whether his mother would have been as desperate to find love if she had been left sufficient money to meet her requirements.

Caroline wearily told him, although she knew full well that he didn't give a damn where she was staying. He just wanted her out of his office. She would be returning having failed. Of course, Alberto would be far too proud to do anything other than shrug his shoulders and say something about having tried, but she would know the truth. She would know that he would be gutted.

'Well, you make sure you try the food market at the Rinascente. You'll enjoy it. Tremendous views. And, of course, the shopping there is good as well.'

'I hate shopping.' Caroline came to a stop in front of the office door and turned around to find that he was virtually on top of her, towering a good eight or nine inches above her and even more intimidating this close up than he had been sitting safely behind his desk or lounging by the window.

The sun glinted from behind, picking out the striking angles of his face and rendering them more scarily beautiful. He had the most amazing eyelashes, long, lush and dark, the sort of eyelashes that most women could only ever have achieved with the help of tons of mascara.

She felt a sickening jolt somewhere in the region of her stomach and was suddenly and uncomfortably aware of her breasts, too big for her height, now sensitive, tingly and weighty as he stared down at her. Her hands wanted to flutter to the neckline of her blouse and draw the lapels tightly together. She flushed with embarrassment; how could she have forgotten that she was the ugly duckling?

'And I don't want to be having this polite conversation with you,' she breathed in a husky, defiant undertone.

'Come again?'

'I'm sorry your parents got divorced, and I'm really sorry that it left such a mark on you, but I think it's horrible that you won't give your father another chance. How do you know exactly what happened between your parents? You were only a child. Your father's ill and you'd rather carry on holding a grudge than try and make the most of the time you have left of him. He might die tomorrow, for all we know!'

That short speech took a lot out of her. She wasn't usually defiant, but this man set her teeth on edge. 'How can you say that, even if you were interested in meeting him, you couldn't possibly get away because you're too important?'

'I said that I have an empire to run.'

'It's the same thing!' She was shaking all over, like a leaf, but she looked up at him with unflinching determination, chin jutting out, her brown eyes, normally mild, flashing fire. 'Okay, I'm not going to see you again…' Caroline drew in a deep breath and impatiently swept her disobedient hair from away her face. 'So I can be really honest with you.'

Giancarlo moved to lounge against the door, arms folded, an expression of lively curiosity on his face. Her cheeks were flushed and her eyes glittered. She was a woman in a rage and he was getting the impression that this was a woman who didn't *do* rages. God, wasn't this turning into one hell of a day?

'I don't suppose *anyone* is really ever honest with you, are they?' She looked around the office, with its mega-expensive fittings, ancient rug, worn bookshelves, the painting on the wall—the only modern one she had glimpsed, which looked vaguely familiar. Who was really ever that honest with someone as wealthy as he appeared to be, as good-looking as he was? He had the arrogance of a man who always got exactly what he wanted.

'It's useful when my man who handles my stocks and shares tells me what he thinks. Although, in fairness, I usually know more than he does. I should get rid of him but—' he shrugged with typical Italian nonchalance '—we go back a long way.'

He shot her a smile that was so unconsciously charming that Caroline was nearly knocked backwards by the force of it. It was like being in a dark room only to be suddenly dazzled by a ray of blistering sunshine. Which didn't distract her from the fact that he refused to see his father, a sick and possibly dying old man. Refused to bury the hatchet, whatever the consequences. Charming smiles counted for nothing when it came to the bigger picture!

'I'm glad you think that this is a big joke,' she said tightly. 'I'm glad that you can laugh about it, but you know what? I feel *sorry* for you! You might think that the only thing that matters is all…all *this*…but none of this counts when it comes to relationships and family. I think you're… you're *arrogant* and *high-handed* and making a huge mistake!'

Outburst over, Caroline yanked open the office door to a surprised Elena, who glanced at her with consternation before looking behind to where her boss, the man who never lost his steely grip on his emotions, was staring at the small, departing brunette with the incredulous expression of someone who has been successfully tackled when least expecting it.

'Stop staring,' Giancarlo said. He shook his head, dazed, and then offered his secretary a wry grin. 'We all lose our cool sometimes.'

CHAPTER TWO

MILAN was a diverse and beautiful city. There were sufficient museums, galleries, basilicas and churches to keep any tourist busy. The Galleria Vittorio was a splendid and elegant arcade, stuffed with cafés and shops. Caroline knew all this because the following day—her last day before she returned to Alberto, when she would have to admit failure—she made sure to read all the literature on a city which she might not visit again. It was tarnished with the miserable experience of having met Giancarlo De Vito.

The more Caroline thought about him, the more arrogant and unbearable he seemed. She just couldn't find a single charitable thing to credit him with. Alberto would be waiting for her, expecting to see her arrive with his son and, failing that, he would be curious for details. Would she be honest and admit to him that she had found his sinfully beautiful son loathsome and overbearing? Would any parent, even an estranged parent, be grateful for information like that?

She looked down to where her ice-cold glass of lemonade was slowly turning warm in the searing heat. She had dutifully spent two hours walking around the Duomo, admiring the stained-glass windows, the impressive statues of saints and the extravagant carvings. But her heart hadn't been in it, and now here she was, in one of the little cafés,

which outside on a hot summer day was packed to the raf-
ters with tourists sitting and lazily people-watching.

Her thoughts were in turmoil. With an impatient sigh,
she glanced down at her watch, wondering how she would
fill the remainder of her day, and was unaware of the
shadow looming over her until she heard Giancarlo's velvety, familiar voice which had become embedded in her
head like an irritating burr.

'You lied to me.'

Caroline looked up, shading her eyes from the glare of
the sun, at about the same time as a wad of papers landed
on the small circular table in front of her.

She was so shocked to see him towering over her, blocking out the sun like a dark avenging angel, that she half-
spilled her drink in her confusion.

'What are you doing here? And how did you find me?'
Belatedly she noticed the papers on the table. 'And what's
all that stuff?'

'We need to have a little chat and this place isn't doing
it for me.'

Caroline felt her heart lift a little. Maybe he was recon-
sidering his original stance. Maybe, just maybe, he had
seen the light and was now prepared to let bygones be bygones. She temporarily forgot his ominous opening words
and the mysterious stack of papers in front of her.

'Of course!' She smiled brightly and then cleared her
throat when there was no reciprocal smile. 'I... You haven't
said how you managed to find me. Where are we going?
Am I supposed to bring all this stuff with me?'

Presumably, yes, as he spun round on his heels and was
scouring the *piazza* through narrowed eyes. Did he notice
the interested stares he was garnering from the tourists,
particularly the women? Or was he immune to that sort of
attention?

Caroline grabbed the papers and scrambled to follow him as he strode away from the café through a series of small roads, leaving the crush of tourists behind.

Today, she had worn the only other outfit she had brought with her, a summer dress with small buttons down the front. Because it left her shoulders bare, and because she was so acutely conscious of her generous breasts, she had a thin pink cardigan slung loosely over her—which wasn't exactly practical, given the weather, but without it she felt too exposed and self-conscious.

With the ease of someone who lived in the city, he weaved his way through the busier areas until they were finally at a small café tucked away from the tourist hotspots, although even here the ancient architecture, the charming square with its sixteenth-century well, the engravings on some of the façades, were all photo opportunities.

She dithered behind him, feeling a bit like a spare part as he spoke in rapid Italian to a short, plump man whom she took to be the owner of the café. Then he motioned her inside where it was blessedly cool and relatively empty.

'You can sit,' Giancarlo said irritably when she continued to hover by the table. What did his father see in the woman? He barely remembered Alberto, but one thing he *did* remember was that he had not been the most docile person in the world. If his mother had been a difficult woman, then she had found her match in her much older husband. What changes had the years wrought, if Alberto was happy to work with someone who had to be the most background woman he had ever met? And once again she was in an outfit that would have been more suitable on a woman twice her age. Truly the English hadn't got a clue when it came to fashion.

He found himself appraising her body and then, surprisingly, lingering on her full breasts pushing against the thin cotton dress, very much in evidence despite the washed-out cardigan she had draped over her shoulders.

'You never said how you managed to find me,' Caroline repeated a little breathlessly as she slid into the chair opposite him.

She shook away the giddy, drowning feeling she had when she looked too hard at him. Something about his animal sex-appeal was horribly unsettling, too hard to ignore and not quite what she was used to.

'You told me where you were staying. I went there first thing this morning and was told by the receptionist that you'd left for the Duomo. It was just a question of time before you followed the herd to one of the cafés outside.'

'So…have you had a rethink?' Caroline asked hopefully. She wondered how it was that he could look so cool and urbane in his cream trousers and white shirt while the rest of the population seemed to be slowly dissolving under the summer sun.

'Have a look at the papers in front of you.'

Caroline dutifully flicked through them. 'I'm sorry, I have no idea what these are—and I'm not very good with numbers.' She had wisely tied her hair back today but still some curling strands found their way to her cheeks and she absent-mindedly tucked them behind her ears while she continued to frown at the pages and pages of bewildering columns and numbers in front of her, finally giving up.

'After I saw you I decided to run a little check on Alberto's company accounts. You're looking at my findings.'

'I don't understand why you've shown me this. I don't know anything about Alberto's financial affairs. He doesn't talk about that at all.'

'Funny, but I never thought him particularly shy when

it came to money. In fact, I would say that he's always had his finger on the button in that area.'

'How would you know, when you haven't seen him for over a decade?'

Giancarlo thought of the way Alberto had short changed his mother and his lips curled cynically. 'Let's move away from that contentious area, shall we? And let's focus on one or two interesting things I unearthed.' He sat back as cold drinks were placed in front of them, along with a plate of delicate little *tortas* and pastries. 'By the way, help yourself...' He gestured to the dish of pastries and cakes and was momentarily sidetracked when she pulled her side plate in front of her and piled a polite mound, but a mound nevertheless, of the delicacies on it.

'You're actually going to eat all of those?' he heard himself ask, fascinated against his will.

'I know, I shouldn't really. But I'm starving.' Caroline sighed at the diet which she had been planning for ages and which had yet to get underway. 'You don't mind, do you? I mean...they're not just here for *show*, are they?'

'No, *di niente*.' He sat back and watched as she nibbled her way through the pastries, politely leaving one, licking the sweet crumbs off her fingers with enjoyment. A rare sight. The stick-thin women he dated pushed food round their plates and would have recoiled in horror at the thought of eating anything as fattening as a pastry.

Of course, he should be getting on with what he wanted to say, but he had been thrown off course and he still was when she shot him an apologetic smile. There was an errant crumb at the side of her mouth and just for an instant he had an overwhelming urge to brush it off. Instead, he gestured to her mouth with his hand.

'I always have big plans for going on a diet.' Caroline blushed. 'Once or twice I actually did, but diets are deadly.

Have you ever been on one? No, I bet you haven't. Well, salads are all well and good, but just try making them interesting. I guess I just really love food.'

'That's…unusual. In a woman. Most of the women I meet do their best to avoid the whole eating experience.'

Of course he would be the type who only associated with model types, Caroline thought sourly. Thin, leggy women who weighed nothing. She wished she hadn't indulged her sweet tooth. Not that it mattered because, although he might be good-looking—well, staggering, really—he wasn't the sort of man she would ever go for. So what did it matter if he thought that she was overweight and greedy into the bargain?

'You were saying something about Alberto's financial affairs?' She glanced down at her watch, because why on earth should he have the monopoly on precious time? 'It's just that I leave tomorrow morning and I want to make sure that I get through as much as possible before I go.'

Giancarlo was, for once in his life, virtually lost for words. Was she *hurrying him along*?

'I think,' he asserted without inflection, 'that your plans will have to take a back seat until I'm finished.'

'You haven't told me whether you've decided to put the past behind you and accompany me back to Lake Como.' She didn't know why she was bothering to ask the question because it was obvious that he had no such intention.

'So you came here to see me for the sole purpose of masterminding a jolly reunion…'

'It wasn't *my* idea.'

'Immaterial. Getting back to the matter in hand, the fact is that Alberto's company accounts show a big, gaping black hole.'

Caroline frowned because she genuinely had no idea what he was talking about.

'*Si,*' Giancarlo imparted without a shade of regret as he continued to watch her so carefully that she could feel the colour mounting in her cheeks. 'He has been leaking money for the past ten years but recently it's become something more akin to a haemorrhage...'

Caroline gasped and stared at him in sudden consternation. 'Oh my goodness... Do you think that that's why he had the heart attack?'

'I beg your pardon?'

'I didn't think he took an active interest in what happened in the company. I mean, he's been pretty much a recluse since I came to live with him.'

'Which would be how long ago?'

'Several months. Originally, I only intended to come for a few weeks, but we got along so well and there were so many things he wanted me to do that I found myself staying on.' She fixed anxious brown eyes on Giancarlo, who seemed sublimely immune to an ounce of compassion at the news he had casually delivered.

'Are you...are you sure you've got your facts right?'

'I'm never wrong,' he said drily. 'It's possible that Alberto hasn't played an active part in running his company for some time now. It's more than possible that he's been merrily living off the dividends and foolishly imagining that his investments are paying off.'

'And what if he only recently found out?' Caroline cried, determined not to become too over-emotional in front of a man who, she knew, would see emotion in a woman as repellent. Besides, she had cried on him yesterday. She still had the handkerchief to prove it. Once had been bad enough but twice would be unforgivable.

'Do you think that that might have contributed to his heart attack? Do you think that he became so stressed that it affected his health?' Horribly rattled at that thought, she distractedly helped herself to the last pastry lying uneaten on her plate.

'No one can ever accuse me of being a gullible man, Signorina Rossi.' Giancarlo was determined to stick to the script. 'One lesson I've learnt in life is that, when it comes to money, there will always be people around who are more than happy to scheme their way into getting their hands on some of it.'

'Yes. Yes, I suppose so. Whatever. Poor Alberto. He never mentioned a word and yet he must have been so worried. Imagine having to deal with that on your own.'

'Yes. Poor Alberto. Still, whilst poring over these findings, it occurred to me that your mission here might very well have been twofold…'

'The doctor said that stress can cause all sorts of health problems.'

'Focus, signorina!'

Caroline fell silent and looked at him. The sun wafting through the pane of glass made his hair look all the more glossy. She vaguely noticed the way it curled at the collar of his shirt. Somehow, it made him look very exotic and very European.

'Now are you with me?'

'There's no need to talk down to me!'

'There's every need. You have the most wandering mind of anyone I've ever met.'

Caroline shot him a look of simmering resentment and added 'rude' to the increasingly long list of things she didn't like about him.

'And you are the *rudest* person I've ever met in my entire life!'

Giancarlo couldn't remember the last time anyone had ever dared to insult him to his face. He didn't think it had ever happened. Rather than be sidetracked, however, he chose to overlook her offensive remark.

'It occurred to me that my father's health, if your story about his heart attack is to be believed, might not be the primary reason for your visit to Milan.'

'If my story is to be believed?' She shook her head with a puzzled frown. 'Why would I lie about something like that?'

'I'll answer a question with a question—why would my father suddenly choose *now* to seek me out? He had more than one opportunity to get in touch. He never bothered. So why now? Shall I put forward a theory? He's wised up to the fact that his wealth has disappeared down the proverbial tubes and has sent you to check out the situation. Perhaps he told you that, if I seemed amenable to the idea of meeting up, you might mention the possibility of a loan?'

Shocked and disturbed by Giancarlo's freewheeling assumptions and cynical, half-baked misunderstandings, Caroline didn't know where to begin. She just stared at him as the colour drained away from her face. She wasn't normally given to anger, but right now she had to stop herself from picking her plate up and smashing it over his arrogant head.

'So maybe I wasn't entirely accurate when I accused you of lying to me. Maybe it would be more accurate to say that you were conveniently economical with the full truth…'

'I can't believe I'm hearing you say these things! How could you accuse your own father of trying to squeeze money out of you?'

Giancarlo flushed darkly under her steady, clear-eyed, incredulous gaze. 'Like I said, money has a nasty habit of bringing out the worst in people. Do you know that it's a given fact that the second someone wins a lottery, they suddenly discover that they have a hell of a lot more close friends and relatives than they ever imagined?'

'Alberto hasn't sent me here on a mission to get money out of you or…or to ask you for a loan!'

'Are you telling me that he had no idea that I was now a wealthy man?'

'That's not the point.' She remembered Alberto's statement that Giancarlo had made something of himself.

'No? You're telling me that there's no link between one semi-bankrupt father who hasn't been on the scene in nearly two decades and his sudden, inexplicable desire to meet the rich son he was happy to kick out of his house once upon a time?'

'Yes!'

'Well, if you really believe that, if you're not in cahoots with Alberto, then you must be incredibly naïve.'

'I feel very sorry for you, Signor De Vito.'

'Call me Giancarlo. I feel as though we almost know each other. Certainly no one can compete with you when it comes to delivering offensive remarks. You are in a league of your own.'

Caroline flushed because she was not given to being offensive. She was placid and easy-going by nature. However, she was certainly not going to apologise for speaking her mind to Giancarlo.

'You are pretty offensive as well,' she retaliated quietly. 'You've just accused me of being a liar. Maybe in *your* world you can never trust anyone…'

'I think it's fair to say that trust is a much over-rated virtue. I have a great deal of money. I've learnt to protect myself, simple as that.' He gave an elegant shrug, dismissing the topic. But Caroline wasn't quite ready to let the matter drop, to allow him to continue believing, unchallenged, that he had somehow been targeted by Alberto. She wouldn't let him walk away thinking the worst of either of them.

'I don't think that trust is an over-rated virtue. I told you that I feel sorry for you and I really do.' She had to steel herself to meet and hold the dark, forbidding depths of his icy eyes. 'I think it's sad to live in a world where you can never allow yourself to believe the best in other people. How can you ever be happy if you're always thinking that the people around you are out to take advantage of you? How can you ever be happy if you don't have faith in the people who are close to you?'

Giancarlo very nearly burst out laughing at that. What planet was this woman from? It was a cutthroat world out there and it became even more cutthroat when money and finances were involved. You had to keep your friends close and your enemies a whole lot closer in order to avoid the risk of being knifed in the back.

'Don't go getting evangelical on me,' he murmured drily and he noted the pink colour rise to her cheeks. 'You're blushing,' he surprised himself by saying.

'Because I'm angry!' But she put her hands to her face and glared at him. 'You're so...so *superior*! What sort of people do you mix with that you would suspect them of trying to use you for what you can give them? I didn't know anything about you when I agreed to come here. I didn't know that you had lots of money. I just knew that Alberto was ill and he wanted to make his peace with you.'

The oddest thing seemed to be happening. Giancarlo could feel himself getting distracted. Was it because of the way those tendrils of curly hair were wisping against her face? Or was it because her anger made her almond-shaped eyes gleam like a furious spitting cat's? Or maybe it was the fact that, when she leant forward like that, the weight and abundance of her breasts brushing against the small table acted like a magnet to his wandering eyes.

It was a strange sensation to experience this slight loss of self-control because it never happened in his dealings with women. And he was a connoisseur when it came to the opposite sex. Without a trace of vanity, he knew that he possessed a combination of looks, power and influence that most women found an irresistible aphrodisiac. Right now, he had only recently broken off a six-month relationship with a model whose stunning looks had graced the covers of a number of magazines. She had begun to make noises about 'taking things further'; had started mentioning friends and relatives who were thinking of tying the knot; had begun to show an unhealthy interest in the engagement-ring section of expensive jewellery shops.

Giancarlo had no interest in going down the matrimonial path. There were two vital lessons he felt he had taken away from his parents: the first was that there was no such thing as a happy-ever-after. The second was that it was very easy for a woman to turn from angel to shrew. The loving woman who was happy to accommodate on every level quickly became the demanding, needy harridan who needed reassurance and attention round the clock.

He had watched his mother contrive to play the perfect partner on so many occasions that he had lost count. He had watched her perform her magic with whatever man happened to be the flavour of the day for a while, had watched her bat her eyelashes and flutter her eyes—but then, when things began winding down, he had seen how she had changed from eager to desperate, from hard-to-get to clingy and dependent. The older she had got, the more pitiful a sight she had made.

Of course, he was a red-blooded man with an extremely healthy libido, but as far as Giancarlo was concerned work was a far better bet when it came to reliability. Women, enjoyable as they might be, became instantly expendable the second they began thinking that they could change him.

He had never let any woman get under his skin and he was surprised now to find his thoughts drifting ever so slightly from the matter at hand.

He had confronted her, having done some background research, simply to have his suspicions confirmed. It had been a simple exercise in proving to her—and via her to Alberto—that he wasn't a mug who could be taken for a ride. At which point, his plan had been to walk away, warning guns sounding just in case they were tempted to try a second approach.

From the very second Caroline had shown up unannounced in his office, he had not allowed a shred of sentiment to colour his judgement. Bitter memories of the stories handed down to him from his mother still cast a long shadow. The truth he had seen with his very own eyes—the way her lack of any kind of robust financial settlement from a man who would have been very wealthy at the time had influenced her behaviour patterns—could not be overlooked.

'You must get bored out there,' Giancarlo heard himself remark when he should have really been thinking of concluding their conversation so that he could return to the various meetings waiting for him back at the office. Without taking his eyes off her, he flicked a finger and more cold drinks were brought to their table.

Caroline could no more follow this change in the conversation than she could have dealt with a snarling crocodile suddenly deciding to smile and offer her a cup of tea. She looked at him warily and wondered whether this was a roundabout lead-up to another scathing attack.

'Why are you interested?' she asked cautiously.

'Why not? It's not every day that a complete stranger waltzes into my office with a bombshell. Even if it turns out to be a bombshell that's easy to defuse. Also—and I'll be completely honest on this score—you don't strike me as the sort of person capable of dealing with the man I remember as being my father.'

Caroline was drawn into the conversation against her will. 'What do you remember?' she asked hesitantly. With another cold drink in front of her, the sight of those remaining pastries was awfully tempting. As though reading her mind, Giancarlo ordered a few more, different ones this time, smiling as they were placed in front of her.

He was amused to watch the struggle on her face as she looked down at them.

'What do I remember of my father? Now, let's think about this. Domineering. Frequently ill-tempered. Controlling. In short, not the easiest person in the world.'

'Like you, in other words.'

Giancarlo's mouth tightened because this was an angle that had never occurred to him and he wasn't about to give it house-room now.

'Sorry. I shouldn't have said that.'

'No, you shouldn't, but I'm already getting used to the idea that you speak before you think. Something else I imagine Alberto would have found unacceptable.'

'I really don't like you *at all*,' Caroline said through gritted teeth. 'And I take back what I said. You're *nothing* like Alberto.'

'I'm thrilled to hear that. So, enlighten me.' He felt a twinge of intense curiosity about this man who had been so thoroughly demonised by his ex-wife.

'Well.' Caroline smiled slowly and Giancarlo was amazed at how that slow, reluctant, suspicious smile altered the contours of her face, turning her into someone strangely beautiful in a lush, ripe way that was even more erotic, given the innocence of everything else about her. It put all sorts of crazy thoughts in his head, although the thoughts lasted only an instant, disappearing fast under the mental discipline that was so much part and parcel of his personality.

'He can be grumpy. He's very grumpy now because he hates being told what he can and can't eat and what time he has to go to bed. He hates me helping him physically, so he's employed a local woman, a nurse from the hospital, to help him instead, and I'm constantly having to tell him that he's got to be less bossy and critical of her.

'He was very polite when I first arrived. I think he knew that he was doing my dad a favour, but he figured that he would only have to be on good behaviour for a few weeks. I don't think he knew what to do with me, to start with. He's not been used to company. He wasn't comfortable making eye contact, but none of that lasted too long. We discovered that we shared so many interests—books, old movies, the garden. In fact, the garden has been invaluable now that Alberto is recovering. Every day we go down to the pond just beyond the walled rose-garden. We sit in the folly, read a bit, chat a bit. He likes me to read to him even though he's forever telling me that I need to put more expression in my voice... I guess all that's going to have to go...'

Giancarlo, who hadn't thought of what he had left behind for a very long time, had a vivid memory of that pond and of the folly, a weird gazebo-style creation with a very comfortable bench inside where he likewise had enjoyed whiling away his time during the long summer months when he had been on holiday. He shook away the memory as if clearing cobwebs from a cupboard that hadn't been opened for a long time.

'What do you mean that you guess that's all "going to have to go"?'

Caroline settled worried eyes on his face. For someone who was clearly so intelligent, she was surprised that he didn't seem to follow her. Then she realised that she couldn't very well explain without risking another attack on Alberto's scruples.

'Nothing,' she mumbled when his questioning silence threatened to become too uncomfortable.

'Tut tut. Are you going to get tongue-tied on me?'

The implication being that she talked far too much, Caroline concluded, hurt.

'What do you mean? And don't bother trying to be coy. It doesn't suit you.'

Caroline didn't think she could feel more loathing for another human being if she tried.

'Well, if Alberto has run into financial difficulties, then he's not going to be able to maintain the house, is he? I mean, it's enormous. Right now, a lot of it isn't used, but he would still have to sell it. And please don't tell me that this is a ploy to try and get money out of you. It isn't.' She sighed in weary resignation. 'I don't know why I'm telling you that. You won't believe me anyway.' Suddenly, she was anxious to leave, to get back to the house on the lake, although she had no idea what she was going to do once she got there. Confront Alberto with his problems? Risk jeopardising his fragile health by piling more stress on his shoulders?

'I'm not even sure your father knows the truth of the situation,' she said miserably. 'I'm certain he would have mentioned something to me.'

'Why would he? You've been around for five seconds. I suggest the first person on his list of confidants would probably have been his accountant.'

'Maybe he's told Father Rafferty. I could go and see him at the church and find out if he knows about any of this. That would be the best thing, because Father Rafferty would be able to put everything into perspective. He's very practical and upbeat.'

'Father Rafferty...?'

'Alberto attends mass at the local church every Sunday. Has done for a long time, I gather. He and Father Rafferty have become close friends. I think your father likes Father Rafferty's Irish sense of humour—and the odd glass of whisky. I should go. All of this...'

'Is probably very unsettling, and probably not what you contemplated when you first decided to come over to Italy.'

'I don't mind!' Caroline was quick to reply. She bit back the temptation to tell him that *someone* had to be there for Alberto.

Giancarlo was realising that his original assumption, which had made perfect sense at the time, had been per-haps a little too hasty. The woman was either an excellent, Oscar-winning actress or else she had been telling the truth all along: her visit had not been instigated for financial pur-poses.

Now his brain was engaged on a different path; he sat back and looked at her as he stroked his chin thoughtfully with one long, brown finger.

'I expect this nurse he's hired is a private nurse?'

Caroline hadn't given that a second's thought, but now she blanched. How much would that be costing? And didn't it prove that Alberto had no idea of the state of his finances? Why, if he did know, would he be spending money on hir-ing a private nurse who would be costing him an arm and a leg?

'And naturally he must be paying *you*,' Giancarlo con-tinued remorselessly. 'How much?' He named a figure that was so ridiculously high that Caroline burst out laughing. She laughed until she felt tears come to her eyes. It was as though she had found a sudden outlet for her stressful, frantic thoughts and her body was reacting of its own volition, even though Giancarlo was now looking at her with the perplexed expression of someone dealing with a complete idiot.

'Sorry.' She hiccupped her way back to some level of seriousness, although she could still feel her mirth lurking close to the surface. 'You've got to be kidding. Take that figure and maybe divide it by four.'

'Don't be ridiculous. No one could survive on that.'

'But I never came here for the money,' Caroline explained patiently. 'I came here to improve my Italian. Alberto was doing me a favour by taking me in, I don't have to pay for food and I don't pay rent. When I return to England, the fact that I will be able to communicate in another language will be a great help to me when it comes to getting a job. Why are you staring at me like that?'

'So it doesn't bother you that you wouldn't be able to have much of a life given that you're paid next to nothing?' *Cheap labour,* Giancarlo thought. *Now, why am I not surprised?* A specialised nurse would hardly donate her services through the goodness of her heart, but a young, clearly inexperienced girl? Why not take advantage? Oh, the old man knew the state of his finances, all right, whatever she exclaimed to the contrary.

'I don't mind. I've never been fussed about money.'

'Guess what?' Giancarlo signalled to the waiter for the bill. When Caroline looked at her watch, it was to find that the time had galloped by. She hadn't even been aware of it passing, even though, disliking him as she did, she should have been counting every agonising minute.

'What?'

'Consider your little mission a success. I think it's time, after all, to return home…'

CHAPTER THREE

GIANCARLO'S last view of his father's house, as he had twisted around in the back of the car, while in the front his mother had sat in stony silence without a backward glance, was of lush gardens and the vast stone edifice which comprised the back of the house. The front of the house sat grandly on the western shores of the lake, perfect positioning for a view of deep blue water, as still as a sheet of glass, that was breathtakingly beautiful.

It was unsettling to be returning now, exactly one week after Caroline had left, seemingly transported with excitement at the fact that she had managed to persuade him to accept the supposed olive-branch that had been extended.

If she was of the opinion that all was joyful in the land of reconciliation, then Giancarlo was equally and coldly reserved about sharing any such optimism. He was under no illusions when it came to human nature. The severity of Alberto's heart attack was open to debate and Giancarlo, for one, was coolly prepared for a man in fairly robust health who may or may not have persuaded a very gullible Caroline otherwise to suit his own purposes. His memories of his father were of a towering man, greatly into discipline and without an emotional bone in his body. He couldn't conceive of him being diminished by ill health, although rapidly disappearing funds might well have played a part in lowering his spirits.

The super-fast sports car had eaten up the miles of motorway and only now, as he slowed to drive through the picturesque towns and villages on the way to his father's house, were vague recollections beginning to surface.

He had forgotten how charming this area was. Lake Como, the third largest and the deepest of the Italian lakes, was picture-postcard perfect, a lush, wealthy area with elegant villas, manicured gardens, towns and villages with cobbled streets and *piazzas* dotted with Romanesque churches and very expensive hotels and restaurants which attracted the more discerning tourist.

He felt a pleasing sense of satisfaction.

This was a homecoming on *his* terms, just the way he liked it. A more in-depth perusal of Alberto's finances had shown a company torn apart by the ravaging effects of an unprecedented economic recession, mismanagement and an unwillingness to move with the times and invest in new markets.

Giancarlo smiled grimly to himself. He had never considered himself a vengeful person but the realisation that he could take over his father's company, rescue the old man and thereby level the scales of justice was a pleasing one. Really, what more bitter pill could his father ever swallow than know that he was indebted, literally, to the son he had turned his back on?

He hadn't mentioned a word of this to Caroline when they had parted company. For a few minutes, Giancarlo found himself distracted by thoughts of the diminutive brunette. She was flaky as hell; unbelievably emotional and prone to tears at the drop of a hat; jaw-droppingly forthright and, frankly, left him speechless. But, as he got closer and closer to the place he had once called his home, he realised that she had managed to get under his skin in a way that was uniquely irritating. In fact, he had never devoted this much time to thinking about any one woman, but that, he reasoned sensibly, was because this particular woman had entered his life in a singularly weird way.

Never again would he rule out the unexpected. Just when you thought you had everything in control, something came along to pull the rug from under your feet.

In this instance, it wasn't all bad. He fiddled with the radio, got to a station he liked and relaxed to enjoy the scenery and the pleasing prospect of what lay ahead.

He gave no house room to nerves. He was on a high, in fact, fuelled by the self-righteous notion of the wheel having turned full circle. Yes, he was curious to reacquaint himself with Alberto, but over the years he had heard so many things about him that he almost felt as though there was nothing left to know. The steady drip, drip, drip of information from a young age had eroded his natural inclination to question.

If anything, he liked to think that Alberto would be the one consumed by nerves. His business was failing and sooner or later, ill health or no ill health, Giancarlo was certain that his father would turn the conversation around to money. Maybe he would try and entice him into some kind of investment. Maybe he would just ditch his pride and ask outright for a loan of some sort. Either approach was possible. Giancarlo relished the prospect of being able to confirm that money would indeed be forthcoming. Wasn't he magnanimous even though, all things considered, he had no reason to be? But a price would have to be paid. He would make his father's company his own. He would take it over lock, stock and barrel. Yes, his father's financial security would rest on the generosity of his disowned son.

He intended to stay at the villa just long enough to convey that message. A couple of days at most. Thereafter it would be enough to know that he had done what he had to do.

He didn't anticipate having anything to say of interest to the old man. Why should he? They would be two strangers, relieved to part company once the nitty-gritty had been sorted out.

He was so wrapped up in his thoughts that he very nearly missed the turning to the villa. This side of the lake was famous for its magnificent villas, most of them eighteenth-century extravaganzas, a few of which had been turned into hotels over the years.

His father's villa was by no means the largest but it was still an impressive old place, approached through forbidding iron gates and a long drive which was surrounded on both sides by magnificent gardens.

He remembered the layout of these glorious spreading lawns more than he had anticipated. To the right, there was the bank of trees in which he had used to play as a child. To the left, the stone wall was barely visible behind rows upon rows of rhododendrons and azaleas, a vibrant wash of colour as bright and as dramatic as a child's painting.

He slowed the car in the circular courtyard, killed the engine and popped the boot, which was just about big enough to fit his small leather overnight case—and, of course, his computer bag in which resided all the necessary documents he would need so that he could begin the takeover process he had in mind for his father's company.

He was an imposing sight. From her bedroom window, which overlooked the courtyard, Caroline felt a sudden sick flutter of nerves.

Over the past seven days, she had done her best to play down the impact he had made on her. He wasn't *that* tall, *that* good-looking or *that* arrogant, she convinced herself.

She had been rattled when she had finally located him and her nerves had thrown everything out of perspective.

Unfortunately, staring down at Giancarlo as he emerged from his sports car, wearing dark sunglasses and walking round to swing two cases out of the miniscule boot of his car, she realised that he really *was* as unbelievably forbidding as she had remembered.

She literally flew down the corridor, took the staircase two steps at a time and reached the sitting-room at the back of the house, breathless.

'He's here!'

Alberto was sitting in a chair by the big bay window that had a charming view of the gardens stretching down to the lake, which was dotted with little boats.

'Anyone would think the Pope was paying a visit. Calm down, girl! Your colour's up.'

'You're going to be nice, aren't you, Alberto?'

'I'm always nice. You just fuss too much, get yourself worked up over small things—it's not good for you. Now, off you go and let the boy in before he climbs back into his car and drives away. And on your way you can tell that nurse of yours that I'm having a glass of whisky before dinner. Whether she likes it or not!'

'I'll do no such thing, Alberto De Vito. If you want to disobey doctor's orders, then you can tell Tessa yourself— and I would love to see how she takes that.' She grinned fondly at the old man, who was backlit by the evening sun glinting through the window. Having met Giancarlo, she found the similarities between them striking. Both had the same proud, aristocratic features and the long, lean lines of natural athletes. Of course, Alberto was elderly now, but it was easy to see that he must have been as striking as his son in his youth.

'Oh, stop that endless chattering, woman, and run along.'

He waved her off and Caroline, steadying her nerves, got to the front door just as the doorbell chimed.

She smoothed nervous hands along her skirt, a black maxi in stretch cotton which she wore with a loose-fitting top and, of course, the ubiquitous cardigan, although at least here it was more appropriate thanks to the cooling breeze that blew off the lake.

She pulled open the door and her mouth went dry. In a snug-fitting cream polo-necked shirt and a pair of tan trousers with very expensive-looking loafers, he was every inch the impeccably dressed Italian. He looked as though he had come straight from a fashion shoot until he raised one sardonic eyebrow and said coolly, 'Were you waiting by the window?'

Remembering that she *had*, actually, been at her window when his car had pulled into the courtyard, Caroline straightened her spine and cleared her throat.

'Of course I wasn't! Although I *was* tempted, just in case you didn't show up.' She stood aside; Giancarlo took a step through the front door and confronted the house in which he had spent the first twelve years of his life. It had changed remarkably little. The hall was a vast expanse of marble, in the centre of which a double staircase spiralled in opposing directions to meet on the impressive galleried landing above. On either side of the hall, a network of rooms radiated like tentacles on an octopus.

Now that he was back, he could place every room in his head: the various reception rooms; the imposing study from which he had always been banned; the dining-room in which portraits of deceased family members glared down at the assembled diners; the gallery in which were hung paintings of great value, another room from which he had been banned.

'Why wouldn't I show up?' Giancarlo turned to face her.

She looked more at home here, less ill at ease, which was hardly surprising, he supposed. Her hair which she had attempted to tie back in Milan was loose, and it flowed over her shoulders and down her back in a tangle of curls, dark brown streaked with caramel where the sun had lightened it.

'You might have had a change of heart,' Caroline admitted in a harried voice, because yet again those dark, cloaked eyes on her were doing weird things to her tummy. 'I mean, you were so adamant that you didn't want to see your father and then all of a sudden you announced that you'd changed your mind. It didn't make sense. So I thought that maybe you might have changed your mind again.'

'Where are the staff?'

'I told you, most of the house is shut off. We have Tessa, the nurse who looks after Alberto. She lives on the premises, and two young girls take care of cleaning the house, but they live in the village. I'm glad you decided to come after all. Shall we go and meet your father? I guess you'll want to be with him on your own.'

'So that we can catch up? Exchange fond memories of the good old days?'

Caroline looked at him in dismay. There was no attempt to disguise the bitterness in his voice. Alberto rarely mentioned the past, and his memoirs, which had taken a back seat over the past few weeks, had mostly got to the state of fond reminiscing about his university days and the places he had travelled as a young man. But she could imagine that Alberto had not been the easiest of fathers. When Giancarlo had agreed to visit, she had naïvely assumed that he had been willing, finally, to overlook whatever mishaps had drastically torn them apart. Now, looking at him, she was uneasily aware that her simple conclusions might have been a little off the mark.

'Or even just agree to put the past behind you and move on,' Caroline offered helpfully.

Giancarlo sighed. Should he let her in to what he had planned? he wondered.

'Why don't you give me a little tour of the house before I meet my father?' he suggested. 'I want to get a feel of the old place. And there are a couple of things I want to talk to you about.'

'Things? What things?'

'If you don't fancy the full tour, you can show me to my bedroom. What I have to say won't take long.'

'I'll show you to your room,' she said stiffly. 'But first I'll go and tell Alberto where we are, so he doesn't worry.'

'Why would he worry?'

'He's been looking forward to seeing you.'

'I'm thinking I will be in my old room,' Giancarlo murmured. 'Left wing. Overlooking the side gardens?'

'The left wing's not really used now.' Making her mind up, she eyed his lack of luggage and began heading up the stairs. 'I'll take you up to where you'll be staying. If we're quick, I'm sure your father won't get too anxious. And you can tell me whatever it is you have to tell me.'

She could feel her heart beating like a sledgehammer inside her as she preceded him up the grand staircase, turning left along the equally grand corridor, which was broad enough to house a *chaise longue* and various highly polished tables on which sat bowls of fresh flowers. Caroline had added that touch soon after she had come to live with Alberto and he had grumpily acquiesced, but not before informing her that flowers inside a house were a waste of time. Why bother when they would die within the week?

'Ah, the Green Room.' Giancarlo looked around him and saw the signs of disrepair. The room looked tired, the wallpaper still elegant but badly faded. The curtains he dimly remembered, although this was one of the many guest rooms into which he had seldom ventured. Nothing had been changed in over two decades. He dumped his overnight bag on the bed and walked across to the window to briefly look down at the exquisite walled garden, before turning to her.

'I feel I ought to tell you that my decision to come here wasn't entirely altruistic,' he told her bluntly. 'I wouldn't want you having any misplaced notions of emotional re-unions, because if you have, then you're in for a crashing disappointment.'

'Not entirely altruistic?'

'Alberto's rocky financial situation has—how shall I put it?—delivered me the perfect opportunity to finally redress certain injustices.'

'What injustices?'

'Nothing you need concern yourself with. Suffice to say that Alberto will not have to fear that the banks are going to repossess this house and all its contents.'

'This house was going to be repossessed?'

'Sooner or later.' Giancarlo shrugged. 'It happens. Debts accumulate. Shareholders get the jitters. Redundancies have to be made. It's a short step until the liquidators start con-verging like vultures, and when that happens possessions get seized to pay off disgruntled creditors who are out of pocket.'

Caroline's eyes were like saucers as she imagined this worst-case scenario.

'That would devastate Alberto,' she whispered. She si-dled towards the bed and sat down. 'Are you sure about all this? No. Forget I asked that. I forgot that you never make mistakes.'

Giancarlo looked at the forlorn figure on the bed and clicked his tongue impatiently. 'Isn't it a good thing that he'll be spared all of that? No bailiffs showing up at the door, demanding the paintings and the hangings? No bank clamouring for the house to be put on the market to the highest bidder, even if the price is way below its worth?'

'Yes.' She looked at him dubiously.

'So you can wipe that pitiful look from your face immediately!'

'You said that you were going to…what, exactly? Give him the money? Won't that be an awful lot of money? Are you *that* rich?'

'I have enough,' Giancarlo stated drily, amused by her question.

'How much is enough?'

'Enough to ensure that Alberto's house and company don't end up in the hands of the receivers. Of course, there's no such thing as a free lunch.'

'What do you mean?'

'I mean…' He pushed himself away from the window and strolled through the bedroom, taking in all those little signs of neglect that were almost impossible to spot unless you were looking for them. God only knew, the house was ancient. It was probably riddled with all manner of damp, dry rot, termites in the woodwork. Having grown up in a house that dated back centuries, Giancarlo had made sure that his own place was unashamedly modern. Dry rot, damp and termites would never be able to get a foothold.

'I *mean* that what is now my father's will inevitably become mine. I will take over his company and return it to its once-thriving state and naturally I will do the same with this villa. It's in dire need of repair anyway. I'll wager that those rooms that have been closed off will be in the process of falling to pieces.'

'And you won't be doing any of that because you care about Alberto,' Caroline spoke her thoughts aloud while

Giancarlo looked at her through narrowed eyes, marvelling at the way every thought running through her head was reflected in the changing nuances of her expressions.

'In fact,' she carried on slowly, her thoughts rearranging themselves in her head to form a complete picture of what was really going on, 'you're not interested in reconciling with your father at all, are you?'

Giancarlo wasn't about to encourage any kind of conversation on what she considered the rights and wrongs of his reasons for coming to the lake, so he maintained a steady silence—although the resigned disappointment in her voice managed to pierce through his rigid self-control in a way that was infuriating. Her huge, accusing eyes were doing the same thing as well and he frowned impatiently.

'It's impossible to reconcile with someone you can barely recall,' he said in a flatly dismissive voice. 'I don't know Alberto.'

'You know him enough to want to hurt him for what you think he did to you.'

'That's a ridiculous assumption!'

'Is it? You said yourself that you were going to buy him out because it would give you the chance to redress injustices.'

Giancarlo was fiercely protective of his private life. He never discussed his past with anyone and many women had tried. They had seen it as a stepping stone to getting to know him better, had mistakenly thought that, with the right amount of encouragement, he would open up and pour his heart out. It was always a fatal flaw.

'Alberto divorced my mother and did everything legally possible to ensure that, whilst the essentials were paid, she was left with the minimum, just enough to get by. From *this*—' he gestured in a sweeping arc to encompass the villa and its fabulous surroundings '—she was reduced to living in a small modern box in the outskirts of Milan. You can see that I carry a certain amount of bitterness towards my father.

'However, it has to be said that, were I a truly vengeful person, I would not have returned here and I certainly would not be contemplating a lucrative buy-out. Lucrative from Alberto's point of view, that is. A lot less lucrative from where I'm standing, because his company will need a great deal of money pouring into it to get it off the starters' gate. Face it, I could have read those financial reports, turned my back, walked away. Waited until I read about the demise of his company in the financial section of the newspapers. Believe me, I seriously considered that option, but then... Let's just say that I opted for the personal touch. So much more satisfying.'

Caroline was finding it impossible to tally up Giancarlo's version of his father with her own experiences of Alberto. Yes, he was undoubtedly difficult and had probably been a thousand times more so when he had been younger, but he wasn't stingy. She just couldn't imagine him being vindictive towards his ex-wife, although how could she know for sure?

One thing she *did* know now was that Giancarlo might justify his actions as redressing a balance but it was revenge of a hands-on variety and no part of her could condone that. He would rescue his father in the certain knowledge that guilt would be Alberto's lifelong companion from then onwards. He would attack Alberto's most vulnerable part: his pride.

She stood up, hands on her hips, and looked at him with blazing eyes.

'I don't care how you put it, that's absolutely *rotten*!'

'*Rotten*, to step in and bail him out?' Giancarlo shook his head grimly and took a couple of steps towards her.

He had his hands in the pockets of his trousers and his movements were leisurely and unhurried, but there was an element of threat in every step he took that brought him closer and Caroline fought to stay her ground. She couldn't wrench her eyes away from him. He had the allure of a dangerous but spectacularly beautiful predator.

Looking down at her, Giancarlo's dark eyes skimmed the hectic flush in her cheeks, her rapid, angry breathing.

'You're a spitfire, aren't you…?' he murmured lazily, which thoroughly disconcerted Caroline. She wasn't used to dealing with men like this. Her experience of the opposite sex was strictly confined to the two men she had dated in the past, both of whom were gentle souls with whom she still shared a comfortable friendship, and work colleagues after she had left school.

'No, I'm not! I never argue. I don't like arguing.'

'You could have fooled me.'

'You do this to me,' she breathed, only belatedly realising that somehow that didn't sound quite right. 'I mean…'

'I get you worked up?'

'Yes! No…'

'Yes? No? Which is it?'

'Stop laughing at me. None of this is funny.' She drew her cardigan tightly around her in a defensive gesture that wasn't lost on him.

'For a young woman, your choice of clothes is very old-fashioned. Cardigans are for women over forty.'

'I don't see what my clothes have to do with anything.' But she stumbled over her words. Was he trying to throw her? He was succeeding. Now, along with anger was a creeping sense of embarrassment.

'Are you self-conscious about your body?' This was the sort of question Giancarlo never asked any woman. He had never been a big fan of soul-searching conversations. He had always preferred to keep it light, and yet he found that he was really curious about the hell cat who claimed not to be a hell cat. Except when in his presence.

Caroline broke the connection and walked towards the door but she was shaking like a leaf.

She stood in the doorway, half-in, half-out of the bedroom, which suddenly seemed as confining as a prison cell when he was towering above her.

'And when do you intend to tell Alberto everything?'

'I should imagine that he will probably be the one who brings up the subject,' Giancarlo said, still looking at her, almost regretful that the conversation was back on a level footing. 'You seem to have a lot of faith in human nature. Take it from me, it's misplaced.'

'I don't want you upsetting him. His doctor says that he's to be as stress-free as possible in order to make a full recovery.'

'Okay. Here's the deal. I won't open the conversation with a casual query about the state of his failing company.'

'You really don't care about anyone but yourself, do you?' Caroline asked in a voice tinged with genuine wonder.

'You have a special knack for saying all the wrong things to me,' Giancarlo muttered with a frown.

'What you mean is that I say things you don't want to hear.' She stepped quickly out into the corridor as he walked towards her. She was beginning to understand that being too close to him physically was like standing too close to an electric field. 'We should go downstairs. Alberto will be wondering where we've got to. He tires easily now, so we'll be having an early supper.'

'And tell me, who does the cooking? The same two girls who come in to clean?' He fell into step alongside her, but even though the conversation had moved on to a more neutral topic he was keenly aware of her still clutching the cardigan around her. His first impression had been of someone very background. Now, he was starting to review that initial impression. Underneath the straightforward personality there seemed to be someone very fiery and not easily intimidated. She had taken a deep breath and stood up to him in a way that not very many people did.

'Sometimes. Now that Alberto is on a restricted diet, Tessa tends to prepare his meals, and I cook for myself and Tessa. It's a daily fight to get Alberto to eat bland food. He's fond of saying that there's no life worth living without salt.'

Giancarlo heard the smile in her voice. For his sins, his father had found himself a very devoted companion.

For the first time he wondered what it would have been like to have had Alberto as a father. The man had clearly mellowed over time. Would they have had that connection? How much had he suffered because of his constant warfare with his wife?

Irritated with himself for being drawn back into a past he could not change, Giancarlo focused on sustaining the conversation with a number of innocuous questions as they walked back down the grand staircase, Caroline leading the way towards the smallest of the sitting-rooms at the back of the house.

Even with the majority of the rooms seemingly closed off, there was still a lot of ground to cover. Yet again he found himself wondering what the appeal was for a young woman. Terrific house, great grounds, pleasing views and interesting walks—but take those things out of the equation and boredom would gradually set in, surely?

How bored had his mother been, surrounded by all this ostentatious wealth, trapped like a bird in a gilded cage?

Alberto had met her on one of his many conferences. She

had been a sparkling, pretty waitress at the only fancy restaurant in a small town on the Amalfi coast where he had gone to grab a couple of days of rest before the remainder of his business trip. She had been plucked from obscurity and catapulted into wealth, but nothing, she had repeatedly complained to her son over the years following her divorce, could compensate for the horror of living with a man who treated her no better than a servant. She had done her very best, but time and again her efforts had been met with a brick wall. Alberto, she had said with bitterness, had turned out to be little more than a difficult, unyielding and unforgiving man, years too old for her, who had thwarted all her attempts at having fun.

Giancarlo had been conditioned to loathe the man whom his mother had held responsible for all her misfortunes.

Except now he was prey to a disturbing sensation of doubt as he heard Caroline chatter on about his father. How disagreeable could the man be if she was so attached to him? Was it possible for a leopard to change its spots to that extreme extent?

Before they reached the sitting-room, she paused to rest one small hand lightly on his arm.

'Do you promise that you won't upset him?'

'I'm not big into making promises.'

'Why is it so hard to get through to you?'

'Believe it or not, most people don't have a problem. In our case, we might just as well be from different planets, occupying different time zones. I told you I won't greet him with an enquiry about the health of his finances, and I won't. Beyond that, I promise nothing.'

'Just try to get to know him,' Caroline pleaded, her huge brown eyes welded to his as she dithered with her hand still on his arm. 'I just can't believe you know the real Alberto.'

Giancarlo's mouth thinned and he stared down pointedly at her hand before looking down at her, his dark eyes as cold and frozen as the lake in winter.

'Don't presume to tell me what I know or don't know,' he said with ice in his voice, and Caroline removed her hand quickly as though she had been burnt suddenly. 'I've come here for a purpose and, whether you like it or not, I will ensure that things are wrapped up before I leave.'

'And how long are you intending to stay? I never asked, but you really haven't come with very much luggage, have you? I mean, one small bag...'

'Put it this way, there will be no need to go shopping for food on my account. I plan on being here no longer than two days. Three at the very most.'

Caroline's heart sank further. This was a business visit, however you dressed it up and tried to call it something else. Two days? Just long enough for Giancarlo to levy his charge for Alberto's past wrongdoings, whatever those might have been, with interest.

She didn't think that he was even prepared to get to know his father. The only thing that interested him, his only motivation for coming to the villa, was to dole out his version of revenge, whether he chose to call it that or not.

'Now, any more questions?' Giancarlo drawled and Caroline shook her head miserably, not trusting herself to speak. Once again, he felt a twinge of uninvited and unwelcome doubt. 'I'm surprised at your level of attachment to Alberto,' he commented brusquely, annoyed at himself, because would her answer change anything? No.

'Why?' Her eyes were wide and clear when she looked at him. 'I didn't have a load of prejudices when I came here. I came with an open mind. I found a lonely old man with a kind heart and a generous nature. Yes, he might be prickly, but it's what's inside that counts. At least, that's how it works for me.'

He really shouldn't have been diverted into encouraging her opinion. He should have known that whatever chirpy, homespun answer she came out with would get on his nerves. He was very tempted to inform her that he was the least prejudiced person on the face of the earth, that if on this single occasion he was prey to a very natural inclination towards one or two preconceived ideas about Alberto, then no one could lay the blame for that at his door. He cut short the infuriating desire to be sidetracked.

'Well, I'm very pleased that he has you around,' Giancarlo said neutrally. Caroline bristled because she could just *sense* that he was being patronising.

'No, you aren't. You're still so mad at him that you probably would much rather have preferred it if he was still on his own in this big, rambling house with no one to talk to. And, if there *was* someone around, then I'm sure you'd rather it wasn't me, because you don't like me at all!'

'What gives you that idea?'

Caroline ignored that question. The promise of what was to come felt like a hangman's noose around her neck. She was fit to explode. 'Well, I don't like you either,' she declared with vehemence. 'And I hope you choke on your plans to ruin Alberto's life.' She spun away from him so that he couldn't witness the tears stinging her eyes. 'He's waiting for you,' she muttered in a driven voice. 'Why don't you go in now and get it over with?'

CHAPTER FOUR

GIANCARLO entered a room that was familiar to him. The smallest of the sitting-rooms at the back of the house had always been the least ornate and hence the cosiest. Out of nowhere came the memory of doing his homework in this very room, always resisting the urge to sneak outside, down to the lake. French doors led out to the sprawling garden that descended to the lake via a series of landscaped staircases. Alberto sat in a chair by one of the bay windows with a plaid rug over his legs even though it was warm in the room.

'So, my boy, you've come.'

Giancarlo looked at his father with a shuttered expression. He wondered if his memory was playing tricks on him, because Alberto looked diminished. In his head, he realised that he had held on to a memory that was nearly two decades old and clearly out of date.

'Father...'

'Caroline. You're gaping. Why don't you offer a drink to our guest? And I will have a whisky while you're about it.'

'You'll have no such thing.' Back on familiar ground, Caroline moved past Giancarlo to adopt a protective stance by her employer, who made feeble attempts to flap her away. Looking at their interaction, Giancarlo could see that it was a game with which they were both comfortable and familiar.

Just for a few seconds, he was the outsider looking in, then that peculiar feeling was gone as the tableau shifted. Caroline walked across to a cupboard which had been re-configured to house a small fridge, various snacks and cartons of juice.

He was aware of her chattering nervously, something about it being time efficient to have stuff at hand for Alberto because this was his favourite room in the house and he just wasn't as yet strong enough to continually make long trips to the kitchen if he needed something to drink.

'Of course, it's all supervised,' she babbled away, while the tension stretched silent and invisible in the room. 'No whisky here. Tessa and I know that that's Alberto's Achilles' heel so we have wine. I put some in earlier, would that be okay?' She kept her eyes firmly averted from the uncomfortable sight of father and son, but in her head she was picturing them circling one another, making their individual, quiet assessments.

Given half a chance, she would have run for cover to another part of the house, but her instinct to protect Alberto kept her rooted to the spot.

When she finally turned around, with drinks and snacks on a little tray, it was to find that Giancarlo had taken up position on one of the chairs. If he was in any way uncomfortable, he wasn't showing it.

'Well, Father, I have been told that you've suffered a heart attack—'

'How was the drive here, Giancarlo? Still too many cars in the villages?'

They both broke into speech at the same time. Caroline drank too much far too quickly to calm her nerves and lapsed into an awkward silence as ultra-polite questions

were fielded with ultra-polite answers. She wondered
if they were aware that many of their mannerisms were
identical—the way they both shifted and leaned forward
when a remark was made; the way they idly held their
glasses, slightly stroking the rim with their fingers. They
should have bonded without question. Instead, Giancarlo's
cool, courteous conversation was the equivalent of a door
being shut.

He was here. He was talking. But he was not convers-
ing.

At least he had kept his word and nothing, so far, had
been mentioned about the state of Alberto's finances, although she knew that her employer must surely be curious
to know why his son had bothered to make the trip out to
Lake Como when he displayed so little enthusiasm for the
end result.

Dinner was a light soup, followed by fish. One of the
local girls had been brought in, along with the two regular
housekeepers, to take care of the cooking and the clearing
away. So, instead of eating in the kitchen, they dined in the
formal dining-room, which proved to be a mistake.

The long table and the austere surroundings were not
conducive to light-hearted conversation. Tessa had volun-
teered to have her meal in the small sitting-room adjoining
her bedroom, in order to give them all some space to chat
without her hovering over Alberto, checking to make sure
he stuck to his diet. Caroline heartily wished she could have
joined her, because the atmosphere was thick with tension.

By the time they had finished their starters and made
adequately polite noises about it, several topics of conversation had been started and quickly abandoned. The changes
in the weather patterns had been discussed, as had the number of tourists at the lakes, the lack of snow the previous
winter and, of course, Alberto asked Giancarlo about his

work, to which he received such brief replies that that too was a subject quickly shelved.

By the time the main course was brought to them—and Alberto had bemoaned the fact that they were to dine on fish rather than something altogether heartier like a slab of red meat—Caroline had frankly had enough of the painfully stilted conversation.

If they didn't want to have any kind of meaningful conversation together, then she would fill in the gaps. She talked about her childhood, growing up in Devon. Her parents were both teachers, very much into being 'green'. She laughed at memories of the chickens they had kept that laid so many eggs at times that her mother would bake cakes a family of three had no possibility of eating just to get rid of some of them. She would contribute them to the church every Sunday and one year was actually awarded a special prize for her efforts.

She talked about exchange students, some of whom had been most peculiar, and joked about her mother's experiments in the kitchen with home-grown produce from their small garden. In the end, she and her father had staged a low-level rebellion until normal food was reintroduced. Alberto chuckled but he was not relaxed. It was there in the nervous flickering of his eyes and his subdued, down-turned mouth. The son he had desperately wanted to see didn't want to see him and he wasn't even bothering to try to hide the fact.

All the while she could feel Giancarlo's dark eyes restively looking at her and she found that she just couldn't look at him. What was it about him that brought her out in goose bumps and made her feel as though she just wasn't comfortable in her own skin? The timbre of his low, husky voice sent shivers down her spine, and when he turned to look at her she was aware of her body in such miniscule detail that she burned with discomfort.

By the time they adjourned for coffee back in the small sitting-room, Caroline was exhausted and she could see that Alberto was flagging. Giancarlo, on the other hand, was as coldly composed as he had been at the start of the evening.

'How long do you plan on staying, my boy? You should get yourself out on the lake. Beautiful weather. And you were always fond of your sailing. Of course, we no longer have the sailboat. What was the point? After, well, after...'

'After what, Father?'

'I think it's time you went to bed, Alberto,' Caroline interjected desperately as the conversation finally threatened to explode. 'You're flagging and you know the doctor said that you really need to take it easy. I'll get hold of Tessa and—'

'After you and your mother left.'

'Ah, so finally you've decided to acknowledge that you ever had a wife. One could be forgiven for thinking that you had erased her from your memory completely.' No mention had been made of Adriana. Not one single word. They had tiptoed around all mention of the past, as though it had never existed. Alberto had been on his best behaviour. Now Giancarlo expected to see his real father, the cold, unforgiving one, the one who, from memory, had never shied away from arguing.

'I've done no such thing, my son,' Alberto surprised Giancarlo by saying quietly.

'It's time you went to bed, Alberto.' Caroline stood up and looked pointedly at Giancarlo. 'I will not allow you to tire your father out any longer,' she said, and in truth Alberto was showing signs of strain around his eyes. 'He's been very ill and this conversation is *not* going to help anything at all.'

'Oh, do stop fussing, Caroline.' But his pocket handkerchief was in his hand and he was patting his forehead wearily.

'*You*—' she jabbed a finger at Giancarlo '—are going to wait *right here* for me while I go to fetch Tessa because I intend to have a little chat with you.'

'The boy wants to talk about his past, Caroline. It's why he's come.'

Caroline snorted without taking her eyes away from Giancarlo's beautiful face. If only Alberto knew!

She spun back around to look at her employer. 'I'm going to fetch Tessa and tomorrow you won't have your routine disrupted. Your son is going to be here for a few days. There will be time enough to take a trip down memory lane.'

'*A few days?*' They both said the same thing at the same time. Giancarlo was appalled and enraged while Alberto was hesitantly hopeful. Caroline decided to favour Giancarlo with a confirming nod.

'Maybe even as long as a week,' she threw at him, because wasn't it better to be hanged for a sheep than a lamb? 'I believe that's what you said to me?' She wondered where on earth this fierce determination was coming from. She always shied away from confrontation!

'So tomorrow,' she continued to both men, 'there will be no need for you to worry about entertaining your son, Alberto. He will be sailing on the lake.'

'I'll be *sailing on the lake*?'

'Correct. With me.' This in case he decided to argue the rules she was confidently laying down, with a silent prayer in her head that he wasn't going to launch into an outraged argument which would devastate Alberto, especially after the gruesome evening they had just spent together.

'I thought you couldn't sail, Caroline,' Alberto murmured and she drew herself up to her unimpressive height of a little over five-three.

'But I've been counting down the days I could start learning.'

'You told me that you had a morbid fear of open water.'

'It's something I've been told I can only overcome by facing it…on open water. It's a well-known fact that, er, that you have to confront your fears to overcome them…'

She backed out of the room before Alberto could pin her down and flew to Tessa's room. She could picture the awkward conversation taking place between Giancarlo and Alberto in her absence, and that was a best-case scenario. The worst-case scenario involved them both taking that trip down memory lane, the one she had temporarily managed to divert. It was a trip that could only lead to the sort of heated argument that would do no good to Alberto's fragile recovery. With that in mind, she ran back to the sitting-room like a bat out of hell and was breathless by the time she reappeared ten minutes later.

It was to discover that Giancarlo had disappeared.

'The boy has work to do,' Alberto told her.

'At this hour?'

'I remember when I was a young man, I used to work all the hours God made. Boy's built like me, which might not be such a good thing. Hard work is fine but the important thing is to know when to stop. He's a fine-looking lad, don't you think?'

'I suppose there might be some who like that sort of look,' Caroline said dismissively. With relief, she heard Tessa approaching. Alberto drew no limits when it came to asking whatever difficult questions he had in his head. It was, he had proclaimed, one of the benefits of being an old bore. The last thing she wanted was to have an in-depth question-and-answer session on what she thought of his son.

'Bright, too.'

Caroline wondered how he could be so clearly generous in his praise for someone who had made scant effort to meet him halfway. She made an inarticulate noise under her breath and tried not to scowl.

'Said he'd meet you by his car at nine tomorrow morning,' Alberto told her, while simultaneously trying to convince Tessa, who had entered the room at a brisk pace, that he didn't need to be treated like a child all the time. 'Think he'll enjoy a spot of sailing. It'll relax him. He seems tense. Of course, I totally understand that, given the circumstances. So don't you mind me, my dear. Think I'll rise and shine, but not with the larks, and the old bat here can take me for my constitutional walk.'

Tessa winked at Caroline and grinned behind Alberto's back as she helped him up.

'Anyone would think he wasn't a complete poppet when I settle him at night,' she said, unfazed.

Having issued her dictate to Giancarlo for 'a chat', Caroline realised that chatting was the last thing she wanted to do with him. All her bravado had seeped out of her. The prospect of a morning in his company now seemed like an uphill climb. Would he listen to her? He hadn't as yet revealed to Alberto the real reason for his visit but he would the following day; she knew it. Just as he would declare that his visit was not going to last beyond forty-eight hours, despite what she had optimistically announced to Alberto.

There was no way that she would be able to persuade Giancarlo into doing anything he didn't want to do and the past few hours had shown her that grasping the olive branch was definitely not on his agenda.

* * *

She had a restless night. The villa was beautiful but no modernisation had taken place for a very long time. Air-conditioning was unheard of and the air was still and sluggish.

She barely felt rested when she opened her eyes the following morning at eight-thirty. It took her a few seconds to remember that her normal routine was out of sync. She wouldn't be having a leisurely breakfast with Alberto before taking him for a walk, then after lunch settling into sifting through some of his first-edition books which, in addition to his memoirs, was one of her jobs for him: sorting them into order so that he could decide which ones might be left to the local museum and which would be kept. He had all manner of historical information about the district, a great deal of which was contained in the various letters and journals of his ancestors. It was a laborious but enjoyable task which she would be missing in favour of a sailing trip with Giancarlo.

She dressed quickly: a pair of trousers, a striped tee shirt and, of course, her cardigan, a blue one this time; covered shoes. She didn't know anything at all about being on a boat, but she knew enough to suspect that a skirt and sandals would not be the required get-up. Impatiently, she tied her hair back in a long braid for the purpose of practicality.

There was no time for breakfast and she walked from one wing of the villa to the other, emerging outside into a blissfully sunny day with cloudless skies, bright turquoise shot through with milk. Giancarlo was standing by his car, sunglasses on, talking into his mobile phone. For a few seconds she stared at him, her heart thudding. He might have severed all ties with his aristocratic background, but he couldn't erase it from the contours of his face. Even in tattered clothes and barefoot he would still look the ultimate sophisticate.

He glanced across, registered her presence and snapped shut his phone to lounge indolently against the car as she walked towards him.

'So,' he drawled, staring down at her when she was finally in front of him. 'I'm apparently here on a one-week vacation.' He removed the sunglasses to dangle them idly between his fingers while he continued to look at her until she felt herself blush to the roots of her hair.

'Yes, well...'

'Maybe you could tell me how I had this week planned out? Bearing in mind that you seemed to have arranged it.'

'You *could* make just a little polite conversation before you start laying into me.'

'Was I doing that?' He pushed himself off the car and swung round to open the door for her, slamming it shut as she clambered into the passenger seat. 'I distinctly recall having told you that the most I would be staying would be a matter of two days. Tell me how you saw fit to extend that into a week?' He had bent down, propping himself against the car with both hands so that he could question her through her open window. He felt so close up and personal that she found herself taking deep breaths and gasping for air.

'Yes, I realise that,' Caroline muttered mutinously when he showed no signs of backing off. 'But you made me mad.'

'I—made—you—mad?'

Caroline nodded mutely and stared straight ahead, keenly aware of his hawk-like eyes boring into her averted profile. She visibly sagged when he strode round to get into the car.

'And how,' he asked softly, 'do you think I felt when you backed me into a corner?'

'Yes, well, you deserved it!'

'Do you know, I can't believe you.' He exited the gravelled courtyard with a screeching of angry tyres and she clenched her fists so tightly that she could feel her nails biting into the palms of her hands. 'I didn't come here for relaxation!'

'I know! Don't you think you made that pretty obvious last night?'

'I gave you my word that I wouldn't introduce the contentious issue of money on day one. I kept my word.'

'*Just about.* You didn't make the slightest effort with Alberto. You just sat there *sneering*, and okay, so maybe I was wrong to imply that you were staying a tiny bit longer than you had planned.'

'You are the master of understatement!'

'But when you mentioned your mother, well, I just wanted to avert an argument, so possibly I said the first thing that came into my head. Look, I'm sorry. I guess you could always tell Alberto that I made a mistake, that I got the dates wrong. I know you have lots of important things to do and probably can't spare a week off, whatever the reason, but just then I didn't think I had a choice. I had to take the sting out of the evening, give Alberto something to hang on to.'

'What a shame you couldn't use your brain and think things through before you jumped in feet first! I take it the little *chat* you had in mind last night has now been covered?'

'It was an awkward evening. Alberto really tried to make conversation. Do you know, after you disappeared to work he actually seemed to understand? It was almost as though he wasn't prepared to see anything wrong in his son coming to see him for the first time in years, barely making an effort and then vanishing to work!'

Giancarlo flushed darkly. The evening had not gone quite as he had envisaged, and now he wasn't entirely sure *what* he had envisaged. He just knew that the argumentative man—the one who had loomed larger than life in his head thanks to Adriana's continuing bitterness; the one who would have made it so easy for him to treat with the patronising contempt he had always assumed would be richly deserved—had not lived up to expectations.

For starters, it was clear that Alberto's ill health was every bit as grave as Caroline had stated, and even more surprising, instead of a conversation spiked with the sort of malice and bitterness to which he had become accustomed with his mother over the years, there had been no mention made of a regrettable past and a miserable marriage. Alberto had been so wildly different from the picture in his head that Giancarlo had spent the time when he should have been working trying to figure out the discrepancies.

Naturally, the question of money, the *raison d'être* for his presence at the villa, would rear its ugly head in due course. He might have been weirdly taken aback at the man he had found, but sooner or later the inevitable begging bowl would emerge. However, not even that certainty could still the uneasy doubt that had crept stealthily through him after he had vacated the sitting-room.

'Perhaps,' he said, glancing around at scenery that felt more familiar with every passing second, 'a few days away from Milan might not be such a terrible idea.' The very second he said it, Giancarlo knew that he had made the right decision.

'Sorry?'

'I wouldn't call it a holiday, but it is certainly more restful here than it is in Milan.' He looked sideways at Caroline. Through the open window, the breeze was wreaking havoc with her attempts at a neat, sensible hair-style, flinging it into disarray.

'I guess you don't really do holidays,' she said tentatively.

Even if his intention was still to consume his father's house and company, a few days spent with Alberto might render him a little less black and white in his judgement, might invest him with sufficient tact so that Alberto wasn't humiliated.

'Time is money.'

'There's more to life than money.'

'Agreed. Unfortunately, it usually takes money to enjoy those things.'

'Why have you decided to stay on? Just a short while ago you were really angry that I had put you in a difficult position.'

'But put me in it you did, and I'm a man who thinks on his feet and adjusts to situations. So I might be here for a bit longer than I had anticipated. It could only work to my advantage when it comes to constructing the sort of business proposal my father will understand. I'll confess that Alberto isn't the man I had expected. I initially thought that talk of his ill health might have been exaggerated.'

His eyes slid across to her face. Predictably, her expression was one of tight-lipped anger. 'Now I see for myself that he is not a well man, which would no doubt explain his unnaturally docile manner. I am not a monster. I had intended to confront him with his financial predicament without bothering with the tedious process of beating around the bush. Now I accept that I might have to tiptoe towards the conclusion I want.'

The scenery rushing past him, the feeling of open space and translucent light, was breathtaking. He was behind the wheel of a car, he was driving through clear open spaces with a view of glittering blue water ahead, and for the first time in years he felt light-headed with a rushing sense of freedom.

'Besides,' he mused lazily, 'I haven't been to this part of the world for a long time.'

He was following signs to one of the many sailing jetties scattered around the lake and now he swerved off the main road, heading down towards the glittering water.

Caroline forgot all her misgivings about Giancarlo's mission. She forgot how angry and upset she was at the thought of Alberto being on the receiving end of a son who had only agreed to see him out of a misplaced desire for revenge.

'I don't think I can go through with this,' she muttered as the car slowed to a stop.

Giancarlo killed the engine and turned to face her. 'Wasn't this whole sailing trip *your* idea?'

'It was supposed to be *your* sailing trip.' There were tourists milling around and the sailing boats bobbed like colourful playthings on the calm water. Out on the lake many more of them skirted over the aquamarine surface. At any given moment, one might very well sink, and where would that leave those happy, smiling tourists on board? She blanched and licked her lips nervously.

'You're white as a sheet.'

'Yes, well…'

'You're seriously scared of water?'

'Of *open* water. Anything could happen. Especially on something as flimsy as a sailboat.'

'Anything could happen to anyone, anywhere. Driving here was probably more of a risk than that boat out there.' He opened his door and swung his long body out, moving round to open the passenger door for her. 'You were right when you said that you can't kill an irrational fear unless you confront it.' He held out one hand and, heart beating fast, Caroline took it. The feel of his fingers as they curled around hers was warm and comforting.

'How would you know?' she asked in a shaky voice as

she eased herself out of the car and half-eyed the lake the way a minnow might eye a patch of shark-infested water. 'I bet you've never been scared of anything in your life.'

'I'll take that as a compliment.' He kept his fingers interlinked with hers as he led her down towards the jetty.

Hell, he never thought he'd live to see the day when there were no thoughts of work, deals to be done or lawyers to meet impinging on his mind. His mother's uncertain finances—the details of which he had never been spared, even when he had been too young to fully understand them—had bred a man to whom the acquisition of money was akin to a primal urge. The fact that he was very, very good at it had only served to strengthen his rampant ambition. Women had come and gone, and would continue to come and go, for his parents were a sad indictment of the institution of marriage, but the challenge of work would always be a constant.

Except, now, it appeared to have taken a back seat.

And he barely recognised the boyish feeling inside him as her fingers tightly squeezed his the closer they got to the jetty.

'Hey, trust me,' he told her. 'It'll be worth it. There's nothing like the freedom of being out on the lake and it's not like being on the sea. The edge of the lake is always visible. You'll always be able to orienteer yourself by the horizon.'

'How deep is it?'

'Don't think about that. Tell me why you're so scared.'

Caroline hesitated. She disapproved of everything about this man and yet his invitation to confide was irresistible. *And* her fingers were still entwined with his. Suddenly conscious of that, she wriggled them, which encouraged him to grasp them slightly harder.

'Well?'

'I fell in a river when I was a child.' She sighed and glanced up at him sheepishly. 'I must have been about seven, just learning how to swim. There were four of us and it was the summer holidays. Our parents had all arranged this picnic in the woods.'

'Sounds idyllic.'

'It was, until the four of us kids went off to do a bit of exploring. We were crossing a bridge, just messing around. Looking back now, the river must not have been more than a metre deep and the bridge was just a low, rickety thing. We were playing that game, the one where you send a twig from one side of the bridge and race to the other side to see it float out. Anyway, I fell, headlong into the river. It was terrifying. Although I could swim enough to get out, it was as though my mind had blanked that out. All I could taste was the water and I could feel floating weeds on my face. I thought I was going to drown. Everyone was screaming. The adults were with us within seconds and there was no harm done, but ever since then I've hated the thought of open water.'

'And when I was fourteen, I tried my hand at horse riding and came off at the first hurdle. Ever since then I've had an irrational fear of horses.'

'No, you haven't.' But she grinned up at him, shading her eyes from the glare of the sun with one hand.

'You're right. I haven't. But it's a possibility. I've never been near a horse in my life. I can ski down any black run but I suspect a horse would have me crying with terror.'

Caroline laughed. She was relaxing, barely noticing that the sailboat was being rented, because Giancarlo had continued to talk to her in the soothing voice of someone intent on calming a skittish animal, describing silly scenarios that made her smile. He was certain that he would have a fear of horses. Spiders brought him out in a sweat. Birds brought to mind certain horror movies. He knew that he would definitely have had a phobia of small aircraft had he not managed to successfully bypass that by owning his own helicopter.

Giancarlo hadn't put this much effort into a woman in a long time. It was baffling, because had someone told him a week ago that he would be held to account by a woman who didn't know the meaning of tact, he would have laughed out loud. And had that someone then said that he would find himself holed up at his father's villa for a week, courtesy of the same woman who didn't know the meaning of tact, he would have called out the little men with strait-jackets because the idea was beyond ridiculous.

Yet here he was: reaching out to help a woman with unruly brown hair streaked with caramel, who didn't seem to give a damn about all the other nonsense other women cared about, onto a sailboat. And enjoying the fact that he had managed to distract her from her fear of water by making her laugh.

Obeying an instinctive need to rationalise his actions, Giancarlo easily justified his uncharacteristic behaviour by assuming that this was simply his creative way of dealing with a situation. So what would have been the point in tearing her off a strip for having coerced him into staying at the villa longer than he had planned? He would still do what he had come to do, and anyway it made a relaxing change to interact with a woman in whom he had no sexual interest. He went for tall, thin blondes with a penchant for high-end designer clothes. So take away the sometimes-tedious game of chase and catch with a woman and it seemed that he was left with something really quite enjoyable.

Caroline was on the sailboat before she really realised what had happened. One minute she was laughing, enjoying his silly remarks with the sun on her face and the breeze running its balmy fingers through her hair and gradually undoing her loose plait—the next minute, terra firma was no longer beneath her feet and the swaying of the boat was forcibly reminding her of everything she feared about being out at sea, or in this case out on the lake.

Did he even know how to handle this thing? Wasn't he supposed to have had a little pep talk from the guys in charge of the rentals—a refresher course in how to make sure this insignificant piece of plywood with a bit of cloth didn't blow over when they were in the middle of the lake?

Giancarlo saw her stricken face, the panicked way she looked over her shoulder at the safety of a shoreline from which they were drifting.

He reacted on pure gut impulse.

He kissed her. He curled his long fingers into her tangle of dark hair and with one hand pulled her towards him. The taste of her full lips was like nectar. He felt her soft, lush body curve into him, felt her full breasts squash softly against his chest. He had taken her utterly by surprise and there was no resistance as the kiss grew deeper and more intimately exploring, tasting every part of her sweet mouth. God, he wanted to do more! His arousal was fast and hard and his fabled self-control disappeared so quickly that he was at the mercy of his senses for the first time in his life.

He wanted to strip off her shirt, tear off her bra, which wouldn't be one of those lacy slips of nothing the women he dated wore but something plainly, resolutely and impossibly sexy. He wanted to lose himself in her generous breasts until he stopped thinking altogether.

Caroline was in the grip of something so intensely powerful that she could barely breathe.

She had never felt like this in her life before. She could feel her body melting, could feel her nipples tightening and straining against her bra, knew that she was hot and wet between her legs…

Her body was behaving in a way it had never behaved before and it thrilled and terrified her at the same time.

When he eventually broke free, she literally felt lost.

'You kissed me,' she breathed, still clutching him by the shirt and looking up at him with huge, searching eyes. She wanted to know *why*. She knew why *she* had responded! Underneath her disapproval for everything he had done and said, there was a strong, irresistible current of pure physical attraction. She had been swept along by it and nothing she had ever experienced in her life before had prepared her for its ferocity. Lust was just something she had read about. Now she knew, firsthand, how powerful it could be. Was he feeling the same thing? Did he want to carry on kissing her as much as she wanted him to?

She gradually became aware of their surroundings and of the fact that, with one hand, he had expertly guided the small sailboat away from shore and out into the open lake. They had become one of the small bright toys she had glimpsed from land.

'You kissed me. Was that to distract me from the fact that we were heading away from land?'

Hell, how did *he* know? He just knew that he had been blown away, had lost all shreds of self-control. It was not something of which he was proud, nor could he understand it. Rallying quickly, he recovered his shattered equilibrium and took a couple of steps back, but then had to look away briefly because her flushed cheeks and parted mouth were continuing to play havoc with his libido.

'It worked, didn't it?' He nodded towards the shore, still not trusting himself to look at her properly. 'You're on the water now and, face it, you're no longer scared.'

CHAPTER FIVE

CAROLINE remained positioned in the centre of the small boat for the next hour. She made sure not to look out to the water, which made her instantly conjure up drowning scenarios in her head. Instead, she looked at Giancarlo. It was blissfully easy to devote all her attention to him. He might not have sailed for a long time but whatever he had learnt as a boy had returned to him with ease.

'It's like riding a bike,' he explained, doing something clever with the rudder. 'Once learnt, never forgotten.'

Caroline found herself staring at his muscular brown legs, sprinkled with dark hair. Having brought just enough clothes to cover a one-night stay, he had, he had admitted when asked, pulled strings and arranged for one of the local shops to open up early for him. At eight that morning, he had taken his car to the nearest small town and bought himself a collection of everyday wear. The khaki shorts and loose-fitting shirt, virtually unbuttoned all the way down, were part of that wardrobe and they offered her an incredible view of his highly toned body. Every time he moved, she could see the ripple of his muscles.

Now he was explaining to her how he had managed to acquire his expertise in a boat. He had always been drawn to the water. He had had his first sailing lesson at the age of five and by the age of ten had been adept enough to sail on his own, although he had not been allowed. By the time he had left the lake for good, he could have crewed his own sailboat, had he been of legal age.

Caroline nodded, murmured and thought about *that kiss*. She had been kissed before but never like that. Neither of the two boyfriends she'd had had ever made her feel as though the ground was spinning and freewheeling under her feet; neither had ever made her feel as if the rules of time and space had altered, throwing her into a wildly different dimension. With an eye for detail she never knew she possessed, she marvelled at how a face so coldly, exquisitely beautiful could inspire such craven weakness deep inside her when she had never previously been drawn to men because of how they looked. She wondered at the way she had fallen headlong into that kiss, never wanting it to stop when she barely liked the guy she had been kissing.

'Hello? Calling Planet Earth…'

'Huh?' Caroline blinked and realised that the sailboat was now practically at a standstill. The sound of the water lapping gently against the sides was mesmeric.

'If you stay in that position any longer, your joints will seize up,' Giancarlo informed her drily. 'Stand up. Walk about.'

'What if I topple the boat over and fall in?'

'Then I'll rescue you. But you'll be easier to rescue if you stripped off to your swimsuit. You *are* wearing a swimsuit underneath those clothes, aren't you?'

'Of course I am!'

'Then, off you go.' To show the way, he dispensed with his shirt, which was damp from his exertions, and laid it flat to dry.

Caroline felt her breath catch painfully in her throat as all her misbehaving senses went into immediate overdrive. Her lips felt swollen and her breasts were tender. She wanted to tell him to look away but knew that that would have been childish. She gave herself a stern little lecture—how many times had she worn this swimsuit? Hundreds! In summer, she would often go down to the beach with her friends. She never went in the water but she lazed and tanned and had never, not once, felt remotely self-conscious.

With a mental shrug, she quickly peeled off her clothes, folding them neatly and accepting the soft towel which Giancarlo had packed in a waterproof bag, then she stood up and took a few tentative steps towards the side of the boat. In truth, she felt much, much calmer than when she had first stepped on the small vessel. There were far too many other things on her mind to focus on her fears.

Watching her, Giancarlo felt a sudden, unexpected rush of pure sexual awareness. She was staring out to sea, her profile to him, offering him a view of the most voluptuous body he had ever laid eyes on, even though her one-piece black swimsuit was the last word in old-fashioned and strove to conceal as much as possible. She had the perfect hourglass figure that would drive most men mad. With the breeze making a nonsense of her plait, she had finally unravelled it and her hair fell in curls almost to her waist. He found that his breathing had become shallow, and his arousal was so prominent and painful that he inhaled sharply and began busying himself with the other towel which he had packed.

A youth spent on water had primed him for certain necessities: towels, drinks, something to snack on and, of course, sun-tan lotion.

He had taken up a safer position, sitting on his towel, when she turned to him with a little frown. He was tempted to tell her to cover herself up as he looked through half-closed eyes at her luscious breasts, which not even her sensible swimsuit could downplay.

'I never even asked,' Caroline said abruptly. 'Are you married?' Proud of herself for having ventured into the unknown and terrifying realms of standing at the side of the boat, she now made her way to where he was sitting and spread her towel alongside his to sit.

'Do I look like a married man?'

Caroline considered her father. 'No,' she admitted. 'And I know that you're not wearing a wedding ring, but lots of married men don't like jewellery of any kind. My dad doesn't.'

'Not married. No intention of ever getting married. You're staring at me as though I've just announced a ban on Christmas Day. Have I shocked you?'

'I just don't understand how you can be so certain of something.'

Giancarlo remained silent for such a long time that she wondered whether he was going to answer. He was now lying down on the towel, his hands folded behind his head, a brooding, dangerous Adonis in repose.

'I don't talk about my private life.'

'I'm not asking you to bare your soul. I was just curious.' She hitched her legs up and wrapped her arms around them. 'You're so... uptight.'

'Me—*uptight*?' Giancarlo looked at her with incredulity.

'It's as though you're scared of ever really letting go.'

'Scared? *Uptight?*'

'I don't mean to be offensive.'

'I never knew I had such a boundless capacity for patience,' Giancarlo confessed in a staggered voice. 'Do you ever think before you speak?'

'I wouldn't have said those things if you had just answered my question but it doesn't matter now.'

Giancarlo sighed heavily and raked his fingers through

his hair in sheer frustration as Caroline stubbornly lay down, closed her eyes and enjoyed the sunshine.

'I've seen firsthand how unreliable the institution of marriage is,' he admitted gruffly. 'And I'm not just talking about the wonderful example set by my parents. The statistics prove conclusively that only an idiot would fall for that fairy-tale nonsense.'

Caroline opened her eyes, propped herself up on one elbow and looked at him with disbelief.

'I'm one of those so-called idiots.'

'Now, I wonder why I'm not entirely surprised?'

'What right do you have to say that?'

Giancarlo held both hands up in surrender. 'I don't want to get into an argument with you, Caroline. The weather's glorious, I haven't been out on a sailboat for the longest while. In fact, this is pretty much the first unscheduled vacation I've had in years. I don't want to spoil it.' He waited for a few seconds and then raised his eyebrows with amusement. 'You mean you aren't going to argue with me?' He shot her a crooked grin that made her go bright red.

'I hate arguing.'

'You could have fooled me.'

But he was still grinning lazily at her. She felt all hot and flustered just looking at him, although she couldn't drag her eyes away. It was impossibly still out here, with just the sound of gentle water and the far-away laughter of people on the nearest sailboat, which was still a good distance away. Suddenly, and for no reason, Caroline felt as though they were a million miles from civilisation, caged in their own intensely private moment. Right now, she wanted nothing more than to be kissed by him again, and that decadent yearning was so shocking that her mouth fell half-open and she found that she was holding her breath.

'Okay, but you have to admit that you give me lots to argue about.'

'I absolutely have to admit that, do I?'

The soft, teasing amusement in his voice made her blush even harder. Suddenly it seemed very important that she remind herself of all the various reasons she had for disliking Giancarlo. She loathed arguing and had never been very good at it, but right now arguing seemed the safest solution to the slow, burning, treacly feeling threatening to send her mind and body off on some weird, scary tangent.

'So, what about girlfriends?' she threw recklessly at him.

'What about *girlfriends*?' Giancarlo couldn't quite believe that she was continuing a conversation which he had deemed to be already closed. She had propped herself up on one elbow so that she was now lying on her side, like a figure from some kind of crazily erotic masterpiece. The most tantalizing thing about her was that he was absolutely convinced that she had no idea of her sensational pulling power.

'Well, I mean, is there someone special in your life at the moment?'

'Why do you ask?'

'I… I just don't want to talk about Alberto…' Caroline clutched at that explanation. In truth, the murky business between Giancarlo and his father seemed a very distant problem as they bobbed on the sailboat, surrounded by the azure blue of the placid lake.

'And nosing where you don't belong is the next best thing?' He should have been outraged at the cavalier way with which she was overstepping his boundaries, but he didn't appear to be. He shrugged. 'No. There's no one special in my life, as you call it, at the moment. The last special woman in my life was two months ago.'

'What was she like?'

'Compliant and undemanding for the first two months. Less so until I called it a day two months later. It happens.'

'I guess most women want more than just a casual fling. Most women like to imagine that things are going to go somewhere after a while.'

'I know. It's a critical mistake.' Giancarlo never made it a habit to enquire about women's pasts. The present was all that interested him. The past was another country, the future a place in which the less interest shown, the better.

Breaking all his own self-imposed restrictions, he asked, with idle curiosity, 'And what about you? Now that we've decided to shelve our arguments over Alberto for a while, you never told me how it is that someone of your age could be tempted to while away an indefinite amount of time in the middle of nowhere with only an old man for company. And forget all that nonsense about enjoying walks in the garden and burying yourself in old books. Did you come to Italy because you were running away from something?'

'Running away from what?' Caroline asked in genuine bewilderment.

'Who knows? Maybe the country idyll proved too much, maybe you got involved with someone who didn't quite fit the image, was that it? Was there some guy lurking in paradise who broke your heart? Was that why you escaped to Italy? Why you're content to hide away in a big, decaying villa? Makes sense. Only child...lots of expectations there...doting parents. Did you decide to rebel? Find yourself the wrong type of man?'

'That's crazy.' She flushed and looked away from those too-penetrating, fabulous bitter-chocolate eyes.

'Is it? Why am I getting a different impression here?'

'I didn't get involved with the wrong type of guy.' Caroline scoffed nervously. 'I'm not attracted to... This is a silly conversation.'

'Okay, maybe you weren't escaping an ill-judged, torrid affair with a married man, but what then? Were the chickens and the sheep and the village-hall dances every Friday night all a little too much?'

Caroline looked at him resentfully from under her lashes and then hurriedly looked away. How had he managed to turn this conversation on its head?

'Well?' Giancarlo asked softly, intrigued. 'You can't make the rules to only suit yourself. Two can play at this little game of going where you don't belong...'

'Oh, for goodness' sake! I *may* have become just a little bored, but so what?' She fidgeted with the edge of the towel and glared at him, because she felt like a traitor to her parents with that admission, and it was *his* fault. 'Italy seemed like a brilliant idea,' she admitted, sliding a sideways look at him, realising that he wasn't smirking as she might have expected. 'London was just too expensive. You need to have a well-paid job to go there and actually be able to afford somewhere to rent, and I didn't want to go to any of the other big cities. When Dad suggested that he get in touch with Alberto, that brushing up on my Italian would be a helpful addition to my CV, I guess I jumped at the chance. And, once I got here, Alberto and I just seemed to click.'

'So why the guilty look when I asked?'

'I think Mum and Dad always expected that I'd stay in the country, live the rural idyll just round the corner from them, maybe get married to one of the local lads...'

'They said so?'

'No, but...'

'They would have wanted you to fly the nest.'

'They wouldn't. We're very close.'

'If they wanted to keep you tied to them, they would never have suggested a move as dramatic as Italy,' Giancarlo told her drily. 'Trust me, they aren't fools. This would have been their gentle way of helping you to find your own space. Shame, though.'

'What do you mean?'

'I was really beginning to warm to the idea of the unsuitable lover.'

Caroline's breath caught sharply in her throat because she was registering how close they were to one another, and lying on her side, she felt even more vulnerable to his watchful dark eyes. Conscious of her every movement, she awkwardly sat up and half-wrapped the towel over her legs.

'I... I'm not attracted to unsuitable men,' she croaked, because he appeared to be waiting for a reply to his murmured statement, head slightly inclined.

'Define *unsuitable*...' He lazily reached over to the cooler bag which he had brought with him, and which she had barely noticed in her panic over the dreaded sailing trip, and pulled out two cold drinks, one of which he handed to her.

Held hostage to a conversation that was running wildly out of control, Caroline could only stare at him in dazed confusion. She pressed the cold can to her heated cheeks.

'Well?' Giancarlo tipped his head back to drink and she found that she couldn't tear her eyes away from him, from the motion of his throat as he swallowed and the play of muscles in his raised arm.

'I like kind, thoughtful, sensitive men,' she breathed.

'Sounds boring.'

'It's not boring to like *good guys*, guys who won't let you down.'

'In which case, where are these guys who don't let you down?'

'I'm not in a relationship at the moment, if that's what

you're asking,' Caroline told him primly, hoping that he wouldn't detect the flustered catch in her voice.

'No. Good guys can be a crashing disappointment, I should imagine.'

'I'm sure some of your past girlfriends wouldn't agree with that!' Bright patches of colour had appeared on her cheeks, and her eyes were locked to his in a way that was invasive and thrilling at the same time. Had he leant closer to her? Or had she somehow managed to shorten the distance between them?

'I've never had any complaints in that department,' Giancarlo murmured. 'Sure, some of them have mistakenly got it into their heads that they could persuade me to be in it for the long term. Sure, they were disappointed when I had to set them straight on that, but complaints? In the sex department? No. In fact—'

'I'm not interested,' Caroline interrupted shrilly.

Giancarlo dealt her a slashing smile tinged with a healthy dose of disbelief.

'I guess you haven't met a lot of Italian studs out here,' he said, shamelessly fishing and enjoying himself in a way that had become alien to him. His high-pressured, high-octane, high-stressed, driven everyday life had been left behind on the shores of Lake Como. He was playing truant now and loving every second of it. His dark eyes drifted down to her full, heaving breasts. She might have modestly half-covered her bare legs with the towel but she couldn't hide what remained on display, nor could he seem to stop himself from appreciating it.

'I didn't come here to meet anyone! That wasn't the point.'

'No, but it might have been a pleasant bonus—unless, of course, you've left someone behind? Is there a local lad waiting for you in the wings? Someone your parents approve heartily of? Maybe a farmer?'

Caroline wondered why he would have picked a *farmer*, of all people. Was it because he considered her the outdoor kind of girl, robust and healthy with pink cheeks and a hearty appetite? The kind of girl he would never have kissed unless he had been obliged to, as a distraction from the embarrassment of having the girl in question make a fool of herself and of him by having a panic attack at the thought of getting into a boat? She sucked her stomach in, gave up the losing battle to look skinny and stood up to move to the side of the boat, where she held the railings and looked out to the lake.

The shore was a distant strip but she wasn't scared. Just like that, her irrational fear of water seemed to have subsided. There wasn't enough room for that silly phobia when Giancarlo was doing crazy things to her senses. And, much as he got under her skin, his presence was weirdly reassuring. How did *that* work?

She was aware that he had moved to stand behind her and in one swift movement she turned around, her back to the waist-high railing. 'It's so peaceful and beautiful here.' She looked at him steadily and tried hard to focus just on his face rather than on his brown, hard torso and its generous sprinkling of dark hair that seemed horribly, unashamedly masculine. 'Do you miss it? I know Milan is very busy and very commercial, but you grew up here. Don't you sometimes long for the tranquillity of the open spaces?'

'I think you're confusing me with one of those sensitive types you claim to like,' Giancarlo murmured. He clasped the railing on either side of her, bracing himself and locking her into a suffocating, non-physical embrace, his lean body only inches away from her. 'I don't do nostalgia. Not, I might add, that I have much to be nostalgic about.'

The smile he shot her sent a heat wave rushing through her body. She was barefoot and her toes curled against the smooth wooden planks of the sailboat. God, she could scarcely breathe! Their eyes tangled and Caroline felt giddy under the shimmering intensity of his midnight-dark eyes.

She could barely remember what they had been talking about. The quiet sounds of the water had receded and she thought she could hear the whoosh of blood rushing through her veins and the frantic pounding of her heart.

She wasn't aware of her eyes half closing, or of her mouth parting on a question that was never asked.

Giancarlo was more than aware of both those things. The powerful scent of lust made his nostrils flare. He realised that this was exactly what he wanted. Her lush, sexy body combined with her wide-eyed innocence had set up a chain reaction in him that he hadn't been able to control.

'And as for getting away from it all…' Some of her long hair blew across his face. She smelled of sun and warmth. 'I have a place on the coast.' From nowhere sprang such a strange notion that he barely registered it. He would like to take her there. He had never had any such inclination with any woman in the past. That was purely his domain, his private getaway from the hassle of everyday life, always maintained, waiting and ready for those very rare occasions when he felt the need to make use of it.

'You have the most amazing hair.' He captured some of it, sank his fingers into its untamed length. 'You should never have it cut.'

Caroline knew that he was going to kiss her and she strained up towards him with a sigh of abandon. She never knew that she could want something so much in her life.

She lifted her hand and trembled as her fingers raked through his fine, dark, silky hair.

With a stifled groan, Giancarlo angled down and lost himself in a kiss that was hungry and exploring. His questing tongue melded with hers and, as the kiss deepened, he spanned her rib cage with urgent, impatient hands. They were out in the open but visible to no one. Other boats, dotted on the sparkling, still water, were too far away to witness his lack of control.

The push of her breasts as she curved her body up to him was explosive to his libido and he hooked his fingers under the straps of her swimsuit. He couldn't pull them down fast enough, and as her breasts spilled out in their glorious abundance he had to control the savage reaction of his throbbing arousal.

'God, you're beautiful,' he growled hoarsely.

'Beautiful' had never been one of those things Caroline had ever considered herself. Friendly, yes. Reasonably attractive, perhaps. But *beautiful*?

Right now, however, as she looked at him with a fevered, slumberous gaze, she believed him and she was infused with a heady, wanton feeling of total recklessness. She wanted to bask in his open admiration. It was a huge turn-on. He looked down and her nipples tightened and ached in immediate response. Her ability to think and to reason had been scattered to the four winds and she moaned and arched her back as his big hands covered her breasts, massaging them, pushing them up so that her swollen nipples were offered up to his scorching inspection. The sun on her half-naked body was beautifully warm. She closed her eyes, hands outstretched on the railing on either side of her.

It was a snapshot of an erotic, abundant goddess with her hair streaming back, and Giancarlo lowered his head to close his mouth over the pulsating pink disc of a surrendered nipple.

Reaching down, Caroline curled her fingers into his hair. She felt like a rag doll and had to stop herself from sinking to the floor of the boat as he plundered her breasts, first one then the other, suckling on her nipple, drawing it into his mouth so that he could tease the distended tip with his tongue. She felt powerful and submissive at the same time as he feasted on her, licking, nipping, sucking, driving her crazy with his mouth.

When his hand clasped her thigh, she nearly fainted. The swimsuit was pulled lower and he trailed kisses over each inch of flesh that was gradually exposed. The paleness of her stomach was a sharp contrast to the golden colour she had acquired over the summer months.

Giancarlo found that he liked that. It was a *real* body, the body of a living, breathing, fulsome woman, unlike the statue-perfect, all-over-bronzed bodies of the stick insects he was accustomed to. He rose to his feet and pushed his leg between her thighs, moving it slowly and insistently which made the boat rock ever so slightly. Caroline, with her phobia of water, barely noticed. She was on a different planet and experiencing sensations that were all new and wonderful.

She only surfaced, abruptly and rudely, when the sound of an outboard motor broke through her blurry, cotton-wool haze. She gasped, shocked at her state of undress and mortified at her rebellious body, which had disobeyed every law of self-preservation to flirt perilously with a situation that instinctively screamed danger.

Struggling to free herself, she felt the boat sway and rock under her and she stumbled to rebalance herself.

'What the hell are you doing? You're going to capsize this thing. Stay still!'

He tried to hold her arms as she frantically endeavoured to pull up her swimsuit and hide the shameful spectacle of her nudity.

'How *could* you?' Caroline was shaking like a leaf as she cautiously made her way back to the centre of the boat. Her huge brown eyes were wide with accusation, and Giancarlo, who had never in living memory experienced any form of rejection from a woman, raked his hand impatiently through his hair.

'How could I *what*?'

'You *know* what!'

He took a couple of steps towards her and was outraged when she shrank back. Did she find him *threatening*?

'What I *know*—' his voice was a whiplash, leaving her no leeway to nurse fanciful notions of being seduced against her will '—is that you *wanted* it, and it's no good huddling there like a virtuous maiden whose virginity has been sullied. Snap out of it, Caroline. You practically threw yourself at me.'

'I did no such *thing*,' Caroline whispered, distraught, because she had, she really *had*, and she couldn't for the life of her understand why.

Giancarlo shook his head with such rampant incredulity that she was forced to look away. When she next sneaked a glance at him, it was to see him preparing to sail back to shore. His face was dark with anger.

With agonising honesty, Caroline licked her lips and cleared her throat. It was no good letting this thing fester in simmering silence. She had had a terrible moment of horrifying misjudgement and she would just have to say something.

'I'm sorry,' she said bravely, addressing his profile, which offered nothing by way of encouragement. 'I know I was partly to blame...'

Giancarlo glanced over to her with a brooding scowl. 'How kind of you to rethink your accusation that I was intent on taking advantage of you.'

'I know you weren't! I never meant to imply that. Look...' With urgent consternation, Caroline leaned towards him. 'I don't know what happened. I don't even *like* you! I disapprove of everything about you.'

'*Everything*, Caroline? Let's not labour that statement too much. You might find that you need to retract it.' Not only was Giancarlo furious at her inexplicable withdrawal, when it had been plain to see that she had been as hot and ready for him as he had been for her, but he was more furious with himself for not being able to look at her for fear of his libido going haywire all over again.

'You took me by surprise.'

'Oh, we're back to that old chestnut, are we? I'm the arch-seducer and you're the shrinking violet!'

'It's the heat,' she countered with increasing desperation. 'And the situation. I've never been on the water like this before. Everything must have just been too much.' She continued to look at him earnestly. 'It's *impossible* for me to be attracted to you.' She sought to impose an explanation for her wildly out-of-character behaviour. 'We don't get along at *all* and I disapprove of why you decided to come here to see Alberto. I don't care about money and I've never been impressed by people who think that making money is the most important thing in the world. And, furthermore, I just don't get it with guys who are scared of commitment. I have no respect for them. So...so...'

'So, despite all of that, you still couldn't resist me. What do you think that says?'

'That's what I'm trying to tell you. It doesn't say *anything*!'

Giancarlo detected the horror in her voice and he didn't

quite know how to deal with it. He would have made love to her right there, on the boat, and he certainly couldn't think of any other woman who wouldn't have relished the experience. The fact that this woman was intent on treating it as something she had to remove herself from as quickly as possible was frankly an insult of the highest order.

Caroline felt that she was finally in possession of her senses once again. 'I think you'll agree that that unfortunate episode is something we'd best put right behind us. Pretend it never happened.'

'You're attracted to me, Caroline.'

'I'm not. Haven't you listened to a word I've just been saying? I got carried away because I'm here, on a boat, out of my comfort zone. I don't go for men like you. I know you probably find that horribly insulting but it happens to be the truth.'

'You're attracted to me, and the faster you face that the better off you'll be.'

'And how do you figure that out, Giancarlo? How?'

'You've spent your life thinking that the local lad who enjoys the barn dance on a Saturday and whose greatest ambition is to have three kids and buy a semi-detached house on the street next to where your parents live is your ideal man. Just as you tried to kid yourself that never leaving the countryside was what you wanted out of life. Wrong on both counts. Your head's telling you what you should want, but here I am, a real man, and you just can't help yourself. Don't worry. Amazingly, it's mutual.'

Caroline went white at his brutal summary of everything she didn't want to face. Her behaviour made no sense to her. She didn't approve of him one bit, yet she had succumbed faster than she could ever have dreamt possible.

It was lust, pure and simple, and he wanted to drag that shameful admission out of her because he had an ego the size of a liner and he didn't care for the fact that she had rejected him. Had he thought that he was complimenting her when he told her that, *amazingly*, he found her attractive? Did he seriously think that it felt good to be somebody's novelty for five minutes before he returned to the sort of woman he usually liked?

Warning bells were ringing so loudly in her head that she would have been a complete idiot not to listen to them. She found that she was gripping the sides of the salty plank of wood sufficiently hard for her knuckles to whiten.

Glancing across at her, Giancarlo could see the slow, painful realisation of the truth sinking in. He had never thought himself the kind of loser who tolerated a woman who blew hot and then blew cold. Women like that were a little too much like hard work. But this woman...

'Okay.' Caroline's words tumbled over one another and she kept her eyes firmly fixed on the fast-approaching shoreline. 'So I find you attractive. You're right. Satisfied? But I'm glad you've dragged that out of me because it's only lust and lust doesn't mean anything. Not to me, anyway. So there. Now it's out in the open and we can both forget about it.'

CHAPTER SIX

IT WAS after five by the time they were finally back at the
villa. The outing on the lake had taken much longer than
she had thought and then, despite its dramatic conclusion,
Giancarlo had insisted on stopping somewhere for them to
have a very late lunch.

To add insult to injury, he had proceeded to talk to her
as naturally as though nothing had happened between
them. He pointed out various interesting landmarks; he
gave her an informative lecture on the Vezio Castle, asking
her whether she had been there. She hadn't. He seemed to
know the history of a lot of the grand mansions, monuments
to the rich and famous, and was a fount of information on
all the local gossip surrounding the illustrious families.

Caroline just wanted to go home. She was bewildered,
confused and in a state of sickening inner turmoil. As
he had talked, gesticulating in a way that was peculiarly
Italian, she had watched those hands and felt giddy at the
thought of where they had been—on her naked body, touching and caressing her in a way that made her breathing
quicken and brought a flush of hectic colour to her cheeks.
She looked at his sensual mouth as he spoke and remembered in graphic detail the feel of his lips on her breasts,
suckling her nipples until she had wanted to scream with
pleasure.

How was she supposed to laugh and chat as though none of that had happened?

And yet, wasn't that precisely what she wanted, what she had told him to do—pretend that nothing had happened? Sweep it all under the carpet and forget about it?

She hated the way he could still manage to penetrate her tight-lipped silence to make her smile at something he said. Obviously, *she* was the only one affected by what had happened out there on the lake.

'Thank you for today,' she told him politely as she opened the car door almost before he had had time to kill the engine.

'Which bit of it are you thanking me for?' Giancarlo rested glittering eyes on her and raised his eyebrows in a telling question that made her blush even more ferociously. She was the perfect portrait of a woman who couldn't wait to flee his company. In fact, she had withstood his polite onslaught over an unnecessarily prolonged lunch with the stoicism of someone obliged to endure a cruel and unusual punishment and, perversely, the fiercer her long-suffering expression, the more he had become intent on obliterating it. Now and again he had succeeded, making her laugh even though he could see that she was fighting the impulse.

Giancarlo didn't understand where his reaction to her was coming from.

She had made a great production of telling him just why she couldn't possibly be attracted to a man like him—all lies, of course, as he had proceeded to prove. But she had had a valid point. Where was the common ground between them? She was gauche, unsophisticated and completely lacking in feminine wiles. In short, nothing like the sort of women he went out with. But, hell, she turned him on. She had even managed to turn him on when she had been sitting there, at the little trattoria, paying attention to everyone around them and only reluctantly looking at him when she'd had no choice.

What was that about? Was his ego so inflated that he couldn't abide the thought of wanting a woman and not having instant and willing gratification? It was not in his nature to dwell on anything, to be remotely introspective, so he quickly shelved that thorny slice of self-examination.

Instead, he chose to focus on the reality of the situation. He was here, dragged back to his past by circumstances he could never have foreseen. Although he had a mission to complete, one that had been handed to him on a plate, it was, he would now concede, a mission that would have to be accomplished with a certain amount of subtlety.

In the meantime, reluctant prisoner though he might be, he found himself in the company of a woman who seemed to possess the knack of wreaking havoc with his self-control. What was he to do about it? Like an itch that had to be scratched, Giancarlo found himself in the awkward and novel position of wanting her beyond reason and knowing that he was prepared to go beyond the call of duty to get her. It was frustrating that he knew she wanted him too and was yet reluctant to dip her toes in the water. Heck, they were both adults, weren't they?

Now, faced with a direct question, she stared at him in mute, embarrassed silence.

'I haven't seen as much of the countryside around here as I would have liked,' Caroline returned politely, averting her eyes to stare just behind his shoulder. 'I have a driving licence, and of course Alberto said that I was more than welcome to use the car, but I haven't been brave enough to do much more than potter into the nearest town. Before he fell ill, we did take a couple of drives out for lunch, but there's still so much left to explore.'

Giancarlo smiled back at her through gritted teeth. He

wanted to turn her face to him and *make* her look him in the eyes. It got on his nerves the way she hovered, as if waiting for permission to be dismissed.

He also hated the way he could feel himself stirring into unwelcome arousal, getting hard at the sight of her, her soft, ultra-feminine curves and her stubborn, pouting full mouth. He wanted to snatch her to him and kiss her into submission, kiss her until she was begging him to have his way with her. He almost laughed at his sudden caveman-like departure from his normal polished behaviour.

'Any time,' he said shortly and she reluctantly looked at him.

'Oh, thanks very much, but I doubt the occasion will arise again. After all, you're not here for much longer and I'll be returning to my usual routine with Alberto from to-morrow. Do you need a hand taking anything in? It's just that I'm really hot and sticky and dying to have a shower...'

'In that case, off you go. I think I can manage a couple of towels and a cool bag.'

Caroline fled. She intended on ducking into the safety of her room, which would give her time to gather herself. Instead, she opened the front door to be confronted with a freshly laundered Alberto emerging from the kitchens, with Tessa in tow.

He paused in the middle of a testy row, which Tessa was enduring with a broad smile, to look shrewdly at Caroline from under beetling brows.

'Been a long time out there, my girl. What have you been getting up to, eh? You look tousled.'

'Leave the poor woman alone, Alberto. It's none of your business *what* she's been getting up to!'

'I haven't been getting up to *anything*!' Caroline addressed both of them in a high voice. 'I mean, it's been a lovely day out...'

'Sailing? I take it my son managed to cure your fear of water?'

'I...I... Turns out I wasn't as scared of the water as I'd thought. You know how it is...childhood trauma...long story. Anyway, I'm awfully hot and sticky. Are you going to be in the sitting-room, Alberto? Shall I join you there as soon as I've had my shower?'

'Where's Giancarlo?'

'Oh, he's just taking some stuff out of the car.' The devil worked on idle hands, and a day spent lazing around had made Alberto frisky. Caroline could spot that devilish glint in his eyes a mile away and she eyed the staircase behind him with longing.

'So you two got along, then, did you? Wasn't sure if you would, as you seem very different characters, but you know what they say about opposites attracting...' Inquisitive eyes twinkled at her as a tide of colour rose into her face. Next to him, Tessa was rolling her eyes to the ceiling and shooting her a look that said, 'Just ignore him—he's in one of his playful moods.'

'I'm not in the *slightest* attracted to your son!' Caroline felt compelled to set the record straight. 'You're one-hundred percent right. We're completely different, *total* opposites. In fact, I'm *surprised* that I managed to put up with him for such a long time. I suppose I must have been so *engrossed* with the whole sailing business that *I barely noticed* him at all.' By the time she had finished that ringing declaration, her voice was shrill and slightly hoarse. She was unaware of Giancarlo behind her and when he spoke it sent shivers of awareness racing up and down her spine, giving her goose bumps.

'Now, now,' he drawled softly. 'It wasn't as bad as all that, was it, Caroline?'

The way he spoke her name was like a caress. Alberto

was looking at them with unconcealed, lively interest. She had to put a stop to this nonsense straight away.

'I never said it was bad. I had a lovely day. Now, if you'll all excuse me...' As an afterthought, she said to Tessa, 'You'll be joining us tonight for dinner, won't you?' But, as luck would have it, Tessa was going to visit her sister and would be back later, in time to make sure that Alberto took his medication—which at least diverted the conversation away from her. She left them to it, with Alberto informing Tessa that he was feeling better and better every day, and he would be in touch with the consultant to see whether he could stop the tablets.

'And then, my dearest harridan, you'll be back to the daily grind at the hospital, tormenting some other poor, innocent soul. You'll miss me, of course, but don't think for a moment that I'll be missing you.' Caroline left him crowing as she hurried towards the staircase.

She took her time having a long, luxurious bath and then carefully choosing what she would wear. Everything, even the most boring and innocuous garments, seemed to be flagrantly revealing. Her tee shirts stretched tautly across her breasts; her jeans clung too tightly to her legs; her blouses were all too low-cut and her skirts made her think how easy it would be for his hand to reach under to the bare skin of her thighs.

In the end she settled for a pair of leggings and a casual black top that screamed 'matronly'.

She found them in the sitting-room where a tense silence greeted her arrival.

Alberto was in his usual position by the window and Giancarlo, on one of the upright chairs, was nursing what looked like a glass of whisky.

Caught off-guard by an atmosphere that was thick and

uncomfortable, Caroline hovered by the door until Alberto waved her impatiently in.

'I can't face the dining-room tonight,' he declared, waving at a platter of snacks on the sideboard. 'I got the girl to bring something light for us to nibble on here. For God's sake, woman, stop standing there like a spectre at the feast and help yourself to something to drink. You know where it all is.'

Caroline slid her eyes across to Giancarlo. His long legs were stretched out, lightly crossed at the ankles. For all the world he looked like a man who was completely relaxed, but there was a threatening stillness about him that made her nervous.

She became even more nervous when Alberto said, with a barb to his voice, 'My son and I were just discussing the state of the world. And, more specifically, the state of *my* world, as evidenced in my business interests.'

Giancarlo watched for her reaction with brooding, lazy interest. So the elephant in the room had been brought out into the open. Why not? If the dancing had to begin, why not be the one to start the music instead of waiting? So much easier to be the one in control and, of course, control was a weapon he had always wielded with ruthless efficiency.

'Your colour's up, Alberto,' Caroline said worriedly. She glared at Giancarlo, who returned her stare evenly. 'Perhaps this isn't the right time to…'

'There is no right time or wrong time when it comes to talking about money, my girl. But maybe we should carry on our little *discussion* later, eh, my boy?' He impatiently gestured for Caroline to bring him the tray of snacks but his sharp eyes were on Giancarlo.

So he'd done it, Caroline thought in a daze, he'd *actually* gone and done it. She could feel it in her bones. Giancarlo had tired of dancing around the purpose for his visit to the villa. Maybe her rejection had hastened thoughts of departure and he had decided that this would be as good a time as any to finally achieve what he had intended to achieve from the very start. Perhaps Alberto's declarations of improving health had persuaded Giancarlo that there was no longer any need to beat around the bush. At any rate, Alberto's flushed face and Giancarlo's cool, guarded silence were saying it all.

Caroline felt crushed by the weight of bitter disappointment. She realised that there had been a part of her that had really hoped that Giancarlo would ditch his stupid desire for revenge and move on, underneath the posturing. She had glimpsed the three-dimensional, complex man behind the façade and had dared to expect more. God, she'd been a fool.

She sank into the deepest, most comfortable chair by the sprawling stone fireplace. From there, she was able to witness, in ever-increasing dismay, the awkwardness between father and son. The subject of money was avoided, but it lay unspoken in the air between them, like a Pandora's box waiting for the lid to be opened.

They talked about the sailing trip. Alberto politely asked what it felt like to be back on the water. Giancarlo replied that, of course, it was an unaccustomed pleasure bearing in mind that life in Milan as a boy had not included such luxuries as sailing trips, not when money had been carefully rationed. In a scrupulously polite voice, he asked Alberto about the villa and then gave a little lecture on the necessity for maintenance of an old property because old properties had a nasty habit of falling apart if left unattended for too long. But of course, he added blandly, old places *did* take money… Had he ever thought of leaving or was possession of one of the area's most picturesque properties just too big a feather in his cap?

After an hour and a half, during which time Ella had removed the snacks and replaced them with a pot of steaming coffee, Caroline was no longer able to bear the crushing discomfort of being caught between two people, one of whom had declared war. She stood up, said something polite about Tessa being back soon and yawned; she would be off to bed. With a forced smile, she parroted something to Alberto about making sure he didn't stay up much longer, that he was to call her on her mobile if Tessa was not back within the hour so that she could help him upstairs. She couldn't look at Giancarlo. His brooding silence frightened her.

'You should maybe come up with me.' She gave it her last best shot to avert the inevitable, but Alberto shook his head briskly.

'My son and I have matters to discuss. I can't pretend there aren't one or two things that need sorting out, and might as well sort them out now. I've never been one to run from the truth!' He was addressing Caroline but staring at Giancarlo. 'It's much better to get the truth out than let things fester.'

Caroline imagined the showdown—well, in Giancarlo's eyes, it was a showdown that had been brewing for the best part of his life and he had come prepared to win it at all costs. She was being dismissed but still she hesitated, searching valiantly for some miracle she could produce from nowhere, like a magician pulling a rabbit from a hat. But there was no miracle and she retreated upstairs. The villa was so extensive that there was no way she could possibly pick up the sound of raised voices, nor could she even hear whether Tessa had returned or not to rescue Alberto from his own son.

She fell into a fitful sleep and awoke with a start to the moon slanting silver light through the window. She had been reading and her book had dropped to the side of the bed. It took a few seconds for her eyes to adjust to the darkness and a few more seconds for her to remember what had been worrying her before she had nodded off: Alberto and Giancarlo. The unbearable tension, like a storm brewing in the distance, waiting to erupt with devastating consequences.

Groaning, she heaved herself out of the four-poster bed, slipped on her dressing gown and headed downstairs, although she wasn't quite sure what she expected to find.

Alberto's suite of rooms lay at the far end of the long corridor, beyond the staircase. Hesitating at the top of the winding staircase, Caroline was tempted to check on him, but first she would go downstairs, make sure that the two of them weren't still locked in a battle to the bitter end. Truth, as Alberto had declared, was something that could take hours to hammer out—and in this case the outcome would be certain defeat for Alberto. He would finally have to bow to Giancarlo and put his destiny in his hands. With financial collapse at his door, what other alternative would there be?

She arrived at the sitting-room to see a slither of light under the shut door. Although she couldn't hear any voices, what else could that light mean except that they were both still in the room? She pushed open the door before she could do what she really wanted to do, which was to run away.

The light came from one of the tall standard lamps that dotted the large room. Sprawled on the chair with his head flung back, eyes closed and a drink cradled loosely in one hand, Giancarlo looked heart-stoppingly handsome and, for once, did not appear to be a man at the top of his game. His hair was tousled, as though he had raked his fingers through it too many times, and he looked ashen and exhausted.

She barely made a sound, but he opened his eyes immediately, although it seemed to take him a few seconds before he could focus on her, and when he did he remained where he was, slumped in the chair.

'Where is Alberto?'

Giancarlo swirled the liquid in his glass without answering and then swallowed back the lot without taking his eyes from her face.

'How much have you *drunk*, Giancarlo?' Galvanised into sudden action, Caroline walked briskly towards him. 'You look terrible.'

'I love a woman who tells it like it is.'

'And you haven't told me where Alberto is.'

'I assure you, he isn't hiding anywhere in this room. You have just me for the pleasure of your company.'

Caroline managed to extract the glass from him. 'You need sobering up.'

'Why? Is there some kind of archaic house rule that prohibits the consumption of alcohol after a certain time?'

'Wait right here. I'm going to go and make a pot of coffee.'

'You have my word. I have no intention of going anywhere, any time soon.'

For once, Caroline failed to be awed by the size and grandeur of the villa. For once, she wished that the kitchens didn't involve a five-minute hike through winding corridors and stately reception rooms. She could barely contain her nerves as she anxiously waited for the kettle to boil, and by the time she made it back to the sitting-room, burdened with a tray on which was piled a mound of buttered toast and a very large pot of black, strong coffee, she half-expected to find that Giancarlo had disappeared.

He hadn't. He had managed to refill his glass and she gently but firmly removed it from him, brought the tray over to place it on the oval table by his chair and then pulled one of the upright, velvet-covered stools towards him.

'What are you doing here, anyway? Did you come down to make sure that the duel at dawn hadn't begun?'

'You should eat something, Giancarlo.' She urged a slice of toast on him and he twirled it thoughtfully between his fingers, examining it as though he had never seen anything like it before.

'You are a very caring person, Caroline Rossi, but I expect you've been told that before. I can't imagine too many women preparing me toast and coffee because they were worried that I'd drunk too much. Although...' He half-leaned towards her, steadying himself on the arm of his chair. 'I've never drunk too much—least of all when in the company of a woman.' He bit into the toast with apparent relish and settled his lustrous dark eyes on her.

'So, what happened? I don't mean to pry...'

'Of course you mean to pry.' He half-closed his eyes, shifted a little in the chair, indicated that he wanted more toast and drank some of the very strong coffee. 'You have my father's welfare at heart.'

'We can talk in the morning, when you're feeling a little less, um, worse for wear.'

'It would take more than half a bottle of whisky to make me feel worse for wear. I've the constitution of an ox. I made a mistake.'

'I know. Well. That's what people always say after they've drunk too much. They also say that they'll never do it again.'

'You're not following me. I made a *mistake*. I screwed up.'

'Giancarlo, I don't know what you're talking about.'

'Of course you don't. Why should you? To summarise—you were right and I was wrong.' He rubbed his eyes, sighed heavily, thought about standing up and discovered that he couldn't be bothered. 'I came here hell-bent on setting the record straight. There were debts to be settled. I was going to be the debt collector. Well, here's one for the book—the invincible Giancarlo didn't get his facts straight.'

'What do you mean?'

'I was always led to believe that Alberto was a bitter ex-husband who had ensured that my mother got as little as possible in her divorce settlement. I was led to believe that he was a monster who had walked away from a difficult situation, having made sure that my mother suffered for the temerity of having a mind of her own. I was drip-fed a series of half-truths! I think another glass of whisky might help the situation.'

'It won't.'

'You told me that there might be another side to the story.'

'There always is.' Her heart constricted in sympathy. Unused to dealing with any kind of emotional doubt, Giancarlo had steadily tried to drink his way out of it. More than anything in the world, Caroline wanted to reach out and smooth away the lines of bitter self-recrimination from his beautiful face.

'My mother had been having affairs. By the time the marriage dissolved, she was involved with a man who turned out to be a con artist. There was a massive settlement. My mother failed to do anything with it. Instead, she handed it over to a certain Bertoldo Monti who persuaded her that he could treble what she'd had. He took the lot and disappeared. Alberto showed me all the documents, the letters my mother wrote begging for more money. Well, he carried on supporting her, and in return she refused to let him see me. She informed him that I was settled, that I didn't want contact. Letters he sent me were returned unopened. He kept them all.'

Giancarlo's voice was raw with emotion. Caroline could feel tears begin to gather at the back of her eyes and she blinked them away, for the last thing a man as proud as Giancarlo would want would be any show of sympathy. Not now, not when his eyes had been ripped open to truths he had never expected.

'I expect that the only reason I received the top education that I did was because the money was paid directly to the school. It was one of those *basics* that Alberto made sure were covered because, certainly, there seems little question that my mother would have spent it or given it away to one of her many lovers, had she had it in her possession.'

'I'm sure, in her own way, she never thought that what she was doing was bad.'

'Ever the cheerful optimist, aren't you?' He laughed harshly, but when he looked at her, his eyes were wearily amused. 'So, it would seem, is my father. Do you know, I used to wonder what you had in common with Alberto. He was a bitter and twisted old man with no time for anyone but himself. You were young and innocent. Seems you two have more in common than I ever imagined. He, too, told me the same thing—my mother was unhappy. He worked too hard. She was bored. He blamed himself for not being around sufficiently to build up a relationship with me and she took advantage of that. She took advantage of his pride, threatened to air all their dirty linen in public if he tried to pursue custody, convinced him that he had failed as a father and that visits would be pointless and disruptive. I was her trump card and she used me to get back at him.

'God, do you know that when she died, Alberto requested to see me via a lawyer and I knocked him back?

She behaved badly, she warped my attitudes, but the truth is she was a simple waitress who was plucked from obscurity and deposited into a lifestyle with which she was unfamiliar and ill at ease. The whole thing was a mess. *Is* still a mess. Alberto didn't know the extent of his financial losses. He's relied on his trusted accountant for the past ten years and he's been kept pretty much in the dark about the true nature of the company accounts. Of course, like a bull in a china shop, that was one of my choice opening observations.'

'Stop blaming yourself, Giancarlo. You were a child when you left here. You weren't to know that things weren't as they seemed. Was…was Alberto okay when he heard? I guess in a way it's quite a good thing that you came along to tell him, because if you hadn't none of these secrets would have ever emerged. He's old. How good is it for the two of you that all these truths have come out? How much better for you both to have reached a place where new beginnings can start, even though the price you've both paid has been so high?'

This time Giancarlo offered her a crooked smile. 'I suppose that's one upbeat way of looking at it.'

'And I know the situation between you hasn't been *ideal*, but when it comes to Alberto and the money, how much worse for him to have been called into an impersonal office somewhere, told that everything he'd spent your life working for had been washed down the tubes?'

'As things turn out.' He closed his eyes briefly, giving her some stolen moments to savour the harsh, stunning contours of his face. Seeing him like this, vulnerable and flawed but brutally, fiercely honest with himself, did something strange inside her. A part of her seemed to connect with him in a way that was scary and thrilling.

'As things turn out?' she prompted, while her mind

drifted to things going on in her head that made her heart beat faster and her pulses race. Could she be *falling* for the guy? Surely not? She would be crazy to do something like that, and she wasn't crazy. But he made her feel *alive*, took her to a different level where all her emotions and senses were amplified in a way that was new and dangerous but also wonderful.

'As things turn out, reparation is long overdue. I don't blame my mother for the things she did. She was who she was, and I have to accept my own portion of responsibility for failing to question when I was old enough to do so.' He held his hand up as though to forestall an argument, although the last thing Caroline was about to do was argue with him. First and foremost, she wanted to get her thoughts in order. She looked at him with a slightly glazed expression.

'Right,' she said slowly, blinking and nodding her head thoughtfully. She noticed that, even having been at the bottle, he was still in control of all his faculties, still able to rationalise his thoughts in a way that many sober people couldn't. He might be ruthless with others who didn't meet his high standards, but he was also ruthless with himself, and that was an indication of his tremendous honesty and fairness. Throw killer looks into the mix, and was it any wonder that her silly, inexperienced head had been well and truly turned? Surely that natural reaction could not be confused with love.

'The least I can do—' he murmured in such a low voice that she had to strain to hear him '—and I have told Alberto this—is to get people in to sort out the company. Old friends and stalwarts are all well and good, but it appears that they have allowed time to do its worst. Whatever it takes, it will be restored to its former glory and an injection of new blood will ensure that it remains there. And there will be no transfer of title. My father will continue to own his company, along with his villa, which I intend to similarly restore.'

Caroline smiled without reservation. 'I'm so glad to hear that, Giancarlo.'

'You mean, you aren't going say "I told you so", even though you did?'

'I would never say anything like that.'

'Do you know, I'm inclined to believe you.'

'I'm really glad I came downstairs,' she confessed honestly. 'It took me ages to fall asleep and then I woke up and wanted to know that everything was all right, but I wasn't sure what to do.'

'Would you believe me if I told you that I'm glad you came downstairs too?'

Caroline found that she was holding her breath. He was staring at her with brooding intensity and she couldn't drag her fascinated eyes away from his face. Without realising it, she was leaning forwards, every nerve in her body straining towards him, like a flower reaching towards a source of heat and light.

'Really?'

'Really,' Giancarlo said wryly. 'I'm not the sort of man who thinks there's anything to be gained by soul searching but you appear to have a talent for listening.'

'And, also, drink lowers inhibitions,' Caroline felt compelled to add, although she was flushed with pleasure.

'This is true.'

'So what happens next?' Caroline asked breathlessly. She envisaged him heading off to sort out companies and a bottomless void seemed to open up at her feet. 'I mean, are you going to be leaving soon?' she heard herself ask.

'For once, work is going to be put on hold.' Giancarlo looked at her lazily. 'I have a house on the coast.'

'So you said.'

'A change of scenery might well work wonders with Alberto and it would give us time to truly put an uncomfortable past behind us.'

'And would I stay here to look after the villa?'

'Would that be what you wanted?'

'No! I…I need to be with Alberto. It's part of my job, you know, to make sure that he's okay.' Silence descended. Into it, memories of that passing passion on the boat dropped until her head was filled with images of them together. Her pupils dilated and she couldn't say a word. She was dimly aware that she was shamelessly staring at him, way beyond the point of politeness.

She was having an out-of-body experience. At least, that was what it seemed like and so it felt perfectly natural to reach out, just extend her hand a little and trace the outline of his face.

'Don't touch, Caroline.' He continued to look at her with driving intensity. 'Unless you're prepared for the consequences. Are you?'

CHAPTER SEVEN

CAROLINE propped herself up on one elbow and stared at Giancarlo. He was dozing. Due to the throes of love-making, the sheets had become a wildly crumpled silken mass that was draped half-on, half-off the bed, and in the silvery moonlight, his long, muscular limbs in repose were like the silhouettes of a perfectly carved fallen statue. She itched to touch them. Indeed, she could feel the tell-tale throb between her legs and the steady build-up of damp-ness that longed for the touch of his mouth, his hands, his exploring fingers.

He had asked her, nearly a fortnight ago, whether she was prepared for the consequences. Yes! Caroline hadn't thought twice. Of course, that first time—and, heck, it seemed like a million years ago—they hadn't made love. Not properly. He was scrupulous when it came to con-traception. No, they had touched each other and she had never known that touching could be so mind-blowing. He had licked every inch of her body, had teased her with his tongue, invaded every private inch of her until she had wanted to pass out.

For Caroline, there had been no turning back.

The few days originally planned by Giancarlo for his visit had extended into two weeks and counting, for he had taken it upon himself to personally oversee the ground changes that needed to be made to Alberto's company. With the authority of command, he had snapped his fingers and in had marched an army of his loyal workforce, who had been released into the company like ants, to work their magic. They stayed at one of the top hotels in the nearby town while Giancarlo remained at the villa, taking his time to try and rebuild a relationship that had been obliterated over time. He would vanish for much of the day, returning early evening, where a routine of sorts had settled into place.

Alberto would always be found in his usual favourite chair in the sitting-room, where Giancarlo would join him for a drink, while upstairs Caroline would ready herself with pounding heart for that first glimpse of Giancarlo of the day.

Alberto didn't suspect a thing. It was in Caroline's nature to be open and honest, and she was guiltily aware that what she was enjoying was anything but a straightforward relationship. The fact that she and Giancarlo had met under very strange circumstances and that, were it not for those strange circumstances, their paths would never have been destined to cross, was an uneasy truth always playing at the back of her mind. She preferred not to dwell on that, however. What was the point? From that very moment when she had closed her eyes and offered her lips to him, there had been no going back.

So late at night, with Alberto safely asleep, she would creep into Giancarlo's bedroom, or he would come to her, and they would talk softly, make love and then make love all over again like randy teenagers who couldn't get enough of one another.

'You're staring at me.' Giancarlo had always found it irritating when women stared at him, as though he was some kind of poster-boy pin-up, the equivalent of the brainless blonde bimbo. He had found, though, that he could quite happily bask in Caroline's openly appreciative gaze. When they were with Alberto and he felt her eyes slide surreptitiously over him, it was a positive turn-on. On more than one occasion he had had to fight the desire to drag her from the room and make love to her wherever happened to be convenient, even if it was a broom cupboard under the stairs. Not that such a place existed in the villa.

'Was I?'

'I like it. Shall I give you a bit more to stare at?' Lazily, he shrugged off the sheet so that his nakedness was fully exposed and Caroline sighed softly and shuddered.

With a groan of rampant appreciation, Giancarlo reached out for her and felt her willingly fall into his arms. He opened his eyes, pulled her on top of him and ground her against him so that she could feel the rock-hard urgency of his erection. As she propped herself up on his chest, her long hair tumbled in a curtain around her heart-shaped face. Roving eyes took in the full pout of her mouth, the sultry passion in her eyes, the soft swing of her generous breasts hanging down, big nipples almost touching his chest.

What was it about this woman's body that drove him to distraction?

They had made love only an hour before and he was ready to go again; incredible. He pulled her down to him so that he could kiss her, and now she no longer needed any prompting to move her body in just the right way so that he felt himself holding on by a slither.

'You're a witch,' he growled, tumbling her under him in one easy move, and Caroline smiled with satisfaction, like the cat that not only had got the cream but had managed to work out where there was an unlimited supply.

He pushed her hair back so that he could sweep kisses along her neck while she squirmed under him.

The thrill of anticipation was running through her like a shot of adrenaline. She couldn't seem to get enough of his mouth on her, and as he closed his lips around one nipple she moaned softly and fell back, arms outstretched, to receive the ministrations of his tongue playing against the erect bud of her nipple. She arched back and curled her fingers in his hair as he sucked and suckled, teasing and nipping until the dampness between her legs became pleasurably painful.

She wrapped her legs around him and as he began moving against her she gave a little cry of satisfaction.

They had arrived at his house on the coast only two days previously, and although it wasn't nearly as big as the villa it was still big enough to ensure perfect privacy when it came to being noisy. Alberto and Tessa were in one wing of the house, she and Giancarlo in the other. It was an arrangement that Caroline had been quick to explain, pointing out in too much detail that it was far more convenient for Tessa to be readily at hand, and the layout of the villa predicated those sleeping arrangements. She had been surprised when Alberto had failed to put up the expected argument, simply shrugging his shoulders and waving her lengthy explanation away.

'Not so fast, my sexy little witch.' Giancarlo paused in his ministrations to stare down at her bare breasts, which never failed to rouse a level of pure primal lust he had hitherto not experienced with any other woman. The circular discs of her nipples were large and dark and he could see the paleness of her skin where the sun hadn't reached. It was incredibly sexy. He leant down and licked the underside of her breasts, enjoying the feel of their weight against his face, then he traced a path down her flat stomach to circle her belly button with his tongue. She was salty with perspiration, as he was, even though it was a cool night and the background whirr of the fan was efficiently circulating the air.

Caroline breathed in sharply, anticipating and thrilling to what was to come, then releasing her breath in one long moan as his tongue flicked along the pulsating sensitised tip of her clitoris, endlessly repeating the motion until she wanted to scream.

In a mindless daze, she looked down at the dark head buried between her thighs and the eroticism of the image was so powerful that she shuddered.

She could barely endure the agony of waiting as, finally, he slipped on protection and entered her in a forceful thrust that sent waves of blissful sensation crashing through her. His hands were under her buttocks as he continued to drive into her, his motions deep and rhythmic. The wave of sensation peaked, and she stiffened and whimpered, her eyes fluttering shut as she was carried away to eventually sag, pleasurably sated, on the bed next to him.

Similarly spent, Giancarlo rolled off her and lay flat, one arm splayed wide, the other clasped around her.

Not for the first time, Caroline was tempted to ask him where they were going, what lay around the corner for the two of them. Surely something that was as good as this wasn't destined to end?

And just as quickly she bit back the temptation. She had long given up on the convenient delusion that what she felt for Giancarlo was nothing more than a spot of healthy lust. Yes, it was lust, but it was lust that was wrapped up in love—and instinctively she knew that love, insofar as it applied to Giancarlo, was a dangerous emotion, best not mentioned.

All she could do was hope that day by day she was becoming an indispensable part of his life.

Certainly, they enjoyed each other's company. He made

her laugh and he had told her countless times that she was unique. Unique and beautiful. Surely that meant something?

She steered clear of perilous thoughts to say drowsily, 'I've got to get back to my room. It's late and I'm really, really tired...'

'Too tired for a bath?'

Caroline giggled and shifted in little movements so that she was curled against him. 'Your baths are not good for a girl who needs to get to sleep.'

'Now, what would make you say that?' But he grinned at her as she delicately hid a yawn.

'Not many women fall asleep on me,' he said sternly and she smiled up at him.

'Is that because you tell them that they're not allowed to?'

'It's because they never get the chance. I've never been a great fan of post-ooital situations.'

'Why is that?' Thin ice stretched out in front of her because she knew that she could easily edge towards a conversation that might be off-limits with him. 'Is that because too much conversation equals too much involvement?'

'What's brought this on?'

Caroline shrugged and flopped back against the pillows. 'I just want to know if I'm another in a long line of women you sleep with but aren't really involved with.'

'I'm not about to get embroiled in a debate on this. Naturally, I've conversed with the women I've dated. Over dinner. After dinner. On social occasions. But my time after we've made love has been for me. I've never encouraged lazing around between the sheets chatting about nothing in particular.'

'Why not? And don't tell me that I ask too many questions. I'm just curious, that's all.'

'Remember what they say about curiosity and cats...'

'Oh, forget it!' Caroline suddenly exploded. 'It was just a simple question. You get so defensive if someone asks you something you don't want to hear.'

Giancarlo discovered that his gut instinct wasn't to ditch the conversation, even though he didn't like where it was going. What did she expect him to say?

'Maybe I've never found the woman I wanted to have chats with in bed...' he murmured softly, drawing her back to him and feeling her relent in his arms. 'Let's not argue,' he said persuasively. 'This riviera is waiting to be explored.'

'Are you sure you can take all that time off work?'

'Surprisingly, I'm beginning to realise the considerable benefits of the World Wide Web. My father may be a dinosaur when it comes to anything technological, but it's working wonders for me. Almost as good as being at an office but with the added advantage of having a sexy woman I can turn to whenever I want.' He smoothed his big hands along her waist then up to gently caress the softness of one of her breasts.

'*And* you're teaching him.' Caroline was glad to put that moment of discomfort behind them. Questions might be jostling for room in her head but she didn't want to argue. She didn't want to explore the outcome of any arguments. 'He's really enjoying those lessons,' she confided, running her hand along his shoulder and liking the hard feel of muscle and sinew. 'I think he finds the whole experience of having a son rather wonderful. In fact, I know *you* feel maybe a bit guilty that you lived with a past that wasn't quite what you thought it was, but he feels guilty too.'

'He's told you that?'

'He called himself a proud old fool the other day when we were out in the garden, which is his way of regretting that he never got in touch with you over the years.' She glanced behind Giancarlo to where the clock on the ornate bedside table was informing her that it was nearly two in the morning. Her eyelids felt heavy. Should she just grab fifteen minutes of sleep before she trudged back to her bedroom? The warmth of Giancarlo's body next to her dulled her senses but she began edging her way out of the bed.

'Stay,' he urged, pulling her back to him.

'Don't be silly.' Caroline yawned.

'Alberto doesn't get up until at least eight in the morning and by the time he gets his act together it's more like nine-thirty before he makes an appearance in the breakfast room. You can be up at seven and back in your room by five past.' He grinned wolfishly at her. 'And isn't the thought of early-morning sex tempting...?' The suggestion had come from nowhere. If he didn't encourage after-sex chat, he'd never encouraged any woman to stay the night. In fact, no one ever had.

He was playing truant from his real life. At least, that was what it felt like, and why shouldn't he enjoy the time out, at least for a little while? Having been driven all his adult life, having poured all his energies into the business of making money, which had been an ambition silently foisted onto him by his mother, why the hell shouldn't he now take time out under these extraordinary circumstances?

Neither he nor his father had been inclined to indulge in lengthy, analytical conversations about the past. In time and at leisure, they could begin to fill in the gaps, and Giancarlo was looking forward to that. For the moment, Alberto had explained what needed to be explained, and his scattered reminiscences had built a picture of sorts for Giancarlo, a more balanced picture than the one he had been given as a child growing up, but the blame game hadn't been played. After an initial surge of anger at his mother and at himself, Giancarlo was now more accepting of the truth that the past couldn't be changed and so why beat himself up over the unchangeable?

However, he could afford to withdraw from the race for a few weeks, and he wanted to. If Alberto had lost his only child for all those years, then Giancarlo had likewise been deprived of his father and it was a space he was keen to fill. Slowly, gradually, with them both treading the same path of discovery and heading in the same direction.

His thoughts turned to Caroline, so much a part of the complex tableau…

Acting out of character by asking her to spend the night with him was just part and parcel of his time out.

He could feel her sleepily deliberating his proposal. To help her along with her decision, he curved one big hand over her breast and softly massaged the generous swell. Tired she might very well be, and spent after their urgent, hungry love-making, but still her nipple began to swell and pulse as he gently rolled his thumb over the tip.

'Not fair,' Caroline murmured.

'Since when would you expect me to play fair?'

'You can't always get what you want.'

'Why not? Don't you want to wake up in the morning with me touching you like this? Or like this?' He slid his hand down to the damp patch between her legs and slowly stroked her, on and on until she felt her breathing begin to quicken.

Giancarlo watched her face as he continued to pleasure her, enjoyed her heightened colour and then, a whole lot more, enjoyed her as she moved against his fingers, her body gently grinding until she came with a soft, startled gasp.

There seemed to be no end to his enjoyment of her body and he had ceased to question the strange pull she had over him. He just knew that he wanted her here with him in his bed because he wanted to wake up next to her.

'Okay. You win and I lose.' Caroline sighed. She shouldn't. She knew that. She was just adding to the house of cards she had fabricated around herself. She loved him and it was just so easy to overlook the fact that the word *love* had never crossed his lips. It shamed her to think how glad she was to have him, whatever the price she would have to pay later.

He kissed her eyelids shut; she was *so* tired...

The next time Caroline opened her eyes, it was to sunshine pouring through the open slats of the wooden shutters. She swam up to full consciousness and to the weight of Giancarlo's arm sprawled possessively over her breasts. Their tangled nakedness galvanised her into immediate action and she leapt out of the bed as he groggily came to and tried to tug her back down to him.

'Giancarlo!' she said with dismay. 'It's after seven! I have to go!'

Fully awake, Giancarlo slung his long legs over the side of the bed and killed the instinct to drag her back to him, to hell with the consequences. She was anxiously scouring the ground for her clothes and he sat for a while on the side of the bed to watch her.

'Are you looking for these, by any chance?' He held up her bra, a very unsexy cotton contraption which led him to think that he would quite like to buy her an entirely new set of lingerie, stuff that he would personally choose, sexy, lacy stuff that would look great on her fabulously lush body.

Caroline tried to swipe them and missed as he whipped them just out of reach.

'You'll have to pay a small penalty charge if you want your bra,' he chided. Sitting on the edge of the bed with her standing in front of him put her at just the perfect height for him to nuzzle her breast.

'We haven't got time!' She tried to slap him away and grab her bra, but put up next to no struggle when he yanked her on top of him and rolled her back on the bed.

'I'll shock you at how fast I can be.'

Fast and just as blissfully, sinfully satisfying. It was past seven-thirty as Caroline quietly opened the bedroom door.

She knew that she was unnecessarily cautious because Giancarlo was right when he had pointed out that his father was a late riser. Very early on in her stay, Alberto had told her that he saw no point in rushing in the morning.

'Lying in bed for as long as you want in the morning,' he had chuckled, 'is the happy prerogative of the teenager and the old man like myself. It's just about the only time I feel like a boy again!'

So the very last thing she expected as she opened the door and let herself very quietly out of Giancarlo's bedroom was to hear Alberto say from behind her, 'And what do we have *here*, my dear?'

Caroline froze and then turned around. She could feel the hot sting of guilt redden her cheeks. Alberto, walking stick in hand, was looking at her with intense curiosity.

'Correct me if I'm wrong, but isn't that my *son's* bedroom?'

He invested the word *bedroom* with such heavy significance that Caroline was lost for words.

'I thought you would still be asleep,' was all she could manage to dredge from her befuddled mind. He raised his bushy eyebrows inquisitively.

'Do you mean that you *hoped* I would still be asleep?'

'Alberto, I can explain…'

As she racked her brains to try and come up with an explanation, she was not aware of Giancarlo quietly opening the bedroom door she had previously shut behind her.

'No point. My father wasn't born yesterday. I'm sure he can jump to all the right conclusions.'

As if to underline his words, Caroline spun round to find that Giancarlo hadn't even bothered to get dressed. He had stuck on his dressing gown, a black silk affair which was only loosely belted at the waist. Was he wearing anything *at all* underneath? she wondered, subduing a frantic temptation to laugh like a maniac. Or would some slight shift expose him in all his wonderful naked glory? Surely not.

The temptation to laugh gave way to the temptation to groan out loud and bash her head against the wall.

Alberto was looking between them. 'I'm not sure how to deal with this shock,' he said weakly, glancing around him for support and finally settling on the dado rail. 'This is not what I expected from either of you!'

'I'm so sorry.' Caroline's voice was thin and pleading. She was suddenly very ashamed of herself. She was in her twenties and yet she felt like a teenager being reprimanded.

'Son, I'll be honest with you—I'm very disappointed.' He shook his head sadly on a heavy sigh and Giancarlo and Caroline remained where they were, stunned. Giancarlo, however, was the first to snap out of it. He took two long strides down the corridor, where a balmy early-morning breeze rustled against the louvres and made the pale voile covering them billow provocatively.

'Papa…'

Alberto, who had turned away, stopped in his unsteady progress back to his wing of the house and tilted his head to one side.

Giancarlo too temporarily paused. It was the first time he had used that word, the first time he had called him 'Papa' as opposed to Alberto.

'Look, I know what you're probably thinking.' Giancarlo raked his fingers through his bed-tousled hair and shook his head in frustration.

'I very much doubt you do, son,' Alberto said mournfully. 'I know I'm a little old-fashioned when it comes to these things, and I do realise that this is your house and you are a grown man fully capable of making his own rules under his own roof, but just tell me this—how long? How long has this been going on? Were you two misbehaving while you were in the villa?'

'*Misbehaving* is not exactly what I would term it,' Giancarlo said roughly, his face darkly flushed, but Alberto was looking past him to where Caroline was dithering on legs that felt like jelly by the louvred window.

'When your parents sent you over to Italy, I very much think that this is not the sort of thing they would have expected,' he told her heavily, which brought on another tidal wave of excruciating guilt in her. 'They entrusted your well-being to me, and by that I'm sure they were not simply referring to your nutritional well-being.'

'Papa, enough.' Giancarlo plunged his hands into the deep pockets of his dressing gown. 'Caroline's well-being is perfectly safe with me. We are both consenting adults and...'

'Pah!' Alberto waved his hand impatiently.

'We're not idiots who haven't stopped to consider the consequences.' Giancarlo's voice was firm and steady and Alberto narrowed his eyes on his son.

'Carry on.'

Caroline was mesmerised. She had inched her way forwards, although Giancarlo's back was still to her, a barrier against the full force of Alberto's disappointment.

'I may have been guilty in the past of fairly random relationships...' Just one confidence shared with his father after several drinks. 'But Caroline and I…er…have something different.' He glanced over his shoulder towards her. 'Don't we?'

'Um?'

'In fact, only yesterday we were discussing where we were going with what we have here…'

'Ah. You mean that you're serious? Well, that's a completely different thing. Caroline, I feel I know you well enough to suspect that you're the marrying kind of girl. I'm taking it that marriage no less is what we're talking about here?' He beamed at them, while a few feet away Caroline's jaw dropped open and she literally goggled like a goldfish.

'Marriage changes everything. I might be old but I'm not unaware of the fact that young people are, shall we say, a little more experimental before marriage than they were in my day. I can't believe you two never breathed a word of this to me.'

He chose to give them no scope for interruption. 'But I have eyes in my head, my boy! Could tell from the way you're relaxed here, a changed man, not to put too fine a point on it. And, as for Caroline, well, she's so skittish when she's around you. All the signs were there. I can't tell you what this means to me, after my brush with the grim reaper!'

'Er, Alberto…'

'You get to my age and you need to have something to hold on to, especially after my heart attack. In fact, I think I might need to rest just now after all this excitement. I wish you'd told me instead of letting me find out for myself, not that the end result isn't the same!'

'We didn't say anything because we didn't want to unduly excite you.' Giancarlo strolled back to her and proceeded to sling his arm over her shoulder, dislodging the robe under which he was thankfully decently clad in some silk boxers. 'It's been a peculiar time, why muddy the waters unnecessarily?'

'Yes, I see that!' Alberto proclaimed with an air of satisfaction. 'I'm thrilled. You must know by now, Giancarlo, that I think the world of your fiancée. Can I call you that now, my dear?'

Fiancée? Engaged? Getting married? Had she been transported into some kind of freaky parallel universe?

'We were going to break it to you over dinner tonight,' Giancarlo announced with such confidence that Caroline could only marvel at his capacity for acting. How much deeper was he going to dig this hole? she wondered.

'Of course, you two will want to have some time off to do the traditional thing—buy a ring. I could come with you,' Alberto tacked on hopefully. 'I know it's a private and personal thing, but I can't think of a single thing that would fill me with more of a sense of hope and optimism, a reason for *going on*.'

'A reason for going on where?' Tessa demanded, striding up towards them. 'You're worse than a puppy off a leash, Alberto! I told you to wait for me and I would help you down to the breakfast room.'

'Do I look as though I need help, woman?' He waggled his cane at her. 'Another week and I won't even need this damnable piece of tomfoolery to get around! And, not that it's part of your job description to be nosing around, but these two love birds are going to be married!'

'When?' Tessa asked excitedly, while she did something with Alberto's shirt, tried to rearrange the collar; predictably he attempted to shoo her away.

'Good question, my shrewish nurse. Have you two set a date yet?'

Finally, Caroline's tongue unglued itself from the roof of her mouth. She stepped out of Giancarlo's embrace and folded her arms. 'No, we certainly haven't, Alberto. And I think we should stop talking about this. It's...um...still in the planning stage.'

'You're right. We'll talk later, perhaps over a dinner, something special.' Alberto glowered at Tessa, who smiled serenely back at him. 'Get in a couple of bottles of the finest champagne, woman, and don't even think of giving me your "demon drink" lecture. Tonight we celebrate and I fully intend to have a glass with something drinkable in it when we make a toast!'

'Okay,' Giancarlo said, once his father and Tessa had safely disappeared down the stairs and out towards the stunning patio that overlooked the crystal-clear blue of the sea from its advantageous perch on the side of the hill. 'So what else was I supposed to do? I feel like I'm meeting my father for the first time. How could I jeopardise his health, ruin his excitement? You heard him, this gives him something to cling to.'

Caroline felt as though she had done several stomach-churning loops on a roller-coaster which had slackened speed, but only temporarily, with the threat of more to come over the horizon.

'What else were you *supposed to do*?' she parroted incredulously. Engagement? Marriage? All the stuff that was so important to her, stuff that she took really seriously, was for Giancarlo no more than a handy way of getting himself out of an awkward situation.

'My mother slept around,' Giancarlo told her abruptly, flushing darkly. 'I knew she wasn't the most virtuous person on the face of the earth. She was never afraid of introducing her lovers to me but she was single, destroyed after a bad marriage, desperate for love and affection. Little did I know at the time that her capacity for sleeping around had started long before her divorce. She was very beautiful and very flighty. My father refrained from using the word *amoral*, but I'm guessing that that's what he thought.

'Here I am now. The estranged son back on the scene. I'm trying to build something out of nothing because I want a relationship with my father. Finding out that we're sleeping together, him thinking that it's nothing but a fly-by-night romance, well, how high do you think his opinion is going to be of me? How soon before he begins drawing parallels between me and my mother?'

'That's silly,' Caroline said gently. 'Alberto's not like that.' But how far had Giancarlo come? It wasn't that long ago that he had agreed to see Alberto purely for the purpose of revenge. He felt himself on fragile ground now. His plans had unravelled on all sides, truths had been exposed and a past rewritten. She could begin to see why he would do anything within his power not to jeopardise the delicate balance.

But at what price?

She had idiotically flung herself into something that had no future and when she should be doing all she could to redress the situation—when, in short, she should be pulling back—here she now was, even more deeply embedded and through no fault of her own.

The smell of him still clinging to her was a forceful reminder of how dangerous he could prove to be emotionally.

'If I dragged you into something you didn't court, then I apologise, but I acted on the spur of the moment.'

'That's all well and good, Giancarlo,' Caroline traded with spirit. 'But it's a *crazy* situation. Alberto believes we're *engaged*! What on earth is he going to do when he finds out that it was all a sham? Did you hear what he said about this giving him something to *carry on for*?'

'I heard,' Giancarlo admitted heavily. 'So the situation

is not ideal. I realise it's a big favour, but I'm asking you to play along with it for a while.'

'Yes, but for how long?' A pretend engagement was a mocking, cruel reminder of what she truly wanted—which, shamefully, was a real engagement, excited plans for the future with the man she loved, *real* plans for a *real* future.

'How long is a piece of string? I'm not asking you to put your life on hold, but to just go with the flow for this window in time—after all, many engagements end in nothing.' Giancarlo propped himself up against the wall and glanced distractedly out towards breathtaking scenery, just snatches of it he could glimpse through the open shutters. 'In the meantime, anything could happen.' Why, he marvelled to himself, was this sitting so comfortably with him?

'You mean Alberto will come to accept that you're nothing like your mother, even though it's in your nature to have flings with women and then chuck them when you get bored?'

'Yet again your special talent for getting right to the heart of the matter,' Giancarlo gritted.

'But it's true, isn't it? Oh, I guess you could soft-soap him with something about us drifting apart, not really being suited to one another.'

'Breaking news—people *do* drift apart, people *do* end up in relationships only to find that they weren't suited to each other in the first place.'

'But you're different.' Caroline stubbornly stood her ground. 'You don't give people a chance. Relationships with you never get to the point where you drift apart because they're rigged to explode long before then!'

'Is this your way of telling me that you have no intention of going along with this? That, although we've been sleeping together, you don't approve of me?'

'That's not what I'm saying!'

'Then explain. Because if you want me to tell Alberto the truth, that we're just having a bit of fun, then I will do that right now and we will both live with the consequences.'

And the consequences would be twofold: the fledgling relationship Giancarlo was building with his father would be damaged—not terminally, although Giancarlo could very well predetermine an outcome he might gloomily predict. And, of course, Alberto would be disappointed in her as well.

'I feel boxed in,' Caroline confessed. 'But I guess it won't be for long.' Would she have been able to sail through the pretence if her heart hadn't been at stake? She would have thought so, but if she felt vulnerable then it was something she would have to put up with, and who else was to blame if not herself? Had she ever thought that what she had with Giancarlo qualified for a happy-ever-after ending? 'I feel awful about deceiving your father, though.'

'Everyone deserves the truth, but sometimes a little white lie is a lot less harmful.'

'But it's not really *little*, is it?'

Giancarlo maintained a steady silence. It was beginning to dawn on him that he didn't know her as well as he had imagined. Or maybe he had arrogantly assumed that their very satisfying physical relationship would have guaranteed her willingness to fall in with what he wanted.

'Nor is it really a lie,' he pointed out softly. 'What we have *is* more than just a bit of fun.'

With all her heart, Caroline wanted to believe him, but caution allied with a keen sense of self-preservation prevented her from exploring that tantalising observation. How much *more* than just a bit of fun? she wanted to ask. How much did he *really* feel for her? Enough to one day love her?

She felt hopelessly vulnerable just thinking like that; she

felt as though he might be able to see straight into her head and pluck out her most shameful, private thoughts and desires. She wondered whether he had not dangled that provocative statement to win her over. Giancarlo would not be averse to a little healthy manipulation if he thought it might suit his own ends. But he needn't have bothered trying to butter her up, she thought gloomily. There was no way that she could ever conceive of jeopardising what had been a truly remarkable turnaround between father and son. She would have had to be downright heartless to have done so.

'Okay,' she agreed reluctantly. 'But not for long, Giancarlo.'

Lush lashes lowered over his eyes, shielding his expression. 'No,' he murmured. 'We'll take it one day at a time.'

CHAPTER EIGHT

CAROLINE wished desperately that this new and artificial dimension to their relationship would somehow wake her up to the fact that they weren't an item. A week ago, when they had launched themselves into this charade, she had tried to get her brain to overrule her rebellious heart and pull back from Giancarlo, but within hours of Alberto's crazy misconceptions all her plans had nosedived in the face of one unavoidable truth.

They were supposedly a couple, madly in love, with the clamour of wedding bells chiming madly in the distance, so gestures of open physical affection were suddenly *de rigeur*. Giancarlo seemed to fling himself into the role of besotted lover with an enthusiasm that struck her as beyond the call of duty.

'How on earth are we ever going to find the right time to break it to your father that we're *drifting apart*, when you keep touching me every time we're together? We're not giving the impression of two people who have made a terrible mistake!' she had cried, three days previously after a lazy day spent by his infinity pool. Those slight brushes against her, the way he had held her in the water under Alberto's watchful gaze, were just brilliant at breaking down all her miserable defences. In fact, she was fast realising that she had no defences left. Now and again, she reminded herself to mutter something pointed to Giancarlo under her breath, but she was slowly succumbing to the myth they had fabricated around themselves.

'One day at a time,' he had reminded her gently.

He was beautifully, staggeringly, wonderfully irresistible and, although she *knew* that it was all a fiction which would of course backfire and injure her, she was lulled with each passing hour deeper and deeper into a feeling of treacherous happiness.

Alberto made no mention of their sleeping arrangements. Ideally, Caroline knew that she and Giancarlo should no longer be sleeping together. Ideally, she should be putting him at a distance, and sleeping with him was just the opposite of that. But every time that little voice of reason popped up, another more strident voice would take charge of the proceedings and tell her that she no longer had anything left to lose. She was with Giancarlo on borrowed time so why not just enjoy herself?

Besides, whether he was aware of it or not, he was burying all her noble intentions with his humour, his intelligence, his charm. Instead of feeling angry with him for putting her in an unenviable position with Alberto, she felt increasingly more vulnerable. With Alberto and Tessa, they explored the coastline, stopping to have lunch at any one of the little towns that clung valiantly to the hilltop from which they could overlook the limpid blue sea. Giancarlo was relaxed and lazily, heart-stoppingly attentive. Just walking hand in hand with him made her toes curl and her heart beat faster.

And now they were going to Milan for three days. The last time she had gone to Milan, her purpose for the visit had been entirely different. Today she was going because Giancarlo had stuff to do that needed his physical presence.

'I think I should stay behind,' she had suggested weakly,

watching while he had unbuttoned her top and vaguely thinking that her protestations were getting weaker with every button undone.

'You're my beloved fiancée.' Giancarlo had given her a slashing smile that brooked no argument. 'You should *want* to see where I work and where I live.'

'Your *pretend* fiancée.'

'Let's not get embroiled in semantics.'

By which time he had completely undone her blouse, rendering her instantly defenceless as he stared with brazen hunger at her abundant, bra-less breasts. As he closed his eyes, spread his hands over her shoulders and took one pouting nipple into his mouth, she completely forgot what she had been saying.

By the time they made it to Milan, Caroline had had ample opportunity to see Giancarlo in work mode. They had taken the train, because Giancarlo found it more relaxing, and also because he wanted the undisturbed time to focus and prepare for the series of meetings awaiting him in Milan. An entire first-class carriage had been reserved for them and they were waited on with the reverential subservience reserved for the very wealthy and the very powerful.

This was no longer the Giancarlo who wore low-slung shorts and loafers without socks and laughed when she tried to keep up with him in the swimming pool. This was a completely different Giancarlo, as evidenced in his smart suit, a charcoal-grey, pin-striped, hand-tailored affair, the jacket of which he had tossed on one of the seats. In front of his laptop computer—frowning as he scrolled down pages and pages of reports; engaging in conference calls which he conducted in a mixture of French, English and Italian, moving fluently between the languages as he spoke with one person then another—he was a different person.

Caroline attempted to appreciate the passing scenery but time and again her eyes were drawn back to him, fascinated at this aspect to the man she loved.

'I'm just going to get in your way,' she said at one point, and he looked up at her with a slow smile.

'I hope so. Especially at night. In my bed. I definitely want you in my way then.'

It was late by the time they made it to Milan. Meetings would start in the morning, which was fine, because there was so much she wanted to see in the city that she had not found the time for on her previous visit. While Giancarlo worked, she would explore the city, and she had brought a number of guide books with her for that purpose.

Right now, as they were ushered into the chauffeur-driven car waiting for them at the station, she was just keen to see where he actually lived.

After the splendid seclusion of his villa on the coast and the peaceful tranquility of the view over the sea, the hectic frenzy of Milan, tourists and workers peopling the streets and pavements like ants on a mission, was an assault on all the senses. But it was temporary, for his apartment was in one of the small winding streets with its stunning eighteenth-century paving with a view of elegant gardens. Caroline didn't need an estate agent to tell her that she was in one of the most prestigious postcodes in the city.

The building in front of which the air-conditioned car finally stopped was the last word in elegance. A historic palace, it had clearly been converted into apartments for the ultra-wealthy and was accessed via wrought-iron gates, as intricate as lace, which led into a beautiful courtyard.

She openly goggled as Giancarlo led the way through the courtyard into the ancient building and up to his penthouse which straddled the top two floors.

He barely seemed to notice the unparalleled, secluded

luxury of his surroundings. In a vibrant city, the financial beating heart of Italy, this was an oasis.

His apartment was not at all what she had expected. Where his villa on the coast was cool and airy, with louvred windows and voile curtains that let the breeze in but kept the ferocity of the sun out, this was all dark, gleaming wooden floors, rich drapes, exquisite furniture and deep, vibrant Persian rugs.

'This is amazing,' she breathed, standing still in one spot and slowly turning round in a circle so that she could take in the full entirety of the vast room into which she had been ushered.

Much more dramatically than ever before, she was struck by the huge, gaping chasm between them. Yes, they were lovers, and yes, he enjoyed her, lusted after her, desired her, couldn't keep his hands off her, but really and truly they inhabited two completely different worlds. Her parents' house was a tiny box compared to this apartment. In fact, the entire ground floor could probably have slotted neatly into the entrance hall in which she was now standing.

'I'm glad you approve.' He moved to stand behind her and wrapped his arms around her, burying his face in her long hair, breathing in the clean smell of her shampoo. She was wearing a flimsy cotton dress, with thin spaghetti straps and he slowly pulled these down, and from behind began unfastening the tiny pearl poppers. She wasn't wearing a bra and he liked that. He had long disbanded any notion of her in fine lingerie. If he had his way, she would never wear any at all.

'Show me the rest of the apartment.' She began doing up the poppers he had undone but it was a wasted mission because as fast as she buttoned them up he proceeded to unbutton them all over again.

'I'm hungry for you. I've had a long train trip with far

too many people hovering in the background, making it impossible for me to touch you.'

Caroline laughed with the familiar pleasure of hearing him say things like that, things that made her feel womanly, desirable, heady and powerful all at the same time.

'Why is sex so important to you?' she murmured with a catch in her voice as he began playing with her breasts, his big body behind her so that she could lean against him, as weak as a kitten as his fingers teased the tips of her nipples into tight little buds.

'Why do you always initiate deep and meaningful conversations when you know that talking is the last thing on my mind?' But he chuckled softly. 'I should be making inroads into my reports but I can't stop wanting you for long enough,' he murmured roughly.

'I'm not sure that's a good thing.' She had arched back and was breathing quickly and unsteadily, eyes fluttering closed as he rolled the sensitised tips of her nipples between gentle fingers.

'I think it's a *very* good thing. Would you like to see my bedroom?'

'I'd like to see the *whole* apartment, Giancarlo.'

He gave an elaborate sigh and released her with grudging reluctance. He had long abandoned the urge to get to the bottom of her appeal. He just knew that, the second he was in her presence, he couldn't seem to keep his hands off her. Hell, even when she wasn't around she somehow still managed to infiltrate his brain so that images of her were never very far away. It was one reason he hadn't hesitated to ask her to accompany him to Milan. He just couldn't quite conceive not having her there when he wanted her. He also couldn't believe how much time he had taken off work. He wondered whether his body had finally caught up with him after years of being chained to the work place.

'Okay.' He stepped back, watched with his hands in his pockets as she primly and regrettably did up all those annoying little pearl buttons that ran the length of her dress. 'Guided tour of the apartment.'

While he was inclined to hurry over the details, Caroline took her time, stopping to admire every small fixture; gasping at the open fireplace in the sitting-room; stroking the soft velvet of the deep burgundy drapes; marvelling at the cunning way the modern appliances in the kitchen sat so comfortably alongside the old hand-painted Italian tiles on the wall and the exquisite kitchen table with its mosaic border and age-worn surface.

His office, likewise, was of the highest specification, geared for a man who was connected to the rest of the working world twenty-four-seven. Yet the desk that dominated the room looked to be centuries old and on the built-in mahogany shelves spanning two of the walls, first-edition books on the history of Italy nestled against law manuals and hardbacks on corporate tax.

Up a small series of squat stairs, four enormous bedrooms shared the upstairs space with a sitting-room in which resided the only television in the apartment.

'Not that I use it much,' Giancarlo commented when he saw her looking at the plasma screen. 'Business news. That's about it.'

'Oh, you're so boring, Giancarlo. *Business news!* Don't you get enough business in your daily life without having to spend your leisure time watching more of it on the telly?'

Giancarlo threw back his head and laughed, looking at her with rich appreciation. 'I don't think anyone's ever called me *boring* before. You're good for me, do you know that?'

'Like a tonic, you mean?' She smiled. 'Well, I don't think anyone has ever told me that before.'

'Come into my bedroom,' he urged her along, restlessly waiting as she poked her head into all of the bedrooms and emitted little cries of delight at something or other, details which he barely noticed from one day to the next. Yes, the tapestry on that wall behind that bed was certainly vibrant in colour; of course that tiffany lamp was beautiful and, sure, those narrow strips of stained glass on either side of the window were amazing. He couldn't wait to get her to his bedroom. He was tormented at the prospect of touching her and feeling her smooth, soft, rounded body under his hands. His loss of self-control whenever she was around still managed to astound him.

'Your mother must have been really proud of you, Giancarlo, to have seen you scale these heights.'

'Mercenary as I now discover she really was?' He shot her a crooked smile and Caroline frowned. 'How long have you been storing up that question?'

'You're so contained and I didn't want to bring up an uncomfortable subject. Not when things have been going so well between you and Alberto, yet I can't help but think that you must be upset at finding out that things weren't as you thought.'

'Less than I might have imagined,' Giancarlo confessed, linking his fingers with hers and leading her away from where she was heading towards one of the windows through which she would certainly exclaim at the view outside. It was one which still managed to impress him, and he was accustomed to it. 'Hell, I should be livid at the fact that my mother rewrote the past and determined my future to suit the rules of her own game, but...'

But he wasn't, because Caroline seemed to cushion him, seemed to be the soothing hand that was making acceptance easier. She was the softly spoken voice that blurred the edges of a bitterness that failed to surface. It made his head spin when he thought about it.

'I'm old enough to be able to put things in perspective. When I was younger, I wasn't. My youth helped determine my hardline attitude to my father but now that I'm older I see that my mother never really grew up. In a funny way, I think she would have been happier if Alberto really had been the guy she portrayed him as being. She would have found toughness easier to handle than understanding. He actually kept supporting her even when she had shown him that she was irresponsible with money, and would have taken everything and thrown it all away had Alberto not had the good sense to lock most of it up. He had bank statements going back for well over a decade.'

He hesitated. 'Three years after we left, she made an attempt to get back with my father. He turned her down. I think that was when she decided that she could punish him by making sure he never saw me.'

'How awful.' Caroline's eyes stung with sympathy but Giancarlo gave an expressive, philosophical shrug.

'It's in the past, and don't feel sorry for me. Adriana might have had dubious motivations for her behaviour—she certainly did her best to screw up whatever relationship I might have had with my father—but she could also be great fun and something of an adventurer. It wasn't all bad. She just spoke without thinking, acted without foreseeing consequences and was a little too gullible when it came to the opposite sex. In the end she was as much a victim of her own bitterness as I was.'

They had reached his bedroom and he pushed open the door, gazing with boyish satisfaction at her look of pleasure as she tentatively stepped into the vast space.

One wall was entirely dominated by a massive arched window that offered a bird's-eye view of Milan. She walked towards it, looked out and then turned round to find him watching her with a smile.

'I know you think I'm gauche.' She blushed.

'Don't worry about it. I happen to like that.'

'Everything's so *grand* in this apartment.'

'I know. I never thought it would be my style. Maybe I find it restful, considering the remainder of my life is so hectic.' He walked slowly towards her and Caroline felt that small frisson of anticipated pleasure as he held her gaze. 'It's easy to forget that the rest of the world exists outside this apartment.' He curved one hand around her waist. With the other, he unhooked the heavy taupe drape from a cord, instantly shrouding the room in semi-darkness.

He gathered her into his arms and they made love slowly. He lingered on her body, drawing every last breath of pleasure out of her, and in turn she lingered over his so that the chocolate-brown sheets and covers on the bed became twisted under their bodies as they repositioned themselves to enjoy one another.

It was dark by the time they eventually surfaced. A single phone call ensured that food was brought to them so that they could eat in the apartment, although Caroline was laughingly appalled at the fact that his fridge was bare of all but the essentials.

Despite the opulence of the decor, this was strictly a bachelor's apartment. Lazing around barefoot in one of his tee shirts, she teased him about his craziness in stocking the finest cheeses in his fridge but lacking eggs; having the best wines and yet no milk; and she pointed to all the shiny, gleaming gadgets and made him list which he was capable of using and which were never touched.

She let herself enjoy the seductive domesticity of being in his space. After a delicious dinner, they washed the dishes together—because he frankly hadn't a clue how to operate the dishwasher—and then she curled into him on the huge sofa in the sitting-room, reading while he flicked through papers with his arm lazily around her.

It all felt so right that it was easy to push away the notion that her love was making a nonsense of her pride and her common sense.

'Wake me up before you leave in the morning,' she made him promise, turning to him in bed and sliding her body against his. She had always covered herself from head to toe whenever she had gone to bed but he had changed all that. Now she slept naked and she loved the feel of his hard body against hers. When she covered his thigh with hers, the pleasure was almost unbearable.

Giancarlo grinned and kissed the corner of her mouth as she tried to disguise a delicate yawn.

'Have I worn you out?'

'You're insatiable, Giancarlo.'

'Only for you, *mi amore*, only for you.'

Caroline fell asleep clutching those words to herself, safeguarding them so that she could pull them out later and examine them for content and meaning.

When she next opened her eyes, it was to bright sunshine trying to force its way through the thick drapes. Next to her the bed was empty and a sleepy examination of the apartment revealed that Giancarlo had left. She wondered what time he had gone, and tried to squash the niggling fear that he might be going off her. Was he? Or was she reading too much in the fact that he had left without saying goodbye? It was hardly nine yet. In the kitchen, prominently displayed on the granite counter, were six eggs, a loaf of bread, some milk and a note informing her that he could be as twenty-first-century as any other man when it came to stocking his larder.

Caroline smiled. It was hardly an outpouring of emotion, but there was something weirdly pleasing about that admission, an admission of change whether he saw it as such or not. She made herself some toast and scrambled eggs, finally headed out with her guide books at a little after ten and, pleasantly exhausted after several hours doing all those touristy things she had missed out on first time around, returned with the warming expectation of seeing him later that evening.

'I might be late,' he had warned her the night before. 'But no later than eight-thirty.'

It gave her oodles of time to have a long, luxurious bath and then to inspect herself in the mirror in the new outfit she had bought that morning. It was a short flared skirt that felt lovely and silky against her bare skin and a matching vest with three tiny buttons down the front. When she left the buttons undone, as she now did, her cleavage was exposed and she knew that without a bra he would be able to see the swing of her heavy breasts and the outline of her nipples against the thin fabric.

Of course she would never go bra-less in public, not in something as thin and flimsy as this top was, but she imagined the flare in his dark eyes when he saw her and felt a lovely shiver of anticipation.

With at least another couple of hours to go, she was thrilled to hear the doorbell ring.

She was smiling as she pulled open the door. Very quickly, her smile disappeared and confusion took over.

'Who are you?'

The towering, leggy blonde with hair falling in a straight sheet to her waist spoke before Caroline had time to marshal her scattered thoughts.

'What are you doing here? Does Giancarlo know that you're here? Are you the maid? Because, if you are, then your dress code is inappropriate. Let me in. Immediately.'

She pushed back the door and Caroline stepped aside in complete bewilderment. She hadn't had time to get a single word in, and now the impossibly beautiful blonde in the elegant short silk shift with the designer bag and the high, high heels that elevated her to over six feet, was in the apartment and staring around her through narrowed, suspicious eyes which finally came to rest once more on Caroline's red, flustered face.

'So.' The blonde folded her arms and looked at Caroline imperiously. 'Explain!'

'Who *are* you?' She had to crane her neck upwards to meet the other woman's eyes. 'Giancarlo didn't tell me that he was expecting anyone.'

'*Giancarlo?* Since when is the maid on first-name terms with her employer? Wait until he hears about this.'

'I'm *not* the maid. I'm…I'm…' There was no way that he would want her to say anything along the lines of 'fiancée', not when it was a relationship fabricated for Alberto's benefit, not when it meant nothing. 'We're…involved.'

The blonde's mouth curled into a smile that got wider and wider until she was laughing with genuine incredulity, while Caroline stood frozen to the spot. Her brain seemed to have shifted down several gears and was in danger of stalling completely. Next to such stupendous beauty, she felt like a complete fool.

'You have *got* to be joking!'

'I'm not, actually.' Caroline pulled herself up to her unimpressive height of a little over five-three. 'We've been seeing each other for a few weeks now.'

'He'd never go out with someone like you,' the blonde said in an exaggeratedly patient voice, the voice of someone trying to convey the obvious to a deluded lunatic.

'Sorry?' Caroline uttered huskily.

'I'm Lucia. Giancarlo and I were an item before I broke

it off a few months ago. Pressure of work. I'm a model, by the way. I hate to tell you this, but *I'm* the sort of woman Giancarlo dates.'

There was an appreciable pause during which Caroline deduced that she was to duly pay heed, take note and join the dots: Giancarlo dated models. He liked them long, leggy and blonde; short, round and brunette was not to his liking. She wished, uncharitably, that she was wearing an engagement ring, a large diamond cluster which she could thrust into the blonde's smirking face, but the trip to the jeweller's had not yet materialised despite Alberto's gentle prodding.

'Look, tell him I called, would you?'

Caroline watched as Lucia—elegant name for an elegant blonde—strutted towards the door.

'Tell him…' Lucia paused. Her cool blue eyes swept over Caroline in a dismissive once-over. 'That he was right. Crazy hours flying all over the world. Tell him that I've decided to take a rest for a while, so he can reach me whenever he wants.'

'Reach you to do *what*?' She forced the question out, although her mouth felt like cotton wool.

'What do you think?' Lucia raised her eyebrows knowingly. Despite her very blonde hair, her eyebrows were dark; a stunning contrast. 'Look, you must think I'm a bitch for saying this, but I'll say it anyway because it's for your own good. Giancarlo might be having a little fun with you because he's broken up about me, but that's all you are and it's not going to last. Do yourself a favour and get out while you can. *Ciao*, darling!'

Caroline remained where she was for a few minutes after Lucia had disappeared. Her brain felt sluggish. It was making connections and the process hurt.

This was Giancarlo's real life—beautiful women who suited his glamorous life. He had taken time out and had somehow ended up in bed with her and now she knew why. In extraordinary circumstances, he had behaved out of character, had fallen into bed with the sort of woman who under normal circumstances he would have overlooked, because she was the sort of woman he might employ as his maid.

Even more terrifying was the suspicion that she had just been *there*, a convenient link between himself and his father. She had bridged a gap that could have been torturously difficult to bridge, and by the way had leapt into bed with him as an added bonus. He had found himself in a win-win situation and, Giancarlo being Giancarlo, he had taken full advantage of the situation. The note she had found, which she had optimistically seen as the sign of someone learning to really share, now seemed casual and dismissive, a few scribbled lines paying lip service to someone who had made his life easier; a willing bed companion who gave him the privileges of a real relationship while conveniently having expectations of none.

Caroline hurt all over. She felt ridiculous in her stupid outfit and was angry and ashamed of having dressed for him. She was mortified at the ease with which she had allowed herself to be taken over body and soul until all her waking moments revolved around him. She had dared to think the impossible—that he would love her back.

She hurried to change. Off came the silly skirt and the even sillier top. She found that her hands were shaking as she rifled through her belongings, picking out a pair of jeans and a tee shirt. It was like stepping back into her old life and back into reality. She stuffed the new outfit—which only hours before had given her such pleasure as she had looked at her reflection in the changing room of the overpriced Italian boutique—into the front pocket of her suitcase which she usually kept for her shoes and dirty clothes.

She very much wanted to run away, but she made herself turn the telly on, and there she was when an hour and a half later she heard Giancarlo slot his key into the door.

She had a horrid image of herself in her silly outfit, scampering to the front door like a perfectly trained puppy greeting its master, and she forced herself to remain exactly where she was in front of the television until he walked into the sitting-room. As he strolled towards her, with that killer smile curving his mouth, he began loosening his tie and unbuttoning his shirt.

Bitter and disillusioned as she was, Caroline still couldn't contain her body's instinctive reaction, and she strove to quell the feverish race of her pulse and the familiar drag on her senses. She pulled up the image of the blonde and focused on that.

'You have no idea how much I've been looking forward to coming back…' Tie undone, he tossed it onto one of the sofas and walked towards her, leaning down over the chair into which she was huddled, his arms braced on either side, caging her in.

Caroline had trouble breathing.

'Really?'

'Really. You're very bad for me. Somehow trying to work out the logistics of due diligence is a lot less fun than thinking about you waiting for me back here.'

Like a faithful, mindless puppy.

'I left my chief in command at the meeting. The option of seeing you here, well, it wasn't a difficult choice.'

Seeing me here…in your bed…

'Food first? My man at the Capello can deliver within the hour.'

Because why would you take me out and cut into the time you can spend in bed with me? Before you get bored, because I'm nothing like the girls you want to date, girls who look good hanging on your arm... Long, leggy girls with waist-length blonde hair and exotic, sexy names like Lucia...

'You're not talking.' Giancarlo vaulted upright and strolled towards the closest chair, where he sat and then leaned forwards, his arms on his thighs. 'I'm sorry I couldn't go sightseeing with you today. Believe me, I would have loved to have shown you my city. Were you bored?'

Caroline unfroze and rediscovered the power of speech. 'I had a very nice time. I visited the Duomo, the museum and I had a very nice lunch in one of the *piazzas*.'

'I'm guessing that there's a 'but' tacked on to that description of your *very nice* day with the *very nice* lunch?' Something was going on here. Giancarlo could feel it, although he was at a loss to explain it.

He had woken next to her at a ridiculously early hour and had paused to look at her perfectly contented face as she slept on her side, one arm flung up, her hands balled into fists, the way a baby would sleep. She had looked incredibly young, and incredibly tempting. He had had to resist the urge to wake her at the ungodly hour of five-thirty to make love. Instead he had taken a cold shower and had spent most of the day counting down to when he would walk through the front door. Never before could he remember having such a craving to return to his apartment. 'Wherever he laid his hat' had never been his definition of home.

He frowned as a sudden thought occurred to him.

'Did something happen today?' he asked slowly. 'I take no responsibility for my fellow Italians, but it's not unheard of for some of them to be forward with tourists. Did you get into some bother while you were sightseeing? Someone follow you? Made a nuisance of himself?' He could feel himself getting hot under the collar, and he clenched and unclenched his fists at the distasteful thought of someone pestering her, making her day out a misery.

'Something *did* happen,' Caroline said quietly, her eyes sliding away from him because even the sight of him was enough to scramble her brains. 'But nothing like what you're saying. I didn't get into any bother when I was out. And, by the way, even if someone *had* made a nuisance of himself I'm not a complete idiot. I would have been able to handle the situation.'

'What, then?'

'I had a visit.' This time she rested her eyes steadily on his beautiful face. A person could drown in those dark, fathomless eyes, she thought. Hadn't *she*?

'A visit *here*?'

Caroline nodded. 'Tall. Leggy. Blonde. You might know who I mean. Her name was Lucia.'

CHAPTER NINE

Giancarlo stilled.

'Lucia was *here*?' he asked tightly. The hard lines of his face reflected his displeasure. Lucia Fontana was history, one of his exes who had taken their break-up with a lot less grace than most. She was a supermodel at the height of her career, accustomed to men lusting after her, paying homage to her beauty, contriving to be in her presence. She was also, in varying degrees, annoying, superficial, vain, self-centred and lacking in anything that could be loosely termed *intelligence*. She had met him at a business function, an art exhibition which had been attended by the glitterati, and she had pursued him. His mistake had been lazily to go along for the ride. 'What the hell was she doing here?'

'Not expecting to find *me*,' Caroline imparted tonelessly. She toyed with the idea of telling him that the blonde had, at first, assumed that she was the maid, the hired help dressed inappropriately for the job of scrubbing floors and cleaning the toilets. She decided to keep that mortifying titbit to herself.

'I apologise for that. Don't worry. It won't happen again.'

Caroline shrugged. Did he expect her to be grateful for that heartening promise, just because she happened to be the flavour of the month, locked in a situation which neither of them could ever have foreseen? She felt an uncharacteristic temptation to snort with disgust.

'I expect there's probably a whole barrel-load of them lurking in the woodwork, waiting to crawl out at any minute.'

'What the hell are you talking about?'

'Women. Exes. Glamorous supermodels you threw over or, in the case of this one, a glamorous supermodel who threw *you* over.'

'Lucia? Did she tell you that she left me?' Giancarlo felt a surge of white-hot rage rip through him. He knew that he had badly dented her ego when he had dumped her, but the thought of her coming to his apartment and lying through her pearly-white teeth made him see red.

'Well, I guess it must have been difficult for her to conduct a relationship with someone when she was travelling all over the place, but she said that she's back now and you can contact her whenever you want. Pick up where you left off.'

No; he was not going to start explaining himself. No way. That was a road he had never been down and he wasn't about to go down it now. It just wasn't in his nature to justify his behaviour, not that he had anything *to* justify!

'And this is what you'll be expecting me to do, is it?' he asked coolly.

Caroline felt her heart breaking in two. She hadn't realised how much she had longed to hear him deny everything the other woman had said. His silence on the subject was telling. Okay, so maybe he wasn't going to race over to Lucia's apartment and fling himself at her feet, but surely if the other woman had been lying he would have denied her story?

'You've gone into a mood because, despite everything, you don't trust me.'

'I'm not in a mood!'

'That's not what my eyes are telling me. Lucia and I were finished months ago.'

'But did you end it or did *she*?'

'What difference does it make? You either trust me or you don't.'

'Why should I trust you, Giancarlo?' She had been determined not to lose her rag, but looking at his proud, aristocratic face she wanted to slap him. Her own crazy love for him, her stupidity in thinking that what they had meant something, rose up like bile to her throat.

'You wouldn't have looked twice at someone like me if we'd met under more normal circumstances, would you?'

'I refuse to get embroiled in a hypothetical discussion of what might or might not have happened. We met and you've had more than ample proof of how attracted I am to you.'

'But I'm not *your type*. I guess I knew that all along— deep down. But your girlfriend made it very clear that—'

'Lucia is *not* my girlfriend. Okay, if it means that much to you to know what happened between us, I'll tell you! I went out with the woman and it turned out to be a mistake. There's only room for one person in Lucia's life and that's Lucia. She's an airhead who can only talk about herself. No mirror is safe when she's around, and aside from that she's got a vicious tongue.'

'But she's beautiful.' Caroline found that she no longer cared about who had done the breaking up. What did it matter? Dig deep and the simple fact was that Lucia was more his type than *she* was. He liked them transient; playthings that wouldn't take up too much of his valuable time and wouldn't make demands of him.

'I dumped her and she took it badly.' He hadn't meant to explain himself but in the end he had been unable *not* to.

'Well, it doesn't matter.'

'It clearly does or you wouldn't be making such a big deal of this.'

Caroline thought that what was nothing to him was a very big deal for her, except there was no way that he would understand that because he hadn't dug himself into the same hole that she had. Every sign of hurt would be just another indication to him of how deeply embedded she had become in their so-called relationship.

What would he do if he discovered that she was in love with him? Laugh out loud? Run a mile? Both? She was determined that he wouldn't find out. At least then she would be able to extract herself with some measure of dignity instead of proving Lucia right, proving that she had made the fatal error of thinking that she meant more to Giancarlo than she did.

Unable to contain her agitation, she stood up and paced restlessly towards the window, peering outside in search of inspiration, then she perched on the broad ledge so that she was sitting on her hands. That way, they kept still.

'I was embarrassed,' Caroline told him. She swallowed back the tears of self-pity that were vying for prevalence over her self-control. 'I hadn't expected to open the door to one of your ex-girlfriends, although it's not your fault that she showed up here. I realise that. She said some pretty hurtful things and that's not your fault either.'

Considering that he was being exonerated of all blame from the sound of it, Giancarlo was disturbed to find that he didn't feel any better. And he didn't like the remote expression on her face. He preferred it when she had been angry, shouting at him, backing him into a corner.

'It *did* make me think, though, that what we're doing is… Well, we need to stop it.'

'Work that one through for me. One stupid woman turns

up uninvited on my doorstep and suddenly you've decided that what we have is a bad idea? We're adults, Caroline. We're attracted to one another.'

'We're deceiving an old man into thinking that this is something that it isn't, and I should have listened to my conscience from the start. It's not just about having fun, never mind the consequences.'

Giancarlo flushed darkly, for once lost for words. If Lucia had been in the room, he would have throttled her. It was unbelievable just how wrong the evening had gone. The worst of it was that he could feel Caroline slipping away from him and there was nothing he could do about it.

'The fact is, that woman was right. I'm not your type.' She couldn't help herself. She left a pause, a heartbeat of silence, something he could fill with a denial. 'You're not my type. We've been having fun, and in the process leading Alberto into thinking that there's more to what we have than there actually is.'

'It's crazy to come back to the hoary subject of *type*.' Even to his own ears he sounded like a man on the back foot, but any talk about the value of 'having fun', which seemed to have become dirty words, would land him even further in the quagmire. He raked frustrated fingers through his hair and glowered at her.

'Maybe if Alberto wasn't involved things might have been a bit different.'

'Isn't it a bit late in the day to start taking the moral high ground?'

'It's never too late in the day to do the right thing.'

'And a woman who meant nothing to me, who was an albatross around my neck after the first week of seeing her, has brought you to this conclusion?'

'I've woken up.' She felt as though she was swallowing

glass and her nerves went into frantic overdrive as he stood up to walk towards her.

Everything about him was achingly familiar, from the smell of him to the supple economy of his movements. Her imagination only had to travel a short distance to picture the feel of his muscular arms under his shirt.

She half-turned but her breathing was fast. More than anything else in the world, she didn't want him to touch her.

'I know it's late, but I really think I'd like to get back to the villa.'

'This is crazy!'

'I need to be—'

'Away from me? Because if you stay too close you're scared that your body might take over?' He muttered a low oath in the face of her continuing silence.

'I don't mind heading back tonight.'

'Forget it! You can leave in the morning, and I'll make sure that I'm not under your feet tonight. I'll instruct my driver to be here for you at nine. My private helicopter will take you back to the villa.' He turned away and began striding towards the bedroom. After a second's hesitation, Caroline followed him, galvanised into action and now terrified of the void opening up at her feet, even though she knew that there was no working her way around it.

'I know you're concerned about Alberto getting the wrong impression of you.'

She hovered by the door, desperate to maintain contact, although she knew that she had lost him. He was turning away, stripping off his shirt to hurl it on the antique chair that sat squarely under the window.

'I'll tell him that your meetings were so intensive that we thought it better for me to head back to the coast, to get out of the stifling heat in Milan.'

Giancarlo didn't answer. She found her feet taking her forwards until she was standing in front of him.

'Giancarlo, please. Don't be like this.'

He paused and looked at her with a shuttered expression. 'What do you want me to say, Caroline?'

She shrugged and stared mutely down at her feet.

'Where are you going to go? I mean, tonight? You said that you'll make sure that you aren't under my feet.' She placed one small hand on his arm and he looked down at it pointedly.

'If you want to touch, then you have to be prepared for the consequences.'

Caroline whipped her hand away and took a couple of unsteady steps back. He had said that before. Once. And back then, light-years ago, she had reached out and touched because she had wanted to fall into bed with him. Now she wanted to run as fast as she could away from him. How had she managed to breach the space between them? It was as if her body, in his presence, had a mind of its own and was drawn to him like a moth to a flame.

'This is your apartment. It's—it's silly for you to go somewhere else for the night,' she stammered.

'What are you suggesting? That I climb into bed next to you and we both go to sleep like chaste babes in the wood?'

'I could use one of the spare bedrooms.'

'I wouldn't trust me if I were you,' Giancarlo murmured, keen eyes watching her as she went a delicate shade of pink. 'You might just wake up to find me a little too close for comfort. Now, I'm going to have a shower. Do you want to continue this conversation in the bathroom?'

Her heart was still beating fast twenty minutes later when Giancarlo reappeared in his sitting-room, showered, changed and with a small overnight bag. He looked refreshed, calm and controlled. She, on the other hand, was perched on the edge of the sofa, her back erect, her hands primly resting on her knees. She looked at him warily.

'You do know,' he said, dropping his bag on one of the sprawling sofas and strolling towards the kitchen, where he proceeded to pour himself a drink, 'that I'll be heading back to the coast once this series of meetings is finished? So I need to know exactly what I'm going to be walking into.'

'Walking into?' She was riveted by the sight of him in a pair of faded jeans and a polo shirt in a similar colour, so different from the businessman who had walked through the door, and all over again she agonised as to whether she had made the right decision. Distressed and disconcerted by Lucia's appearance, had she overreacted? She loved Giancarlo! Had she blown whatever chance she had of somehow getting him to feel the way she felt? If they had continued seeing one another, would love eventually have replaced lust?

As soon as she started thinking like that, another scenario rushed up in her head. It was a scenario in which he became bored and disinterested, in which she became more and more needy and clingy. It was a scenario in which another Lucia clone came along, leggy, blonde and dimwitted, to lure him away from the challenge of someone who spoke too freely. He might find her frankness a novelty now, but it was not a trait he was used to—and did a leopard ever change its spots?

But the way he looked…

She swallowed and told herself just to *focus*.

'Now that you've seen the light, are you even planning on being there at the end of the week?'

'Of course I am! I told you that I'm prepared to go along with this for a short while longer, but we're going to have to show your father that we're drifting apart so that he won't be upset when we announce that it's over between us.'

'And any clues on how we should do that? Maybe we could stage a few arguments? Or you could play with the truth and tell him that you met one of my past girlfriends and you didn't like what you saw.'

Caroline thought of Lucia and she glanced hesitantly at Giancarlo. 'Were all your girlfriends like that?'

'Come again?'

'All your girlfriends, were they like Lucia?'

Giancarlo frowned, taken aback by the directness of the question and the gentle criticism he could detect underlying it.

'I know that Lucia might have annoyed you,' she continued. 'But were they all like her? Have you ever been out with someone who wasn't a model? Or an actress? I mean, do you just go out with women because of the way they look?'

'I don't see the relevance of the question.' Nor could he explain how it was that a beautiful, intellectually unchallenging woman could be less of a distraction than the other way around. But that was indeed the case as far as he was concerned. He had not been programmed for distraction. Somewhere along the line, that hard-wiring had just failed.

'No. It's not relevant.' She looked away from him and he was savagely tempted to force himself into her line of vision and bring her back to his presence.

Instead, he slung his holdall over his shoulder and began heading towards the front door.

Caroline forced herself to stay put, but it was hard because her disobedient feet wanted to fly behind him and cling, keep him there with a few more questions. She wanted to ask him what he ever saw in her. She wasn't beautiful, so was there something else that attracted him?

She wanted to prise anything favourable out of him but she bit back the words before they could tumble out of her mouth.

She thought of this so-called distancing that would have to take place and immediately missed the physical contact and the easy camaraderie. And the laughter. And everything else that had hooked her in.

She heard the quiet click of the front door shutting and the apartment suddenly felt very big and very, very empty.

With her mind in complete turmoil, she had no idea how she was ever going to get to sleep, but in actual fact she fell asleep easily and woke to thin grey light filtering through the crack in the heavy curtains. It took her a few seconds for the links in her mind to join up. Giancarlo wasn't there. The bed was empty. It hadn't been slept in. He was gone. For a few seconds more, she replayed events of the evening before. She was a spectator at a film, condemned to watch it even though she knew the ending and hated it.

The chauffeur was there promptly at nine, and Caroline was waiting for him, her bags packed. Right up until the last minute, she half-hoped to see Giancarlo appear. She guiltily allowed herself the fantasy of him appearing with a huge bouquet of flowers, red roses, full of apologies and possibly with a ring in a small box.

In the absence of any of that, she spent both the drive and the brief helicopter ride sickeningly scared at the very real possibility that he had left the apartment to seek solace in someone else's arms.

Would he do that? She didn't know. But then, how well did she know him, after all?

She had sworn that she had seen the complete man, but she had been living in a bubble. The Giancarlo she had known was not the same Giancarlo who dated supermodels because they were undemanding and because they looked good on his arm.

She felt a pang of agonising emptiness as finally, with both the drive and the helicopter ride behind her, the villa at last approached, cresting the top of the cliff like an imperious master ruling the waves beneath it.

What they had shared was over. She had been so busy dwelling on that that she had given scant thought as to what she would actually say to Alberto when she saw him.

Now, as she stepped out of the taxi which had taken her from the helipad close by to the house, her thoughts shifted into another gear.

They had as left the happy couple. How easy was it going to be to convince Alberto that in the space of only a few hours that had all begun unravelling?

As she frantically grappled with the prospect of yet more half-truths, and before she could slot the spare key which she had been given when they first arrived at the villa into the lock, the front door was pulled open and she was confronted with the sight of a fairly flabbergasted Alberto.

Caroline smiled weakly as he peered around her in search of Giancarlo.

'What's going on? Shouldn't you be in Milan on the roof terraces of the Duomo with the rest of the tourists, making a nuisance of yourself with your camera and your guide book and getting in the way of the locals?' He frowned keenly at her. 'Something you want to tell me?' He stood aside. 'I was just on my way out for a little stroll in the gardens, to take a breather from the harridan, but from the looks of it we need to talk…'

Giancarlo looked at his watch for the third time. He was battle-hardened when it came to meetings, but this particular one seemed to be dragging its feet. It was now nearly four in the afternoon and they had been at it since six-thirty that morning, a breakfast meeting where strong coffee had made sure all participants were raring to go. There was a hell of a lot to get through.

Unfortunately, his mind was almost entirely preoccupied with the woman he had left the previous evening.

He scowled at the memory and distractedly began tapping his pen on the conference table until all eyes were focused on him in anticipation of something very important being said. This was just the sort of awestruck respect to which he had become accustomed over time and which he now found a little irritating. Didn't any of these people have minds of their own? Was there a single one present who would dare risk contradicting anything he had to say? Or did he just have to tap a pen inadvertently to have them gape at him and fall silent?

He pushed his papers aside and stood up. Several half-rose and then resumed their seats.

Having spent the day in the grip of indecision, with his mind caught up in the last conversation he'd had with Caroline, Giancarlo had now reached a decision, and was already beginning to regain some of his usual self-assured buoyancy.

Step one was to announce to the assembled crew that he would be leaving, which was met with varying degrees of shock and surprise. Giancarlo walking out of a meeting was unheard of.

'Roberto.' He looked at the youngest member of the team, a promising lad who had no fear of long hours. 'This is your big chance for centre stage. You're well filled-in on the details of this deal. I will be contactable on my mobile, but I'm trusting you can handle the technicalities. Naturally, nothing will proceed without my final say-so.'

Which made at least one person extremely happy.

Step two involved a call to his secretary. Within minutes he was ready for the trip back to the coast. The helicopter was available but Giancarlo chose instead the longer option of the train. He needed to think.

Once on the train he checked his mobile for messages, stashed his computer bag away, because the last thing he needed was the distraction of work, and then gazed out of the window as the scenery flashed past him in an ever-changing riot of colour.

He was feeling better and better about his decision to leave Milan. Halfway through his trip, he reached the decision that he would start being more proactive in training up people who could stand in for him. Yes, he had a solid, dependable and capable network of employees, but he was still far too much the figurehead of the company, the one they all turned to for direction. Hell, he hadn't had time out for years!

It was dark by the time he arrived at the villa, and as he stood in front of it he paused to look at its perfect positioning and exquisite architectural detail. As getaways went, it was one that had seldom been used. He had just never seemed to find the down time. Getaways had been things for other people.

He let himself in and headed straight for the breezy patio at the front of the house. He knew the routine. His father would be outside, enjoying the fresh air, which he claimed to find more invigorating than the stuffiness of the lakes.

'Must be the salt!' he had declared authoritatively on day one, and Giancarlo had laughed and asked for medical proof to back up that sweeping statement.

It was a minute or two before Alberto was alerted to Giancarlo's shadowy figure approaching, and a few more seconds for Caroline to realise that they were no longer alone.

They had not switched on the bank of outside lights, preferring instead the soothing calm of the evening sky as the colours of the day faded into greys, reds and purples before being extinguished by black.

'Giancarlo!' Caroline was the first to break the silence. She stood up, shocked to see him silhouetted in front of her, tall and even more dramatically commanding because he was backlit, making it impossible for her to clearly see his face.

'We weren't expecting you.' Alberto looked shrewdly between them and waved Caroline back down. 'No need to stand, my girl. You're not in the presence of royalty.'

'What are you doing here?'

'Since when do I need a reason to come to my own house?'

'I just thought that in the light of what's happened you would remain in Milan.'

'In the light of what's happened?'

'I've told your father everything, Giancarlo. There's no need to pretend any longer.'

A thick silence greeted this flat statement and it stretched on and on until Caroline could feel herself begin to perspire with nervous tension. She wished he would move out to the patio. Anything but stand there like a sentinel, watching them both with a stillness that sent a shiver through her.

Caroline glanced over to Alberto for some assistance and was relieved when he rose to the occasion.

'Of course, I was deeply upset by this turn of events,' Alberto said sadly. 'I'm an old man with health problems, and perhaps I placed undue pressure on the both of you to feign something just for the purpose of keeping me happy. If that was the case, son, then it was inexcusable.'

'Aren't you being a little over-dramatic, Alberto?'

Giancarlo stepped out to the patio and shoved his hands in his pockets.

'There is nothing over-dramatic about admitting to being a misguided old fool, Giancarlo. I can only hope that my age and frailty excuse me.' He stood up and gripped the arm of the chair, steadying himself and flapping Caroline away when she rose to help him.

'I'm old, but I'm not dead yet,' he said with a return of his feisty spirit. 'Now I suppose you two should do some talking. Sort out arrangements. I believe you mentioned to me that you would be thinking of heading back to foreign shores, my girl?'

Caroline frantically tried to remember whether she had said any such thing. Had she? Perhaps she had voiced that thought out loud. It certainly hadn't been one playing on her mind. In fact, she hadn't really considered her next move at all, although now that the suggestion was out in the open didn't it make horrible sense? Why would she want to stick around when the guy who had broken her heart would always be there on the sidelines, popping in to see his father?

Besides, surely she had a life to lead?

'Er...'

'In fact, it might be appropriate for us to leave the coast, come to think of it. Head back to the lakes. We wouldn't want to take advantage of your hospitality, given the circumstances.'

'Papa, please. Sit down.'

'And I could have sworn that you two had chemistry. Just goes to show what a hopeful fool I was.'

'We got along fine.' Caroline waded in before Alberto could really put his foot in it. She had confessed everything to her employer, including how she felt about his son. Those were details with which he had been sworn to secrecy. 'We...we... We're just... I'm sure we'll remain friends.'

Giancarlo threw her a ferocious scowl and she wilted. So, not even friendship. It had been an impractical suggestion, anyway. There was no way she could remain friends with him. It would always hurt far too much.

'I'll toddle off now. Tessa will probably be fretting. Damn woman thinks I'm going off the rails if I'm not in bed by ten.'

Mesmerised by Giancarlo's unforgiving figure, Caroline was only dimly aware of Alberto making his way towards the sitting-room by the kitchen, where Tessa was watching her favourite soap on the television. Alberto would join her. Caroline was convinced that he was becoming hooked on it even though he had always been the first to decry anything as lightweight as a soap opera.

'So,' Giancarlo drawled, slowly covering the space between them until he was standing right in front of her.

'I know I said I wouldn't say anything to Alberto, but I got here and it all just poured out. I'm sorry. He was okay with it. We underestimated him. I don't understand why you came back, Giancarlo.'

'Disappointed, are you?' he asked fiercely. He stepped away from her and walked towards the wooden railing to lean heavily against it and stare out at the glittering silver ocean below.

He turned round to face her.

'Just surprised. I thought you had so much to do in Milan.'

'And if I hadn't shown up here tonight, would you have disappeared back to England without saying a word?'

'I don't know,' Caroline confessed truthfully. She bowed her head and stared down at her feet.

'Well, at least that's more honest than the last lot of assurances you gave me—when you said that you'd say nothing to my father. I can't talk to you here. I keep expecting

Alberto to pop out at any minute and join in the conversation.'

'What's there to talk about?'

'Walk with me on the beach. Please.'

'I'd rather not. Now that your father has no expectations of us getting married or anything of the sort, we need to put what we had behind us and move on.'

'Is that what you want?' Giancarlo asked roughly. 'If I recall, you said that, were it not for Alberto, you would consider us… Well, Alberto is now out of the picture.'

'There's more to it than that,' Caroline mumbled. The breeze lifted her hair, cooled her hot face. Beneath her, the sound of the waves crashing against rocks was as soothing as an orchestral beat, although she didn't feel in the least soothed.

'I need more than just a physical relationship, Giancarlo, and I suppose that was what I finally faced up to when your ex-girlfriend paid a visit to your apartment. She's reality. She's the life you lead. I was just a step out of time. When you decided, for whatever reason, to return to Lake Como to see your father, you were doing something totally out of the ordinary. I was just part and parcel of your time out. It was fun but I want more than to just be someone's temporary time-out girl.'

'Don't tell me we're not suited to one another. I can't accept that.'

'Because you just can't imagine someone turning you down? I believe you when you say that you dumped Lucia— and yet there she was, a woman who could snap her fingers and have anyone she wanted, ready to do whatever it took to get you back.'

'And now the boot's on the other foot,' Giancarlo said

in a husky undertone. 'Now I've found out what it's like to be that person who is willing to do whatever it takes to get someone back.'

'YOU'RE just saying that,' Caroline whispered tautly. 'You just can't bear the thought of someone walking away from you.'

'I don't care who walks away from me. I just can't bear the thought that that person would be *you*.'

Caroline didn't want to give house room to any hope. One false move and it would begin taking over, like a pernicious weed, suffocating all her common sense and noble intentions. And then where would she be?

'Look, let's go down to the beach. It's private there.'

Caroline thought that that was exactly what she was scared of. Too much privacy with Giancarlo had always proved to be a disaster. On the other hand, what had he meant when he'd said that he would do whatever it took to get her back? Had she misheard?

'Okay,' she agreed, dragging that one word out with a pointed show of reluctance, just in case he got it into his head that he might have the upper hand. 'But I want to get to bed early. In the morning I think it would be best all round for us to leave, return to the lakes, and then I can start thinking about heading back to the U.K.' Her mind instantly went blank and she felt a sense of vague panic.

'I've already been in Italy far too long!' she babbled on

brightly. 'Mum's started asking when I plan to return. It's been a brilliant experience over here. I may not be incredibly fluent but I can hold my own now in Italian. I think it's going to be so much easier to get a really good job.'

'I'm not all that interested in your prospective CV.'

'I'm just saying that I have lots of stuff planned for when I return home and, now that Alberto is back on his feet and this silliness between us is over, there's no reason for me to stay on.'

'Do you really think that what we had could be termed *silly*?'

Caroline fell silent. When on a frustrated sigh Giancarlo began heading towards the lawns, to the side gate that opened onto a series of steps that had been carved into the hillside so that the cove beneath could be accessed, she followed him. It was dark, but the walk down was lit and the steps, in a graceful arch, were broad, shallow and easily manoeuvred thanks to iron railings on either side. She had no idea what the cove was like. The walk was a bit too challenging for Alberto and she had hesitated to go on her own. In Giancarlo's presence, her fear of open water was miraculously nonexistent. Without him around, she had been dubious at the prospect of the small beach on her own. What if the tide rushed up and took her away?

'The water is very shallow here,' Giancarlo said, reading her mind. 'And very calm.'

'I wasn't scared.'

He paused to turn around and look at her. 'No. Why would you be? I'm here.'

Her heart skipped a beat and she licked her lips nervously. Although it was after nine, it was still warm. In the distance, the sea beyond the protected cove glinted silver and black, constantly changing as the waves rose, fell, crashed against rocks and ebbed away. It was an atmosphere that was intimate and romantic but all she felt was trepidation and an incredible sadness that her last memories of Giancarlo would probably be of him right here, on his own private beach. Whatever he said about doing whatever it took, she would know what he meant: he didn't want to lose.

The cove was small and private. Giancarlo slipped off his shoes and he felt the sand under his feet with remembered delight. Then he walked to the water's edge and looked out to the black, barely visible horizon.

Behind him, Caroline was as still as the night. In fact, he could hardly hear her breathing. What was she talking about, leaving the country, returning to the U.K.? Uncertainty made him unusually hesitant. She had confessed everything to Alberto. For him, that said it all. He turned round to see her perched on a flat slab of rock, her knees drawn up, her arms wrapped around herself. She was staring out to sea but as he walked towards her she looked up at him warily.

'I don't want you to leave,' he said roughly, staring down at her. 'I came back here because I had to see you. I couldn't concentrate. Hell, that's never happened to me before.'

'I'm sorry.'

He sat next to her on the sand. 'Is that all you have to say? That you're sorry? What about the bit where I told you that I don't want you to leave?'

'Why don't you? Want me to leave, that is?'

'Isn't it obvious?'

'No. It's not.' Caroline shifted her gaze back to the inky sea. 'This is all about you being attracted to me,' she said in a low, even voice. 'I don't suppose you expected that to happen when you first came to see your father. In fact, I don't suppose you expected lots of things to happen.'

'If by that you mean that I didn't expect to reconcile with Alberto, then you're right.'

'I'm just part of an unexpected chain of events.'

'I have no idea what you're talking about.'

'That's the problem.' Caroline sighed. 'You don't know what I'm talking about.'

'Then why don't you enlighten me?'

Caroline wondered how she could phrase her deeply held fear that she had been no more than a novelty. How many times, as they had laughed and made love and laughed again, had he marvelled at the feeling of having taken time out of his ordinary life? Like someone going on holiday for the first time, he had picked her up and enjoyed a holiday romance with her, but had he ever mentioned anything permanent? Had he ever made plans for a future? Now that she had found the strength to walk away from him, he had come dashing back because she hadn't quite outstayed her welcome. But she would.

'I feel that my life's been on hold and now it's time for me to move on,' she said in a low voice. 'I never really meant to stay for this length of time in Italy in the first place, but Alberto and I got along so well together, and then when he fell ill I didn't want to leave him to on his own.'

'What does that have to do with us?' A cold chill was settling in the pit of his stomach. This had all the signs of a Dear John letter and he didn't like it. He refused to accept it.

'I don't want to just hang around here, living with Alberto, waiting for the occasional weekend when you decide to come down to visit until you get sick of me and go back to the sort of life you've always led.'

'What if I don't want to go back to the life I've always led?'

'What are you saying?'

'Maybe I've realised that the life I've always led isn't all that it's cracked up to be.'

Caroline gave him a smile of genuine amusement. 'So you've decided that you'll take to the lakes and become a sailing instructor?'

'You're so perfect for me. You never take me seriously.'

On the contrary, Caroline thought that she took him *far* too seriously.

'You swore to me that you weren't going to say a word to my father.'

How did they get back to this place? Caroline frowned her puzzlement but then she gave an imperceptible shrug. 'I hadn't planned to,' she confessed truthfully. 'But Alberto was at the front door when I got back. I think if I'd had time to get my thoughts in order—I don't know… But he opened the door to me and I took one look at him and I just knew that I couldn't carry on with the deception. He deserved the truth. It doesn't matter now, anyway.'

'It matters to me. I came here to try and persuade you that I didn't want us to break up. We're good for one another.'

For that, Caroline read 'we're good in bed together'. She looked at him sceptically.

'You don't believe me.'

'I believe that you've had a good time with me, and maybe you'd like the good time to continue a little bit longer, but it's crazy to confuse that with something else.'

'Something else like what?' he asked swiftly and Caroline was suddenly hot and flustered.

'Like a reason for not breaking up,' she muttered. 'Like a reason for trying to persuade me to stay on in Italy when I'm long overdue for my return trip. Like a reason for persuading me to think that it's okay to put my life on hold because we're good in bed together.'

'And let's just say that I want you in my life for longer than a few weeks? Or a few months? Or a few years? Let's just say that I want you in my life for ever?'

Caroline was so shocked that she held her breath and stared at him wide-eyed and unblinking.

'You're not the marrying sort. You don't even like women getting their feet through your front door.'

'You have an annoying habit of quoting me back to myself.' But he shot her a rueful grin and raked his fingers through his hair. 'You also have an annoying habit of making me feel nervous.'

'*I* make *you* feel nervous?' But her mind was still wrapped up with what he had said about wanting her in his life for ever. She desperately wanted to rewind so that she could dwell on that a bit longer. Well, a lot longer. What had he meant? Had she misheard or was that his way of proposing to her in a roundabout manner? Really proposing? Not just asking her to marry him as a pretence...?

Logically, there was no need for him to continue the farce of trying to pull the wool over Alberto's eyes. And Giancarlo was all about logic. Which meant...

Her brain failed to compute.

'I'm nervous now,' Giancarlo said roughly.

'Why?'

'Because there are things I want to say to you. No, things I *need* to say to you. Hell, have I mentioned that that's another annoying trait you have? You make me say things I never thought I would.'

'It's good to be open.'

'I love your homespun pearls of wisdom.' He held up one hand as though to prevent her from interrupting, although in truth she couldn't have interrupted if she had wanted to, not when that little word *love* had been uttered by him, albeit not exactly in the context she would have liked.

'I never knew how much I had been affected by my past until you came along,' he said in such a low voice that she had to lean forward in the darkness to follow him.

'Sure, I remembered my childhood, but it had been coloured by my mother and after a while her bitterness just became my reality. I accepted it. The financial insecurity was all my father's fault and my job was to know exactly where the blame lay and to make sure that I began rectifying the situation as soon as I was capable of doing that. I never questioned the rights or wrongs of being driven to climb to the top. It felt like my destiny, and anyway I enjoyed it. I was good at it. Making money came naturally to me and if I recognised my mother's inability to control her expenditures then I ignored it. The fact is, in the process, I forgot what it meant to just take each day at a time and learn to enjoy the little things that had nothing to do with making money.

'Am I boring you?' He smiled crookedly at her and Caroline's heart constricted.

'You could never do that,' she breathed huskily, not wanting to disturb the strange, thrilling atmosphere between them.

Giancarlo, who had never suffered a moment's hesitation in his life before, took comfort from that assertion.

'Ditto.' He badly wanted to reach out and touch her. It was an all-consuming craving that he had to fight to keep at bay.

'But you never got involved with anyone. Never had the urge to settle down?' It was a question she desperately needed answering. Yes, he might have been driven to make money—it might have been an ambition that had been planted in him from a young age, when he had been too young to question it and then too old to debate its value—

but that didn't mean that he couldn't have formed a lasting relationship somewhere along the way.

'My mother,' Giancarlo said wryly. 'Volatile, embittered, seduced by men who made empty promises and then vanished without a backward glance. I don't suppose she was the ideal role-model. Don't get me wrong, I accepted her and I loved her, but it never occurred to me that I would want someone like that in my life as a partner. I worked all the hours God made, and in a highly stressed environment the last thing I needed was a woman who was high maintenance and I was quietly certain that all women were. Until I met you.'

'I'm not sure that I should take that as a compliment.' But she was beaming. She could barely think straight and her heart was beating like a sledgehammer inside her. Take it as a compliment? She was on a high! She felt as though she had received the greatest compliment of her life! She had felt so inadequate thinking about the exciting, glamorous women he had dated. How could she ever hope to measure up? And yet here he was, reaching deep to find the true essence of her, and filling her with a heady sense of self-confidence that was frankly amazing.

'You're fishing.'

'Okay, you're right. I am. But can you blame me? I've spent weeks trying not to tell you how crazy I am about you.'

Giancarlo grinned and at last reached out and linked his fingers through hers. Warmth spread through him like treacle, heating every part of his body. He rubbed his thumb over hers.

'You're crazy about me,' he murmured with lazy satisfaction and Caroline blushed madly. Liberated from having to hold back what she would otherwise have confessed because she was so open by nature, she felt as though she was walking on cloud nine.

'Madly,' she admitted on a sigh, and when he pulled her towards him she relaxed against his hard body with a sensation of bliss and utter completion. 'I thought you were the most arrogant person on the face of the earth, to start with, but then I don't know what happened. You made me laugh and I began to see a side to you that was so wonderfully complex and fascinating.'

'Complex and fascinating. I like it. Carry on.'

She twisted to look up at him and smiled when he kissed her, his lips tracing hers gently at first, then with hungry urgency. Her breathing quickened and she moaned as he pushed up her top, quickly followed by her bra. He bent his legs slightly, supporting her so that she could lean back in a graceful arch as he began suckling on her nipples, pulling one then the other into his mouth, greedy to taste her.

She understood sufficient Italian now to know that his hoarse utterances were mind-blowingly erotic, although nothing was as erotic as when, temporarily sated, he looked down seriously at her flushed face to say with such fierce tenderness that her heart flipped over, 'I love you. I don't know when it started. I just knew when I was in Milan that I couldn't stand not being close to you. I missed everything about you.

'Meetings and conferences and lawyers and stockpiling wealth faded into insignificance. I was broken up by the way things had ended between us, and I had to get here as quickly as I could because I was so damned scared that I was on the verge of losing you. Damn it, I wondered whether I'd ever had you in the first place!'

It was unbearably touching to know that this big, strong man, so self-assured and controlled, had been uncertain.

'I love you so much,' she whispered.

'Enough to marry me? Nothing short of that will ever be enough.'

EPILOGUE

CAROLINE looked at the assembled guests with a smile. It wasn't a big wedding. Neither of them had wanted that, although they had had to restrain Alberto from his vigorous efforts to have a full-blown wedding of the century.

'Let's wake up these old bores in their big houses,' he had argued with devilish amusement. 'Give them something to talk about for the next ten years!'

They had chosen to be married in the small church close to where Alberto lived and where Giancarlo had grown up. It felt like home to Caroline, especially over the past two months, when the giddy swirl of having her parents over and planning the wedding had swept her off her feet.

She had never been happier. Giancarlo had proven himself to be a convert to the art of working from home and, along with all the marvellous renovations to the villa, had installed an office in one of the rooms from which he could work at his own chosen pace. Which included a great deal of down time with his bride to be.

Her gaze shifted to the man who was now her husband. Amongst the hundred or so guests—friends, family and neighbours who had delightedly enjoyed reconnecting with Alberto, who had become something of a recluse over the years—he stood head and shoulders above them all.

Right now, he was smiling, chatting to her parents,

doubtless charming them even more than they had already been charmed, she thought.

Unconsciously, she placed a hand on her stomach, and just at that instant their eyes connected. And this time his smile was all for her, locking her into that secret, loving world she shared with him and him alone.

As everyone began moving towards the formal dining-room, onto which a magnificent marquee had been cleverly attached so that the guests could all be seated comfortably for the five-course meal, he strode across to her, pulling her into the small sitting-room, now empty of guests.

'Have I told you how much I love you?' He curved his hand behind the nape of her neck and tilted her face to his.

'You have. But you need to remind me how much of this is down to Alberto.'

'The wily old fox.' Giancarlo grinned. 'To think that he knew exactly what he was doing when he decided that we were going to be married. Anyone would be forgiven for thinking, listening to his little speech in the drawing-room, that he had masterminded the whole thing.'

Caroline laughed and thought back affectionately to Alberto's smug declaration that anyone in need of match-making should seek him out.

'I know. Still, how can you do anything but smile when you see how thrilled he is that everything worked out according to his plans, if he's to be believed? I heard him telling Tessa the day before yesterday that there was no way he was going to allow us to go our separate ways because we were pig-headed. He would sooner have summoned the ambulance and threatened to jump in unless we came to our senses.'

'He now has a son and a daughter-in-law and you can bet that I'll be raising my glass to him during my after-dinner speech. He deserves it. You look spectacular tonight. Have I already mentioned that?'

'Yes, but I've always loved it when you repeat yourself.' Her eyes danced with amusement for he never tired of reminding her of his love.

'Have I also told you that I'm hard for you right now?' As if any proof were needed, he guided her hand to where his erection was pressing painfully against his zip. 'It's awkward having to constantly think of trivia to distract myself from the fact that I've spent the past four hours wanting to rip that dress off you.'

Caroline giggled and glanced down at her ivory dress, which was simple but elegant and had cost a small fortune. She was horrified at the thought of Giancarlo ripping it off her, and amazingly turned on by the image at the same time.

'But I guess I'll have to wait for a few more hours until I have you all to myself.' He curved his hand over her breast, gently massaged it just enough for her to feel that tell-tale moisture dampening between her legs, just enough for her eyelids to flutter drowsily and her pulses to begin their steady race.

He kissed the side of her mouth and then dipped his tongue inside to explore further until she was gasping, so tempted to pull him towards her, even though she knew that there was no way they could abandon their own reception even for the shortest of time.

But she wanted him to herself just for a few moments longer. Just long enough to tell him her news.

'I can't wait for us to be alone,' he murmured fervently, before she could speak. He relinquished his hold with evident regret and then primly smoothed the ruffled neckline of her dress. 'Talking and laughing, and making love and making babies, because in case you didn't know that cunning father of mine has already started making noises about wanting grandchildren while he still has the energy to play with them. And he's not above pulling any stunt he wants if it means he can get his way.'

'That seems to be a family trait but, now that you mention it...' Caroline couldn't contain her happiness a second longer. She smiled radiantly up at him and reached to stroke his cheek, allowing her hand to be captured by his. 'You might find that there's not much need to try on the making babies front.'

'What are you telling me?'

'I'm telling you that I'm a week late with my period, and I just couldn't hold off any longer so I did a pregnancy test this morning—and we're going to have a baby. Are you happy?'

Silly question. She knew that he would be. From the man who had made a habit of walking away from involvement, he had become a devoted partner; he would be a devoted husband and she couldn't think of anyone who would be a more devoted father.

The answer in his eyes confirmed everything she already knew.

'My darling,' he said brokenly. 'I am the happiest man on the face of the earth.' He took both her hands in his and kissed them tenderly. 'And my mission is to make sure that you never forget that.'

* * * * *

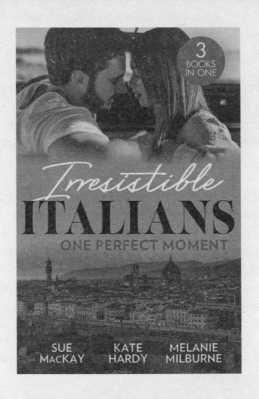

LET'S TALK

Romance

For exclusive extracts, competitions
and special offers, find us online:

- f facebook.com/millsandboon
- 🐦 @MillsandBoon
- 📷 @MillsandBoonUK
- ♪ @MillsandBoonUK

Get in touch on 01413 063 232

MILLS & BOON

THE HEART OF ROMANCE

A ROMANCE FOR EVERY READER

MODERN
Prepare to be swept off your feet by sophisticated, sexy and seductive heroes, in some of the world's most glamourous and romantic locations, where power and passion collide.

HISTORICAL
Escape with historical heroes from time gone by. Whether your passion is for wicked Regency Rakes, muscled Vikings or rugged Highlanders, awaken the romance of the past.

MEDICAL
Set your pulse racing with dedicated, delectable doctors in the high-pressure world of medicine, where emotions run high and passion, comfort and love are the best medicine.

True Love
Celebrate true love with tender stories of heartfelt romance, from the rush of falling in love to the joy a new baby can bring, and a focus on the emotional heart of a relationship.

Desire
Indulge in secrets and scandal, intense drama and sizzling hot action with heroes who have it all: wealth, status, good looks…everything but the right woman.

HEROES
The excitement of a gripping thriller, with intense romance at its heart. Resourceful, true-to-life women and strong, fearless men face danger and desire - a killer combination!

To see which titles are coming soon, please visit

millsandboon.co.uk/nextmonth

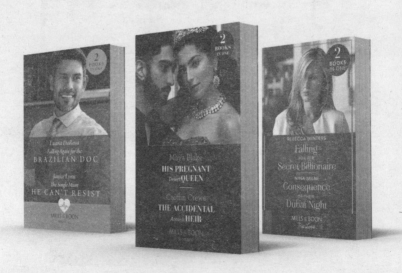

GET YOUR ROMANCE FIX!

Get the latest romance news,
exclusive author interviews, story
extracts and much more!

MILLS & BOON
MODERN
Power and Passion

Prepare to be swept off your feet by sophisticated, sexy and seductive heroes, in some of the world's most glamourous and romantic locations, where power and passion collide.

MILLS & BOON

MEDICAL

Pulse-Racing Passion

Set your pulse racing with dedicated, delectable doctors in the high-pressure world of medicine, where emotions run high and passion, comfort and love are the best medicine.

MILLS & BOON
Desire

Indulge in secrets and scandal, intense drama and plenty of sizzling hot action with powerful and passionate heroes who have it all: wealth, status, good looks…everything but the right woman.

MILLS & BOON

HEROES

At Your Service

Experience all the excitement of a gripping thriller, with an intense romance at its heart. Resourceful, true-to-life women and strong, fearless men face danger and desire – a killer combination!